Gallantry

Gallantry

James Branch Cabell

MINT EDITIONS

Gallantry was first published in 1907.

This edition published by Mint Editions 2021.

ISBN 9781513295732 | E-ISBN 9781513297231

Published by Mint Editions®

MINT
EDITIONS
minteditionbooks.com

Publishing Director: Jennifer Newens
Design & Production: Rachel Lopez Metzger
Project Manager: Micaela Clark
Typesetting: Westchester Publishing Services

Contents

The Epistle Dedicatory

To Mrs. Grundy

Madam,—It is surely fitting that a book which harks back to the manners of the second George should have its dedication and its patron. And these comedies claim naturally your protection, since it likewise appears a custom of that era for the poet to dedicate his book to his most influential acquaintance and the one least likely to value it.

Indeed, it is as proper that the plaudits of great persons be reserved for great performances as it is undeniable these

> *tiny pictures of that tiny time*
> *Aim little at the lofty and sublime.*

Yet cognoscenti still esteem it an error in the accomplished Shakespeare that he introduced a game of billiards into his portrayal of Queen Cleopatra's court; and the impropriety had been equal had I linked the extreme of any passion with an age and circle wherein abandonment to the emotions was adjudged bucolic, nay, Madam, the Eumenides were very terrifying at Delphi, no doubt, but deck them with paint, patch, and panniers, send them howling among the *beau monde* on the Pantiles, and they are only figures of fun; nor may, in reason, the high woes of a second Lear, or of a new Prometheus, be adequately lighted by the flambeaux of Louis Quinze.

Conceive, then, the overture begun, and fear not, if the action of the play demand a lion, but that he shall be a beast of Peter Quince's picking. The ladies shall not be frighted, for our chief comedians will enact modish people of a time when gallantry prevailed.

Now the essence of gallantry, I take it, was to accept the pleasures of life leisurely and its inconveniences with a shrug. As requisites, a gallant person will, of course, be "amorous, but not too constant, have a pleasant voice, and possess a talent for love-letters." He will always bear in mind that in love-affairs success is less the Ultima Thule of desire than its *coup de grâce*, and he will be careful never to admit the fact, especially to himself. He will value ceremony, but rather for its comeliness than for its utility, as one esteeming the lily, say, to be a more applaudable bulb than the onion. He will prink; and he will be at his best after sunset. He will dare to acknowledge the shapeliness of a thief's leg, to contend that the commission of murder does not necessarily impair the agreeableness of the assassin's conversation; and to insist that at bottom God is kindlier than the genteel would regard as rational. He will, in fine, sin on sufficient provocation, and repent within the moment, quite sincerely, and be not unconscionably surprised when he repeats the progression: and he will consider the world with a smile of toleration, and his own doings with a smile of honest amusement, and Heaven with a smile that is not distrustful.

This particular attitude toward life may have its merits, but it is not conducive to meticulous morality; therefore, in advance, I warn you that my *Dramatis Personæ* will in their display of the cardinal virtues evince a certain parsimony. Theirs were, in effect, not virtuous days. And the great man who knew these times *au fond*, and loved them, and wrote of them as no other man may ever hope to do, has said of these same times, with perfect truth:

"Fiddles sing all through them; wax-lights, fine dresses, fine jokes, fine plate, fine equipages, glitter and sparkle: never was there such a brilliant, jigging, smirking Vanity Fair. But wandering through that city of the dead, that dreadfully selfish time, through those godless intrigues and feasts, through those crowds, pushing, and eager, and struggling,—rouged, and lying, and fawning,—I have wanted some one to be friends with. I have said, *Show me some good person about that Court; find me, among those selfish courtiers, those dissolute gay people, some one being that I can love and regard.*" And Thackeray confesses that, for all his research, he could not find anybody living irreproachably, at this especial period. . .

Where a giant fails one may in reason hesitate to essay. I present, then, people who, as people normally do, accepted their times and made the best of them, since the most estimable needs conform a little to the custom of his day, whether it be Caractacus painting himself sky-blue or Galileo on his knees at Santa Maria. And accordingly, many of my comedians will lie when it seems advisable, and will not haggle over a misdemeanor when there is anything to be gained by it; at times their virtues will get them what they want, and at times their vices, and at other times they will be neither punished nor rewarded; in fine, Madam, they will be just human beings stumbling through illogical lives with precisely that lack of common-sense which so pre-eminently distinguishes all our neighbors from ourselves.

For the life that moved in old Manuel of Poictesme finds hereinafter in his descendants, in these later Allonbys and Bulmers and Heleighs and Floyers, a new *milieu* to conform and curb that life in externes rather than in essentials. What this life made of chivalrous conditions has elsewhere been recorded: with its renewal in gallant circumstances, the stage is differently furnished and lighted, the costumes are dissimilar; but the comedy, I think, works toward the same *dénouement*, and certainly the protagonist remains unchanged. My protagonist is still the life of Manuel, as this life was perpetuated in his descendants; and my endeavor is (still) to show you what this life made (and omitted to make) of its tenancy of earth. 'Tis a drama enactable in any setting.

Yet the comedy of gallantry has its conventions. There must be quite invaluable papers to be stolen and juggled with; an involuntary marriage either threatened or consummated; elopements, highwaymen, and despatch-boxes; and a continual indulgence in soliloquy and eavesdropping. Everybody must pretend to be somebody else, and young girls, in particular, must go disguised as boys, amid much cut-and-thrust work, both ferric and verbal. For upon the whole, the comedy of gallantry tends to unfold itself in dialogue, and yet more dialogue, with just the notice of a change of scene or a brief stage direction inserted here and there. All these conventions, Madam, I observe.

A word more: the progress of an author who alternates, in turn, between fact and his private fancies (like unequal crutches) cannot in reason be undisfigured by false steps. Therefore it is judicious to confess, Madam, that more than once I have pieced the opulence of my subject with the poverty of my inventions. Indisputably, to thrust words into a dead man's mouth is in the ultimate as unpardonable as the axiomatic offence of stealing the pennies from his eyes; yet if I have sometimes erred in my surmise at what Ormskirk or de Puysange or Louis de Soyecourt really said at certain moments of their lives, the misstep was due, Madam, less to malevolence than to inability to replevin their superior utterance; and the accomplished shade of Garendon, at least, I have not travestied, unless it were through some too prudent item of excision.

Remains but to subscribe myself—in the approved formula of dedicators—as,

MADAM,
    Your ladyship's most humble and most obedient servant,
                            THE AUTHOR

THE PROLOGUE

Spoken by Lady Allonby, Who Enters in a Flurry

The author bade we come—Lud, I protest!—
He bade me come—and I forget the rest.
But 'tis no matter; he's an arrant fool
That ever bade a woman speak by rule.

Besides, his Prologue was, at best, dull stuff,
And of dull writing we have, sure, enough.
A book will do when you've a vacant minute,
But, la! who cares what is, and isn't, in it?

And since I'm but the Prologue of a book,
What I've omitted all will overlook,
And owe me for it, too, some gratitude,
Seeing in reason it cannot be good
Whose author has as much but now confessed,—
For, *Who'd excel when few can make a test*
Betwixt indifferent writing and the best?
He said but now.

              And I:—La, why excel,
When mediocrity does quite as well?
'Tis women buy the books,—and read 'em, say,
What time a person nods, en négligée,
And in default of gossip, cards, or dance,
Resolves t' incite a nap with some romance.

The fool replied in verse,—I think he said
'Twas verses the ingenious Dryden made,
And trust 'twill save me from entire disgrace
To cite 'em in his foolish Prologue's place.
    Yet, scattered here and there, I some behold,
Who can discern the tinsel from the gold;

To these he writes; and if by them allowed,
'Tis their prerogative to rule the crowd,
For he more fears, like, a presuming man,
Their votes who cannot judge, than theirs can.

I

SIMON'S HOUR

As Played at Stornoway Crag, March 25, 1750

You're a woman—one to whom Heaven gave beauty, when it grafted roses on a briar. You are the reflection of Heaven in a pond, and he that leaps at you is sunk. You were all white, a sheet of lovely spotless paper, when you first were born; but you are to be scrawled and blotted by every goose's quill."

Dramatis Personæ

Lord Rokesle, a loose-living, Impoverished nobleman, and
loves Lady Allonby.

Simon Orts, Vicar of Heriz Magna, a debauched fellow, and
Rokesle's creature.

Punshon, servant to Rokesle.

Lady Allonby, a pleasure-loving, luxurious woman, a widow,
and rich.

Scene
The Mancini Chamber at Stornoway Crag, on Usk.

Simon's Hour

Proem:—The Age and a Product of It

W e begin at a time when George the Second was permitting Ormskirk and the Pelhams to govern England, and the Jacobites had not yet ceased to hope for another Stuart Restoration, and Mr. Washington was a promising young surveyor in the most loyal colony of Virginia; when abroad the Marquise de Pompadour ruled France and all its appurtenances, and the King of Prussia and the Empress Maria Theresa had, between them, set entire Europe by the ears; when at home the ladies, if rumor may be credited, were less unapproachable than their hoop-petticoats caused them to appear,* and gentlemen wore swords, and some of the more reckless bloods were daringly beginning to discard the Ramillie-tie and the pigtail for their own hair; when politeness was obligatory, and morality a matter of taste, and when well-bred people went about the day's work with an ample leisure and very few scruples. In fine, we begin toward the end of March, in the year 1750, when Lady Allonby and her brother, Mr. Henry Heleigh, of Trevor's Folly, were the guests of Lord Rokesle, at Stornoway Crag, on Usk.

As any person of *ton* could have informed you, Anastasia Allonby was the widow (by his second marriage) of Lord Stephen Allonby, the Marquis of Falmouth's younger brother; and it was conceded by the most sedate that Lord Stephen's widow, in consideration of her liberal jointure, possessed inordinate comeliness.

She was tall for a woman. Her hair, tonight unpowdered, had the color of amber and something, too, of its glow; her eyes, though not profound, were large and in hue varied, as the light fell or her emotions shifted, through a wide gamut of blue shades. But it was her mouth you remembered: the fulness and brevity of it, the deep indentation of its upper lip, the curves of it and its vivid crimson—these roused you to wildish speculation as to its probable softness when Lady Allonby and Fate were beyond ordinary lenient. Pink was the color most favorable to her complexion, and this she wore tonight; the gown was voluminous,

---

* "Oft have we known that sevenfold fence to fail, Though stiff with hoops, and armed with ribs of whale."

with a profusion of lace, and afforded everybody an ample opportunity to appraise her neck and bosom. Lady Allonby had no reason to be ashamed of either, and the last mode in these matters was not prudish.

To such a person, enters Simon Orts, chaplain in ordinary to Lord Rokesle, and Vicar of Heriz Magna, one of Lord Rokesle's livings.

I

"Now of a truth," said Simon Orts, "that is curious—undeniably that is curious."

He stayed at the door for a moment staring back into the ill-lit corridor. Presently he shut the door, and came forward toward the fireplace.

Lady Allonby, half-hidden in the depths of the big chair beside the chimney-piece, a book in her lap, looked up inquiringly. "What is curious, Mr. Orts?"

The clergyman stood upon the hearth, warming his hands, and diffusing an odor of tobacco and stale alcohol. "Faith, that damned rascal—I beg your pardon, Anastasia; our life upon Usk is not conducive to a mincing nicety of speech. That rascal Punshon made some difficulty over admitting me; you might have taken him for a sentinel, with Stornoway in a state of siege. He ruffled me,—and I don't like it," Simon Orts said, reflectively, looking down upon her. "No, I don't like it. Where's your brother?" he demanded on a sudden.

"Harry and Lord Rokesle are at cards, I believe. And Mrs. Morfit has retired to her apartments with one of her usual headaches, so that I have been alone these two hours. You visit Stornoway somewhat late, Mr. Orts," Anastasia Allonby added, without any particular concealment of the fact that she considered his doing so a nuisance.

He jerked his thumb ceilingward. "The cloth is at any rascal's beck and call. Old Holles, my Lord's man, is dying up yonder, and the whim seized him to have a clergyman in. God knows why, for it appears to me that one knave might very easily make his way to hell without having another knave to help him. And Holles?—eh, well, from what I myself know of him, the rogue is triply damned." His mouth puckered as he set about unbuttoning his long, rain-spattered cloak, which, with his big hat, he flung aside upon a table. "Gad!" said Simon Orts, "we are most of us damned on Usk; and that is why I don't like it—" He struck his hand against his thigh. "I don't like it, Anastasia."

"You must pardon me," she languidly retorted, "but I was never good at riddles."

He turned and glanced about the hall, debating. Lady Allonby meanwhile regarded him, as she might have looked at a frog or a hurtless snake. A small, slim, anxious man, she found him; always fidgeting, always placating some one, but never without a covert sneer. The fellow was venomous; his eyes only were honest, for even while his lips were about their wheedling, these eyes flashed malice at you; and their shifting was so unremittent that afterward you recalled them as an absolute shining which had not any color. On Usk and thereabouts they said it was the glare from within of his damned soul, already at white heat; but they were a plain-spoken lot on Usk. Tonight Simon Orts was all in black; and his hair, too, and his gross eyebrows were black, and well-nigh to the cheek-bones of his clean-shaven countenance the thick beard, showed black through the skin.

Now he kept silence for a lengthy interval, his arms crossed on his breast, gnawing meanwhile at the fingernails of his left hand in an unattractive fashion he had of meditating. When words came it was in a torrent.

"I will read you my riddle, then. You are a widow, rich; as women go, you are not so unpleasant to look at as most of 'em. If it became a clergyman to dwell upon such matters, I would say that your fleshly habitation is too fine for its tenant, since I know you to be a good-for-nothing jilt. However, you are God's handiwork, and doubtless He had His reasons for constructing you. My Lord is poor; last summer at Tunbridge you declined to marry him. I am in his confidence, you observe. He took your decision in silence—'ware Rokesle when he is quiet! Eh, I know the man,—'tisn't for nothing that these ten years past I have studied his whims, pampered his vanity, lied to him, toadied him! You admire my candor?—faith, yes, I am very candid. I am Rokesle's hanger-on; he took me out of the gutter, and in my fashion I am grateful. And you?—Anastasia, had you treated me more equitably fifteen years ago, I would have gone to the stake for you, singing; now I don't value you the flip of a farthing. But, for old time's sake, I warn you. You and your brother are Rokesle's guests—on Usk! Harry Heleigh* can handle

---

* Henry Heleigh, thirteenth Earl of Brudenel, who succeeded his cousin the twelfth Earl in 1759, and lived to a great age. Bavois, writing in 1797, calls him "a very fine, strong old gentleman."

a sword, I grant you,—but you are on Usk! And Mrs. Morfit is here to play propriety—propriety on Usk, God save the mark! And besides, Rokesle can twist his sister about his little finger, as the phrase runs. And I find sentinels at the door! I don't like it, Anastasia. In his way Rokesle loves you; more than that, you are an ideal match to retrieve his battered fortunes; and the name of my worthy patron, I regret to say, is not likely ever to embellish the Calendar of Saints."

Simon Orts paused with a short laugh. The woman had risen to her feet, her eyes widening and a thought troubled, though her lips smiled contemptuously.

"La, I should have comprehended that this late in the evening you would be in no condition to converse with ladies. Believe me, though, Mr. Orts, I would be glad to credit your warning to officious friendliness, were it not that the odor about your person compels me to attribute it to gin."

"Oh, I have been drinking," he conceded; "I have been drinking with a most commendable perseverance for these fifteen years. But at present I am far from drunk." Simon Orts took a turn about the hall; in an instant he faced her with an odd, almost tender smile, "You adorable, empty-headed, pink-and-white fool," said Simon Orts, "what madness induced you to come to Usk? You know that Rokesle wants you; you know that you don't mean to marry him. Then why come to Usk? Do you know who is king in this sea-washed scrap of earth?—Rokesle. German George reigns yonder in England, but here, in the Isle of Usk, Vincent Floyer is king. And it is not precisely a convent that he directs. The men of Usk, I gather, after ten years' experience in the administering of spiritual consolation hereabouts"—and his teeth made their appearance in honor of the jest,—"are part fisherman, part smuggler, part pirate, and part devil. Since the last ingredient predominates, they have no very unreasonable apprehension of hell, and would cheerfully invade it if Rokesle bade 'em do so. As I have pointed out, my worthy patron is subject to the frailties of the flesh. Oh, I am candid, for if you report me to his Lordship I shall lie out of it. I have had practice enough to do it handsomely. But Rokesle—do you not know what Rokesle is—?"

The Vicar of Heriz Magna would have gone on, but Lady Allonby had interrupted, her cheeks flaming. "Yes, yes," she cried;' "I know him to be a worthy gentleman. 'Tis true I could not find it in my heart to marry him, yet I am proud to rank Lord Rokesle among my friends." She waved her hand toward the chimney-piece, where hung—and hangs today,—the sword of Aluric Floyer, the founder of the house of Rokesle. "Do you see that old sword, Mr. Orts? The man who wielded it long ago was a gallant gentleman and a stalwart captain. And my Lord, as he told me but on Thursday afternoon, hung it there that he might always have in mind the fact that he bore the name of this man, and must bear it meritoriously. My Lord is a gentleman. La, believe me, if you, too, were a gentleman, Mr. Orts, you would understand! But a gentleman is not a talebearer; a gentleman does not defame any person behind his back, far less the person to whom he owes his daily bread."

"So he has been gulling you?" said Simon Orts; then he added quite inconsequently: "I had not thought anything you could say would hurt me. I discover I was wrong. Perhaps I am not a gentleman. Faith, no; I am only a shabby drunkard, a disgrace to my cloth, am I not, Anastasia? Accordingly, I fail to perceive what old Aluric Floyer has to do with the matter in hand. He was reasonably virtuous, I suppose; putting aside a disastrous appetite for fruit, so was Adam: but, viewing their descendants, I ruefully admit that in each case the strain has deteriorated."

There was a brief silence; then Lady Allonby observed: "Perhaps I was discourteous. I ask your forgiveness, Mr. Orts. And now, if you will pardon the suggestion, I think you had better go to your dying parishioner."

But she had touched the man to the quick. "I am a drunkard; who made me so? Who was it used to cuddle me with so many soft words and kisses—yes, kisses, my Lady!—till a wealthier man came a-wooing, and then flung me aside like an old shoe?"

This drenched her cheeks with crimson, "I think we had better not refer to that boy-and-girl affair. You cannot blame me for your debauched manner of living. I found before it was too late that I did not love you. I was only a girl, and 'twas natural that at first I should be mistaken in my fancies."

The Vicar had caught her by each wrist. "You don't understand, of course. You never understood, for you have no more heart than one of those pink-and-white bisque figures that you resemble. You don't love me, and therefore I will go to the devil' may not be an all-rational deduction, but 'tis very human logic. You don't understand that, do you, Anastasia? You don't understand how when one is acutely miserable one remembers that at the bottom of a wineglass—or even at the bottom of a tumbler of gin,—one may come upon happiness, or at least upon acquiescence to whatever the niggling gods may send. You don't understand how one remembers, when the desired woman is lost, that there are other women whose lips are equally red and whose hearts are tenderer and—yes, whose virtue is less exigent. No; women never understand these things: and in any event, you would not understand, because you are only an adorable pink-and-white fool."

"Oh, oh!" she cried, struggling, "How dare you? You insult me, you coward!"

"Well, you can always comfort yourself with the reflection that it scarcely matters what a sot like me may elect to say. And, since you understand me now no more than formerly, Anastasia, I tell you that the lover turned adrift may well profit by the example of his predecessors. Other lovers have been left forsaken, both in trousers and in ripped petticoats; and I have heard that when Chryseis was reft away from Agamemnon, the *cnax andrôn* made himself tolerably comfortable with Briseis; and that, when Theseus sneaked off in the night, Ariadne, after having wept for a decent period, managed in the ultimate to console herself with Theban Bacchus,—which I suppose to be a courteous method of stating that the daughter of Minos took to drink. So the forsaken lover has his choice of consolation—in wine or in that dearer danger, woman. I have tried both, Anastasia. And I tell you—"

He dropped her hands as though they had been embers. Lord Rokesle had come quietly into the hall.

"Why, what's this?" Lord Rokesle demanded. "Simon, you aren't making love to Lady Allonby, I hope? Fie, man! remember your cloth."

Simon Orts wheeled—a different being, servile and cringing. "Your Lordship is pleased to be pleasant. Indeed, though, I fear that your ears must burn, sir, for I was but now expatiating upon the manifold kindnesses your Lordship has been so generous as to confer upon your unworthy friend. I was admiring Lady Allonby's ruffle, sir,— Valenciennes, I take it, and very choice."

Lord Rokesle laughed. "So I am to thank you for blowing my trumpet, am I?" said Lord Rokesle. "Well, you are not a bad fellow, Simon, so long as you are sober. And now be off with you to Holles— the rascal is dying, they tell me. My luck, Simon! He made up a cravat better than any one in the kingdom."

"The ways of Providence are inscrutable," Simon Orts considered; "and if Providence has in verity elected to chasten your Lordship, doubtless it shall be, as anciently in the case of Job the Patriarch, repaid by a recompense, by a thousandfold recompense." And after a meaning glance toward Lady Allonby,—a glance that said: "I, too, have a tongue,"—he was mounting the stairway to the upper corridor when Lord Rokesle called to him.

"By my conscience! I forgot," said Lord Rokesle; "don't leave Stornoway without seeing me again, I shall want you by and by."

II

LORD ROKESLE SAT DOWN UPON the long, high-backed bench, beside the fire, and facing Lady Allonby's arm-chair.

Neither he nor Lady Allonby spoke for a while.

In a sombre way Lord Rokesle was a handsome man, and tonight, in brown and gold, very stately. His bearing savored faintly of the hidalgo; indeed, his mother was a foreign woman, cast ashore on Usk, from a wrecked Spanish vessel, and incontinently married by the despot of the island. For her, Death had delayed his advent unmercifully; but her reason survived the marriage by two years only, and there were those familiar with the late Lord Rokesle's* peculiarities who considered that in this, at least, the crazed lady was fortunate. Among these gossips it was also esteemed a matter deserving comment that in the shipwrecks not infrequent about Usk the women sometimes survived, but the men never.

Now Lord Rokesle regarded Lady Allonby, the while that she displayed conspicuous interest in the play of the flames. But by and by, "O vulgarity!" said Lady Allonby. "Pray endeavor to look a little more cheerful. Positively, you are glaring at me like one of those disagreeable beggars one so often sees staring at bakery windows."

He smiled. "Do you remember what the Frenchman wrote—*et pain ne voyent qu'aux fenêtres?* There is not an enormous difference between me and the tattered rascal of Chepe, for we both stare longingly at what we most desire. And were I minded to hunt the simile to the foot of the letter, I would liken your coquetry to the intervening window-pane,— not easily broken through, but very, very transparent, Anastasia."

---

* Born 1685, and accidentally killed by Sir Piers Sabiston in 1738; an accurate account of this notorious duellist, profligate, charlatan, and playwright is given in Ireson's *Letters*.

"You are not overwhelmingly polite," she said, reflectively; "but, then, I suppose, living in the country is sure to damage a man's manners. Still, my dear Orson, you smack too much of the forest."

"Anastasia," said Lord Rokesle, bending toward her, "will you always be thus cruel? Do you not understand that in this world you are the only thing I care for? You think me a boor; perhaps I am,—and yet it rests with you, my Lady, to make me what you will. For I love you, Anastasia—"

"Why, how delightful of you!" said she, languidly.

"It is not a matter for jesting. I tell you that I love you." My Lord's color was rising.

But Lady Allonby yawned. "Your honor's most devoted," she declared herself; "still, you need not boast of your affection as if falling in love with me were an uncommonly difficult achievement. That, too, is scarcely polite."

"For the tenth time I ask you will you marry me?" said Lord Rokesle.

"Is't only the tenth time? Dear me, it seems like the thousandth. Of course, I couldn't think of it. Heavens, my Lord, how can you expect me to marry a man who glares at me like that? Positively you look as ferocious as the blackamoor in the tragedy,—the fellow who smothered his wife because she misplaced a handkerchief, you remember."

Lord Rokesle had risen, and he paced the hall, as if fighting down resentment. "I am no Othello," he said at last; "though, indeed, I think that the love I bear you is of a sort which rarely stirs our English blood. 'Tis not for nothing I am half-Spaniard, I warn you, Anastasia, my love is a consuming blaze that will not pause for considerations of policy nor even of honor. And you madden me, Anastasia! Today you hear my protestations with sighs and glances and faint denials; tomorrow you have only taunts for me. Sometimes, I think, 'tis hatred rather than love I bear you. Sometimes—" He clutched at his breast with a wild gesture. "I burn!" he said. "Woman, give me back a human heart in place of this flame you have kindled here, or I shall go mad! Last night I dreamed of hell, and of souls toasted on burning forks and fed with sops of bale-fire,—and you were there, Anastasia, where the flames leaped and curled like red-blazoned snakes about the poor damned. And I, too, was there. And through eternity I heard you cry to God in vain, O dear, wonderful, golden-haired woman! and we could see Him, somehow,— see Him, a great way off, with straight, white brows that frowned upon you pitilessly. And I was glad. For I knew then that I hated you. And even now, when I think I must go mad for love of you, I yet hate you with a fervor that shakes and thrills in every fibre of me. Oh, I burn, I burn!" he cried, with the same frantic clutching at his breast.

Lady Allonby had risen.

"Positively, I must ask you to open a window if you intend to continue in this strain. D'ye mean to suffocate me, my Lord, with your flames and your blazes and your brimstone and so on? You breathe conflagrations, like a devil in a pantomime. I had as soon converse with a piece of fireworks. So, if you'll pardon me, I will go to my brother."

At the sound of her high, crisp speech his frenzy fell from him like a mantle. "And you let me kiss you yesterday! Oh, I know you struggled, but you did not struggle very hard, did you, Anastasia?"

"Why, what a notion!" cried Lady Allonby; "as if a person should bother seriously one way or the other about the antics of an amorous clodhopper! Meanwhile, I repeat, my Lord, I wish to go to my brother."

"Egad!" Lord Rokesle retorted, "that reminds me I have been notably remiss. I bear you a message from Harry. He had tonight a letter from Job Nangle, who, it seems, has a purchaser for Trevor's Folly at last. The fellow is with our excellent Nangle at Peniston Friars, and offers liberal terms if the sale be instant. The chance was too promising to let slip, so Harry left the island an hour ago. It happened by a rare chance that some of my fellows were on the point of setting out for the mainland,—and he knew that he could safely entrust you to Mrs. Morfit's duennaship, he said."

"He should not have done so," Lady Allonby observed, as if in a contention of mind. "He—I will go to Mrs. Morfit, then, to confess to her in frankness that, after all these rockets and bonfires—"

"Why, that's the unfortunate part of the whole affair," said Lord Rokesle. "The same boat brought Sabina a letter which summoned her to the bedside of her husband,* who, it appears, lies desperately ill at Kuyper Manor. It happened by a rare chance that some of my fellows were on the point of setting out for the mainland—from Heriz pier yonder, not from the end of the island whence Harry sailed,—so she and her maid embarked instanter. Of course, there was your brother here to play propriety, she said. And by the oddest misfortune in the

---

* Archibald Morfit, M.P. for Salop, and in 1753 elected Speaker, which office he declined on account of ill-health. He was created a baronet in 1758 through the Duke of Ormskirk's influence.

world," Lord Rokesle sighed, "I forgot to tell her that Harry Heleigh had left Usk a half-hour earlier. My memory is lamentably treacherous."

But Lady Allonby had dropped all affectation. "You coward! You planned this!"

"Candidly, yes. Nangle is my agent as well as Harry's, you may remember. I have any quantity of his letters, and of course an equal number of Archibald's. So I spent the morning in my own apartments, Anastasia,—tracing letters against the window-pane, which was, I suppose, a childish recreation, but then what would you have? As you very justly observe, country life invariably coarsens a man's tastes; and accordingly, as you may now recall, I actually declined a game of *écarté* with you in order to indulge in these little forgeries. Decidedly, my dear, you must train your husband's imagination for superior flights—when you are Lady Rokesle."

She was staring at him as though he had been a portent. "I am alone," she said. "Alone—in this place—with you! Alone! you devil!"

"Your epithets increase in vigor. Just now I was only a clodhopper. Well, I can but repeat that it rests with you to make me what you will. Though, indeed, you are to all intent alone upon Usk, and upon Usk there are many devils. There are ten of them on guard yonder, by the way, in case your brother should return inopportunely, though that's scarcely probable. Obedient devils, you observe, Anastasia,—devils who exert and check their deviltry as I bid 'em, for they esteem me Lucifer's lieutenant. And I grant the present situation is an outrage to propriety, yet the evil is not incurable. Lady Allonby may not, if she value her reputation, pass tonight at Stornoway; but here am I, all willingness, and upstairs is the parson. Believe me, Anastasia, the most vinegarish prude could never object to Lady Rokesle's spending tonight at Stornoway."

"Let me think, let me think!" Lady Allonby said, and her hands plucked now at her hair, now at her dress. She appeared dazed. "I can't think!" she wailed on a sudden. "I am afraid. I—O Vincent, Vincent, you cannot do this thing! I trusted you, Vincent. I know I let you make love to me, and I relished having you make love to me. Women are like that. But I cannot marry you, Vincent. There is a man, yonder in England, whom I love. He does not care for me any more,—he is in love with my step-daughter. That is very amusing, is it not, Vincent? Some day I may be his mother-in-law. Why don't you laugh, Vincent? Come, let us both laugh—first at this and then at the jest you have just played on me. Do you know, for an instant, I believed you were in earnest? But Harry went to sleep over the cards, didn't he? And Mrs. Morfit has gone to bed with one of her usual headaches? Of course; and you thought you would retaliate upon me for teasing you. You were quite right, 'Twas an excellent jest. Now let us laugh at it. Laugh, Vincent! Oh!" she said now, more shrilly, "for the love of God, laugh, laugh!—or I shall go mad!"

But Lord Rokesle was a man of ice, "Matrimony is a serious matter, Anastasia; 'tis not becoming in those who are about to enter it to exhibit undue levity. I wonder what's keeping Simon?"

"Simon Orts!" she said, in a half-whisper. Then she came toward Lord Rokesle, smiling. "Why, of course, I teased you, Vincent, but there was never any hard feeling, was there? And you really wish me to marry you? Well, we must see, Vincent. But, as you say, matrimony is a serious matter. D'ye know you say very sensible things, Vincent?— not at all like those silly fops yonder in London. I dare say you and I would be very happy together. But you wouldn't have any respect for me if I married you on a sudden like this, would you? Of course not. So you will let me consider it. Come to me a month from now, say,—is that too long to wait? Well, I think 'tis too long myself. Say a week, then. I must have my wedding-finery, you comprehend. We women are such vain creatures—not big and brave and sensible like you men. See, for example, how much bigger your hand is than mine— mine's quite lost in it, isn't it? So—since I am only a vain, chattering, helpless female thing,—you are going to indulge me and let me go up to London for some new clothes, aren't you, Vincent? Of course you will; and we will be married in a week. But you will let me go to London first, won't you?—away from this dreadful place, away—I didn't mean that. I suppose it is a very agreeable place when you get accustomed to it. And 'tis only for clothes—Oh, I swear it is only for clothes, Vincent! And you said you would—yes, only a moment ago you distinctly said you would let me go. 'Tis not as if I were not coming back—who said I would not come back? Of course I will. But you must give me time, Vincent dear,—you must, you must, I tell you! O God!" she sobbed, and flung from her the loathed hand she was fondling, "it's no use!"

"No," said Lord Rokesle, rather sadly. "I am not Samson, nor are you Delilah to cajole me. It's of no use, Anastasia. I would have preferred that you came to me voluntarily, but since you cannot, I mean to take you unwilling. Simon," he called, loudly, "does that rascal intend to spin out his dying interminably? Charon's waiting, man."

From above, "Coming, my Lord," said Simon Orts.

III

THE VICAR OF HERIZ MAGNA descended the stairway with deliberation. His eyes twitched from the sobbing woman to Lord Rokesle, and then back again, in that furtive way Orts had of glancing about a room, without moving his head; he seemed to lie in ambush under his gross brows; and whatever his thoughts may have been, he gave them no utterance.

"Simon," said Lord Rokesle, "Lady Allonby is about to make me the happiest of men. Have you a prayer-book about you, Master Parson?— for here's a loving couple desirous of entering the blessed state of matrimony."

"The match is somewhat of the suddenest," said Simon Orts. "But I have known these impromptu marriages to turn out very happily— very happily, indeed." he repeated, rubbing his hands together, and smiling horribly. "I gather that Mr. Heleigh will not grace the ceremony with his presence?"

They understood each other, these two. Lord Rokesle grinned, and in a few words told the ecclesiastic of the trick which had insured the absence of the other guests; and Simon Orts also grinned, but respectfully,—the grin, of the true lackey wearing his master's emotions like his master's clothes, at second-hand.

"A very pretty stratagem," said Simon Orts; "unconventional, I must confess, but it is proverbially known that all's fair in love."

At this Lady Allonby came to him, catching his hand. "There is only you, Simon. Oh, there is no hope in that lustful devil yonder. But you are not all base, Simon. You are a man,—ah, God! if I were a man I would rip out that devil's heart—his defiled and infamous heart! I would trample upon it, I would feed it to dogs—!" She paused. Her impotent fury was jerking at every muscle, was choking her. "But I am only a woman. Simon, you used to love me. You cannot have forgotten, Simon. Oh, haven't you any pity on a woman? Remember, Simon— remember how happy we were! Don't you remember how the night-jars used to call to one another when we sat on moonlit evenings under the elm-tree? And d'ye remember the cottage we planned, Simon?—where we were going to live on bread and cheese and kisses? And how we quarrelled because I wanted to train vines over it? You said the rooms would be too dark. You said—oh, Simon, Simon! if only I had gone to live with you in that little cottage we planned and never builded!" Lady Allonby was at his feet now. She fawned upon him in somewhat the manner of a spaniel expectant of a thrashing.

The Vicar of Heriz Magna dispassionately ran over the leaves of his prayer-book, till he had found the marriage service, and then closed the book, his forefinger marking the place. Lord Rokesle stood apart, and with a sly and meditative smile observed them.

"Your plea is a remarkable one," said Simon Orts. "As I understand it, you appeal to me to meddle in your affairs on the ground that you once made a fool of me. I think the obligation is largely optional. I remember quite clearly the incidents to which you refer; and it shames even an old sot like me to think that I was ever so utterly at the mercy of a good-for-nothing jilt. I remember every vow you ever made to me, Anastasia, and I know they were all lies. I remember every kiss, every glance, every caress—all lies, Anastasia! And gad! the only emotion it rouses in me is wonder as to why my worthy patron here should want to marry you. Of course you are wealthy, but, personally, I would not have you for double the money. I must ask you to rise, Lady Rokesle.—Pardon me if I somewhat anticipate your title."

Lady Allonby stumbled to her feet. "Is there no manhood in the world?" she asked, with a puzzled voice. "Has neither of you ever heard of manhood, though but as distantly as men hear summer thunder? Had neither of you a woman for a mother—a woman, as I am—or a father who was not—O God!—not as you are?"

"These rhetorical passages," said Lord Rokesle, "while very elegantly expressed, are scarcely to the point. So you and Simon went a-philandering once? Egad, that lends quite a touch of romance to the affair. But despatch, Parson Simon,—your lady's for your betters now."

"Dearly beloved,—" said Simon Orts.

"Simon, you are not all base. I am helpless, Simon, utterly helpless. There was a Simon once would not have seen me weep. There was a Simon—"

"—we are gathered together here in the sight of God—"

"You cannot do it, Simon,—do I not know you to the marrow? Remember—not me—not the vain folly of my girlhood!—but do you remember the man you have been, Simon Orts!" Fiercely Lady Allonby caught him by the shoulder. "For you do remember! You do remember, don't you, Simon?"

The Vicar stared at her. "The man I have been," said Simon Orts, "yes!—the man I have been!" Something clicked in his throat with sharp distinctness.

"Upon my word," said Lord Rokesle, yawning, "this getting married appears to be an uncommonly tedious business."

Then Simon Orts laid aside his prayer-book and said: "I cannot do it, my Lord. The woman's right."

She clapped her hands to her breast, and stood thus, reeling upon her feet. You would have thought her in the crisis of some physical agony; immediately she breathed again, deeply but with a flinching inhalation, as though the contact of the air scorched her lungs, and, swaying, fell. It was the Vicar who caught her as she fell.

"I entreat your pardon?" said Lord Rokesle, and without study of Lady Allonby's condition. This was men's business now, and over it Rokesle's brow began to pucker.

Simon Orts bore Lady Allonby to the settie. He passed behind it to arrange a cushion under her head, with an awkward, grudging tenderness; and then rose to face Lord Rokesle across the disordered pink fripperies.

"The woman's right, my Lord. There is such a thing as manhood. Manhood!" Simon Orts repeated, with a sort of wonder; "why, I might have boasted it once. Then came this cuddling bitch to trick me into a fool's paradise—to trick me into utter happiness, till Stephen Allonby, a marquis' son, clapped eyes on her and whistled,— and within the moment she had flung me aside. May God forgive me, I forgot I was His servant then! I set out to go to the devil, but I went farther; for I went to you, Vincent Floyer. You gave me bread when I was starving,—but 'twas at a price. Ay, the price was that I dance attendance on you, to aid and applaud your knaveries, to be your pander, your lackey, your confederate,—that I puff out, in effect, the last spark of manhood in my sot's body. Oh, I am indeed beholden to you two! to her for making me a sot, and to you for making me a lackey. But I will save her from you, Vincent Floyer. Not for her sake"—Orts looked down upon the prostrate woman and snarled. "Christ, no! But I'll do it for the sake of the boy I have been, since I owe that boy some reparation. I have ruined his nimble body, I have dulled the wits he gloried in, I have made his name a foul thing that honesty spits out of her mouth; but, if God yet reigns in heaven, I cleanse that name tonight!"

"Oh, bless me," Lord Rokesle observed; "I begin to fear these heroics are contagious. Possibly I, too, shall begin to rant in a moment. Meanwhile, as I understand it, you decline to perform the ceremony. I have had to warn you before this, Simon, that you mustn't take too much gin when I am apt to need you. You are very pitifully drunk, man. So you defy me and my evil courses! You defy me!" Rokesle laughed, genially, for the notion amused him. "Wine is a mocker, Simon. But come, despatch, Parson Tosspot, and let's have no more of these lofty sentiments."

"I cannot do it. I—O my Lord, my Lord! You wouldn't kill an unarmed man!" Simon Orts whined, with a sudden alteration of tone; for Lord Rokesle had composedly drawn his sword, and its point was now not far from the Vicar's breast.

"I trust that I shall not be compelled to. Egad, it is a very ludicrous business when the bridegroom is forced to hold a sword to the parson's bosom all during the ceremony; but a ceremony we must have, Simon, for Lady Allonby's jointure is considerable. Otherwise—Harkee, my man, don't play the fool! there are my fellows yonder, any one of whom would twist your neck at a word from me. And do you think I would boggle at a word? Gad, Simon, I believed you knew me better!"

The Vicar of Heriz Magna kept silence for an instant; his eyes were twitching about the hall, in that stealthy way of his. Finally, "It is no use," said he. "A poor knave cannot afford the luxury of honesty. My life is not a valuable one, perhaps, but even vermin have an aversion to death. I resume my lackeyship, Lord Rokesle. Perhaps 'twas only the gin. Perhaps—In any event, I am once more at your service. And as guaranty of this I warn you that you are exhibiting in the affair scant forethought. Mr. Heleigh is but three miles distant. If he, by any chance, get wind of this business, Denstroude will find a boat for him readily enough—ay, and men, too, now that the Colonel is at feud with you. Many of your people visit the mainland every night, and in their cups the inhabitants of Usk are not taciturn. An idle word spoken over an inn-table may bring an armed company thundering about your gates. You should have set sentinels, my Lord."

"I have already done so," Rokesle said; "there are ten of 'em yonder. Still there is something in what you say. We will make this affair certain."

Lord Rokesle crossed the hall to the foot of the stairway and struck thrice upon the gong hanging there. Presently the door leading to the corridor was opened, and a man came into the hall.

"Punshon," said Lord Rokesle, "have any boats left the island tonight?"

"No, my Lord."

"You will see that none do. Also, no man is to leave Stornoway tonight, either for Heriz Magna or the mainland; and nobody is to enter Stornoway. Do you understand, Punshon?"

"Yes, my Lord."

"If you will pardon me," said Simon Orts, with a grin, "I have an appointment tonight. You'd not have me break faith with a lady?"

"You are a lecherous rascal, Simon. But do as you are bid and I indulge you. I am not afraid of your going to Harry Heleigh—after performing the ceremony. Nay, my lad, for you are thereby *particeps criminis*. You will pass Mr. Orts, Punshon, to the embraces of his whore. Nobody else."

Simon Orts waved his hand toward Lady Allonby. "'Twere only kindness to warn Mr. Punshon there may be some disturbance shortly. A lamentation or so."

At this Lord Rokesle clapped him upon the shoulder and heartily laughed. "That's the old Simon—always on the alert. Punshon, no one is to enter this wing of the castle, on any pretext—no one, you understand. Whatever noises you may hear, you will pay no attention. Now go."

He went toward Lady Allonby and took her hand. "Come, Anastasia!" said he. "Hold, she has really swooned! Why, what the devil, Simon—!"

Simon Orts had flung the gong into the fire. "She will be sounding that when she comes to," said Simon Orts. "You don't want a rumpus fit to vex the dead yonder in the Chapel." Simon Orts stood before the fire, turning the leaves of his prayer-book. He seemed to have difficulty in finding again the marriage service. You heard the outer door of the corridor closing, heard chains dragged ponderously, the heavy falling of a bolt. Orts dropped the book and, springing into the arm-chair, wrested Aluric Floyer's sword from its fastening. "Tricked, tricked!" said Simon Orts. "You were always a fool, Vincent Floyer."

Lord Rokesle blinked at him, as if dazzled by unexpected light. "What d'ye mean?"

"I have the honor to repeat—you are a fool, I did not know the place was guarded—you told me. I needed privacy; by your orders no one is to enter here tonight. I needed a sword—you had it hanging here, ready for the first comer. Oh, beyond doubt, you are a fool, Vincent Floyer!" Standing in the arm-chair, Simon Orts bowed fantastically, and then leaped to the ground with the agility of an imp.

"You have tricked me neatly," Lord Rokesle conceded, and his tone did not lack honest admiration. "By gad, I have even given them orders to pass you—after you have murdered me! Exceedingly clever, Simon,—but one thing you overlooked. You are very far from my match at fencing. So I shall presently kill you. And afterward, ceremony or no ceremony, the woman's mine."

"I am not convinced of that," the Vicar observed. "'Tis true I am no swordsman; but there are behind my sword forces superior to any which skill might muster. The sword of your fathers fights against you, my Lord—against you that are their disgrace. They loved honor and truth; you betrayed honor, you knew not truth. They revered womanhood; you reverence nothing, and your life smirches your mother's memory. Ah, believe me, they all fight against you! Can you not see them, my Lord?—yonder at my back?—old Aluric Floyer and all those honest gentlemen, whose blood now blushes in your body— ay, blushes to be confined in a vessel so ignoble! Their armament fights against you, a host of gallant phantoms. And my hatred, too, fights against you—the cur's bitter hatred for the mastering hand it dares not bite. I dare now. You made me your pander, you slew my manhood; in return, body and soul, I demolish you. Even my hatred for that woman fights against you; she robbed me of my honor—is it not a tragical revenge to save her honor, to hold it in my hand, mine, to dispose of as I elect,—and then fling it to her as a thing contemptible? Between you, you have ruined me; but it is Simon's hour tonight. I shame you both, and past the reach of thought, for presently I shall take your life—in the high-tide of your iniquity, praise God!—and presently I shall give my life for hers. Ah, I a fey, my Lord! You are a dead man, Vincent Floyer, for the powers of good and the powers of evil alike contend against you."

He spoke rather sadly than otherwise; and there was a vague trouble in Lord Rokesle's face, though he shook his head impatiently. "These are fine words to come from the dirtiest knave unhanged in England."

"Great ends may be attained by petty instruments, my Lord; a filthy turtle quenched the genius of Æschylus, and they were only common soldiers who shed the blood that redeemed the world."

Lord Rokesle pished at this. Yet he was strangely unruffled. He saluted with quietude, as equal to equal, and the two crossed blades.

Simon Orts fought clumsily, but his encroachment was unwavering. From the first he pressed his opponent with a contained resolution. The Vicar was as a man fighting in a dream—with a drugged obstinacy, unswerving. Lord Rokesle had wounded him in the arm, but Orts did not seem aware of this. He crowded upon his master. Now there were little beads of sweat on Lord Rokesle's brow, and his tongue protruded from his mouth, licking at it ravenously. Step by step Lord Rokesle drew back; there was no withstanding this dumb fanatic, who did not know when he was wounded, who scarcely parried attack.

"Even on earth you shall have a taste of hell," said Simon Orts. "There is terror in your eyes, my worthy patron."

Lord Rokesle flung up his arms as the sword dug into his breast. "I am afraid! I am afraid!" he wailed. Then he coughed, and seemed with his straining hands to push a great weight from him as the blood frothed about his lips and nostrils. "O Simon, I am afraid! Help me, Simon!"

Old custom spoke there. Followed silence, and presently the empty body sprawled upon the floor. Vincent Floyer had done with it.

IV

Simon Orts knelt, abstractedly wiping Aluric Floyer's sword upon the corner of a rug. It may be that he derived comfort from this manual employment which necessitated attention without demanding that it concentrate his mind; it may have enabled him to forget how solitary the place was, how viciously his garments rustled when he moved: the fact is certain that he cleaned the sword, over and over again.

Then a scraping of silks made him wince. Turning, he found Lady Allonby half-erect upon the settle. She stared about her with a kind of infantile wonder; her glance swept, over Lord Rokesle's body, without to all appearance finding it an object of remarkable interest. "Is he dead?"

"Yes," said Simon Orts; "get up!" His voice had a rasp; she might from his tone have been a refractory dog. But Lady Allonby obeyed him.

"We are in a devil of a mess," said Simon Orts; "yet I see a way out of it—if you can keep your head. Can you?"

"I am past fear," she said, dully. "I drown, Simon, in a sea of feathers. I can get no foothold, I clutch nothing that is steadfast, and I smother. I have been like this in dreams. I am very tired, Simon."

He took her hand, collectedly appraising her pulse. He put his own hand upon her bared bosom, and felt the beat of her heart. "No," said Simon Orts, "you are not afraid. Now, listen: You lack time to drown in a sea of feathers. You are upon Usk, among men who differ from beasts by being a thought more devilish, and from devils by being a little more bestial; it is my opinion that the earlier you get away the better. Punshon has orders to pass Simon Orts. Very well; put on this."

He caught up his long cloak and wrapped it about her. Lady Allonby stood rigid. But immediately he frowned and removed the garment from her shoulders.

"That won't do. Your skirts are too big. Take 'em off."

Submissively she did so, and presently stood before him in her under-petticoat.

"You cut just now a very ludicrous figure, Anastasia. I dare assert that the nobleman who formerly inhabited yonder carcass would still be its tenant if he had known how greatly the beauty he went mad for was beholden to the haberdasher and the mantua-maker, and quite possibly the chemist. *Persicos odi*, Anastasia; 'tis a humiliating reflection that the hair of a dead woman artfully disposed about a living head should have the power to set men squabbling, and murder be at times engendered in a paint-pot. However, wrap yourself in the cloak. Now turn up the collar,—so. Now pull down the hatbrim. Um—a—pretty well. Chance favors us unblushingly. You may thank your stars it is a rainy night and that I am a little man. You detest little men, don't you? Yes, I remember." Simon Orts now gave his orders, emphasizing each with a not over-clean forefinger. "When I open this door you will go out into the corridor. Punshon or one of the others will be on guard at the farther end. Pay no attention to him. There is only one light—on the left. Keep to the right, in the shadow. Stagger as you go; if you can manage a hiccough, the imitation will be all the more lifelike. Punshon will expect something of the sort, and he will not trouble you, for he knows that when I am fuddled I am quarrelsome. 'Tis a diverting world, Anastasia, wherein, you now perceive, habitual drunkenness and an unbridled temper may sometimes prove commendable,—as they do tonight, when they aid persecuted innocence!" Here Simon Orts gave an unpleasant laugh.

"But I do not understand—"

"You understand very little except coquetry and the proper disposition of a ruffle. Yet this is simple. My horse is tied at the postern. Mount—astride, mind. You know the way to the Vicarage, so does the horse; you will find that posturing half-brother of mine at the Vicarage. Tell Frank what has happened. Tell him to row you to the mainland; tell him to conduct you to Colonel Denstroude's. Then you must shift for yourself; but Denstroude is a gentleman, and Denstroude would protect Beelzebub if he came to him a fugitive from Vincent Floyer. Now do you understand?"

"Yes," said Lady Allonby, and seated herself before the fire,—"yes, I understand. I am to slip away in the darkness and leave you here to answer for Lord Rokesle's death—to those devils. La, do you really think me as base as that?"

Now Simon Orts was kneeling at her side. The black cloak enveloped her from head to foot, and the turned-up collar screened her sunny hair; in the shadow of the broad hatbrim you could see only her eyes, resplendent and defiant, and in them the reflection of the vaulting flames. "You would stay, Anastasia?"

"I will not purchase my life at the cost of yours. I will be indebted to you for nothing, Simon Orts."

The Vicar chuckled. "Nor appeared Less than archangel ruined," he said. "No, faith, not a whit less! We are much of a piece, Anastasia. Do you know—if affairs had fallen out differently—I think I might have been a man and you a woman? As it is—" Kneeling still, his glance devoured her. "Yes, you would stay. And you comprehend what staying signifies. 'Tis pride, your damnable pride, that moves you,—but I rejoice, for it proves you a brave woman. Courage, at least, you possess, and this is the first virtue I have discovered in you for a long while. However, there is no necessity for your staying. The men of Usk will not hurt Simon Orts."

She was very eager to believe this. Lady Allonby had found the world a pleasant place since her widowhood. "They will not kill you? You swear it, Simon?"

"Why, the man was their tyrant. They obeyed him—yes, through fear. I am their deliverer, Anastasia. But if they found a woman here—a woman not ill-looking—" Simon Orts snapped his fingers. "Faith, I leave you to conjecture," said he.

They had both risen, he smiling, the woman in a turbulence of hope and terror. "Swear to it, Simon!"

"Anastasia, were affairs as you suppose them, I would have a curt while to live. Were affairs as you suppose them, I would stand now at the threshold of eternity. And I swear to you, upon my soul's salvation, that I have nothing to fear. Nothing will ever hurt me any more."

"No, you would not dare to lie in the moment of death," she said, after a considerable pause. "I believe you. I will go. Good-bye, Simon." Lady Allonby went toward the door opening into the corridor, but turned there and came back to him. "I shall never see you again. And, la, I think that I rather hate you than otherwise, for you remind me of things I would willingly forget. But, Simon, I wish we had gone to live in that little cottage we planned, and quarrelled over, and never built! I think we would have been happy."

Simon Orts raised her hand to his lips. "Yes," said he, "we would have been happy. I would have been by this a man doing a man's work in the world, and you a matron, grizzling, perhaps, but rich in content, and in love opulent. As it is, you have your flatterers, your gossip, and your cards; I have my gin. Good-bye, Anastasia."

"Simon, why have you done—this?"

The Vicar of Heriz Magna flung out his hands in a gesture of impotence. "I dare confess now that which even to myself I have never dared confess. I suppose the truth of it is that I have loved you all my life."

"I am sorry. I am not worth it, Simon."

"No; you are immeasurably far from being worth it. But one does not justify these fancies by mathematics. Good-bye, Anastasia."

V

Holding the door ajar, the Vicar of Heriz Magna heard a horse's hoofs slap their leisurely way down the hillside. Presently the sound died and he turned back into the hall.

"A brave woman, that! Oh, a trifling, shallow-hearted jilt, but a brave creature!

"I had to lie to her. She would have stayed else. And perhaps it is true that, in reality, I have loved her all my life,—or in any event, have hankered after the pink-and-white flesh of her as any gentleman might. Pschutt! a pox on all lechery says the dying man,—since it is now necessary to put that strapping yellow-haired trollop out of your mind, Simon Orts—yes, after all these years, to put her quite out of your mind. Faith, she might wheedle me now to her heart's content, and my pulse would never budge; for I must devote what trivial time there is to hoping they will kill me quickly. He was their god, that man!"

Simon Orts went toward the dead body, looking down into the distorted face. "And I, too, loved him. Yes, such as he was, he was the only friend I had. And I think he liked me," Simon Orts said aloud, with a touch of shy pride. "Yes, and you trusted me, didn't you, Vincent? Wait for me, then, my Lord,—I shall not be long. And now I'll serve you faithfully. I had to play the man's part, you know,—you mustn't grudge old Simon his one hour of manhood. You wouldn't, I think. And in any event, I shall be with you presently, and you can cuff me for it if you like—just as you used to do."

He covered the dead face with his handkerchief, but in the instant he drew it away. "No, not this coarse cambric. You were too much of a fop, Vincent. I will use yours—the finest linen, my Lord. You see old Simon knows your tastes."

He drew himself erect exultantly.

"They will come at dawn to kill me; but I have had my hour. God, the man I might have been! And now—well, perhaps He would not be offended if I said a bit of a prayer for Vincent."

So the Vicar of Heriz Magna knelt beside the flesh that had been Lord Rokesle, and there they found him in the morning.

II

LOVE AT MARTINMAS

As Played at Tunbridge Wells, April 1, 1750

"He to love an altar built
Of twelve vast French romances, neatly gilt.
There lay three garters, half a pair of gloves,
And all the trophies of his former loves;
With tender billet-doux he lights the pyre,
And breathes three amorous sighs to raise the fire;
Then prostrate falls, and begs with ardent eyes
Soon to obtain, and long possess the prize."

Dramatis Personæ

Mr. Erwyn, a gentleman of the town, ceremonious and a coxcomb, but a man of honor.

Lady Allonby, a woman of fashion, and widow to Lord Stephen Allonby.

Miss Allonby, daughter to Lord Stephen by a former marriage, of a considerable fortune in her own hands.

Footmen to Lady Allonby; and in the Proem Francis Orts, commonly know as Francis Vanbingham, a dissolute play-actor.

Scene
A drawing-room in Lady Allonby's villa at Tunbridge Wells.

LOVE AT MARTINMAS

PROEM:—To be Filed for Reference Hereafter

L ady Allonby followed in all respects the Vicar's instructions; and midnight found her upon the pier of Bishops Onslow, Colonel Denstroude's big and dilapidated country-residence. Frank Orts had assisted her from the rowboat without speaking; indeed, he had uttered scarcely a word, save to issue some necessary direction, since the woman first came to him at the Vicarage with her news of the night's events. Now he composedly stepped back into the boat.

"You've only to go forward," said Frank Orts. "I regret that for my own part I'm no longer an acceptable visitor here, since the Colonel and I fought last summer over one Molly Yates. Nay, I beseech you, put up your purse, my Lady."

"Then I can but render you my heartfelt thanks," replied Lady Allonby, "and incessantly remember you in daily prayers for the two gallant men who have this night saved a woman from great misery. Yet there is that in your voice which is curiously familiar, Mr. Orts, and I think that somewhere you and I have met before this."

"Ay," he responded, "you have squandered many a shilling on me here in England, where Francis Vanringham bellows and makes faces with the rest of the Globe Company. On Usk, you understand, I'm still Frank Orts, just as I was christened; but elsewhere the name of Vanringham was long ago esteemed more apt to embellish and adorn the bill of a heroic play. Ay, you've been pleased to applaud my grimaces behind the footlights, more than once; your mother-in-law, indeed, the revered Marchioness-Dowager of Falmouth, is among my staunchest patrons."

"Heavens! then we shall all again see one another at Tunbridge!" said Lady Allonby, who was recovering her spirits; "and I shall have a Heaven-sent opportunity, to confirm my protestations that I am not ungrateful. Mr. Vanringham, I explicitly command you to open in *The Orphan*, since: as Castalio in that piece you are the most elegant and moving thing in the universal world."*

---

* This was the opinion of others as well. Thorsby (*Roscius Anglicanus*) says, "Mr. Vanringham was good in tragedy, as well as in comedy, especially as Castalio in Otway's *Orphan*, and

"Your command shall be obeyed," said the actor. "And meantime, my Lady, I bid you an *au revoir*, with many millions of regrets for the inconveniences to which you've been subjected this evening, Oho, we are lamentably rustic hereabout."

And afterward as he rowed through the dark the man gave a grunt of dissatisfaction.

"I was too abrupt with her. But it vexes me to have Brother Simon butchered like this. . . These natural instincts are damnably inconvenient,—and expensive, at times, Mr. Vanringham,—beside being ruinous to one's sense of humor, Mr. Vanringham. Why, to think that she alone should go scot-free! and of her ordering a stage-box within the hour of two men's destruction on her account! Upon reflection, I admire the woman to the very tips of my toes. Eh, well! I trust to have need of her gratitude before the month is up."

I

Since Colonel Denstroude proved a profane and dissolute and helpful person, Lady Allonby was shortly re-established in her villa at Tunbridge Wells, on the Sussex side, where she had resolved to find a breathing-space prior to the full season in London. And thereupon she put all thoughts of Usk quite out of her mind: it had been an unhappy business, but it was over. In the meanwhile her wardrobe needed replenishing now that spring was coming in; the company at the Wells was gay enough; and Lady Allonby had always sedulously avoided anything that was disagreeable.

Mr. Erwyn Lady Allonby was far from cataloguing under that head. Mr. George Erwyn had been for years a major-general, at the very least, in Fashion's army, and was concededly a connoisseur of all the elegancies.

Mr. Erwyn sighed as he ended his recital—half for pity of the misguided folk who had afforded Tunbridge its latest scandal, half for relief that, in spite of many difficulties, the story had been set forth in discreet language which veiled, without at all causing you to miss, the more unsavory details.

---

the more famous Garrick came, in that part, far short of him." Vanringham was also noted for his Valentine in *Love for Love* and for his Beaugard in *The Soldier's Fortune*.

"And so," said he, "poor Harry is run through the lungs, and Mrs. Anstruther has recovered her shape and is to be allowed a separate maintenance."

"'Tis shocking!" said Lady Allonby.

"'Tis incredible," said Mr. Erwyn, "to my mind, at least, that the bonds of matrimony should be slipped thus lightly. But the age is somewhat lax and the world now views with complaisance the mad antics of half-grown lads and wenches who trip toward the altar as carelessly as if the partnership were for a country-dance."

Lady Allonby stirred her tea and said nothing. Notoriously her marriage had been unhappy; and her two years of widowhood (dating from the unlamented seizure, brought on by an inherited tendency to apoplexy and French brandy, which carried off Lord Stephen Allonby of Prestonwoode) had to all appearance never tempered her distrust of the matrimonial state. Certain it was that she had refused many advantageous offers during this period, for her jointure was considerable, and, though in candid moments she confessed to thirty-three, her dearest friends could not question Lady Allonby's good looks. She was used to say that she would never re-marry, because she desired to devote herself to her step-daughter, but, as gossip had it at Tunbridge, she was soon to be deprived of this subterfuge; for Miss Allonby had reached her twentieth year, and was nowadays rarely seen in public save in the company of Mr. Erwyn, who, it was generally conceded, stood high in the girl's favor and was desirous of rounding off his career as a leader of fashion with the approved comoedic *dénouement* of marriage with a young heiress.

For these reasons Lady Allonby heard with interest his feeling allusion to the laxity of the age, and through a moment pondered thereon, for it seemed now tolerably apparent that Mr. Erwyn had lingered, after the departure of her other guests, in order to make a disclosure which Tunbridge had for many months expected.

"I had not thought," said she, at length, "that you, of all men, would ever cast a serious eye toward marriage. Indeed, Mr. Erwyn, you have loved women so long that I must dispute your ability to love a woman— and your amours have been a byword these twenty years."

"Dear lady," said Mr. Erwyn, "surely you would not confound amour with love? Believe me, the translation is inadequate. Amour is but the summer wave that lifts and glitters and laughs in the sunlight, and within the instant disappears; but love is the unfathomed eternal sea itself. Or—to shift the metaphor—Amour is a general under whom youth must serve: Curiosity and Lustiness are his recruiting officers, and it is well to fight under his colors, for it is against Ennui that he marshals his forces. 'Tis a resplendent conflict, and young blood cannot but stir and exult as paradoxes, marching and countermarching at the command of their gay generalissimo, make way for one another in iridescent squadrons, while through the steady musketry of epigram one hears the clash of contending repartees, or the cry of a wailing sonnet. But this lord of laughter may be served by the young alone; and by and by each veteran—scarred, it may be, but not maimed, dear lady—is well content to relinquish the glory and adventure of such colorful campaigns for some quiet inglenook, where, with love to make a third, he prattles of past days and deeds with one that goes hand in hand with him toward the tomb."

Lady Allonby accorded this conceit the tribute of a sigh; then glanced, in the direction of four impassive footmen to make sure they were out of earshot.

"And so—?" said she.

"Split me!" said Mr. Erwyn, "I thought you had noted it long ago."

"Indeed," she observed, reflectively, "I suppose it is quite time."

"I am not," said Mr. Erwyn, "in the heyday of my youth, I grant you; but I am not for that reason necessarily unmoved by the attractions of an advantageous person, a fine sensibility and all the graces."

He sipped his tea with an air of resentment; and Lady Allonby, in view of the disparity of age which existed between Mr. Erwyn and her step-daughter, had cause to feel that she had blundered into *gaucherie*; and to await with contrition the proposal for her step-daughter's hand that the man was (at last) about to broach to her, as the head of the family.

"Who is she?" said Lady Allonby, all friendly interest.

"An angel," said Mr. Erwyn, fencing.

"Beware," Lady Allonby exhorted, "lest she prove a recording angel; a wife who takes too deep an interest in your movements will scarcely suit you."

"Oh, I am assured," said Mr. Erwyn, smiling, "that on Saturdays she will allow me the customary half-holiday."

Lady Allonby, rebuffed, sought consolation among the conserves.

"Yet, as postscript," said Mr. Erwyn, "I do not desire a wife who will take her morning chocolate with me and sup with Heaven knows whom. I have seen, too much of *mariage à la mode*, and I come to her, if not with the transports of an Amadis, at least with an entire affection and respect."

"Then," said Lady Allonby, "you love this woman?"

"Very tenderly," said Mr. Erwyn; "and, indeed, I would, for her sake, that the errors of my past life were not so numerous, nor the frailty of my aspiring resolutions rendered apparent—ah, so many times!—to a gaping and censorious world. For, as you are aware, I cannot offer her an untried heart; 'tis somewhat worn by many barterings. But I know that this heart beats with accentuation in her presence; and when I come to her some day and clasp her in my arms, as I aspire to do, I trust that her lips may not turn away from mine and that she may be more glad because I am so near and that her stainless heart may sound an echoing chime. For, with a great and troubled adoration, I love her as I have loved no other woman; and this much, I submit, you cannot doubt."

"I?" said Lady Allonby, with extreme innocence. "La, how should I know?"

"Unless you are blind," Mr. Erwyn observed—"and I apprehend those spacious shining eyes to be more keen than the tongue of a dowager,—you must have seen of late that I have presumed to hope—to think—that she whom I love so tenderly might deign to be the affectionate, the condescending friend who would assist me to retrieve the indiscretions of my youth—"

The confusion of his utterance, his approach to positive agitation as he waved his teaspoon, moved Lady Allonby. "It is true," she said, "that I have not been wholly blind—"

"Anastasia," said Mr. Erwyn, with yet more feeling, "is not our friendship of an age to justify sincerity?"

"Oh, bless me, you toad! but let us not talk of things that happened under the Tudors. Well, I have not been unreasonably blind,—and I do not object,—and I do not believe that Dorothy will prove obdurate."

"You render me the happiest of men," Mr. Erwyn stated, rapturously. "You have, then, already discussed this matter with Miss Allonby?"

"Not precisely," said she, laughing; "since I had thought it apparent to the most timid lover that the first announcement came with best grace from him."

"O' my conscience, then, I shall be a veritable Demosthenes," said Mr. Erwyn, laughing likewise; "and in common decency she will consent."

"Your conceit," said Lady Allonby, "is appalling."

"'Tis beyond conception," Mr. Erwyn admitted; "and I propose to try marriage as a remedy. I have heard that nothing so takes down a man."

"Impertinent!" cried Lady Allonby; "now of whatever can the creature be talking!"

"I mean that, as your widowship well knows, marrying puts a man in his proper place. And that the outcome is salutary for proud, puffed-up fellows I would be the last to dispute. Indeed, I incline to dispute nothing, for I find that perfect felicity is more potent than wine. I am now all pastoral raptures, and were it not for the footmen there, I do not know to what lengths I might go."

"In that event," Lady Allonby decided, "I shall fetch Dorothy, that the crown may be set upon your well-being. And previously I will dismiss the footmen." She did so with a sign toward those lordly beings.

"Believe me," said Mr. Erwyn, "'tis what I have long wished for. And when Miss Allonby honors me with her attention I shall, since my life's happiness depends upon the issue, plead with all the eloquence of a starveling barrister, big with the import of his first case. May I, indeed, rest assured that any triumph over her possible objections may be viewed with not unfavorable eyes?"

"O sir," said Lady Allonby, "believe me, there is nothing I more earnestly desire than that you may obtain all which is necessary for your welfare. I will fetch Dorothy."

The largest footman but one removed Mr. Erwyn's cup.

II

Mr. Erwyn, left alone, smiled at his own reflection in the mirror; rearranged his ruffles with a deft and shapely hand; consulted his watch; made sure that the padding which enhanced the calves of his most notable legs was all as it should be; seated himself and hummed a merry air, in meditative wise; and was in such posture when the crimson hangings that shielded the hall-door quivered and broke into tumultuous waves and yielded up Miss Dorothy Allonby.

Being an heiress, Miss Allonby was by an ancient custom brevetted a great beauty; and it is equitable to add that the sourest misogynist could hardly have refused, pointblank, to countersign the commission. They said of Dorothy Allonby that her eyes were as large as her bank account, and nearly as formidable as her tongue; and it is undeniable that on provocation there was in her speech a tang of acidity, such (let us say) as renders a salad none the less palatable. In a word, Miss Allonby pitied the limitations of masculine humanity more readily than its amorous pangs, and cuddled her women friends as she did kittens, with a wary and candid apprehension of their power to scratch; and decision was her key-note; continually she knew to the quarter-width of a cobweb what she wanted, and invariably she got it.

Such was the person who, with a habitual emphasis which dowagers found hoydenish and all young men adorable, demanded without prelude:

"Heavens! What can it be, Mr. Erwyn, that has cast Mother into this unprecedented state of excitement?"

"What, indeed?" said he, and bowed above her proffered hand.

"For like a hurricane, she burst into my room and cried, 'Mr. Erwyn has something of importance to declare to you—why did you put on that gown?—bless you, my child—' all in one eager breath; then kissed me, and powdered my nose, and despatched me to you without any explanation. And why?" said Miss Allonby.

"Why, indeed?" said Mr. Erwyn.

"It is very annoying," said she, decisively.

"Sending you to me?" said Mr. Erwyn, a magnitude of reproach in his voice.

"That," said Miss Allonby, "I can pardon—and easily. But I dislike all mysteries, and being termed a child, and being—"

"Yes?" said Mr. Erwyn.

"—and being powdered on the nose," said Miss Allonby, with firmness. She went to the mirror, and, standing on the tips of her toes, peered anxiously into its depths. She rubbed her nose, as if in disapproval, and frowned, perhaps involuntarily pursing up her lips,—which Mr. Erwyn intently regarded, and then wandered to the extreme end of the apartment, where he evinced a sudden interest in bric-à-brac.

"Is there any powder on my nose?" said Miss Allonby.

"I fail to perceive any," said Mr. Erwyn.

"Come closer," said she.

"I dare not," said he.

Miss Allonby wheeled about. "Fie!" she cried; "one who has served against the French,* and afraid of powder!"

---

* This was not absolutely so. Mr. Erwyn had, however, in an outburst of patriotism, embarked, as a sort of cabin passenger, with his friend Sir John Morris, and possessed

"It is not the powder that I fear."

"What, then?" said she, in sinking to the divan beside the disordered tea-table.

"There are two of them," said Mr. Erwyn, "and they are so red—"

"Nonsense!" cried Miss Allonby, with heightened color.

"'Tis best to avoid temptation," said Mr. Erwyn, virtuously.

"Undoubtedly," she assented, "it is best to avoid having your ears boxed."

Mr. Erwyn sighed as if in the relinquishment of an empire. Miss Allonby moved to the farther end of the divan.

"What was it," she demanded, "that you had to tell me?"

"'Tis a matter of some importance—" said Mr. Erwyn.

"Heavens!" said Miss Allonby, and absent-mindedly drew aside her skirts; "one would think you about to make a declaration."

Mr. Erwyn sat down beside her, "I have been known," said he, "to do such things."

The divan was strewn with cushions in the Oriental fashion. Miss Allonby, with some adroitness, slipped one of them between her person and the locality of her neighbor. "Oh!" said Miss Allonby.

"Yes," said he, smiling over the dragon-embroidered barrier; "I admit that I am even now shuddering upon the verge of matrimony."

"Indeed!" she marvelled, secure in her fortress. "Have you selected an accomplice?"

"Split me, yes!" said Mr. Erwyn.

"And have I the honor of her acquaintance?" said Miss Allonby.

"Provoking!" said Mr. Erwyn; "no woman knows her better."

Miss Allonby smiled. "Dear Mr. Erwyn," she stated, "this is a disclosure I have looked for these six months."

"Split me!" said Mr. Erwyn.

"Heavens, yes!" said she. "You have been a rather dilatory lover—"

"I am inexpressibly grieved, that I should have kept you waiting—"

"—and in fact, I had frequently thought of reproaching you for your tardiness—"

"Nay, in that case," said Mr. Erwyn, "the matter could, no doubt, have been more expeditiously arranged."

"—since your intentions have been quite apparent."

---

in consequence some claim to share such honor as was won by the glorious fiasco of Dungeness.

Mr. Erwyn removed the cushion. "You do not, then, disapprove," said he, "of my intentions?"

"Indeed, no," said Miss Allonby; "I think you will make an excellent step-father."

The cushion fell to the floor. Mr. Erwyn replaced it and smiled.

"And so," Miss Allonby continued, "Mother, believing me in ignorance, has deputed you to inform me of this most transparent secret? How strange is the blindness of lovers! But I suppose," sighed Miss Allonby, "we are all much alike."

"We?" said Mr. Erwyn, softly.

"I meant—" said Miss Allonby, flushing somewhat.

"Yes?" said Mr. Erwyn. His voice sank to a pleading cadence. "Dear child, am I not worthy of trust?"

There was a microscopic pause.

"I am going to the Pantiles this afternoon," declared Miss Allonby, at length, "to feed the swans."

"Ah," said Mr. Erwyn, and with comprehension; "surely, he, too, is rather tardy."

"Oh," said she, "then you know?"

"I know," he announced, "that there is a tasteful and secluded summer-house near the Fountain of Neptune."

"I was never allowed," said Miss Allonby, unconvincingly, "to go into secluded summer-houses with any one; and, besides, the gardeners keep their beer jugs there—under the biggest bench."

Mr. Erwyn beamed upon her paternally. "I was not, till this, aware," said he, "that Captain Audaine was so much interested in ornithology. Yet what if, even when he is seated upon that biggest bench, your Captain does not utterly lose the head he is contributing to the *tête-à-tête*?"

"Oh, but he will," said Miss Allonby, with confidence; then she reflectively added: "I shall have again to be painfully surprised by his declaration, for, after all, it will only be his seventh."

"Doubtless," Mr. Erwyn considered, "your astonishment will be extreme when you rebuke him, there above hortensial beer jugs—"

"And I shall be deeply grieved that he has so utterly misunderstood my friendly interest in his welfare; and I shall be highly indignant after he has—in effect, after he has—"

"But not until afterward?" said Mr. Erwyn, holding up a forefinger. "Well, I have told you their redness is fatal to good resolutions."

"—after he has astounded me by his seventh avowal. And I shall behave in precisely the same manner the eighth time he recurs to the repugnant subject."

"But the ninth time?" said Mr. Erwyn.

"He has remarkably expressive eyes," Miss Allonby stated, "and really, Mr. Erwyn, it is the most lovable creature when it raves about my flint-heartedness and cutting its poor throat and murdering every man I ever nodded to!"

"Ah, youth, youth!" sighed Mr. Erwyn. "Dear child, I pray you, do not trifle with the happiness that is within your grasp! *Si jeunesse savait*—the proverb is somewhat musty. But we who have attained the St. Martin's summer of our lives and have grown capable of but a calm and tempered affection at the utmost—we cannot but look wistfully upon the raptures and ignorance of youth, and we would warn you, were it possible, of the many dangers whereby you are encompassed. For Love is a deity that must not be trifled with; his voice may chaunt the requiem of all which is bravest in our mingled natures, or sound a stave of such nobility as heartens us through life. He is kindly, but implacable; beneficent, a bestower of all gifts upon the faithful, a bestower of very terrible gifts upon those that flout him; and I who speak to you have seen my own contentment blighted, by just such flippant jesting with Love's omnipotence, before the edge of my first razor had been dulled. 'Tis true, I have lived since in indifferent comfort; yet it is but a dreary banquet where there is no platter laid for Love, and within the chambers of my heart—dust-gathering now, my dear!—he has gone unfed these fifteen years or more."

"Ah, goodness!" sighed Miss Allonby, touched by the ardor of his speech. "And so, you have loved Mother all of fifteen years?"

"Nay, split me—!" said Mr. Erwyn.

"Your servant, sir," said the voice of Lady Allonby; "I trust you young people have adjusted matters to your satisfaction?"

III

"DEAR MADAM," CRIED MISS ALLONBY, "I am overjoyed!" then kissed her step-mother vigorously and left the room, casting in passage an arch glance at Mr. Erwyn.

"O vulgarity!" said Lady Allonby, recovering her somewhat rumpled dignity, "the sweet child is yet unpolished. But, I suppose, we may regard the matter as settled?"

"Yes," said Mr. Erwyn, "I think, dear lady, we may with safety regard the matter as settled."

"Dorothy is of an excitable nature," she observed, and seated herself upon the divan; "and you, dear Mr. Erwyn, who know women so thoroughly, will overlook the agitation of an artless girl placed in quite unaccustomed circumstances. Nay, I myself was affected by my first declaration."

"Doubtless," said Mr. Erwyn, and sank beside her. "Lord Stephen was very moving."

"I can assure you," said she, smiling, "that he was not the first."

"I gad," said he, "I remember perfectly, in the old days, when you were betrothed to that black-visaged young parson—"

"Well, I do not remember anything of the sort," Lady Allonby stated; and she flushed.

"You wore a blue gown," he said.

"Indeed?" said she.

"And—"

"La, if I did," said Lady Allonby, "I have quite forgotten it, and it is now your manifest duty to do likewise."

"Never in all these years," said Mr. Erwyn, sighing, "have I been able to forget it."

"I was but a girl, and 'twas natural that at first I should be mistaken in my fancies," Lady Allonby told him, precisely as she had told Simon Orts: "and at all events, there is nothing less well-bred than a good memory. I would decline to remain in the same room with one were it not that Dorothy has deserted you in this strange fashion. Whither, pray, has she gone?"

Mr. Erwyn smiled. "Her tender heart," said Mr. Erwyn, "is affected by the pathetic and moving spectacle of the poor hungry swans, pining for their native land and made a raree-show for visitors in the Pantiles; and she has gone to stay them with biscuits and to comfort them with cakes."

"Really!" said Lady Allonby.

"And," Mr. Erwyn continued, "to defend her from the possible ferocity of the gold-fish, Captain Audaine had obligingly afforded service as an escort."

"Oh," said Lady Allonby; then added, "in the circumstances she might permissibly have broken the engagement."

"But there is no engagement," said Mr. Erwyn—"as yet."

"Indeed?" said she.

"Harkee," said he; "should he make a declaration this afternoon she will refuse him."

"Why, but of course!" Lady Allonby marveled.

"And the eighth time," said he.

"Undoubtedly," said she; "but at whatever are you hinting?"

"Yet the ninth time—"

"Well, what is it, you grinning monster?"

Mr. Erwyn allowed himself a noiseless chuckle. "After the ninth time," Mr. Erwyn declared, "there will be an engagement."

"Mr. Erwyn!" cried Lady Allonby, with widened eyes, "I had understood that Dorothy looked favorably upon your suit."

"Anastasia!" cried he; and then his finger-tips lightly caressed his brow. "'Tis the first I had heard of it," said Mr. Erwyn.

"Surely—" she began.

"Nay, but far more surely," said he, "in consideration of the fact that, not a half-hour since, you deigned to promise me your hand in marriage—"

"O la now!" cried Lady Allonby; and, recovering herself, smiled courteously. "'Tis the first I had heard of it," said she.

They stared at each other in wonderment. Then Lady Allonby burst into laughter.

"D'ye mean—?" said she.

"Indeed," said Mr. Erwyn, "so unintentional was I of aspiring to Miss Allonby's affections that all my soul was set upon possessing the heart and person of a lady, in my humble opinion, far more desirable."

"I had not dreamed—" she commenced.

"Behold," said Mr. Erwyn, bitterly, "how rightly is my presumption punished. For I, with a fop's audacity, had thought my love for you of sufficient moment to have been long since observed; and, strong in my conceit, had scorned a pleasing declaration made up of faint phrases and whining ballad-endings. I spoke as my heart prompted me; but the heart has proven a poor counsellor, dear lady, and now am I rewarded. For you had not even known of my passion, and that which my presumption had taken for a reciprocal tenderness proves in the ultimate but a kindly aspiration to further my union with another."

"D'ye love me, toad?" said Lady Allonby, and very softly.

"Indeed," said Mr. Erwyn, "I have loved you all my life, first with a boyish inclination that I scarce knew was love, and, after your marriage with an honorable man had severed us, as I thought, irrevocably, with such lore as an ingenuous person may bear a woman whom both circumstances and the respect in which he holds her have placed beyond his reach,—a love that might not be spoken, but of which I had considered you could never be ignorant."

"Mr. Erwyn," said she, "at least I have not been ignorant—"

"They had each one of them some feature that reminded me of you. That was the truth of it, a truth so patent that we will not discuss it. Instead, dear madam, do you for the moment grant a losing gamester the right to rail at adverse fate! for I shall trouble you no more. Since your widowhood I have pursued you with attentions which, I now perceive, must at many times have proven distasteful. But my adoration had blinded me; and I shall trouble you no more. I have been too serious, I did not know that our affair was but a comedy of the eternal duel between man and woman; nor am I sorry, dear opponent, that you have conquered. For how valorously you fought! Eh, let it be! for you have triumphed in this duel, O puissant lady, and I yield the victor—a devoted and, it may be, a rather heavy heart; and I shall trouble you no more."

"Ah, sir," said Lady Allonby, "you are aware that once—"

"Indeed," said Mr. Erwyn, "'twas the sand on which I builded. But I am wiser now, and I perceive that the feeling you entertain toward me is but the pallid shadow of a youthful inclination. I shall not presume upon it. Oh, I am somewhat proud, dear Anastasia; I have freely given you my heart, such as it is; and were you minded to accept it, even at the eleventh hour, through friendship or through pity only, I would refuse. For my love of you has been the one pure and quite unselfish, emotion of my life, and I may not barter it for an affection of lesser magnitude either in kind or in degree. And so, farewell!"

"Yet hold, dear sir—" said Lady Allonby. "Lord, but will you never let me have the woman's privilege of talking!"

"Nay, but I am, as ever, at your service," said Mr. Erwyn, and he paused in transit for the door.

"—since, as this betokens—"

"'Tis a tasteful handkerchief," said Mr. Erwyn—"but somewhat moist!"

"And—my eyes?"

"Red," said Mr. Erwyn.

"I have been weeping, toad, with my head on the pin-cushion, and the maid trying to tipsify me with brandy."

"Why?" said Mr. Erwyn.

"I thought you were to marry Dorothy."

Mr. Erwyn resumed his seat. "You objected?" he said.

"I think, old monster," Lady Allonby replied, "that I would entertain the same objection to seeing any woman thus sacrificed—"

"Well?" said Mr. Erwyn.

"—except—"

"Incomparable Anastasia!" said Mr. Erwyn.

IV

AFTERWARD THESE TWO SAT LONG in the twilight, talking very little, and with their eyes rarely meeting, although their hands met frequently at quite irrelevant intervals. Just the graze of a butterfly to make it certain that the other was there: but all the while they both regarded the tiny fire which had set each content of the room a-dancing in the companionable darkness. For each, I take it, preferred to think of the other as being still the naïve young person each remembered; and the firelight made such thinking easier.

"D'ye remember—?" was woven like a refrain through their placid duo. . .

It was, one estimates, their highest hour. Frivolous and trivial persons you might have called them and have justified the accusation; but even to the fop and the coquette was granted an hour wherein all human happenings seemed to be ordered by supernal wisdom lovingly. Very soon they would forget this hour; meanwhile there was a wonderful sense of dreams come true.

III

THE CASUAL HONEYMOON

As Played at Tunbridge Wells, April 1, 1750

B ut this is the most cruel thing, to marry one does not know how, nor why, nor wherefore.—Gad, I never liked anybody less in my life. Poor woman!—Gad, I'm sorry for her, too; for I have no reason to hate her neither; but I wish we could keep it secret! why, I don't believe any of this company would speak of it."

Dramatis Personæ

Captain Audaine, of a pompous and handsome person, and loves Miss Allonby.

Lord Humphrey Degge, younger son to the Marquis of Venour, makes love to Miss Allonby.

Gerald Allonby, brother to Miss Allonby, a true raw Squire.

Mr. Erwyn, betrothed to Lady Allonby.

Vanringham, an impudent tragedian of the Globe Company.

Quarmby, Vanringham's associate.

Miss Allonby, an heiress, of a petulant humor, in love with Audaine.

Marchioness of Falmouth, an impertinent affected dowager, and grandmother to Miss Allonby.

Lady Allonby, step-mother to Miss Allonby and Gerald.

Postilions, Servants, Etc.

Scene

Tunbridge Wells, thence shifting to Chetwode Lodge, Mr. Babington-Herle's house, on Rusthall Common, within two miles of the town.

The Casual Honeymoon

Proem:—Introductive of Captain Francis Audaine

It appears convenient here to pursue Miss Allonby on her stroll about the Pantiles in company with Captain Audaine. The latter has been at pains to record the events of the afternoon and evening, so that I give you his own account of them, though I abridge in consideration of his leisured style. Pompous and verbose I grant the Captain, even in curtailment; but you are to remember these were the faults of his age, ingrained and defiant of deletion; and should you elect to peruse his memoirs* you will find that I have considerably spared you a majority of the digressions to which the future Earl of Garendon was lamentably addicted.

For the purpose of my tale you are to view him as Tunbridge did at this particular time: as a handsome and formal person, twenty-eight years old or thereabouts, of whom nobody knew anything quite definite—beyond the genealogic inference to be drawn from a smatch of the brogue—save that after a correspondence of gallantries, of some three weeks' duration, he was the manifest slave of Miss Dorothy Allonby, and had already fought three duels behind Ormerod House,—with Will Pratchet, Lord Humphrey Degge, and Sir Eugene Harrabie, respectively, each one of whom was a declared suitor for her hand.

And with this prelude I begin on my transcription.

I

Miss Allonby (says Captain Audaine) was that afternoon in a mighty cruel humor. Though I had omitted no reasonable method to convince her of the immensity of my passion, 'twas without the twitch of an eyelash she endured the volley of my sighs and the fusillade of my respectful protestations; and candor compels me to admit that toward the end her silvery laughter disrupted the periods of a most elegant and sensible peroration. And when the affair was concluded, and for the

---

* There appears to have been no American edition since that, in 1836, printed in Philadelphia, "for Thomas Wardle, No. 15 Minor Street." In England the memoirs of Lord Garendon are to all appearance equally hard to come by, and seem to have been out of print since 1907.

seventh time I had implored her to make me the happiest of men, the rogue merely observed: "But I don't want to marry you. Why on earth should I?"

"For the sake of peace," I replied, "and in self-protection, since as long as you stay obdurate I shall continue to importune, and by and by I shall pester you to death."

"Indeed, I think it more than probable," she returned; "for you dog me like a bailiff. I am cordially a-weary, Captain Audaine, of your incessant persecutions; and, after all, marrying you is perhaps the civilest way to be rid of both them and you."

But by this I held each velvet-soft and tiny hand. "Nay," I dissented; "the subject is somewhat too sacred for jest. I am no modish lover, dearest and best of creatures, to regard marriage as the thrifty purchase of an estate, and the lady as so much bed-furniture thrown in with the mansion. I love you with completeness: and give me leave to assure you, madam, with a freedom which I think permissible on so serious an occasion that, even as beautiful as you are, I could never be contented with your person without your heart."

She sat with eyes downcast, all one blush. Miss Dorothy Allonby was in the bloom of nineteen, and shone with every charm peculiar to her sex. But I have no mind to weary you with poetical rhodomontades till, as most lovers do, I have proven her a paragon and myself an imbecile: it suffices to say that her face, and shape, and mien, and wit, alike astounded and engaged all those who had the happiness to know her; and had long ago rendered her the object of my entire adoration and the target of my daily rhapsodies. Now I viewed her with a dissension of the liveliest hopes and fears; for she had hesitated, and had by this hesitation conceded my addresses to be not irretrievably repugnant; and within the instant I knew that any life undevoted to her service and protection could be but a lingering disease.

But by and by, "You shall have your answer this evening," she said, and so left me.

I fathomed the meaning of "this evening" well enough. For my adored Dorothy was all romance, and by preference granted me rendezvous in the back garden, where she would tantalize me nightly, from her balcony, after the example of the Veronese lady in Shakespeare's spirited tragedy, which she prodigiously admired. As concerns myself, a reasonable liking for romance had been of late somewhat tempered by the inclemency of the weather and the obvious unfriendliness of the dog; but there is no resisting a lady's commands; and clear or foul, you might at any twilight's death have found me under her window, where a host of lyric phrases asserted the devotion which a cold in the head confirmed.

This night was black as a coal-pit. Strolling beneath the casement, well wrapt in my cloak (for it drizzled), I meditated impartially upon the perfections of my dear mistress and the tyrannic despotism of love. Being the source of our existence, 'tis not unreasonably, perhaps, that this passion assumes the proprietorship of our destinies and exacts of all mankind a common tribute. Tonight, at least, I viewed the world as a brave pavilion, lighted by the stars and swept by the clean winds of heaven, wherein we enacted varied rôles with God as audience; where, in turn, we strutted or cringed about the stage, where, in turn, we were beset and rent by an infinity of passions; but where every man must play the part of lover. That passion alone, I said, is universal; it set wise Solomon a-jigging in criminal byways, and sinewy Hercules himself was no stranger to its inquietudes and joys. And I cried aloud with the Roman, *Parce precor!* and afterward upon high Heaven to make me a little worthier of Dorothy.

II

ENGROSSED IN MEDITATIONS SUCH AS these, I was fetched earthward by the clicking of a lock, and, turning, saw the door beneath her balcony unclose and afford egress to a slender and hooded figure. My amazement was considerable and my felicity beyond rhetoric.

"Dorothy—!" I whispered.

"Come!" was her response; and her finger-tips rested upon my arm the while that she guided me toward the gateway opening into Jervis Lane. I followed with a trepidation you may not easily conceive; nor was this diminished when I found awaiting us a post-chaise, into which my angel hastily tripped.

I babbled I know not what inarticulate nonsense. But, "Heavens!" she retorted, "d'ye mean to keep the parson waiting all night?"

This was her answer, then. Well, 'twas more than I could have hoped for, though to a man of any sensibility this summary disposal of our love-affair could not but vaguely smack of the distasteful. Say what you will, every gentleman has about him somewhere a tincture of that venerable and artless age when wives were taken by capture and were retained by force; he prefers to have the lady hold off until the very last; and properly, her tongue must sound defiance long after melting eyes have signalled that the traitorous heart of her, like an anatomical Tarpeia, is ready to betray the citadel and yield the treasury of her charms.

Nevertheless, I stepped into the vehicle. The postilion was off in a twinkling, as the saying is, over the roughest road in England. Conversation was impossible, for Dorothy and I were jostling like two pills in a box; and as the first observation I attempted resulted in a badly bitten tongue, I prudently held my peace.

This endured for, perhaps, a quarter of an hour, at the end of which period the post-chaise on a sudden stopped, and I assisted my companion to alight. Before us was a villa of considerable dimension, and situate, so far as I could immediately detect, in the midst of a vast and desolate moor; there was no trace of human habitation within the radius of the eye; and the house itself presented not a glimpse of tenancy or illumination.

"O Lord, madam—" I began.

"Hasten!" spoke a voice from within the Parsonage. And Dorothy drew me toward a side door, overhung with ivy, where, sure enough, a dim light burned, 'Twas but a solitary candle stuck upon a dresser at the remoter end of a large and low-ceiled apartment; and in this flickering obscurity we found a tremulous parson in full canonicals, who had united our hands and gabbled half-way through the marriage service before I had the slightest notion of what was befalling me.

And such is the unreasonable disposition of mankind that the attainment of my most ardent desires aroused a feeling not altogether unakin to irritation. This skulking celerity, this hole-and-corner business, I thought, was in ill-accord with the respect due to a sacrament; and I could have wished my marriage to have borne a less striking resemblance to the conference of three thieves in a cellar. But 'twas over in two twos. Within scantier time than it takes to tell of it, Francis and Dorothy were made one, and I had turned to salute my wife.

She gave a shriek of intolerable anguish. "Heavens!" said she, "I have married the wrong man!"

III

WITHOUT DELAY I SNATCHED UP the guttering candle and held it to my wife's countenance. You can conceive that 'twas with no pleasurable emotion I discovered I had inadvertently espoused the Dowager Marchioness of Falmouth, my adored Dorothy's grandmother; and in frankness I can't deny that the lady seemed equally dissatisfied: words failed us; and the newly wedded couple stared at each other in silence.

"Captain Audaine," said she, at last, "the situation is awkward."

"Sure, madam," I returned, "and that is the precise thought which has just occurred to me."

"And I am of the opinion," she continued, "that you owe me some sort of explanation. For I had planned to elope with Mr. Vanringham—"

"Do I understand your Ladyship to allude to Mr. Francis Vanringham, the play-actor, at present the talk of Tunbridge?"

She bowed a grave response.

"This is surprising news," said I, "and grant me leave to tell you that a woman of mature years, possessed of an abundant fortune and unassailable gentility, does not by ordinary sneak out of the kitchen door to meet a raddle-faced actor in the middle of the night. 'Tis, indeed, a circumstance to stagger human credulity. Oh, believe me, madam, for a virtuous woman the back garden is not a fitting approach to the altar, nor is a comedian an appropriate companion there at eleven o'clock in the evening."

"Hey, my fine fellow," says my wife, "and what were you doing in the back garden?"

"Among all true lovers," I returned, "it is an immemorial custom to prowl like sentinels beneath the windows of the beauteous adored. And I, madam, had the temerity to aspire toward an honorable union with your granddaughter."

She wrung her withered hands. "That any reputable woman should have nocturnal appointments with gentlemen in the back garden, and beguile her own grandmother into an odious marriage! I protest, Captain Audaine, the degenerate world of today is no longer a suitable residence for a lady!"

"Look you, sir, this is a cruel bad business," the Parson here put in. He was pacing the apartment in an altercation of dubiety and amaze. "Mr. Vanringham will be vexed."

"You will pardon me," I retorted, "if I lack pity to waste upon your Mr. Vanringham. At present I devote all funds of compassion to my own affairs. Am I, indeed, to understand that this lady and I are legally married?"

He rubbed his chin. "By the Lord Harry," says he, "'tis a case that lacks precedents! But the coincidence of the Christian names is devilish awkward; the service takes no cognizance of surnames; and I have merely united a Francis and a Dorothy."

"O Lord, Mr. What-d'ye-call-um," said I, "then there is but one remedy and that is an immediate divorce."

My wife shrieked. "Have you no sense of decency, Captain Audaine? Never has there been a divorce in my family. And shall I be the first to drag that honored name into a public court,—to have my reputation worried at the bar by a parcel of sniggering lawyers, while the town wits buzz about it like flies around carrion? I pray you, do not suggest any such hideous thing."

"Here's the other Francis," says the Parson, at this point. And it was,—a raffish, handsome, slender, red-haired fellow, somewhat suggestive of the royal duke, yet rather more like a sneak-thief, and with a whiff somewhere of the dancing-master. At first glance you recognized in the actor a personage, for he compelled the eye with a monstrous vividness of color and gesture. Tonight he had missed his lady at their rendezvous, owing to my premature appearance, and had followed us post-haste.

"My Castalio!" she screamed. "My Beaugard!"* She ran to him, and with disjointed talk and quavering utterance disclosed the present lamentable posture of affairs.

And I found the tableau they presented singular. My wife had been a toast, they tell me, in Queen Anne's time, and even now the lean and restless gentlewoman showed as the abandoned house of youth and wit and beauty, with here and there a trace of the old occupancy; always her furtive eyes shone with a cold and shifting glitter, as though a frightened imp peeped through a mask of Hecuba; and in every movement there was an ineffable touch of something loosely hinged and fantastic. In a word, the Marchioness was not unconscionably sane, and was known far and wide as a gallant woman resolutely oblivious to the batterings of time, and so avid of flattery that she was ready to smile on any man who durst give the lie to her looking-glass. Demented landlady of her heart, she would sublet that antiquated chamber to the first adventurer who came prepared to pay his scot in the false coin of compliment; and

---

* I never saw the rascal act, thank Heaven, since in that event, report assures me, I might conceivably have accredited him with the possession of some meritorious qualities, however trivial; but, it appears, these two above-mentioned rôles were the especial puppetry in which Mr. Vanringham was most successful in wringing tears and laughter from the injudicious.—F.A.

'twas not difficult to comprehend how this young Thespian had acquired its tenancy.

But now the face of Mr. Vanringham was attenuated by her revelations, and the wried mouth of Mr. Vanringham suggested that the party be seated, in order to consider more at ease the unfortunate *contretemps*. Fresh lights were kindled, as one and all were past fear of discovery by this; and we four assembled about a table which occupied the centre of the apartment.

IV

"THE SITUATION," MR. VANRINGHAM, BEGAN, "MAY reasonably be described as desperate. Here we sit, four ruined beings. For Dr. Quarmby has betrayed an unoffending couple into involuntary matrimony, an act of which his Bishop can scarcely fail to take official notice; Captain Audaine and the Marchioness are entrapped into a loveless marriage, than which there mayn't be a greater misery in life; and my own future, I needn't add, is irrevocably blighted by the loss of my respected Dorothy, without whom continued animation must necessarily be a hideous and hollow mockery. Yet there occurs to me a panacea for these disasters."

"Then, indeed, Mr. Vanringham," said I, "there is one of us who will be uncommonly glad to know the name of it."

He faced me with a kind of compassion in his wide-set brown eyes, "You, sir, have caused a sweet and innocent lady to marry you against her will—Oho, beyond doubt, your intentions were immaculate; but the outcome remains in its stark enormity, and the hand of an inquisitive child is not ordinarily salved by its previous ignorance as to the corrosive properties of fire. You have betrayed confiding womanhood, an act abhorrent to all notions of gentility. There is but one conclusive proof of your repentance.—Need I mention that I allude to self-destruction?"

"O Lord, sir," I observed, "suicide is a deadly sin, and I would not willingly insult any gentlewoman by evincing so marked a desire for the devil's company in preference to hers."

"Your argument is sophistry," he returned, "since 'tis your death alone that can endear you to your bride. Death is the ultimate and skilled assayer of alloyed humanity: and by his art our gross constituents—our foibles, our pettinesses, nay, our very crimes—are precipitated into the coffin, the while that his crucible sets free the volatile pure essence, and shows as undefiled by all life's accidents that part of divinity which harbors in the vilest bosom. This only is remembered: this only mounts, like an ethereal spirit, to hallow the finished-with blunderer's renown, and reverently to enshrine his body's resting-place. Ah, no, Captain Audaine! death alone may canonize the husband. Once you're dead, your wife will adore you; once you're dead, your wife and I have before us an open road to connubial felicity, a road which, living, you sadly encumber; and only when he has delivered your funeral oration may Dr. Quarmby be exempt from apprehension lest his part in your marriage ceremony bring about his defrockment. I urge the greatest good for the greatest number, Captain; living, you plunge all four of us into suffering; whereas the nobility of an immediate *felo-de-se* will in common decency exalt your soul to Heaven accompanied and endorsed by the fervent prayers of three grateful hearts."

"And by the Lord Harry," says the Parson, "while no clergyman extant has a more cordial aversion to suicide, I cannot understand why a prolonged existence should tempt you. You love Miss Dorothy Allonby, as all Tunbridge knows; and to a person of sensibility, what can be more awkward than to have thrust upon him grandfathership of the adored one? You must in this position necessarily be exposed to the committal of a thousand *gaucheries*; and if you insist upon your irreligious project of procuring a divorce, what, I ask, can be your standing with the lady? Can she smile upon the suit of an individual who has publicly cast aside the sworn love and obedience of the being to whom she owes her very existence? or will any clergyman in England participate in the union of a woman to her ex-grandfather? Nay, believe me, sir, 'tis less the selfishness than the folly of your clinging to this vale of tears which I deplore. And I protest that this rope"—he fished up a coil from the corner—"appears to have been deposited here by a benign and all-seeing Providence to Suggest the manifold advantages of hanging yourself as compared with the untidy operation of cutting one's throat."

"And conceive, sir," says my wife, "what must be the universal grief for the bridegroom so untimelily taken off in the primal crescence of his honeymoon! Your funeral will be unparalleled both for sympathy and splendor; all Tunbridge will attend in tears; and 'twill afford me a melancholy but sincere pleasure to extend to you the hospitality of the Allonby mausoleum, which many connoisseurs have accounted the finest in the three kingdoms."

JAMES BRANCH CABELL

"I must venture," said I, "to terminate this very singular conversation. You have, one and all, set forth the advantages of my immediate demise; your logic is unassailable and has proven suicide my plain duty; and my rebuttal is confined to the statement that I will see everyone of you damned before I'll do it."

Mr. Francis Vanringham rose with a little bow. "You have insulted both womanhood and the Established Church by the spitting out of that ribald oath; and me you have with equal levity wronged by the theft of my affianced bride. I am only a play-actor, but in inflicting an insult a gentleman must either lift his inferior to his own station or else forfeit his gentility. I wear a sword, Captain Audaine. Heyho, will you grant me the usual satisfaction?"

"My fascinating comedian," said I, "if 'tis a fight you are desirous of, I can assure you that in my present state I would cross swords with a costermonger, or the devil, or the Archbishop of Canterbury, with equal impartiality. But scarcely in the view of a lady, and, therefore, as you boast the greater influence in that quarter, will you kindly advise the withdrawal of yonder unexpected addition to my family?"

"There's an inner room," says he, pointing to the door behind me; and I held it open as my wife swept through.

"You are the epitome of selfishness," she flung out, in passing; "for had you possessed an ounce of gallantry, you would long ago have freed me from this odious marriage."

"Sure, madam," I returned, with a *congée*; "and is it not rather a compliment that I so willingly forfeit a superlunar bliss in order to retain the pleasure of your society?"

She sniffed, and I closed the door; and within the moment the two men fell upon me, from the rear, and presently had me trussed like a fowl and bound with that abominable Parson's coil of rope.

V

"Believe me," says Mr. Vanringham, now seated upon the table and indolently dangling his heels,—the ecclesiastical monstrosity, having locked the door upon Mrs. Audaine, had occupied a chair and was composedly smoking a churchwarden,—"believe me, I lament the necessity of this uncouth proceeding. But heyho! man is a selfish animal. You take me, sir, my affection for yonder venerable lady does not keep me awake o' nights; yet is a rich marriage the only method to amend my threadbare fortunes, so that I cheerfully avail myself of her credulity. By God!" cried he, with a quick raising of the voice, "tomorrow I had been a landed gentleman but for you, you blundering omadhaun! And is a shabby merry-andrew from the devil knows where to pop in and spoil the prettiest plot was ever hatched?"

'Twas like a flare of lightning, this sudden outburst of malignity; for you saw in it, quintessentialized, the man's stark and venomous hatred of a world which had ill-used him; and 'twas over with too as quickly as the lightning, yielding to the pleasantest smile imaginable. Meanwhile you are to picture me, and my emotions, as I lay beneath his oscillating toes, entirely helpless. "'Twas not that I lacked the courage to fight you," he continues, "nor the skill, either. But there is always the possibility that by some awkward thrust or other you might deprive the stage of a distinguished ornament; and as a sincere admirer of my genius, I must, in decency, avoid such risks. 'Twas necessary to me, of course, that you be got out of this world speedily, since a further continuance of your blunderings would interfere with my plans for the future; having gone thus far, I cannot reasonably be expected to cede my interest in the Marchioness and her estate. Accordingly I decide upon the handiest method and tip the wink to Quarmby here; the lady quits the apartment in order to afford us opportunity to settle our pretensions, with cutlery as arbiter; and she will return to find your perforated carcass artistically displayed in yonder extremity of the room. Slain in an affair of honor, my dear Captain! The disputed damsel will think none the worse of me, a man of demonstrated valor and affection; Quarmby and I'll bury you in the cellar; and being freed from her recent and unfortunate alliance, my esteemed Dorothy will seek consolation in the embraces of a more acceptable spouse. Confess, sir, is it not a scheme of Arcadian simplicity?"

'Twas the most extraordinary sensation to note the utterly urbane and cheerful countenance with which Mr. Vanringham disclosed the meditated atrocity. This unprincipled young man was about to run me through with no more compunction than a naturalist in the act of pinning a new beetle among his collection may momentarily be aware of.

Then my quickened faculties were stirred on a sudden, and for the first time I opened my mouth. Whatever claim I had upon Vanringham, there was no need to advance it now.

"You were about to say—?" he queried.

"I was about to relieve a certain surplusage of emotion," I retorted, "by observing that I regret to find you, sir, a chattering, lean-witted fool—a vain and improvident fool!"

"Harsh words, my Captain," says he, with lifted eyebrows.

"O Lord, sir, but not of an undeserved asperity!" I returned, "D'ye think the Marchioness, her flighty head crammed with scraps of idiotic romance, would elope without regard for the canons of romance? Not so; depend upon it, a letter was left upon her pin-cushion announcing her removal with you, and in the most approved heroic style arraigning the obduracy of her unsympathetic grandchildren. D'ye think Gerald Allonby will not follow her? Sure, and he will; and the proof is," I added, "that you may hear his horses yonder on the heath, as I heard them some moments ago."

Vanringham leaped to the floor and stood thus, all tension. He raised clenched, quivering hands toward the ceiling. "O King of Jesters!" he cried, in horrid blasphemy; and then again, "O King of Jesters!"

And by this time men were shouting without, and at the door there was a prodigious and augmenting hammering. And the Parson wrung his hands and began to shake like a dish of jelly in a thunder-storm.

"Captain Audaine," Mr. Vanringham resumed, with more tranquillity, "you are correct. Clidamira and Parthenissa would never have fled into the night without leaving a note upon the pin-cushion. The folly I kindled in your wife's addled pate has proven my ruin. Remains to make the best of Hobson's choice." He unlocked the door. "Gentlemen, gentlemen!" says he, with deprecating hand, "surely this disturbance is somewhat *outré*, a trifle misplaced, upon the threshold of a bridal-chamber?"

Then Gerald Allonby thrust into the room, followed by Lord Humphrey Degge,* my abhorred rival for Dorothy's affection, and two attendants.

"My grandmother!" shrieks Gerald. "Villain, what have you done with my grandmother?"

"The query were more fitly put," Vanringham retorts, "to the lady's husband." And he waves his hand toward me.

---

* I must in this place entreat my reader's profound discredit of any aspersions I may rashly seem to cast upon this honest gentleman, whose friendship I today esteem as invaluable; but I wrote, as always, *currente calamo*, and the above was penned in an amorous misery, *sub Venire*, be it remembered; and in such cases a wrong bias is easily hung upon the mind.—F.A.

Thereupon the new-comers unbound me with various exclamations of wonder. "And now," I observed, "I would suggest that you bestow upon Mr. Vanringham and yonder blot upon the Church of England the bonds from which I have been recently manumitted, or, at the very least, keep a vigilant watch upon those more than suspicious characters, the while that I narrate the surprising events of this evening."

VI

SUBSEQUENTLY I MADE A CLEAN breast of affairs to Gerald and Lord Humphrey Degge. They heard me with attentive, even sympathetic, countenances; but by and by the face of Lord Humphrey brightened as he saw a not unformidable rival thus jockeyed from the field; and when I had ended, Gerald rose and with an oath struck his open palm upon the table.

"This is the most fortunate coincidence," he swears, "that I have ever known of. I come prepared to find my grandmother the wife of a beggarly play-actor, and I discover that, to the contrary, she has contracted an alliance with a gentleman for whom I entertain sincere affection."

"Surely," I cried, aghast, "you cannot deliberate acceptance of this iniquitous and inadvertent match!"

"What is your meaning, Captain Audaine?" says the boy, sharply. "What other course is possible?"

"O Lord!" said I, "after tonight's imbroglio I have nothing to observe concerning the possibility of anything; but if this marriage prove a legal one, I am most indissuadably resolved to rectify matters without delay in the divorce court."

Now Gerald's brows were uglily compressed. "A divorce," said he, with an extreme of deliberation, "means the airing of tonight's doings in the open. I take it, 'tis the duty of a man of honor to preserve the reputation of his grandmother stainless; whether she be a housemaid or the Queen of Portugal, her frailties are equally entitled to endurance, her eccentricities to toleration: can a gentleman, then, sanction any proceeding of a nature calculated to make his grandmother the laughing-stock of England? The point is a nice one."

"For, conceive," said Lord Humphrey, with the most knavish grin I ever knew a human countenance to pollute itself with, "that the entire matter will be convoyed by the short-hand writers to the public press, and after this will be hawked about the streets; and that the venders will yell particulars of your grandmother's folly under your very windows; and that you must hear them in impotence, and that for some months the three kingdoms will hear of nothing else. Gad, I quite feel for you, my dear."

"I have fallen into a nest of madmen," I cried. "You know, both of you, how profoundly I adore Mr. Gerald's sister, the accomplished and bewitching Miss Allonby; and in any event, I demand of you, as rational beings, is it equitable that I be fettered for life to an old woman's apron-strings because a doctor of divinity is parsimonious of his candles?"

But Gerald had drawn with a flourish. "You have repudiated my kinswoman," says he, "and you cannot deny me the customary satisfaction. Harkee, my fine fellow, Dorothy will marry my friend Lord Humphrey if she will be advised by me; or if she prefer it, she may marry the Man in the Iron Mask or the piper that played before Moses, so far as I am concerned: but as for you, I hereby offer you your choice between quitting this apartment as my grandfather or as a corpse."

"I won't fight you!" I shouted. "Keep the boy off, Degge!" But when the infuriate lad rushed upon me, I was forced, in self-protection, to draw, and after a brief engagement to knock his sword across the room.

"Gerald," I pleaded, "for the love of reason, consider! I cannot fight you. Heaven knows this tragic farce hath robbed me of all pretension toward your sister, and that I am just now but little better than a madman; yet 'tis her blood which exhilarates your veins, and with such dear and precious fluid I cannot willingly imbrue my hands. Nay, you are no swordsman, lad,—keep off!"

And there I had blundered irretrievably.

"No swordsman! By God, I fling the words in your face, Frank Audaine! must I send the candlestick after them?" And within the instant he had caught up his weapon and had hurled himself upon me, in an abandoned fury. I had not moved. The boy spitted himself upon my sword and fell with a horrid gasping.

"You will bear me witness, Lord Humphrey," said I, "that the quarrel was not of my provokement."

But at this juncture the outer door reopened and Dorothy tripped into the room, preceding Lady Allonby and Mr. George Erwyn. They had followed in the family coach to dissuade the Marchioness from her contemplated match by force or by argument, as the cat might jump;

and so it came about that my dear mistress and I stared at each other across her brother's lifeless body.

And 'twas in this poignant moment I first saw her truly. In a storm you have doubtless had some utterly familiar scene leap from the darkness, under the lash of lightning, and be for the instant made visible and strange; and I beheld her with much that awful clarity. Formerly 'twas her beauty had ensnared me, and this I now perceived to be a fortuitous and happy medley of color and glow and curve, indeed, yet nothing more. 'Twas the woman I loved, not her trappings; and her eyes were no more part of her than were the jewels in her ears. But the sweet mirth of her, the brave heart, the clean soul, the girl herself, how good and generous and kind and tender,—'twas this that I now beheld, and knew that this, too, was lost;—and, in beholding, the little love of yesterday fled whimpering before the sacred passion which had possessed my being. And I began to laugh.

"My dear," said I, "'twas tonight that you promised me your answer, and tonight you observe in me alike your grandfather and your brother's murderer."

VII

LADY ALLONBY FELL TO WRINGING her hands, but Dorothy had knelt beside the prostrate form and was inspecting the ravages of my fratricidal sword. "Oh, fy! fy!" says she immediately, and wrinkles her saucy nose; "had none of you the sense to perceive that Gerald was tipsy? And as for the wound, 'tis only a scratch here on the left shoulder. Get water, somebody." And her command being obeyed, she cleansed the hurt composedly and bandaged it with the ruffle of her petticoat.

Meanwhile we hulking men stood thick about her, fidgeting and foolishly gaping like a basket of fish; and presently a sibilance of relief went about our circle as Gerald opened his eyes. "Sister," says he, with a profoundly tragic face, "remember—remember that I perished to preserve the honor of our family."

"To preserve a fiddlestick!" said my adored Dorothy. And, rising, she confronted me, a tinted statuette of decision. "Now, Frank," says she, "I would like to know the meaning of this nonsense."

And thereupon, for the second time, I recounted the dreadful and huddled action of the night.

When I had ended, "The first thing," says she, "is to let Grandmother out of that room. And the second is to show me the Parson." This was done; the Dowager entered in an extremity of sulkiness, and the Parson, on being pointed out, lowered his eyes and intensified his complexion.

"As I anticipated," says my charmer, "you are, one and all, a parcel of credulous infants. 'Tis a parson, indeed, but merely the parson out of Vanbrugh's *Relapse*; only last Friday, sir, we heartily commended your fine performance. Why, Frank, the man is one of the play-actors."

"I fancy," Mr. Vanringham here interpolates, "that I owe the assembled company some modicum of explanation. 'Tis true that at the beginning of our friendship I had contemplated matrimony with our amiable Marchioness, but, I confess, 'twas the lady's property rather than her person which was the allure. And reflection dissuaded me; a legal union left me, a young and not unhandsome man, irrevocably fettered to an old woman; whereas a mock-marriage afforded an eternal option to compound the match—for a consideration—with the lady's relatives, to whom, I had instinctively divined, her alliance with me would prove distasteful. Accordingly I had availed myself of my colleague's skill* in the portrayal of clerical parts rather than resort to any parson whose authority was unrestricted by the footlights. And accordingly—"

"And accordingly my marriage," I interrupted, "is not binding?"

"I can assure you," he replied, "that you might trade your lawful right in the lady for a twopenny whistle and not lose by the bargain."

"And what about my marriage?" says the Marchioness—"the marriage which was never to be legalized?—'twas merely that you might sell me afterward, like so much mutton, was it, you jumping-jack—!"

But I spare you her ensuing gloss upon this text.

The man heard her through, without a muscle twitching. "It is more than probable," he conceded, "that I have merited each and every fate your Ladyship is pleased to invoke. Indeed, I consider the extent of your distresses to be equaled only by that of your vocabulary. Yet by ordinary the heart of woman is not obdurate, and upon one lady here I have some claim—"

---

* I witnessed this same Quarmby's hanging in 1754, and for a burglary, I think, with an extraordinary relish.—F. A.

Dorothy had drawn away from him, with an odd and frightened cry. "Not upon me, sir! I never saw you except across the footlights. You know I never saw you except across the footlights, Mr. Vanringham!"

Fixedly he regarded her, with a curious yet not unpleasing smile. "I am the more unfortunate," he said, at last. "Nay, 'twas to Lady Allonby I addressed my appeal."

The person he named had been whispering with George Erwyn, but now she turned toward the actor. "Heavens!" said Lady Allonby, "to think I should be able to repay you this soon! La, of course, you are at liberty, Mr. Vanringham, and we may treat the whole series of events as a frolic suited to the day. For I am under obligations to you, and, besides, your punishment would breed a scandal, and, above all, anything is preferable to being talked about in the wrong way."

Having reasons of my own, I was elated by the upshot of this rather remarkable affair. Yet in justice to my own perspicacity, I must declare that it occurred to me, at this very time, that Mr. Vanringham had proven himself not entirely worthy of unlimited confidence, I reflected, however, that I had my instructions, and that, if a bad king may prove a good husband, a knave may surely carry a letter with fidelity, the more so if it be to his interest to do it.

VIII

I rode back to Tunbridge in the coach, with Dorothy at my side and with Gerald recumbent upon the front seat,—where, after ten minutes' driving the boy very philanthropically fell asleep.

"And you have not," I immediately asserted—"after all, you have not given me the answer which was tonight to decide whether I be of all mankind the most fortunate or the most miserable. And 'tis nearing twelve."

"What choice have I?" she murmured; "after tonight is it not doubly apparent that you need some one to take care of you? And, besides, this is your eighth proposal, and the ninth I had always rather meant to accept, because I have been in love with you for two whole weeks."

My heart stood still. And shall I confess that for an instant my wits, too, paused to play the gourmet with my emotions? She sat beside me in the darkness, you understand, waiting, mine to touch. And everywhere the world was filled with beautiful, kind people, and overhead God smiled down upon His world, and a careless seraph had left open the door of Heaven, so that quite a deal of its splendor flooded the world about us. And the snoring of Gerald was now inaudible because of a stately music which was playing somewhere.

"Frank—!" she breathed. And I noted that her voice was no less tender than her lips.

IV

THE RHYME TO PORRINGER

As Played at Tunbridge Wells, April 2, 1750

"Ye gods, why are not hearts first paired above,
But still some interfere in others' love,
Ere each for each by certain marks are known?
You mould them up in haste, and drop them down,
And while we seek what carelessly you sort,
You sit in state, and make our pains your sport."

Dramatis Personæ

Captain Audaine, an ingenious, well-accomplished gentleman.
Lord Humphrey Degge, an airy young gentleman, loves Miss
    Allonby for her money.
Vanringham, emissary and confederate of Audaine.
Miss Allonby, a young lady of wit and fortune.
Attendants to Lord Humphrey, Etc.

Scene
Tunbridge Wells, first in and about Lord Humphrey's lodgings, then shifting to a drawing-room in Lady Allonby's villa.

The Rhyme to Porringer

Proem:—Merely to Serve as Intermezzo

Next morning Captain Audaine was closeted with Mr. Vanringham in the latter's apartments at the *Three Gudgeons*. I abridge the Captain's relation of their interview, and merely tell you that it ended in the actor's looking up, with a puzzled face, from a certain document.

"You might have let me have a whiff of this," Mr. Vanringham began. "You might have breathed, say, a syllable or two last night—"

"I had my instructions, sir, but yesterday," replied the Captain; "and surely, Mr. Vanringham, to have presumed last night upon my possession of this paper, so far as to have demanded any favor of you, were unreasonable, even had it not savored of cowardice. For, as it has been very finely observed, it is the nicest part of commerce in the world, that of doing and receiving benefits. O Lord, sir! there are so many thousand circumstances, with respect to time, person, and place, which either heighten or allay the value of the obligation—"

"I take your point," said the other, with some haste, "and concede that you are, beyond any reasonable doubt, in the right. Within the hour I am off."

"Then all is well," said Captain Audaine.

But he was wrong in this opinion, so wrong that I confute him by subjoining his own account of what befell, somewhat later in the day.

I

'Twas hard upon ten in the evening (the Captain estimates) when I left Lady Culcheth's,* and I protest that at the time there was not a happier man in all Tunbridge than Francis Audaine.

"You haven't the king?" Miss Allonby was saying, as I made my adieus to the company. "Then I play queen, knave, and ace, which gives me the game, Lord Humphrey."

---

* Sir Henry Muskerry's daughter, of whom I have already spoken, and by common consent an estimable lady and a person of fine wit; but my infatuation for Lady Betty had by this time, after three nights with her, been puffed out; and this fortunate extinction, through the affair of the broken snuffbox, had left me now entirely indifferent to all her raptures, panegyrics, and premeditated artlessnesses.—F. A.

And afterward she shuffled the cards and flashed across the room a glance whose brilliance shamed the tawdry candles about her, and, as you can readily conceive, roused a prodigious trepidation in my adoring breast.

"Dorothy!—O Dorothy!" I said over and over again when I had reached the street; and so went homeward with constant repetitions of her dear name.

I suppose it was an idiotic piece of business; but you are to remember that I loved her with an entire heart, and that, as yet, I could scarcely believe the confession of a reciprocal attachment, which I had wrung from her overnight, to the accompaniment of Gerald's snoring, had been other than an unusually delectable and audacious dream upon the part of Frank Audaine.

I found it, then, as I went homeward, a heady joy to ponder on her loveliness. Oh, the wonder of her voice, that is a love-song! cried my heart. Oh, the candid eyes of her, more beautiful than the June heavens, more blue than the very bluest speedwell-flower! Oh, the tilt of her tiny chin, and the incredible gold of her hair, and the quite unbelievable pink-and-white of her little flower-soft face! And, oh, the scrap of crimson that is her mouth.

In a word, my pulses throbbed with a sort of divine insanity, and Frank Audaine was as much out of his senses as any madman now in Bedlam, and as deliriously perturbed as any lover is by ordinary when he meditates upon the object of his affections.

But there was other work than sonneting afoot that night, and shortly I set about it. Yet such was my felicity that I went to my nocturnal labors singing. Yes, it rang in my ears, somehow, that silly old Scotch song, and under my breath I hummed odd snatches of it as I went about the night's business.

Sang I:

> *"Ken ye the rhyme to porringer?*
> *Ken ye the rhyme to porringer?*
> *King James the Seventh had ae daughter,*
> *And he gave her to an Oranger.*
>
> *"Ken ye how he requited him?*
> *Ken ye how he requited him?*
> *The dog has into England come,*
> *And ta'en the crown in spite of him!*

> "*The rogue he salna keep it lang,*
> *To budge we'll make him fain again;*
> *We'll hang him high upon a tree,*
> *And King James shall hae his ain again!*"

II

WELL! MATTERS WENT SMOOTHLY ENOUGH at the start. With a diamond Vanringham dexterously cut out a pane of glass, so that we had little difficulty in opening the window; and I climbed into a room black as a pocket, leaving him without to act as a sentinel, since, so far as I could detect, the house was now untenanted.

But some twenty minutes later, when I had finally succeeded in forcing the escritoire I found in the back room upon the second story, I heard the street door unclose. And I had my candle extinguished in that self same instant. You can conceive that 'twas with no pleasurable anticipation I peered into the hall, for I was fairly trapped. I saw some five or six men of an ugly aspect, who carried among them a burden, the nature of which I could not determine in the uncertain light. But I heaved a sigh of relief as they bore their cargo past me, to the front room, (which opened on the one I occupied), without apparent recognition of my presence.

"Now," thinks I, "is the time for my departure." And having already selected the papers I had need of from the rifled desk, I was about to run for it, when I heard a well-known voice.

"Rat the parson!" it cried; "he should have been here an hour ago. Here's the door left open for him, endangering the whole venture, and whey-face han't plucked up heart to come! Do some of you rogues fetch him without delay; and do all of you meet me tomorrow at the *Mitre*, to be paid in full for this business, before reporting to his Grace."

"Here," thinks I, "is beyond doubt a romance." And as the men tumbled down-stairs and into the street, I resolved to see the adventure through, by the light of those candles which were now burning in the next room.

I waited for perhaps ten minutes, during which period I was aware of divers movements near at hand; and, judging that in any case there was but one man's anger to be apprehended, I crept toward the intervening door and found it luckily ajar.

So I peered through the crack into the adjoining room, and there, as I had anticipated, discovered Lord Humphrey Degge, whom I had last seen at Lady Culcheth's wrangling over a game of *écarté* with the fairest antagonist the universe could afford.

Just now my Lord was in a state of high emotion, and the cause of it was evident when I perceived his ruffians had borne into the house a swooning lady, whom merciful unconsciousness had rendered oblivious to her present surroundings, and whose wrists his Lordship was vigorously slapping in the intervals between his frequent applications to her nostrils of a flask, which, as I more lately learned, contained sal volatile.

Here was an unlucky turn, since I had no desire to announce my whereabouts, my business in the house being of a sort that necessitated secrecy; whereas, upon the other hand, I could not but misdoubt my Lord's intention toward the unknown fair was of discreditable kinship, and such as a gentleman might not countenance with self-esteem.

Accordingly I devoted the moments during which the lady was recovering from her swoon, to serious reflection concerning the course that I should preferably adopt. But now, Miss came to, and, as is the custom of all females similarly situated, rubbed her eyes and said, "Where am I?"

And when she rose from the divan I saw that 'twas my adored Dorothy.

"In the presence of your infatuated slave," says my Lord. "Ah, divine Miss Allonby—!"

But being now aware of her deplorable circumstances, she began to weep, and, in spite of the amorous rhetoric with which his Lordship was prompt to comfort her, rebuked him for unmanly conduct, with sublimity and fire, and depicted the horrors of her present predicament in terms that were both just and elegant.

From their disjointed talk I soon determined that, Lord Humphrey's suit being rejected by my angel, he had laid a trap for her (by bribing her coachman, as I subsequently learned), and had so far succeeded in his nefarious scheme that she, on leaving Lady Culcheth's, had been driven to this house, in the conviction she rode homeward; and this course my Lord endeavored to justify, with a certain eloquence, and attributed the irregularity of his behavior solely to the colossal vehemence of his affection.

His oratory, however, was of little avail, for Dorothy told him plainly that she had rather hear the protestations of a toad than listen to his far more nauseous flattery; and bade him at once restore her to her natural guardians.

"*Ma charmante*," said he, "tomorrow your good step-mother may, if you will, share with your husband the privilege of saluting Lady Humphrey Degge; but as for Miss Allonby, I question if in the future her dearest friends are likely to see much of her."

"What do you mean?" cries she.

"That the parson will be here directly," said he.

"Infamous!" she observes; "and is the world run mad, that these extempore weddings should be foisted upon every woman in the Allonby connection!"

"Ah, but, my dear," he answered airily, "'twas those two fiascos which begot my notion, and yet hearten me. For in every approved romance the third adventurer gets the victory; so that I am, I take it, predestinate to win where Vanringham and Rokesle failed."

She did not chop logic with him, but instead retorted in a more primitive fashion by beginning to scream at the top of her voice.

I doubt if any man of honor was ever placed under a more great embarrass. Yonder was the object of my devotion, exposed to all the diabolical machinations of a heartless villain; and here was I concealed in my Lord's bedroom, his desk broken open, and his papers in my pocket. To remain quiet was impossible, since 'twas to expose her to a fate worse than death; yet to reveal myself was to confess Frank Audaine a thief, and to lose her perhaps beyond redemption.

Then I thought of the mask which I had brought in case of emergency; and, clapping it on, resolved to brazen out the affair. Meanwhile I saw all notions of gallantry turned topsy-turvy, for my Lord was laughing quietly, while my adored Dorothy called aloud upon the name of her Maker.

"The neighborhood is not unaccustomed to such sounds," said he, "and I hardly think we need fear any interruption. I must tell you, my dear creature, you have, by an evil chance, arrived in a most evil locality, for this quarter of the town is the devil's own country, and he is scarcely like to make you free of it."

"O Lord, sir!" said I, and pushed the door wide open, "surely you forget that the devil is a gentleman?"

III

HAD I DROPPED A HAND-GRENADE into the apartment the astonishment of its occupants would not have been excessive. My Lord's face, as he clapped his hand to his sword, was neither tranquil nor altogether agreeable to contemplate; but as for Dorothy, she gave a frightened little cry, and ran toward the masked intruder with a piteous confidence which wrung my heart.

"The devil!" says my Lord.

"Not precisely," I amended, and bowed in my best manner, "though 'tis undeniable I come to act as his representative."

"Oh, joy to your success!" his Lordship sneered.

"Harkee, sir," said I, "as you, with perfect justice, have stated, this is the devil's stronghold, and hereabouts his will is paramount; and, as I have had the honor to add, the devil is a gentleman. Sure, and as such, he cannot be expected to countenance your present behavior? Nay, never fear! Lucifer, already up to the ears in the affairs of this mundane sphere, lacks leisure to express his disapproval in sulphuric person. He tenders his apologies, sir, and sends in his stead your servant, with whose capabilities he is indifferently acquainted."

"To drop this mummery," says Lord Humphrey, "what are you doing in my lodgings?"

"O Lord, sir!" I responded, "I came thither, I confess, without invitation. And with equal candor I will admit that my present need is of your Lordship's banknotes and jewels, and such-like trifles, rather than—you force me, sir, to say it,—rather than of your company."

Thus speaking, I drew and placed myself on guard, while my Lord gasped.

"You're the most impudent rogue," says he, after he had recovered himself a little, "that I have had the privilege of meeting—"

"Your Lordship is all kindness," I protested.

"—but your impudence is worth the price of whatever you may have pilfered. Go, my good man—or devil, if you so prefer to style yourself! Tell Lucifer that he is well served; and obligingly return to the infernal regions without delay. For, as you have doubtless learned, Miss and I have many private matters to discuss. And, gad, Mr. Moloch,* pleasant as is your conversation, you must acknowledge I can't allow evil spirits about the house without getting it an ill reputation. So pardon me if I exorcise you with this."

---

* A deity of, I believe, Ammonitish origin. His traditional character as represented by our immortal Milton is both taking to the fancy and finely romantic; and is, I am informed, no less remarkable for many happy turns of speech than for conformity throughout to the most famous legends of Talmudic fabrication.—F.A.

JAMES BRANCH CABELL

He spoke boldly, and, as he ended, tossed me a purse. I let it lie where it fell, for I had by no means ended my argument.

"Yet, sir," said I, "my errand, which began with the acquisition of your pins, studs and other jewelry, now reaches toward treasure far more precious—"

"Enough!" he cried, impatiently, "Begone! and do you render thanks—that my present business is so urgent as to prevent my furnishing the rope which will one day adorn your neck."

"That's as may be," quoth I; "and, indeed, I doubt if I could abide drowning, for 'tis a damp, unwholesome, and very permanent sort of death. But my fixed purpose, to cut short all debate, is to escort Miss Allonby homeward."

"Come," sneers my Lord,—"come, Mr. Moloch, I have borne with your insolence for a quarter of an hour—"

"Twenty minutes," said I, after consulting my watch.

"—but I mean to put up with it no longer; and in consequence I take the boorish liberty of suggesting that this is none of your affair."

"Good sir," I conceded, "your Lordship speaks with considerable justice, and we must leave the final decision to Miss here."

I bowed toward her. In her face there was a curious bewilderment that made me fear lest, for all my mask, for all my unnatural intonations, and for all the room's half-light, my worshipped mistress had come near to recognizing this caught thief.

"Miss Allonby," said I, in a falsetto voice which trembled, "since I am unknown to you, may I trust you will permit me to present myself? My name—though, indeed, I have a multitude of names—is for the occasion Frederick Thomasson. With my father's appellation and estates I cannot accommodate you, for the reason that a mystery attaches to his identity. As for my mother, let it suffice to say that she was a vivacious brunette of a large acquaintance, and generally known to the public as Black Moll O'Reilly. I began life as a pickpocket. Since then I have so far improved my natural gifts that the police are flattering enough to value my person at several hundred pounds. My rank in society, as you perceive, is not exalted; yet, if my luck by any chance should fail, I do not question that I shall, upon some subsequent Friday, move in loftier circles than any nobleman who happens at the time to be on Tyburn Hill.—So much for my poor self. And since by this late hour Lady Allonby is beyond doubt beginning to grow uneasy, let us have done with further exposition, and remember that 'tis high time you selected an escort to her residence. May I implore that you choose between the son of the Marquis of Venour and Black Molly's bastard?"

She looked us over,—first one, then the other. More lately she laughed; and if I had never seen her before, I could have found it in my heart to love her for the sweet insolence of her demeanor.

"After all," said my adored Dorothy, "I prefer the rogue who when he goes about his knaveries has at least the decency to wear a mask."

"That, my Lord," said I, "is fairly conclusive; and so we will be journeying."

"Over my dead body!" says he.

"Sure, and what's beneath the feet," I protested, "is equally beneath consideration."

The witticism stung him like a wasp, and, with an oath, he drew, as I was heartily glad to observe, for I cannot help thinking that when it comes to the last pinch, and one gentleman is excessively annoyed by the existence of another, steel is your only arbiter, and charitable allowances for the dead make the one rational peroration. So we crossed blades; and, pursuing my usual tactics, I began upon a flow of words, which course, as I have learned by old experience, is apt to disconcert an adversary far more than any trick of the sword can do.

I pressed him sorely, and he continued to give way, but clearly for tactical purposes, and without permitting the bright flash of steel that protected him to swerve an instant from the proper line.

"Miss Allonby," said I, growing impatient, "have you never seen a venomous insect pinned to the wall? In that case, I pray you to attend more closely. For one has only to parry—thus! And to thrust—in this fashion! And behold, the thing is done!"

In fact, having been run through the chest, my Lord was for the moment affixed to the panelling at the extreme end of the apartment, where he writhed, much in the manner of a cockchafer which mischievous urchins have pinned to a card,—his mien and his gesticulations, however, being rather more suggestive of the torments of the damned, as they are so strikingly depicted by the Italian Dante.*

---

* I allude, of course, to the famous Florentine, who excels no less in his detailed depictions of infernal anguish than in his eloquent portrayal of the graduated and equitable emoluments of an eternal glorification.—F.A.

He tumbled in a heap, though, when I sheathed my sword and bowed toward my charmer.

"Miss Allonby," said I, "thus quickly ends this evil quarter of an hour; and with, equal expedition, I think, should we be leaving this evil quarter of the town."

She had watched the combat with staring and frightened eyes. Now she had drawn nearer, and she looked curiously at her over-presumptuous lover where he had fallen.

"Have you killed him?" she asked, in a hushed voice.

"O Lord, no!" I protested. "The life of a peer's son is too valuable a matter; he will be little the worse for it in a week."

"The dog!" cries she, overcome with pardonable indignation at the affront which the misguided nobleman had put upon her; and afterward, with a ferocity the more astounding in an individual whose demeanor was by ordinary of an aspect so amiable and so engaging, she said, "Oh, the lewd thieving dog!"

"My adorable Miss Allonby," said I, "do not, I pray you, thus slander the canine species! Meanwhile, permit me to remind you that 'tis inexpedient to loiter in these parts, for the parson will presently be at hand; and if it be to inter rather than to marry Lord Humphrey—well, after all, the peerage is a populous estate! But, either way, time presses."

"Come!" said she, and took my arm; and together we went down-stairs and into the street.

IV

ON THE WAY HOMEWARD SHE spoke never a word. Vanringham had made a hasty flitting when my Lord's people arrived, so that we saw nothing of him. But when we had come safely to Lady Allonby's villa, Dorothy began to laugh.

"Captain Audaine," says she, in a wearied and scornful voice, "I know that the hour is very late, yet there are certain matters to be settled between as which will, I think, scarcely admit of delay. I pray you, then, grant me ten minutes' conversation."

She had known me all along, you see. Trust the dullest woman to play Oedipus when love sets the riddle. So there was nothing to do save clap my mask into my pocket and follow her, sheepishly enough, toward one of the salons, where at Dorothy's solicitation a gaping footman made a light for us.

She left me there to kick my heels through a solitude of some moments' extent. But in a while my dear mistress came into the room, with her arms full of trinkets and knick-knacks, which she flung upon a table.

"Here's your ring, Captain Audaine," says she, and drew it from her finger. "I did not wear it long, did I? And here's the miniature you gave me, too. I used to kiss it every night, you know. And here's a flower you dropped at Lady Pevensey's. I picked it up—oh, very secretly!— because you had worn it, you understand. And here's—"

But at this point she fairly broke down; and she cast her round white arms about the heap of trinkets, and strained them close to her, and bowed her imperious golden head above them in anguish.

"Oh, how I loved you—how I loved you!" she sobbed. "And all the while you were only a common thief!"

"Dorothy—!" I pleaded.

"You shame me—you shame me past utterance!" she cried, in a storm of mingled tears and laughter. "Here's this bold Captain Audaine, who comes to Tunbridge from nobody knows where, and wins a maid's love, and proves in the end a beggarly house-breaker! Mr. Garrick might make a mirthful comedy of this, might he not?" Then she rose to her feet very stiffly. "Take your gifts, Mr. Thief," says she, pointing,—"take them. And for God's sake let me not see you again!"

So I was forced to make a clean breast of it.

"Dorothy," said I, "ken ye the rhyme to porringer?" But she only stared at me through unshed tears.

Presently, though, I hummed over the old song:

> *"Ken ye the rhyme to porringer?*
> *Ken ye the rhyme to porringer?*
> *King James the Seventh had ae daughter,*
> *And he gave her to an Oranger."*

"And the Oranger filched his crown," said I, "and drove King James— God bless him!—out of his kingdom. This was a while and a half ago, my dear; but Dutch William left the stolen crown to Anne, and Anne, in turn, left it to German George. So that now the Elector of Hanover reigns at St. James's, while the true King's son must skulk in France, with never a roof to shelter him. And there are certain gentlemen, Dorothy, who do not consider that this is right."

"You are a Jacobite?" said she. "Well! and what have your politics to do with the matter?"

"Simply that Lord Humphrey is not of my way of thinking, my dearest dear. Lord Humphrey—pah!—this Degge is Ormskirk's spy, I tell you! He followed Vanringham to Tunbridge on account of our business. And today, when Vanringham set out for Avignon, he was stopped a mile from the Wells by some six of Lord Humphrey's fellows, disguised as highwaymen, and all his papers were stolen. Oho, but Lord Humphrey is a thrifty fellow: so when Ormskirk puts six bandits at his disposal he employs them in double infamy, to steal you as well as Vanringham's despatches. Tomorrow they would have been in Ormskirk's hands. And then—" I paused to allow myself a whistle.

She came a little toward me, in the prettiest possible glow of bewilderment, "I do not understand," she murmured. "Oh, Frank, Frank, for the love of God, beware of trusting Vanringham in anything! And you are not a thief, after all? Are you really not named Thomasson?"

"I am most assuredly not Frederick Thomasson," said I, "nor do I know if any such person exists, for I never heard the name before tonight. Yet, in spite of this, I am an unmitigated thief. Why, d'ye not understand? What Vanringham carried was a petition from some two hundred Scotch and English gentlemen that our gracious Prince Charlie be pleased to come over and take back his own from the Elector. 'Twas rebellion, flat rebellion, and the very highest treason! Had Ormskirk seen the paper, within a month our heads had all been blackening over Temple Bar. So I stole it,—I, Francis Audaine, stole it in the King's cause, God bless him! 'Twas burglary, no less, but it saved two hundred lives, my own included; and I look to be a deal older than I am before I regret the deed with any sincerity."

Afterward I showed her the papers, and then burned them one by one over a candle. She said nothing. So by and by I turned toward her with a little bow.

"Madam," said I, "you have forced my secret from me. I know that your family is staunch on the Whig side; and yet, ere the thief goes, may he not trust you will ne'er betray him?"

And now she came to me, all penitence and dimples.

"But it was you who said you were a thief," my dear mistress pointed out.

"O Lord, madam!" said I, "'twas very necessary that Degge should think me so. A house-breaker they would have only hanged, but a Jacobite they would have hanged and quartered afterward."

"Ah, Frank, do not speak of such fearful matters, but forgive me instantly!" she wailed.

And I was about to do so in what I considered the most agreeable and appropriate manner when the madcap broke away from me, and sprang upon a footstool and waved her fan defiantly.

"Down with the Elector!" she cried, in her high, sweet voice. "Long live King James!"

And then, with a most lovely wildness of mien, she began to sing:

> *"Ken ye the rhyme to porringer?*
> *Ken ye the rhyme to porringer?*
> *King James the Seventh had ae daughter—"*

until I interrupted her. For, "Extraordinary creature!" I pleaded, "you will rouse the house."

"I don't care! I intend to be a Jacobite if you are one!"

"Eh, well," said I, "Frank Audaine is not the man to coerce his wife in a political matter. Nevertheless, I know of a certain Jacobite who is not unlikely to have a bad time of it if by any chance Lord Humphrey recognized him tonight. Nay, Miss, you may live to be a widow yet."

"But he didn't recognize you. And if he did"—she snapped her fingers,—"why, we'll fight him again, you and I won't we, my dear? For he stole our secret, you know. And he stole me, too. Very pretty behavior, wasn't it?" And here Miss Allonby stamped the tiniest, the most infinitesimal of red-heeled slippers.

> *"The rogue he didna keep me lang,*
> *To budge we made him fain again—*

"that's you, Frank, and your great, long sword. And now:

> *"We'll hang him high, upon a tree,*
> *And King Frank shall hae his ain again!"*

Afterward my adored Dorothy jumped from the footstool, and came toward me, lifting up the crimson trifle that she calls her mouth, "So take your own, my king," she breathed, with a wonderful gesture of surrender.

And a gentleman could do no less.

JAMES BRANCH CABELL

V

ACTORS ALL

As Played at Tunbridge Wells, April 3, 1750

I am thinking if some little, filching, inquisitive poet should get my story, and represent it to the stage, what those ladies who are never precise but at a play would say of me now,—that I were a confident, coming piece, I warrant, and they would damn the poor poet for libelling the sex."

DRAMATIS PERSONÆ

DUKE OF ORMSKIRK.
COLONEL DENSTROUDE,   }
SIR GRESLEY CARNE,   } Gentlemen of the town.
MR. BABINGTON-HERLE,   }
VANRINGHAM, a play-actor and a Jacobite emissary.
MR. LANGTON, secretary to Ormskirk.
MISS ALLONBY, an heiress, loves Captain Audaine.
LOTTRUM, maid to Miss Allonby.
BENYON, MINCHIN, and OTHER SERVANTS to Ormskirk.

SCENE

Tunbridge Wells, shifting from Ormskirk's lodgings at the *Mitre* to Vanringham's apartments in the *Three Gudgeons*.

Actors All

Proem.—To Explain Why the Heroine of
This Comedy Must Wear Her Best

I quit pilfering from the writings of Francis Audaine, since in the happenings which now concern us he plays but a subsidiary part. The Captain had an utter faith in decorum, and therefore it was, as he records, an earth-staggering shock when the following day, on the Pantiles, in full sight of the best company at the Wells, Captain Audaine was apprehended. He met disaster like an old acquaintance, and hummed a scrap of song—"*O, gin I were a bonny bird*,"—and shrugged; but when Miss Allonby, with whom he had been chatting, swayed and fell, the Captain caught her in his arms, and standing thus, turned angrily upon the emissaries of the law.

"Look you, you rascals," said he, "you have spoiled a lady's afternoon with your foolish warrant!"

He then relinquished the unconscious girl to her brother's keeping, tenderly kissed one insensate hand, and afterward strolled off to jail *en route* for a perfunctory trial and a subsequent traffic with the executioner that Audaine did not care to think of.

Tunbridge buzzed like a fly-trap with the ensuing rumors. The Captain was at the head of a most heinous Jacobitical uprising. The great Duke of Ormskirk was come hastily from London on the business. Highlanders were swarming over the Border, ten thousand French troops had landed at Pevensey, commanded by the Chevalier St. George in person, and twenty thousand friars and pilgrims from Coruña had sailed for Milford Haven, under the admiralty of young Henry Stuart. The King was locked in the Tower; the King had been assassinated that morning by a Spanish monk, with horse-pistols and a cast in his left eye; and the King and the Countess of Yarmouth had escaped three days ago, in disguise, and were now on their way to Hanover.

These were the reports which went about Tunbridge, while Dorothy Allonby wept a little and presently called for cold water and a powder-puff, and afterward for a sedan chair.

I

Miss Allonby found my Lord Duke of Ormskirk deep in an infinity of papers. But at her entrance he rose and with a sign dismissed his secretary.

It appears appropriate here to afford you some notion of Ormskirk's exterior. I pilfer from Löwe's memoir of him, where Horace Calverley, who first saw Ormskirk at about this time, is quoted:

"His Grace was in blue-and-silver, which became him, though he is somewhat stomachy for such conspicuous colors. A handsome man, I would have said, honest but not particularly intelligent. . . Walpole, in a fit of spleen, once called him 'a porcelain sphinx,' and the phrase sticks; but, indeed, there is more of the china-doll about him. He possesses the same too-perfect complexion, his blue eyes have the same spick-and-span vacuity; and the fact that the right orb is a trifle larger than its fellow gives his countenance, in repose, much the same expression of placid astonishment. . . Very plump, very sleepy-looking, immaculate as a cat, you would never have accorded him a second glance: covert whisperings that the stout gentleman yonder is the great Duke of Ormskirk have, I think, taxed human belief more than once during these ten years past."

They said of Ormskirk that he manifested a certain excitement on the day after Culloden, when he had seventy-two prisoners shot *en masse*,* but this was doubted; and in any event, such *battues* being comparatively rare, he by ordinary appeared to regard the universe with a composed and feline indifference.

II

"Child, child!" Ormskirk began, and made a tiny gesture of deprecation, "I perceive you are about to appeal to my better nature, and so I warn you in advance that the idiotic business has worked me into a temper absolutely ogreish."

---

* But for all that, when, near Rossinish (see Löwe), he captured Flora Macdonald and her ostensibly female companion, Ormskirk flatly declined to recognize Prince Charles. "They may well call you the Pretender, madam," he observed to "Bettie Burke,"—"since as concerns my party you are the most desirable Pretender we could possibly imagine." And thereupon he gave the Prince a pass out of Scotland.

"The Jacobite conspiracy, you mean?" said Miss Allonby. "Oh, I suppose so. I am not particularly interested in such matters, though; I came, you understand, for a warrant, or an order, or whatever you call it, for them to let Frank out of that horrid filthy gaol."

The Duke's face was gravely humorous as he gazed at her for a moment or two in silence, "You know quite well," he said at last, "that I can give you nothing of the sort."

Miss Allonby said: "Upon my word, I never heard of such nonsense! How else is he to take me to Lady Mackworth's ball tonight?"

"It is deplorable," his Grace of Ormskirk conceded, "that Captain Audaine should be thus snatched from circles which he, no doubt, adorns. Still, I fear you must look for another escort; and frankly, child, if you will be advised by me, you will permit us to follow out our present intentions and take off his head—not a great deprivation when you consider he has so plainly demonstrated its contents to be of such inferior quality."

She had drawn close to him, with widening, pitiable eyes. "You mean, then," she demanded, "that Frank's very life is in danger?"

"This is unfair," the Duke complained. "You are about to go into hysterics forthwith and thus bully me into letting the man escape. You are a minx. You presume upon the fact that in the autumn I am to wed your kinswoman and bosom companion, and that my affection for her is widely known to go well past the frontier of common-sense; and also upon the fact that Marian will give me the devil if I don't do exactly as you ask. I consider you to abuse your power unconscionably, I consider you to be a second Delilah. However, since you insist upon it, this Captain Audaine must, of course, be spared the fate he very richly merits."

Miss Allonby had seated herself beside a table and was pensively looking up at him. "Naturally," she said, "Marian and I, between us, will badger you into saving Frank. I shall not worry, therefore, and I must trust to Providence, I suppose, to arrange matters so that the poor boy will not catch his death of cold in your leaky gaol yonder. And now I would like to be informed of what he has been most unjustly accused."

"His crime," the Duke retorted, "is the not unusual one of being a fool. Oh, I am candid! All Jacobites are fools. We gave the Stuarts a fair trial, Heaven knows, and nobody but a fool would want them back."

"I am not here to discuss politics," a dignified Miss Allonby stated, "but simply to find out in what way Frank has been slandered."

Ormskirk lifted one eyebrow. "It is not altogether a matter of politics. Rather, as I see it, it is a matter of common-sense. Under the Stuarts England was a prostitute among the nations, lackey in turn to Spain and France and Italy; under the Guelph the Three-per-cents. are today at par. The question as to which is preferable thus resolves itself into a choice between common-sense and bedlamite folly. But, unhappily, you cannot argue with a Jacobite: only four years ago Cumberland and Hawley and I rode from Aberdeen to the Highlands and left all the intervening country bare as the palm of your hand; I forget how many Jacobites we killed, but evidently not enough to convince the others. Very well: we intend to have no more such nonsense, and we must settle this particular affair by the simple device of hanging or beheading every man—Jack concerned in it." He spoke without vehemence—rather regretfully than otherwise.

Miss Allonby was patient, yet resolute to keep to the one really important point. "But what has Frank been accused of doing when it never even entered his head?"

"He has been conspiring," said the Duke, "and with conspicuous clumsiness. It appears, child, that it was their common idiocy which of late brought together some two hundred gentlemen in Lancashire. Being everyone of them most unmitigated fools, they desired that sot at Avignon to come over once more and 'take back his own,' as the saying is. He would not stir without definite assurances. So these men drew up a petition pledging their all to the Chevalier's cause and—God help us!—signed it. I protest," the Duke sighed, "I cannot understand these people! A couple of penstrokes, you observe, and there is your life at the mercy of chance, at the disposal of a puff of wind or the first blunderer who stumbles on the paper."

"Doubtless that is entirely true," said Miss Allonby, "but what about Frank?"

Ormskirk shrugged his shoulders and began to laugh. "You are an incomparable actress, you rogue you. But let us be candid, for all that, since as it happens Lord Humphrey is not the only person in my employ. What occurred last night I now partly know, and in part guess, Degge played a bold game, and your Captain gambled even more impudently,— only the stakes, as it today transpires, were of somewhat less importance than either of them surmised. For years Mr. Vanringham has been a Jacobite emissary; now he tires of it; and so he devoted the entire morning, yesterday to making a copy of this absurd petition."

"I do not understand," said Miss Allonby; and in appearance, at least, she was no whit disconcerted.

"He carried only the copy. You burned only the copy. Mr. Vanringham, it develops, knew well enough what that bungling Degge had been deputed to do, and he preferred to treat directly with Lord Humphrey's principal. Mr. Vanringham is an intelligent fellow. I dare make this assertion, because I am fresh from an interview with Mr. Vanringham," his Grace of Ormskirk ended, and allowed himself a reminiscent chuckle.

She had risen. "O ungenerous! this Vanringham has been bribed!"

"I pray you," said the Duke, "give vent to no such scandal. Vanringham's life would not be worth a farthing if he had done such a thing, and he knows it. Nay, I have planned it more neatly. Tonight Mr. Vanringham will be arrested—merely on suspicion, mind you,—and all his papers will be brought to me; and it is possible that among them we may find the petition. And it is possible that, somehow, when he is tried with the others, Mr. Vanringham alone may be acquitted. And it is possible that an aunt—in Wales, say,—may die about this time and leave him a legacy of some five thousand pounds. Oh, yes, all this is quite possible," said the Duke; "but should we therefore shriek *Bribery*? For my own part, I esteem Mr. Vanringham, as the one sensible man in the two hundred."

"He has turned King's evidence," she said, "and his papers will be brought to you—" Miss Allonby paused. "All his papers!" said Miss Allonby.

"And very curious they will prove, no doubt," said his Grace. "So many love-sick misses write to actors. I can assure you, child, I look forward with a deal of interest to my inspection of Mr. Vanringham's correspondence."

"Eh?—Oh, yes!" Miss Allonby assented—"all his papers! Yes, they should be diverting, I must be going home though, to make ready for Lady Mackworth's ball. And if I have nobody to dance with me, I shall know quite well whose fault it is. How soon will Frank be freed, you odious tyrant?"

"My child, but in these matters we are all slaves to red tape! I can promise you, however, that your Captain will be released from prison before this month is out, so you are not to worry."

III

WHEN SHE HAD LEFT HIM the Duke sat for a while in meditation.

"That is an admirable girl, I would I could oblige her in the matter and let this Audaine live. But such folly is out of the question. The man is the heart of the conspiracy.

"No, Captain Audaine, I am afraid we must have that handsome head of yours, and set your spirit free before this month is out. And your head also, Mr. Vanringham, when we are done with using your evidence. This affair must be the last; hitherto we have tried leniency, and it has failed; now we will try extermination. Not one of these men must escape.

"I shall have trouble with Marian, since the two girls are inseparable. Yes, this Audaine will cause me some trouble with Marian. I heartily wish the fellow had never been born."

Ormskirk took a miniature from his pocket and sat thus in the dusk regarding it. It was the portrait of a young girl with hazel eyes and abundant hair the color of a dead oak-leaf. And now his sleepy face was curiously moved.

"I shall have to lie to you. And you will believe me, for you are not disastrously clever. But I wish it were not necessary, my dear. I wish it were possible to make you understand that my concern is to save England rather than a twopenny captain. As it is, I shall lie to you, and you will believe. And Dorothy will get over it in time, as one gets over everything in time. But I wish it were not necessary, sweetheart.

"I wish. . . I wish that I were not so happy when I think of you. I become so happy that I grow afraid. It is not right that anyone should be so happy.

"Bah! I am probably falling into my dotage."

Ormskirk struck upon the gong. "And now, Mr. Langton, let us get back to business."

IV

LATER IN THE AFTERNOON MISS Allonby demanded of her maid if Gerald Allonby were within, and received a negative response. "Nothing could be better," said Miss Allonby. "You know that new suit of Master Gerald's, Lottrum—the pink-and-silver? Very well; then you will do thus, and thus, and thus—" And she poured forth a series of directions that astonished her maid not a little.

"Law you now!" said Lottrum, "whatever—?"

"If you ask me any questions," said Dorothy, "I will discharge you on the spot. And if you betray me, I shall probably kill you."

Lottrum said, "O Gemini!" and did as her mistress ordered.

Miss Allonby made a handsome boy, and such was her one comfort. Her mirror showed an epicene denizen of romance,—Rosalind or Bellario, a frail and lovely travesty of boyhood; but it is likely that the girl's heart showed stark terror. Here was imminent no jaunt into Arden, but into the gross jaws of even bodily destruction. Here was probable dishonor, a guaranteeable death. She could fence well enough, thanks to many bouts with Gerald; but when the foils were unbuttoned, there was a difference which the girl could appreciate.

"In consequence," said Dorothy, "I had better hurry before I am still more afraid."

V

So THERE CAME THAT EVENING, after dusk, to Mr. Francis Vanringham's apartments, at the *Three Gudgeons*, a young spark in pink-and-silver. He appeared startled at the sight of so much company, recovered his composure with a gulp, and presented himself to the assembled gentlemen as Mr. Osric Allonby, unexpectedly summoned from Cambridge, and in search of his brother, Squire Gerald. At his step-mother's villa they had imagined Gerald might be spending the evening with Mr. Vanringham. Mr. Osric Allonby apologized for the intrusion; was their humble servant; and with a profusion of *congées* made as though to withdraw.

Mr. Vanringham lounged forward. The comedian had a vogue among the younger men, since at all games of chance they found him untiring and tolerably honest; and his apartments were, in effect, a gambling parlor.

Vanringham now took the boy's hand very genially. "You have somewhat the look of your sister," he observed, after a prolonged appraisal; "though, in nature, 'tis not expected of us trousered folk to be so beautiful. And by your leave, you'll not quit us thus unceremoniously, Master Osric. I am by way of being a friend of your brother's, and 'tis more than possible that he may during the evening honor us with his presence. Will you not linger awhile on the off-chance?" And Osric Allonby admitted he had no other engagements.

He was in due form made known to the three gentlemen—Colonel Denstroude,* Mr. Babington-Herle, and Sir Gresley Carne—who sat over a bowl of punch. Sir Gresley was then permitted to conclude the narrative which Mr. Allonby's entrance had interrupted: the evening previous, being a little tipsy, Sir Gresley had strolled about Tunbridge in search of recreation and, with perhaps excessive playfulness, had slapped a passer-by, broken the fellow's nose, and gouged both thumbs into the rascal's eyes. The young baronet conceded the introduction of these London pastimes into the rural quiet of Tunbridge to have been an error in taste, especially as the man proved upon inquiry to be a respectable haberdasher and the sole dependence of four children; and having thus unfortunately blinded the little tradesman, Sir Gresley wished to ask of the assembled company what in their opinion was a reasonable reparation. "For I sincerely regret the entire affair," Sir Gresley concluded, "and am desirous to follow a course approvable by all men of honor."

"Heyho!" said Mr. Vanringham, "I'm afraid the rape of both eyes was a trifle extreme; for by ordinary a haberdasher is neither a potato nor an Argus, and, remembering that, even the high frivolity of brandy-and-water should have respected his limitations."

The hands of Mr. Allonby had screened his face during the recital, "Oh, the poor man!" he said, "I cannot bear—" And then, with swift alteration, he tossed back his head, and laughed. "Are we gentlemen to be denied all amusement? Sir Gresley acted quite within his privilege, and in terming him severe you have lied, Mr. Vanringham. I repeat, sir, you have lied!"

Vanringham was on his feet within the instant, but Colonel Denstroude, who sat beside him, laid a heavy hand upon Vanringham's arm. "'Oons, man," says the Colonel, "infanticide is a crime."

The actor shrugged his shoulders, "Doubtless you are in the right, Mr. Allonby," he said; "though, as you were of course going on to remark, you express yourself somewhat obscurely. Your meaning, I take

---

* He and Vanringham had just been reconciled by Molly Yates' elopement with Tom Stoach, the Colonel's footman. Garendon has a curious anecdote concerning this lady, apropos of his notorious duel with Denstroude, in '61.

JAMES BRANCH CABELL

it, is that I mayn't criticise the doings, of my guests? I stand corrected, and concede Sir Gresley acted with commendable moderation, and that Cambridge is, beyond question, the paramount expositor of morals and manners."

The lad stared about him: with a bewildered face. "La, will he not fight me now?" he demanded of Colonel Denstroude,—"now, after I have called him a liar?"

"My dear," the Colonel retorted, "he may possibly deprive you of your nursing-bottle, or he may even birch you, but he will most assuredly not fight you, so long as I have any say in the affair. I' cod, we are all friends here, I hope. D'ye think Mr. Vanringham has so often enacted Richard III that to strangle infants is habitual with him? Fight you, indeed! 'Sdeath and devils!" roared the Colonel, "I will cut the throat of any man who dares to speak of fighting in this amicable company! Gi'me some more punch," said the Colonel.

And thereupon in silence Mr. Allonby resumed his seat.

Now, to relieve the somewhat awkward tension, Mr. Vanringham cried: "So being neighborly again, let us think no more of the recent difference in opinion. Pay your damned haberdasher what you like, Gresley; or, rather, let Osric here fix the remuneration. I confess to all and sundry," he added, with a smile, "that I daren't say another word in the matter. Frankly, I'm afraid of this youngster. He breathes fire like Ætna."

"He is a lad of spirit," said Mr. Babington-Herle, with an extreme sobriety. "He's a lad eshtrornary spirit. Let's have game hazard."

"Agreed, good sir," said Vanringham, "and I warn you, you will find me a daring antagonist. I had today an extraordinary—the usual prejudice, my dear Herle, is, I believe, somewhat inclined to that pronunciation of the word,—the most extraordinary windfall. I am rich, and I protest King Croesus himself sha'n't intimidate me tonight. Come!" he cried, and he drew from his pocket a plump purse and emptied its contents upon the table; "come, lay your wager!"

"Hell and furies," the Colonel groaned, "there's that tomfool boy again! Gi'me some more punch."

For Osric Allonby had risen to his feet and had swept the littered gold and notes toward him. He stood thus, his pink-tipped fingers caressing the money, while his eyes fixed those of Mr. Vanringham. "And the chief priests," observed Osric Allonby, "took the silver pieces and said, 'It is not lawful for to put them into the treasury, because it is the price of blood.' Are they, then, fit to be touched by gentlemen, Mr.—ah, but I forget your given name?"

Vanringham, too, had risen, his face changed. "My sponsors in baptism were pleased to christen me Francis."

"I entreat your pardon," the boy drawled, "but I have the oddest fancies. I had thought it was Judas." And so they stood, warily regarding each the other, very much as strange dogs are wont to do at meeting.

"Boy is drunk," Mr. Babington-Herle explained at large, "and presents to pitying eye of disinterested spectator most deplorable results incidental to combination of immaturity and brandy. As to money, now, in Suetonius—" And he launched upon a hiccough-punctuated anecdote of Vespasian, which to record here is not convenient. "And moral of it is," Mr. Babington-Herle perorated, "that all money is always fine thing to have. *Non olet!* Classical scholar, by Jove! Now let's have game hazard."

Meanwhile those two had stood like statues. Vanringham seemed half-frightened, half persuaded that this unaccountable boy spoke at random. Talk, either way, the actor knew, was dangerous. . .

"I ask your forgiveness, gentlemen," said Francis Vanringham, "but I'm suddenly ill. If you'll permit me to retire—"

"Not at all," said. Mr. Babington-Herle; "late in evening, as it is. We will go,—Colonel and old Carne and I will go kill watchman. Persevorate him, by Jove,—like sieve."

"I thank you," said Mr. Vanringham, withdrawing up the stairway toward his bedroom. "I thank you. Mr. Allonby," he called, in a firmer tone, "you and I have had some words together and you were the aggressor. Oho, I think we may pass it over. I think—"

Below, the four gentlemen were unhooking their swords from the wall. Mr. Allonby now smiled with cherubic sweetness. "I, too," said he, "think that all our differences might be arranged by ten minutes' private talk." He came back, came up the stairs. "You had left your sword," he said to Mr. Vanringham, "but I fetched it, you see."

Vanringham stared, his lips working oddly. "I am no Siegfried," said he, "and ordinarily my bedfellow is not cold and—deplorable defect in such capacity!—somewhat unsympathetic steel."

"But you forget," the boy urged, "that the room is public. And see, the hilt is set with jewels. Ah, Mr. Vanringham, let us beware how we lead others into temptation—" The door closed behind them.

　　　　　　　　　　　　　　　　JAMES BRANCH CABELL

VI

Said Mr. Babington-Herle, judicially, "That's eshtrornary boy—most eshtrornary boy, and precisely unlike brother."

"You must remember," the Colonel pointed out, "that since his marriage Gerald is a reformed man; he has quite given up punks and hazard, they say, for beer and cattle-raising."

"Well, but it is a sad thing to have a spirited tall rogue turn pimp to balls and rams, and Mrs. Lascelles will be inconsolable," Sir Gresley considered.—"Hey, what's that? Did you not hear a noise up-stairs?"

"I do not think," said the Colonel, "that Mallison finds her so.—Yes, i'cod! I suppose that tipsy boy has turned over a table."

"But you astound me," Sir Gresley interrupted. "The constant Mallison, of all persons!"

"Nevertheless, my dear, they assure me that he has made over to her the heart and lodgings until lately occupied by Mrs. Roydon—Oh, the devil!" cried Colonel Denstroude, "they are fighting above!"

"Good for Frank!" observed Mr. Babington-Herle. "Hip-hip! Stick young rascal! Persevorate him, by Jove!"

But the other men had run hastily up the stairway and were battering at the door of Vanringham's chamber. "Locked!" said the Colonel. "Oh, the unutterable cur! Open, open, I tell you, Vanringham! By God, I'll have your blood for this if you have hurt the boy!"

"Break in the door!" said a voice from below. The Colonel paused in his objurgations, and found that the Duke of Ormskirk, followed by four attendants, had entered the hallway of the *Three Gudgeons*. "Benyon," said the Duke, more sharply, and wheeled upon his men, "you have had my orders, I believe. Break in yonder door!"

This was done. They found Mr. Francis Vanringham upon the hearthrug a tousled heap of flesh and finery, insensible, with his mouth gaping, in a great puddle of blood. To the rear of the room was a boy in pink-and-silver, beside the writing-desk he had just got into with the co-operation of a poker. Hugged to his breast he held a brown despatch-box.

Ormskirk strode toward the boy and with an inhalation paused. The Duke stood tense for a moment. Then silently he knelt beside the prostrate actor and inspected Vanringham's injury. "You have killed him," the Duke said at last.

"I think so," said the boy. "But 'twas in fair fight."

The Duke rose. "Benyon," he rapped out, "do you and Minchin take this body to the room below. Let a surgeon be sent for. Bring word if he find any sign of life. Gentlemen, I must ask you to avoid the chamber. This is a state matter. I am responsible for yonder person."

"Then your Grace is responsible for perfectly irresponsible young villain!" said Mr. Babington-Herle. "He's murderer Frank Vanringham, of poor dear Frank, like a brother to me, by Jove! Hang him high's Haman, your Grace, and then we'll have another bottle."

"Colonel Denstroude," said the Duke, "I will ask you to assist your friend in retiring. The stairs are steep, and his conviviality, I fear, has by a pint or so excceded his capacity. And in fine—I wish you a good-evening, gentlemen."

VII

ORMSKIRK CLOSED THE DOOR; THEN he turned, "I lack words," the Duke said. "Oh, believe me, speech fails before this spectacle. To find you, here, at this hour! To find you—my betrothed wife's kinswoman and life-long associate,—here, in this garb! A slain man at your feet, his blood yet reeking upon that stolen sword! His papers—pardon me!"

Ormskirk sprang forward and caught the despatch-box from her grasp as she strove to empty its contents into the fire. "Pardon me," he repeated; "you have unsexed yourself; do not add high treason to the list of your misdemeanors. Mr. Vanringham's papers, as I have previously had the honor to inform you, are the state's property."

She stood with void and inefficient hands that groped vaguely. "I could trust no one," she said. "I have fenced so often with Gerald. I was not afraid—at least, I was not very much afraid.. And 'twas so difficult to draw him into a quarrel,—he wanted to live, because at last he had the money his dirty little soul had craved. Ah, I had sacrificed so many things to get these papers, my Lord Duke,—and now you rob me of them. You!"

The Duke bent pitiless brows upon her. "I rob you of them," he said,—"ay, I am discourteous and I rob, but not for myself alone. For your confusion tells me that I hold here between my hands the salvation of England. Child, child!" he cried, in sudden tenderness, "I trusted you today, and could you not trust me? I promised you the life of the man you love. I promised you—" He broke off, as if in a rivalry of rage and horror. "And you betrayed me! You came hither, trousered and shameless, to save these hare-brained traitors! Well, but at worst your treachery has very happily released me from my promise to meddle in the fate of this Audaine. I shall not lift a finger now. And I warn you that within the week your precious Captain will have become the associate of seraphim."

She had heard him, with defiant eyes; her head was flung back and she laughed. "You thought I had come to destroy the Jacobite petition! Heavens, what had I to do with all such nonsense? You had promised me Frank's pardon, and the other men I had never seen. Harkee, my Lord Duke, do all you politicians jump so wildly in your guess work? Did you in truth believe that the poor fool who lies dead below would have entrusted the paper which meant life and wealth to the keeping of a flimsy despatch-box?"

"Indeed, no," his Grace of Ormskirk replied, and appeared a thought abashed; "I was certain it would be concealed somewhere about his person, and I have already given Benyon orders to search for it. Still, I confess that for the moment your agitation misled me into believing these were the important papers; and I admit, my dear creature, that unless you came hither prompted by a mad design somehow to destroy the incriminating documents and thereby to ensure your lover's life— why, otherwise, I repeat, I am quite unable to divine your motive."

She was silent for a while. Presently, "You told me this afternoon," she began, in a dull voice, "that you anticipated much amusement from your perusal of Mr. Vanringham's correspondence. All his papers were to be seized, you said; and they all were to be brought to you, you said. And so many love-sick misses write to actors, you said."

"As I recall the conversation," his Grace conceded, "that which you have stated is quite true." He spoke with admirable languor, but his countenance was vaguely troubled.

And now the girl came to him and laid her finger-tips ever so lightly upon his. "Trust me," she pleaded. "Give me again the trust I have not merited. Ay, in spite of reason, my Lord Duke, restore to me these papers unread, that I may destroy them. For otherwise, I swear to you that without gain to yourself—without gain, O God!—you wreck alike the happiness of an innocent woman and of an honest gentleman. And otherwise—O infatuate!" she wailed, and wrung impotent hands.

But Ormskirk shook his head. "I cannot leap in the dark."

She found no comfort in his face, and presently lowered her eyes. He remained motionless. The girl went to the farther end of the apartment, and then, her form straightening on a sudden, turned and came back toward him.

"I think God has some grudge against you," Dorothy said, without any emotion, "and—hardens your heart, as of old He hardened Pharaoh's heart, to your own destruction. I have done my utmost to save you. My woman's modesty I have put aside, and death and worse than death I have dared to encounter tonight,—ah, my Lord, I have walked through hell this night for your sake and another's. And in the end 'tis yourself who rob me of what I had so nearly gained. Beyond doubt God has some grudge against you. Take your fate, then."

"*Integer vitæ*—" said the Duke of Ormskirk; and with more acerbity, "Go on!" For momentarily she had paused.

"The man who lies dead below was loved by many women. God pity them! But women are not sensible like men, you know. And always the footlights made a halo about him; and when you saw him as Castalio or Romeo, all beauty and love and vigor and nobility, how was a woman to understand his splendor was a sham, taken off with his wig, removed with his pinchbeck jewelry, and as false? No, they thought it native, poor wretches. Yet one of them at least, my Lord—a young girl—found out her error before it was too late. The man was a villain through and through. God grant he sups in hell tonight!"

"Go on," said Ormskirk. But by this time he knew all that she had to tell.

"Afterward he demanded money of her. He had letters, you understand—mad, foolish letters,—and these he offered to sell back to her at his own price. And their publicity meant ruin. And, my Lord, we had so nearly saved the money—pinching day by day, a little by a little, for his price was very high, and it was necessary the sum be got in secrecy,— and that in the end they should be read by you—" Her voice broke.

"Go on," said Ormskirk.

But her composure was shattered. "I would have given my life to save her," the girl babbled. "Ah, you know that I have tried to save her. I was not very much afraid. And it seemed the only way. So I came hither, my Lord, as you see me, to get back the letters before you, too, had come."

"There is but one woman in the world," the Duke said, quietly, "for whom you would have done this thing. You and Marian were reared together. Always you have been inseparable, always you have been to each other as sisters. Is this not what you are about to tell me?"

JAMES BRANCH CABELL

"Yes," she answered.

"Well, you may spare yourself the pains of such unprofitable lying. That Marian Heleigh should have been guilty of a vulgar *liaison* with, an actor is to me, who know her, unthinkable. No, madam! It was fear, not love, which drove you hither tonight, and now a baser terror urges you to screen yourself by vilifying her. The woman of whom you speak is yourself. The letters were written by you."

She raised one arm as though a physical blow impended. "No, no!" she cried.

"Madam," the Duke said, "let us have done with these dexterities. I have the vanity to believe I am not unreasonably obtuse—nor, I submit, unreasonably self-righteous. Love is a monstrous force, as irrational, I sometimes think, as the force of the thunderbolt; it appears neither to select nor to eschew, but merely to strike; and it is not my duty to asperse or to commend its victims. You have loved unworthily. From the bottom of my heart I pity you, and I would that you had trusted me—had trusted me enough—" His voice was not quite steady. "Ah, my dear," said Ormskirk, "you should have confided all to me this afternoon. It hurts me that you did not, for I am no Pharisee and—God knows!—my own past is not immaculate. I would have understood, I think. Yet as it is, take back your letters, child,—nay, in Heaven's name, take them in pledge of an old man's love for Dorothy Allonby."

The girl obeyed, turning them in her hands, the while that her eyes were riveted to Ormskirk's face. And in Aprilian fashion she began to smile through her tears. "You are superb, my Lord Duke. You comprehend that Marian wrote these letters, and that if you read them—and I knew of it,—your pride would force you to break off the match, because your notions as to what is befitting in a Duchess of Ormskirk are precise. But you want Marian, you want her even more than I had feared. Therefore, you give me all these letters, because you know that I will destroy them, and thus an inconvenient knowledge will be spared you. Oh, beyond doubt, you are superb."

"I give them to you," Ormskirk answered, "because I have seen through your cowardly and clumsy lie, and have only pity for a thing so base as you. I give them to you because to read one syllable of their contents would be to admit I had some faith in your preposterous fabrication."

But she shook her head. "Words, words, my Lord Duke! I understand you to the marrow. And, in part, I think that I admire you."

He was angry now. "Eh! for the love of God," cried the Duke of Ormskirk, "let us burn the accursed things and have no more verbiage!" He seized the papers and flung them into the fire.

Then these two watched the papers consume to ashes, and stood a while in silence, the gaze of neither lifting higher than the andirons; and presently there was a tapping at the door.

"That will be Benyon," the Duke said, with careful modulations. "Enter, man! What news is there of this Vanringham?"

"He will recover, your Grace, though he has lost much blood. Mr. Vanringham has regained consciousness and took occasion to whisper me your Grace would find the needful papers in his escritoire, in the brown despatch-box."

"That is well," the Duke retorted, "You may go, Benyon." And when the door had closed, he began, incuriously: "Then you are not a murderess at least, Miss Allonby. At least—" He made a queer noise as he gazed, at the despatch-box in his hand. "The brown box!" It fell to the floor. Ormskirk drew near to her, staring, moving stiffly like a hinged toy, "I must have the truth," he said, without a trace of any human passion. This was the Ormskirk men had known in Scotland.

"Yes," she answered, "they were the Jacobite papers. You burned them."

"I!" said the Duke.

Presently he said: "Do you not understand what this farce has cost? Thanks to you, I have no iota of proof against these men. I cannot touch these rebels. O madam, I pray Heaven that you have not by this night's trickery destroyed England!"

"I did it to save the man I love," she proudly said.

"I had promised you his life."

"But would you have kept that promise?"

"No," he answered, simply.

"Then are we quits, my Lord. You lied to me, and I to you. Oh, I know that were I a man you would kill me within the moment. But you respect my womanhood. Ah, goodness!" the girl cried, shrilly, "what very edifying respect for womanhood have you, who burned those papers because you believed my dearest Marian had stooped to a painted mountebank!"

"I burned them—yes, in the belief that I was saving you."

She laughed in his face. "You never believed that,—not for an instant."

But by this time Ormskirk had regained his composure. "The hour is somewhat late, and the discussion—if you will pardon the suggestion,—not likely to be profitable. The upshot of the whole matter is that I am now powerless to harm anybody—I submit the simile of the fangless snake,—and that Captain Audaine will have his release in the morning. Accordingly you will now permit me to wish you a pleasant night's rest. Benyon!" he called, "you will escort Mr. Osric Allonby homeward. I remain to clear up this affair."

He held open the door for her, and, bowing, stood aside that she might pass.

VIII

But afterward the great Duke of Ormskirk continued for a long while motionless and faintly smiling as he gazed into the fire. Tricked and ignominiously defeated! Ay, but that was a trifle now, scarcely worthy of consideration. The girl had hoodwinked him, had lied more skilfully than he, yet in the fact that she had lied he found a prodigal atonement. Whigs and Jacobites might have their uses in the cosmic scheme, he reflected, as house-flies have, but what really mattered was that at Halvergate yonder Marian awaited his coming. And in place of statecraft he fell to thinking of two hazel eyes and of abundant hair the color of a dead oak-leaf.

VI

APRIL'S MESSAGE

As Played at Halvergate House, April 9, 1750

"You cannot love, nor pleasure take, nor give,
But life begin when 'tis too late to live.
On a tired courser you pursue delight,
Let slip your morning, and set out at night.
If you have lived, take thankfully the past;
Make, as you can, the sweet remembrance last.
If you have not enjoyed what youth could give,
But life sunk through you, like a leaky sieve."

Dramatis Personæ

Duke of Ormskikk.

Earl of Brudenel, father to Lady Marian Heleigh, who has retired sometime into the country.

Lord Humphrey Degge, a gamester, and Ormskirk's hireling.

Mr. Langton, secretary to Ormskirk.

Lady Marian Heleigh, betrothed to Ormskirk, a young, beautiful girl of a mild and tender disposition.

Scene
The east terrace of Halvergate House.

April's Message

Proem:—Apologia pro Auctore

It occurs to me that we here assume intimacy with a man of unusual achievement, and therefore tread upon quaggy premises. Yet I do but avail myself of today's privilege. . . It is an odd thing that people will facilely assent to Don Adriano's protestation against a certain travestying of Hector,—"Sweet chucks, beat not the bones of the dead, for when he breathed he was a man,"—even while through the instant the tide of romance will be setting quite otherwhither, with their condonation. For in all the best approved romances the more sumptuous persons of antiquity are very guilty of twaddle on at least one printed page in ten, and nobody remonstrates; and here is John Bulmer, too, lugged from the grave for your delectation.

I presume, however, to palliate the offence. The curious may find the gist of what I narrate concerning Ormskirk in Heinrich Löwe's biography of the man, and will there discover that with established facts I have not made bold to juggle. Only when knowledge failed have I bridged the void with speculation. Perhaps I have guessed wrongly: the feat is not unhuman, and in provision against detection therein I can only protest that this lack of omniscience was never due to malice; faithfully I have endeavored to deduce from the known the probable, and in nothing to misrepresent to you this big man of a little age, this trout among a school of minnows.

Trout, mark you; I claim for Ormskirk no leviathan-ship. Rather I would remind you of a passage from somewhat anterior memoirs: "The Emperor of Lilliput is taller, by almost the breadth of my nail, than any of his court, which alone is enough to strike an awe into his beholders."

This, however, is not the place to expatiate on Ormskirk's extraordinary career; his rise from penury and obscurity, tempered indeed by gentle birth, to the priviest secrets of his Majesty's council,—climbing the peerage step by step, as though that institution had been a garden-ladder,—may be read of in the history books.

"I collect titles as an entomologist does butterflies," he is recorded to have said: "and I find the gaudier ones the cheapest. My barony I got for a very heinous piece of perjury, my earldom for not running away until the latter end of a certain battle, my marquisate for hoodwinking a half-senile Frenchman, and my dukedom for fetching in a quack doctor when he was sore needed by a lady whom the King at that time delighted to honor."

It was, you observe, a day of candors.

I

THE DUKE OF ORMSKIRK, THEN (one gleans from Löwe's pages), dismissed from mind the Audaine conspiracy. It was a pity to miss the salutary effect of a few political executions just then, but after all there was nothing to be done about it. So the Duke turned to the one consolation offered by the affair, and set out for Halvergate House, the home of Marian Heleigh's father. There one finds him, six days later, deep in a consultation with his secretary, which in consideration of the unseasonable warmth was held upon the east terrace.

"Yes, I think we had better have the fellow hanged on the thirteenth," said Ormskirk, as he leisurely affixed his signature. "The date seems eminently appropriate. Now the papers concerning the French treaty, if you please, Mr. Langton."

The impassive-faced young man who sat opposite placed a despatch-box between them. "These were sent down from London only last night, sir. Mr. Morfit* has been somewhat dilatory."

"Eh, it scarcely matters. I looked them over in bed this morning and found them quite correct, Mr. Langton, quite—Why, heyday!" the Duke demanded, "what's this? You have brought me the despatch-box from my dresser—not, as I distinctly told you, from the table by my bed. Nay, I have had quite enough of mistakes concerning despatch-boxes, Mr. Langton."

Mr. Langton stammered that the error was natural. Two despatch-boxes were in appearances so similar—

"Never make excuses, Mr. Langton. '*Qui s'excuse*—' You can complete the proverb, I suppose. Bring me Morfit's report this afternoon, then. Yes, that appears to be all. You may go now, Mr. Langton. No, you may leave that box, I think, since it is here. O man, man, a mistake isn't high treason! Go away, Mr. Langton! you annoy me."

---

* Perhaps the most adroit of all the many spies in Ormskirk's employment. It was this same Morfit who in 1756 accompanied Damiens into France as far as Calais; and see page 16.

Left alone, the Duke of Ormskirk sat for a while, tapping his fingers irresolutely against the open despatch-box. He frowned a little, for, with fair reason to believe Tom Langton his son, he found the boy too stolid, too unimaginative, to go far. It seemed to Ormskirk that none of his illegitimate children displayed any particular promise, and he sighed. Then he took a paper from the despatch-box, and began to read.

He sat, as one had said, upon the east terrace of Halvergate House. Behind him a tall yew-hedge shut off the sunlight from the table where he and Tom Langton had earlier completed divers businesses; in front of him a balustrade, ivy-covered, and set with flower-pots of stone, empty as yet, half screened the terraced gardens that sank to the artificial lake below.

The Duke could see only a vast expanse of sky and a stray bit of Halvergate printing the horizon with turrets, all sober gray save where the two big copper cupolas of the south façade burned in the April sun; but by bending forward you glimpsed close-shaven lawns dotted with clipped trees and statues,—as though, he reflected, Glumdalclitch had left her toys scattered haphazard about a green blanket—and the white of the broad marble stairway descending to the sunlit lake, and, at times, the flash of a swan's deliberate passage across the lake's surface. All white and green and blue the vista was, and of a monastic tranquillity, save for the plashing of a fountain behind the yew-hedge and the grumblings of an occasional bee that lurched complainingly on some by-errand of the hive.

Presently his Grace of Ormskirk replaced the papers in the despatch-box, and, leaning forward, sighed. "*Non sum qualis eram sub bonæ regno Cynaræ,*" said his Grace of Ormskirk. He had a statesman-like partiality for the fag-end of an alcaic.

Then he lifted his head at the sound of a girl's voice. Somewhere rearward to the hedge the girl idly sang—an old song of Thomas Heywood's,—in a serene contralto, low-pitched and effortless, but very sweet. Smilingly the Duke beat time.

Sang the girl:

> "*Pack clouds away, and welcome, day!*
> *With night we banish sorrow:*
> *Sweet air, blow soft; mount, lark, aloft,*
> *To give my love good-morrow.*
> *Wings from the wind to please her mind,*

> *Notes from the lark I'll borrow:*
> *Bird, prune thy wing; nightingale, sing,*
> *To give my love good-morrow."*

And here the Duke chimed in with a sufficiently pleasing baritone:

> *"To give my love good-morrow,*
> *Notes from them all I'll borrow."*

"O heavens!" spoke the possessor of the contralto, "I would have thought you were far too busy sending people to gaol and arranging their execution, and so on, to have any time for music. I am going for a walk in the forest, Jack." Considering for a moment, she added, "You may come, too, if you like."

But the concession was made so half-heartedly that in the instant the Duke of Ormskirk raised a dissenting hand. "I would not annoy you for an emperor's ransom. Go in peace, my child."

Lady Marian Heleigh stood at an opening in the yew-hedge and regarded him for a lengthy interval in silence. Slender, men called her, and women "a bean pole." There was about her a great deal of the child and something of the wood-nymph. She had abundant hair, the color of a dead oak-leaf, and her skin was clear, with a brown tinge. Her eyes puzzled you by being neither brown nor green consistently; no sooner had you convicted them of verdancy than they shifted to the hue of polished maple, and vice versa; but they were too large for her face, which narrowed rather abruptly beneath a broad, low forehead, and they flavored her aspect with the shrewd innocence of a kitten. She was by ordinary grave; but, animated, her countenance quickened with somewhat the glow of a brown diamond; then her generous eyes flashed and filmed like waters moving under starlight, then you knew she was beautiful. All in all, you saw in Marian a woman designed to be petted, a Columbine rather than a Cleopatra; her lures would never shake the stability of a kingdom, but would inevitably gut its toy-shops; and her departure left you meditative less of high enterprises than of buying something for her.

Now Marian considered her betrothed, and seemed to come at last to a conclusion that skirted platitude. "Jack, two people can be fond of each other without wanting to be together all the time. And I really am fond of you, Jack."

JAMES BRANCH CABELL

"I would be a fool if I questioned the first statement," rejoined the Duke; "and if I questioned the second, very miserable. Nevertheless, you go in pursuit of strange gods, and I decline to follow."

Her eyebrows interrogated him.

"You are going," the Duke continued, "in pursuit of gods beside whom I esteem Zidonian Ashtoreth, and Chemosh, and Milcom, the abomination of the Ammonites, to be commendable objects of worship. You will pardon my pedantic display of learning, for my feelings are strong. You are going to sit in the woods. You will probably sit under a youngish tree, and its branches will sway almost to the ground and make a green, sun-steeped tent about you, as though you sat at the heart of an emerald. You will hear the kindly wood-gods go steathily about the forest, and you will know that they are watching you, but you will never see them. From behind every tree-bole they will watch you; you feel it, but you never, never quite see them. Presently the sweet, warm odors of the place and its perpetual whispering and the illimitably idiotic boasting of the birds,—that any living creature should be proud of having constructed one of their nasty little nests is a reflection to baffle understanding,—this hodge-podge of sensations, I say, will intoxicate you. Yes, it will thoroughly intoxicate you, Marian, and you sit there quite still, in a sort of stupor, drugged into the inebriate's magnanimity, firmly believing that the remainder of your life will be throughout of finer texture,—earth-spurning, free from all pettiness, and at worst vexed only by the noblest sorrows. Bah!" cried the Duke; "I have no patience with such nonsense! You will believe it to the tiniest syllable, that wonderful lying message which April whispers to every living creature that is young,—then you will return to me, a slim, star-eyed Mænad, and will see that I am wrinkled. But do you go your ways, none the less, for April is waiting for you yonder,—beautiful, mendacious, splendid April. And I? Faith, April has no message for me, my dear."

He laughed, but with a touch of wistfulness; and the girl came to him, laying her hand upon his arm, surprised into a sort of hesitant affection.

"How did you know, Jack? How did you, know that—things, invisible, gracious things, went about the spring woods? I never thought that you knew of them. You always seemed so sensible. I have reasoned it out, though," Marian went on, sagaciously wrinkled as to the brow. "They are probably the heathen fauns and satyrs and such,—one feels somehow that they are all men. Don't you, Jack? Well, when the elder gods were sent packing from Olympus there was naturally no employment left for these sylvan folk. So April took them into her service. Each year she sends them about every forest on her errands: she sends them to make up daffodil-cups, for instance, which I suppose is difficult, for evidently they make them out of sunshine; or to pencil the eyelids of the narcissi—narcissi are brazen creatures, Jack, and use a deal of kohl; or to marshal the fleecy young clouds about the sky; or to whistle the birds up from the south. Oh, she keeps them busy, does April! And 'tis true that if you be quite still you can hear them tripping among the dead leaves; and they watch you—with very bright, twinkling little eyes, I think,—but you never see them. And always, always there is that enormous whispering,—half-friendly, half-menacing,—as if the woods were trying to tell you something. 'Tis not only the foliage rustling. . . No, I have often thought it sounded like some gigantic foreigner—some Titan probably,—trying in his own queer and outlandish language to tell you something very important, something that means a deal to you, and to you in particular. Has not anybody ever understood him?"

He smiled. "And I, too, have dwelt in Arcadia," said his Grace of Ormskirk. "Yes, I once heard April's message, Marian, for all my crow's-feet. But that was a long while ago, and perhaps I have forgotten it. I cannot tell, my dear. It is only from April in her own person that one hears this immemorial message. And as for me? Eh, I go into the April woods, and I find trees there of various sizes that pay no attention to me, and shrill, dingy little birds that deafen me, and it may be a gaudy flower or two, and, in any event, I find a vast quantity of sodden, decaying leaves to warn me the place is no fitting haunt for a gentleman afflicted with rheumatism. So I come away, my dear."

Marian looked him over for a moment. "You are not really old," she said, with rather conscious politeness. "And you are wonderfully well-preserved. Why, Jack, do you mind—not being foolish?" she demanded, on a sudden.

He debated the matter. Then, "Yes," the Duke of Ormskirk conceded, "I suppose I do, at the bottom of my heart, regret that lost folly. A part of me died, you understand, when it vanished, and it is not exhilarating to think of one's self as even partially dead. Once—I hardly know"—he sought the phrase,—"once this was a spacious and inexplicable world, with a mystery up every lane and an adventure around each street-corner; a world inhabited by most marvelous men and women,—some amiable, and some detestable, but everyone of them very interesting. And now I miss the wonder of it all. You will presently discover, my dear, that youth is only an ingenious prologue to whet one's appetite for a rather dull play. Eh, I am no pessimist,—one may still find satisfaction in the exercise of mind and body, in the pleasures of thought and taste and in other titillations of one's faculties. Dinner is good and sleep, too, is excellent. But we men and women tend, upon too close inspection, to appear rather paltry flies that buzz and bustle aimlessly about, and breed perhaps, and eventually die, and rot, and are swept away from this fragile window-pane of time that opens on eternity."

"If you are, indeed, the sort of person you describe," said Marian, reflectively, "I do not at all blame April for having no communication with anyone possessed of such extremely unpleasant opinions. But for my own part, I shall never cease to wonder what it is that the woods whisper about."

Appraising her, he hazarded a cryptic question, "Vase of delights, and have you never—cared?"

"Why, yes, I think so," she answered, readily enough. "At least, I used to be very fond of Humphrey Degge,—that is the Marquis of Venour's place yonder, you know, just past the spur of the forest,—but he was only a younger son, so of course Father wouldn't hear of it. That was rather fortunate, as Humphrey by and by went mad about Dorothy's blue eyes and fine shape,—I think her money had a deal to do with it, too, and in any event, she will be fat as a pig at thirty,—and so we quarrelled. And I minded it—at first. And now—well, I scarcely know." Marian hesitated. "He was a handsome man, but that ridiculous cavalry moustache of his was so bristly—"

"I beg your pardon?" said the Duke.

"—that it disfigured him dreadfully," said she, with firmness. She had colored.

His Grace of Ormskirk was moved to mirth. "Child, child, you are so deliciously young it appears a monstrous crime to marry you to an old fellow like me!" He took her firm, soft hand in his. "Are you quite sure you can endure me, Marian?"

"Why, but of course I want to marry you," she said, naïvely surprised. "How else could I be Duchess of Ormskirk?"

Again he chuckled. "You are a worldly little wretch," he stated; "but if you want my title for a new toy, it is at your service. And now be off with you,—you and your foolish woods, indeed!"

Marian went a slight distance and then turned about, troubled. "I am really very fond of you, Jack," she said, conscientiously.

"Be off with you!" the Duke scolded. "You should be ashamed of yourself to practice such flatteries and blandishments on a defenceless old gentleman. You had best hurry, too, for if you don't I shall probably kiss you," he threatened. "I, also," he added, with point.

She blew him a kiss from her finger-tips and went away singing. Sang Marian:

> *"Blackbird and thrush, in every bush,*
> *Stare, linnet, and cock-sparrow,*
> *You pretty elves, amongst yourselves,*
> *Sing my fair love good-morrow.*
> *To give my love good-morrow,*
> *Sing birds, in every furrow."*

II

LEFT TO HIS OWN RESOURCES, the Duke of Ormskirk sat down beside the table and fell to making irrelevant marks upon a bit of paper. He hummed the air of Marian's song. There was a vague contention in his face. Once he put out his hand toward the open despatch-box, but immediately he sighed and pushed, it farther from him. Presently he propped his chin upon both hands and stayed in the attitude for a long while, staring past the balustrade at the clear, pale sky of April.

Thus Marian's father, the Earl of Brudenel, found Ormskirk. The Earl was lean and gray, though only three years older than his prospective son-in-law, and had been Ormskirk's intimate since boyhood. Ormskirk had for Lord Brudenel's society the liking that a successful person usually preserves for posturing in the gaze of his outrivalled school-fellows: Brudenel was an embodied and flattering commentary as to what a less able man might make of chances far more auspicious than Ormskirk ever enjoyed. All failure the Earl's life had been; in London they had long ago forgotten handsome Harry Heleigh and the composure with which he nightly shoved his dwindling patrimony across the gaming-table; about Halvergate men called him "the muddled Earl," and said of him that his heart died, with his young wife some eighteen years back. Now he

JAMES BRANCH CABELL

vegetated in the home of his fathers, contentedly, a veteran of life, retaining still a mild pride in his past vagaries;* and kindly time had armed him with the benumbing, impenetrable indifference of the confessed failure. He was abstractedly courteous to servants, and he would not, you felt, have given even to an emperor his undivided attention. For the rest, the former wastrel had turned miser, and went noticeably shabby as a rule, but this morning he was trimly clothed, for he was returning homeward from the quarter-sessions at Winstead.

"Dreamer!" said the Earl. "I do not wonder that you grow fat."

The Duke smiled up at him. "Confound you, Harry!" said he, "I had just overreached myself into believing I had made what the world calls a mess of my career and was supremely happy. There are disturbing influences abroad today." He waved his hand toward the green-and-white gardens. "Old friend, you permit disreputable trespassers about Halvergate. 'See you not Goldy-locks there, in her yellow gown and green sleeves? the profane pipes, the tinkling timbrels?' Spring is at her wiles yonder,—Spring, the liar, the queen-cheat, Spring that tricks all men into happiness."

"'Fore Gad," the Earl capped his quotation, "if the heathen man could stop his ears with wax against the singing woman of the sea, then do you the like with your fingers against the trollop of the forest."

"Faith, time seals them firmlier than wax. You and I may sit snug now with never a quicker heart-beat for all her lures. Yet I seem to remember,—once a long while ago when we old fellows were somewhat sprier,—I, too, seem to remember this Spring-magic."

"Indeed," observed the Earl, seating himself ponderously, "if you refer to a certain inclination at that period of the year toward the likeliest wench in the neighborhood, so do I 'Tis an obvious provision of nature, I take it, to secure the perpetuation of the species. Spring comes, and she sets us all a-mating—humanity, partridges, poultry, pigs, every blessed one of us she sets a-mating. Propagation, Jack—propagation is necessary, d'ye see; because," the

---

* It was then well said of him by Claridge, "It is Lord Henry Heleigh's vanity to show that he is a man of pleasure as well as of business; and thus, in settlement, the expedition he displays toward a fellow-gambler is equitably balanced by his tardiness toward a too-credulous shoemaker."

Earl conclusively demanded, "what on earth would become of us if we didn't propagate?"

"The argument is unanswerable," the Duke conceded. "Yet I miss it,—this Spring magic that no longer sets the blood of us staid fellows a-fret."

"And I," said Lord Brudenel, "do not. It got me into the deuce of a scrape more than once."

"Yours is the sensible view, no doubt. . . Yet I miss it. Ah, it is not only the wenches and the red lips of old years,—it is not only that at this season lasses' hearts grow tender. There are some verses—" The Duke quoted, with a half-guilty air:

> *"Now I loiter, and dream to the branches swaying*
> *In furtive conference,—high overhead—*
> *Atingle with rumors that Winter is sped*
> *And over his ruins a world goes Maying.*
>
> *"Somewhere—impressively,—people are saying*
> *Intelligent things (which their grandmothers said),*
> *While I loiter, and dream to the branches swaying*
> *In furtive conference, high overhead."*

"Verses!" The Earl snorted. "At your age!"

> *"Here the hand of April, unwashed from slaying*
> *Earth's fallen tyrant—for Winter is dead,—*
> *Uncloses anemones, staining them red:*
> *And her daffodils guard me in squads,—displaying*
> *Intrepid lances lest wisdom tread*
> *Where I loiter and dream to the branches' swaying—*

"Well, Harry, and today I cannot do so any longer. That is what I most miss,—the ability to lie a-sprawl in the spring grass and dream out an uncharted world,—a dream so vivid that, beside it, reality grew tenuous, and the actual world became one of childhood's shrug-provoking bugbears dimly remembered."

"I do not understand poetry," the Earl apologetically observed. "It appears to me unreasonable to advance a statement simply because it happens to rhyme with a statement you have previously made. And that is what all you poets do. Why, this is very remarkable," said Lord Brudenel, with a change of tone; "yonder is young Humphrey Degge with Marian. I had thought him in bed at Tunbridge. Did I not hear something of an affair with a house-breaker—?"

Then the Earl gave an exclamation, for in full view of them Lord Humphrey Degge was kissing Lord Brudenel's daughter.

"Oh, the devil!" said the Earl. "Oh, the insolent young ape!"

"Nay," said the Duke, restraining him; "not particularly insolent, Harry. If you will observe more closely you will see that Marian does not exactly object to his caresses—quite the contrary, I would say, I told you that you should not permit Spring about the premises."

The Earl wheeled in an extreme of astonishment. "Come, come, sir! she is your betrothed wife! Do you not intend to kill the fellow?"

"My faith, why?" said his Grace of Ormskirk, with a shrug. "As for betrothals, do you not see that she is already very happily paired?"

In answer Brudenel raised his hands toward heaven, in just the contention of despair and rage appropriate to parental affection when an excellent match is imperilled by a chit's idiocy.

Marian and Lord Humphrey Degge were mounting from the scrap of forest that juts from Pevis Hill, like a spur from a man's heel, between Agard Court and Halvergate. Their progress was not conspicuous for celerity. Now they had attained to the tiny, elm-shadowed plateau beyond the yew-hedge, and there Marian paused. Two daffodils had fallen from the great green-and-yellow cluster in her left hand. Humphrey Degge lifted them, and then raised to his mouth the slender fingers that reached toward the flowers. The man's pallor, you would have said, was not altogether due to his recent wound.

She stood looking up at him, smiling a little timidly, her teeth glinting through parted lips, her eyes star-fire, her cheeks blazoning gules in his honor; she seemed not to breathe at all. A faint twinge woke in the Duke of Ormskirk's heart. Most women smiled upon him, but they smiled beneath furtive eyes, sometimes beneath rapacious eyes, and many smiled with reddened lips which strove, uneasily, to provoke a rental; how long was it he wondered, simply, since any woman had smiled as Marian smiled now, for him?

"I think it is a dream," said Marian.

From the vantage of the yew-hedge, "I would to Heaven I could think so, too," observed her father.

III

THE YOUNGER PEOPLE HAD PASSED out of sight. But from the rear of the hedge came to the Duke and Lord Brudenel, staring blankly at each other across the paper-littered table, a sort of duet. First tenor, then contralto, then tenor again,—and so on, with many long intervals of silence, during which you heard the plashing of the fountain, grown doubly audible, and, it might be, the sharp, plaintive cry of a bird intensified by the stillness.

"I think it is a dream," said Marian. . .

"What eyes you have, Marian!"

"But you have not kissed the littlest finger of all. See, it is quite stiff with indignation."

"They are green, and brown, and yellow—O Marian, there are little gold specks in them like those in *eau de Dantzig*! They are quite wonderful eyes, Marian. And your hair is all streaky gold-and-brown. You should not have two colors in your hair, Marian. Marian, did any one ever tell you that you are very beautiful?"

Silence. "Pee-weet!" said a bird. "Tweet?"

And Marian replied: "I am devoted to Dorothy, of course, but I have never admired her fashion of making advances to every man she meets. Yes, she does."

"Nay, 'twas only her money that lured me, to do her justice. It appeared so very sensible to marry an heiress. . . But how can any man be sensible so long as he is haunted by the memory of your eyes? For see how bright they are,—see, here in the water. Two stars have fallen into the fountain, Marian."

"You are handsomer so. Your nose is too short, but here in the fountain you are quite handsome—"

"Marian,—"

"I wonder how many other women's fingers you have kissed—like that. Ah, don't tell me, Humphrey! Humphrey, promise me that you will always lie to me when I ask you about those other women. Lie to me, my dear, and I will know that you are lying and love you all the better for it. . . You should not have told me about Dorothy. How often did you kiss all of Dorothy's finger-tips one by one, in just that foolish, dear way?"

"But who was this Dorothy you speak of, Marian? I have forgotten. Oh, yes—we quarrelled—over some woman,—and I went away. I left you for a mere heiress, Marian. You! And five days, ago while I lay abed, wounded, they told me that you, were to marry Ormskirk. I thought I would go mad. . . Eh, I remember now. But what do these things matter? Is it not of far greater importance that the sunlight turns your hair to pure topaz?"

"Ah, my hair, my eyes! Is it these you care for? You would not love me, then, if I were old and ugly?"

"Eh,—I love you."

"Animal!"

There was a longer silence now. "Tweet!" said a bird, pertly.

Then Marian said, "Let us go to my father."

"To tell him—?"

"Why, that I love you, I suppose, and that I cannot marry Jack, not even to be a duchess. Oh, I did so much want to be a duchess! But when you came back to me yonder in the forest, somehow I stopped wanting anything more. Something—I hardly know—something seemed to say, as you came striding through the dead leaves, laughing and so very pale,—something seemed to say, 'You love him'—oh, quite audibly."

"Audibly! Why, the woods whispered it, the birds trilled it, screamed it, the very leaves underfoot crackled assent. Only they said, 'You love her—the girl yonder with glad, frightened eyes, Spring's daughter.' Oh, I too, heard it, Marian! 'Follow,' the birds sang, 'follow, follow, follow, for yonder is the heart's desire!'"

The Duke of Ormskirk raised his head, his lips sketching a whistle. "Ah! ah!" he muttered. "Eureka! I have recaptured it—the message of April."

IV

WHEN THESE TWO HAD GONE the Duke flung out his hands in a comprehensive gesture of giving up the entire matter. "Well," said he, "you see how it is!"

"I do," Lord Brudenel assented. "And if you intend to sit patient under it, I, at least, wear a sword. Confound it, Jack, do you suppose I am going to have promiscuous young men dropping out of the skies and embracing my daughter?" The Earl became forceful in his language.

"Harry,—" the Duke began.

"The fellow hasn't a penny—not a stick or a stiver to his name! He's only a rascally, impudent younger son—and even Venour has nothing except Agard Court yonder! That—that crow's nest!" Lord Brudenel spluttered. "They mooned about together a great deal a year ago, but I thought nothing of it; then he went away, and she never spoke of him again. Never spoke of him—oh, the jade!"

The Duke of Ormskirk considered the affair, a mild amusement waking in his plump face.

"Old friend," said he, at length, "it is my opinion that we are perilously near to being a couple of fools. We planned this marriage, you and I—dear, dear, we planned it when Marian was scarcely out of her cradle! But we failed to take nature into the plot, Harry. It was sensible—Oh, granted! I obtained a suitable mistress for Ingilby and Bottreaux Towers, a magnificent ornament for my coach and my opera-box; while you—your pardon, old friend, if I word it somewhat grossly,—you, in effect, obtained a wealthy and not uninfluential husband for your daughter. Nay, I think you are fond of me, but that is beside the mark; it was not Jack Bulmer who was to marry your daughter, but the Duke of Ormskirk. The thing was as logical as a sale of bullocks,—value for value. But now nature intervenes, and"—he snapped his fingers,—"eh, well, since she wants this Humphrey Degge, of course she must have him."

Lord Brudenel mentioned several penalties which he would voluntarily incur in case of any such preposterous marriage.

"Your style," the Duke regretfully observed, "is somewhat more original than your subject. You have a handsome daughter to barter, and you want your price. The thing is far from uncommon. Yet you shall have your price, Harry. What estate do you demand of your son-in-law?"

"What the devil are you driving at?" said Lord Brudenel.

Composedly the Duke of Ormskirk spread out his hands. "You have, in effect, placed Marian in the market," he said, "and I offer to give Lord Humphrey Degge the money with which to purchase her."

"'Tis evident," the Earl considered, "that you are demented!"

"Because I willingly part with money? But then I have a great deal of money. I have money, and I have power, and the King occasionally pats me upon the shoulder, and men call me 'your Grace,' instead of 'my Lord,' as they do you. So I ought to be very happy, ought I not, Harry? Ah, yes, I ought to be entirely happy, because I have had everything, with the unimportant exception of the one thing I wanted."

JAMES BRANCH CABELL

But Lord Brudenel had drawn himself erect, stiffly. "I am to understand, then, from this farrago, that on account of the—um—a—incident we have just witnessed you decline to marry my daughter?"

"I would sooner cut off my right hand," said the Duke, "for I am fonder of Marian than I am of any other living creature."

"Oh, very well!" the Earl conceded, sulkily. "Umfraville wants her. He is only a marquis, of course, but so far as money is concerned, I believe he is a thought better off than you. I would have preferred you as a son-in-law, you understand, but since you withdraw—why, then, let it be Umfraville."

Now the Duke looked up into his face for some while. "You would do that! You would sell Marian to Umfraville—* to a person who unites the continence of a partridge with the graces of a Berkshire hog—to that lean whoremonger, to that disease-rotted goat! Because he has the money! Why, Harry, what a car you are!"

Lord Brudenel bowed, "My Lord Duke, you are today my guest. I apprehend you will presently be leaving Halvergate, however, and as soon—as that regrettable event takes place, I shall see to it a friend wait upon you with the length of my sword. Meanwhile I venture to reserve the privilege of managing my family affairs at my own discretion."

"I do not fight with hucksters," the Duke flung at him, "and you are one. Oh, you peddler! Can you not understand that I am trying to buy your daughter's happiness?"

"I intend that my daughter shall make a suitable match," replied the Earl, stubbornly, "and she shall. If Marian is a sensible girl—and, barring today, I have always esteemed her such,—she will find happiness in obeying her father's mandates: otherwise—" He waved the improbable contingency aside.

"Sensible! Faith, can you not see, even now, that to be sensible is not the highest wisdom? You and I are sensible as the world goes,—and in God's name, what good does it do us? Here we sit, two miserable and empty-veined old men squabbling across a deal-table, breaking up a friendship of thirty years. And yonder Marian and this Humphrey Degge—who are within a measurable distance of insanity, if their conversation be the touchstone,—yet tread the pinnacles of some seventh heaven of happiness. April has brought them love, Harry. Oh, I concede their love is folly! But it is all folly, Harry Heleigh. Purses,

---

* "Whose entrance blushing Satan did deny Lest hell be thought no better than a sty."

titles, blue ribbons, and the envy of our fellows are the toys which we struggle for, we sensible men; and in the end we find them only toys, and, gaining them, we gain only weariness. And love, too, is a toy; but, gaining love, we gain, at least, a temporary happiness. There is the difference, Harry Heleigh."

"Oh, have done with your, balderdash!" said Lord Brudenel. He spoke irritably, for he knew his position to be guaranteed by common-sense, and his slow wrath was kindling at opposition.

His Grace of Ormskirk rose to his feet, all tension. In the act his hand struck against the open despatch-box; afterward, with a swift alteration of countenance, he overturned this box and scattered the contents about the table. For a moment he seemed to forget Lord Brudenel; quite without warning Ormskirk flared into rage.

"Harry Heleigh, Harry Heleigh!" he cried, as he strode across the terrace, and caught Lord Brudenel roughly by the shoulder, "are you not content to go to your grave without killing another woman? Oh, you dotard miser!—you haberdasher!—haven't I offered you money, an isn't money the only thing you are now capable of caring for? Give the girl to Degge, you huckster!"

Lord Brudenel broke from the Duke's grasp. Brudenel was asplutter with anger. "I will see you damned first. You offer money,—I fling the money in your fat face. Look you, you have just insulted, me, and now you offer—money! Another insult. John Bulmer, I would not accept an affront like this from an archangel. You are my guest, but I am only flesh and blood. I swear to you this is the most deliberate act of my life." Lord Brudenel struck him full upon the cheek.

"Pardon," said the Duke of Ormskirk. He stood rigid, his arms held stiff at his sides, his hands clenched; the red mark showed plain against an ashy countenance. "Pardon me for a moment." Once or twice he opened and shut his eyes like an automaton. "And stop behaving so ridiculously. I cannot fight you. I have other matters to attend to. We are wise, Harry,—you and I We know that love sometimes does not endure; sometimes it flares up at a girl's glance, quite suddenly, and afterward smoulders out into indifference or even into hatred. So, say we, let all sensible people marry for money, for then in any event you get what you marry for,—a material benefit, a tangible good, which does no vanish when the first squabble, or perhaps the first gray hair, arrives. That is sensible; but women, Harry, are not always sensible—"

"Draw, you coward!" Lord Brudenel snarled at him. The Earl had already lugged out his ineffectual dress sword, and would have been, as he stood on guard, a ludicrous figure had he not been rather terrible. His rage shook him visibly, and his obstinate mouth twitched and snapped like that of a beast cornered. All gray he was, and the sun glistened on his gray tye-wig as he waited. His eyes were coals.

But Ormskirk had regained composure. "You know that I am not a coward," the Duke said, equably. "I have proven it many times. Besides, you overlook two details. One is that I have no sword with me, I am quite unarmed. The other detail is that only gentlemen fight duels, and just now we are hucksters, you and I, chaffering over Marian's happiness. So I return to my bargaining. You will not sell Marian's happiness to me for money? Why, then—remember, we are only hucksters, you and I,—I will purchase it by a dishonorable action. I will show you a woman's letters,—some letters I was going to burn romantically before I married—Instead, I wish you to read them."

He pushed the papers lying upon the table toward Lord Brudenel. Afterward Ormskirk turned away and stood looking over the ivy-covered balustrade into the gardens below. All white and green and blue the vista was, and of a monastic tranquillity, save for the plashing of the fountain behind the yew-hedge. From the gardens at his feet irresolute gusts brought tepid woodland odors. He heard the rustling of papers, heard Lord Brudenel's sword fall jangling to the ground. The Duke turned.

"And for twenty years I have been eating my heart out with longing for her," the Earl said. "And—and I thought you were my friend, Jack."

"She was not your wife when I first knew her. But John Bulmer was a penniless nobody,—so they gave her to you, an earl's heir, those sensible parents of hers. I never saw her again, though—as you see,—she wrote to me sometimes. And her parents did the sensible thing; but I think they killed her, Harry."

"Killed her?" Lord Brudenel echoed, stupidly. Then on a sudden it was singular to see the glare in his eyes puffed out like a candle. "I killed her," he whispered; "why, I killed Alison,—I!" He began to laugh. "Now that is amusing, because she was the one thing in the world I ever loved. I remember that she used to shudder when I kissed her. I thought it was because she was only a brown and thin and timid child, who would be wiser in love's tricks by and by. Now I comprehend 'twas because every kiss was torment to her, because every time I touched her 'twas torment. So she died very slowly, did Alison,—and always I was at hand with my kisses, my pet names, and my paddlings,—killing her, you observe, always urging her graveward. Yes, and yet there is nothing in these letters to show how much she must have loathed me!" he said, in a mild sort of wonder. He appeared senile now, the shrunken and calamitous shell of the man he had been within the moment.

The Duke of Ormskirk put an arm about him. "Old friend, old friend!" said he.

"Why did you not tell me?" the Earl said. "I loved you, Jack. I worshipped her. I would never willingly have seen you two unhappy."

"Her parents would have done as you planned to do,—they would have given their daughter to the next richest suitor. I was nobody then. So the wisdom of the aged slew us, Harry,—slew Alison utterly, and left me with a living body, indeed, but with little more. I do not say that body has not amused itself. Yet I too, loved her, Harry Heleigh. And when I saw this new Alison—for Marian is her mother, face, heart, and soul,—why, some wraith of emotion stirred in me, some thrill, some not quite forgotten pulse. It seemed Alison come back from the grave. Love did not reawaken, for youth's fervor was gone out of me, yet presently I fell a-dreaming over my Madeira on long winter evenings,— sedate and tranquil dreams of this new Alison flitting about Ingilby, making the splendid, desolate place into a home. Am old man's fancies, Harry,—fancies bred of my loneliness, for I am lonely nowadays. But my dreams, I find, were not sufficiently comprehensive; for they did not anticipate April,—and nature,—and Lord Humphrey Degge. We must yield to that triumvirate, we sensible old men. Nay, we are wise as the world goes, but we have learned, you and I, that to be sensible is not the highest wisdom. Marian is her mother in soul, heart, and feature. Don't let the old tragedy be repeated, Harry. Let her have this Degge! Let Marian have her chance of being happy, for a year or two. . ."

But Lord Brudenel had paid very little attention. "I suppose so," he said, when the Duke had ended. "Oh, I suppose so. Jack, she was always kind and patient and gentle, you understand, but she used to shudder when I kissed her," he repeated, dully,—"shudder, Jack." He sat staring at his sword lying there on the ground, as though it fascinated him.

"Ah, but,—old friend," the Duke cried, with his hand upon Lord Brudenel's shoulder, "forgive me! It was the only way."

Lord Brudenel rose to his feet. "Oh, yes! why, yes, I forgive you, if that is any particular comfort to you. It scarcely seems of any importance, though. The one thing which really matters is that I loved her, and I killed her. Oh, beyond doubt, I forgive you. But now that you have made my whole past a hideous stench to me, and have proven the love I was so proud of—the one quite clean, quite unselfish thing in my life, I thought it, Jack,—to have been only my lust vented on a defenceless woman,—why, just now, I have not time to think of forgiveness. Yes, Marian may marry Degge if she cares to. And I am sorry I took her mother away from you. I would not have done it if I had known."

Brudenel started away drearily, but when he had gone a little distance turned back.

"And the point of it is," he said, with a smile, "that I shall go on living just as if nothing had happened, and shall probably live for a long, long time. My body is so confoundedly healthy. How the deuce did you have the courage to go on living?" he demanded, enviously. "You loved her and you lost her. I'd have thought you would have killed yourself long ago."

The Duke shrugged. "Yes, people do that in books. In books they have such strong emotions—"

Then Ormskirk paused for a heart-beat, looking down into the gardens. Wonderfully virginal it all seemed to Ormskirk, that small portion of a world upon the brink of renaissance: a tessellation of clean colors, where the gravelled walkways were snow beneath the sun, and were in shadow transmuted to dim violet tints; and for the rest, green ranging from the sober foliage of yew and box and ilex to the pale glow of young grass In the full sunlight; all green, save where the lake shone, a sapphire green-girdled. Spring triumphed with a vaunting pageant. And in the forest, in the air, even in the unplumbed sea-depths, woke the mating impulse,—irresistible, borne as it might seem on the slow-rising tide of grass that now rippled about the world. Everywhere they were mating; everywhere glances allured and mouth met mouth, while John Bulmer went alone without any mate or intimacy with anyone.

Everywhere people were having emotions which Ormskirk envied. He had so few emotions nowadays. Even all this posturing and talk about Alison Heleigh in which he had just indulged began to savor somehow of play-acting. He had loved Alison, of course, and that which he had said was true enough—in a way,—but, after all, he had over-colored it. There had been in his life so many interesting matters, and so many other women too, that the loss of Alison could not be said to have blighted his existence quite satisfactorily. No, John Bulmer had again been playing at the big emotions which he heard about and coveted, just as at this very moment John Bulmer was playing at being sophisticated and *blasé*. . . with only poor old Harry for audience. . .

"A great deal of me did die," the Duke heard this John Bulmer saying,—"all, I suppose, except my carcass, Harry. And it seemed hardly worth the trouble to butcher that also."

"No," Lord Brudenel conceded, "I suppose not. I wonder, d'ye know, will anything ever again seem really worth the trouble of doing it?"

The Duke of Ormskirk took his arm. "Fy, Harry, bid the daws seek their food elsewhere, for a gentleman may not wear his heart upon his sleeve. Empires crumble, and hearts break, and we are blessed or damned, as Fate elects; but through it all we find comfort in the reflection that dinner is good, and sleep, too, is excellent. As for the future—eh, well, if it mean little to us, it means a deal to Alison's daughter. Let us go to them, Harry."

IN THE SECOND APRIL

As Played at Bellegarde, in the April of 1750

This passion is in honest minds the strongest incentive that can move the soul of man to laudable accomplishments. Is a man just? Let him fall in love and grow generous. It immediately makes the good which is in him shine forth in new excellencies, and the ill vanish away without the pain of contrition, but with a sudden amendment of heart."

Dramatis Personæ

Duke of Ormskisk.

Duc de Puysange, a true Frenchman, a pert, railing fribble, but at bottom a man of parts.

Marquis de Soyecourt, a brisk, conceited rake, and distant cousin to de Puysange.

Cazaio, captain of brigands.

Dom Michel Frégose, a lewd, rascally friar.

Guiton, steward to de Puysange.

Pawsey, Ormskirk's man.

Achon, a knave.

Michault, another knave.

Duchesse de Puysange.

Claire, sister to de Puysange, a woman of beauty and resolution, of a literal humor.

Attendants, Brigands, and Dragoons; and, in the Proem, Lord Humphrey Degge and Lady Marian Heleigh.

Scene

First at Dover, thence shifting to Bellegarde-en-Poictesme and the adjacent country.

In the Second April

Proem:—More Properly an Apologue, and
Treats of the Fallibility of Soap

The Duke of Ormskirk left Halvergate on the following day, after participation in two dialogues, which I abridge.

Said the Duke to Lord Humphrey Degge:

"You have been favored, sir, vastly beyond your deserts. I acquiesce, since Fate is proverbially a lady, and to dissent were in consequence ungallant. Shortly I shall find you more employment, at Dover, whither I am now going to gull my old opponent and dear friend, Gaston de Puysange, in the matter of this new compact between France and England. I shall look for you at Dover, then, in three days' time."

"And in vain, my Lord Duke," said the other.

Now Ormskirk raised one eyebrow, after a fashion that he had.

"Because I love Marian," said Lord Humphrey, "and because I mean to be less unworthy of Marian than I have been heretofore. So that I can no longer be your spy. Besides, in nature I lack aptitude for the trade. Eh, my Lord Duke, have you already forgotten how I bungled the affair of Captain Audaine and his associates?"

"But that was a maiden effort. And as I find—at alas! the cost of decrepitude,—the one thing life teaches us is that many truisms are true. 'Practice makes perfect' is one of them. And faith, when you come to my age, Lord Humphrey, you will not grumble at having to soil your hands occasionally in the cause of common-sense."

The younger man shook his head. "A week ago you would have found me amenable enough to reason, since I was then a sensible person, and to be of service to his Grace of Ormskirk was very sensible,—just as to marry Miss Allonby, the young and beautiful heiress, was then the course pre-eminently sensible. All the while I loved Marian, you understand. But I clung to common-sense. Desperately I clung to common-sense. And yet—" He flung out his hands.

"Yes, there is by ordinary some plaguy *yet*," the Duke interpolated.

"There is," cried Lord Humphrey Degge, "the swift and heart-grappling recollection of the woman you gave up in the cause of common-sense,—roused by some melody she liked, or some shade of color she was wont to wear, or by hearing from other lips some turn of speech to which she was addicted. My Lord Duke, that memory wakes on a sudden and clutches you by the throat, and it chokes you. And one swears that common-sense—"

"One swears that common-sense may go to the devil," said his Grace of Ormskirk, "whence I don't say it didn't emanate! And one swears that, after all, there is excellent stuff in you! Your idiotic conduct, sir, makes me far happier than you know!"

After some ten paces he turned, with a smile. "In the matter of soiling one's hands—Personally I prefer them clean, sir, and particularly in the case of Marian's husband. Had it been I, he must have stuck to prosaic soap; with you in the rôle there is a difference. Faith, Lord Humphrey, there is a decided difference, and if you be other than a monster of depravity you will henceforth, I think, preserve your hands immaculate."

To Marian the Duke said a vast number of things, prompted by a complaisant thrill over the fact that, in view of the circumstances, his magnanimity must to the unprejudiced appear profuse and his behavior tolerably heroic.

"These are very absurd phrases," Marian considered, "since you will never love anyone, I think—however much you may admire the color of her eyes,—one-quarter so earnestly as you will always marvel at John Bulmer. Or perhaps you have only to wait a little, Jack, till in her time and season the elect woman shall come to you, just as she comes to all men,—and then, for once in your existence, you will be sincere."

"I go, provisionally, to seek this paragon at Dover," said his Grace of Ormskirk, and he lifted her fingers toward his smiling lips; "but I shall bear in mind, my dear, even in Dover, that sincerity is a devilishly expensive virtue."

I

IT WAS ON THE THIRTEENTH day of April that they signed the Second Treaty of Dover, which not only confirmed its predecessor of Aix-la-Chapelle, but in addition, with the brevity of lightning, demolished the last Stuarts' hope of any further aid from France. And the French ambassador subscribed the terms with a chuckle.

"For on this occasion, Jean," he observed, as he pushed the paper from him, "I think that honors are fairly even. You obtain peace at home, and in India we obtain assistance for Dupleix; good, the benefit is quite mutual; and accordingly, my friend, I must still owe you one requiting for that Bavarian business."

Ormskirk was silent until he had the churchwarden which he had just ignited aglow. "That was the evening I had you robbed and beaten by footpads, was it not? Faith, Gaston, I think you should rather be obliged to me, since it taught you never to carry important papers in your pocket when you go about your affairs of gallantry."

"That beating with great sticks," the Duc de Puysange considered, "was the height of unnecessity."

And the Duke of Ormskirk shrugged. "A mere touch of verisimilitude, Gaston; footpads invariably beat their victims. Besides, you had attempted to murder me at Aix, you may remember."

De Puysange was horrified. "My dear friend, when I set Villaneuve upon you it was with express orders only to run you through the shoulder. Figure to yourself: that abominable St. Severin had bribed your *chef* to feed you powdered glass in a ragout! But I dissented. 'Jean and I have been the dearest enemies these ten years past,' I said. 'At every Court in Europe we have lied to each other. If you kill him I shall beyond doubt presently perish of ennui.' So, that France might escape a blow so crushing as the loss of my services, St. Severin consented to disable you."

"Believe me, I appreciate your intervention," Ormskirk stated, with his usual sleepy smile; before this he had found amusement in the naïveté of his friend's self-approbation.

"Not so! Rather you are a monument of ingratitude," the other complained. "You conceive, Villaneuve was in price exorbitant. I snap my fingers. 'For a comrade so dear,' I remark, 'I gladly employ the most expensive of assassins.' Yet before the face of such magnanimity you grumble." The Duc de Puysange spread out his shapely hands. "I murder you! My adored Jean, I had as lief make love to my wife."

Ormskirk struck his finger-tips upon the table. "Faith, I knew there was something I intended to ask of you, I want you to get me a wife."

"In fact," de Puysange observed, "warfare being now at an end, it is only natural that you should resort to matrimony. I can assure you it is an admirable substitute. But who is the lucky Miss, my little villain?"

"Why, that is for you to settle," Ormskirk said. "I had hoped you might know of some suitable person."

"*Ma foi*, my friend, if I were arbiter and any wife would suit you, I would cordially desire you to take mine, for when a woman so incessantly resembles an angel in conduct, her husband inevitably desires to see her one in reality."

"You misinterpret me, Gaston. This is not a jest. I had always intended to marry as soon as I could spare the time, and now that this treaty is disposed of, my opportunity has beyond doubt arrived. I am practically at leisure until the autumn. At latest, though, I must marry by August, in order to get the honeymoon off my hands before the convocation of Parliament. For there will have to be a honeymoon, I suppose."

"It is customary," de Puysange said. He appeared to deliberate something entirely alien to this reply, however, and now sat silent for a matter of four seconds, his countenance profoundly grave. He was a hideous man,* with black beetling eyebrows, an enormous nose, and an under-lip excessively full; his face had all the calculated ill-proportion of a gargoyle, an ugliness so consummate and merry that in ultimate effect it captivated.

At last de Puysange began: "I think I follow you. It is quite proper that you should marry. It is quite proper that a man who has done so much for England should leave descendants to perpetuate his name, and with perhaps some portion of his ability—no, Jean, I do not flatter,—serve the England which is to his heart so dear. As a Frenchman I cannot but deplore that our next generation may have to face another Ormskirk; as your friend who loves you I say that this marriage will appropriately round a successful and honorable and intelligent life. Eh, we are only men, you and I, and it is advisable that all men should marry, since otherwise they might be so happy in this colorful world that getting to heaven would not particularly tempt them. Thus is matrimony a bulwark of religion."

"You are growing scurrilous," Ormskirk complained, "whereas I am in perfect earnest."

"I, too, speak to the foot of the letter, Jean, as you will soon learn. I comprehend that you cannot with agreeability marry an Englishwoman. You are too much the personage. Possessing, as you notoriously possess, your pick among the women of gentle degree—for none of them would her guardians nor her good taste permit to refuse the great Duke of Ormskirk,—any choice must therefore be a too robustious affrontment

---

* For a consideration of the vexed and delicate question whether or no Gaston de Puysange was grandson to King Charles the Second of England, the reader is referred to the third chapter of La Vrillière's *De Puysange et son temps*. The Duke's resemblance in person to that monarch was undeniable.

JAMES BRANCH CABELL

to all the others. If you select a Howard, the Skirlaws have pepper in the nose; if a Beaufort, you lose Umfraville's support,—and so on. Hey, I know, my dear Jean; your affair with the Earl of Brudenel's daughter cost you seven seats in Parliament, you may remember. How am I aware of this?—why, because I habitually have your mail intercepted. You intercept mine, do you not? Naturally; you would be a very gross and intolerable scion of the pig if you did otherwise. *Eh bien*, let us get on. You might, of course, play King Cophetua, but I doubt if it would amuse you, since Penelophons are rare; it follows in logic that your wife must come from abroad. And whence? Without question, from France, the land of adorable women. The thing is plainly demonstrated; and in France, my dear, I have to an eyelash the proper person for you."

"Then we may consider the affair as settled," Ormskirk replied, "and should you arrange to have the marriage take place upon the first of August,—if possible, a trifle earlier,—I would be trebly your debtor."

De Puysange retorted: "Beyond doubt I can adjust these matters. And yet, my dear Jean, I must submit that it is not quite the act of a gentleman to plunge into matrimony without even inquiring as to the dowry of your future bride."

"It is true," said Ormskirk, with a grimace; "I had not thought of her portion. You must remember my attention is at present pre-empted by that idiotic Ferrers business. How much am I to marry, then, Gaston?"

"I had in mind," said the other, "my sister, the Demoiselle Claire de Puysange,—"

It was a day of courtesy when the minor graces were paramount. Ormskirk rose and accorded de Puysange a salutation fitted to an emperor. "I entreat your pardon, sir, for any *gaucherie* of which I may have been guilty, and desire to extend to you my appreciation of the honor you have done me."

"It is sufficient, monsieur," de Puysange replied. And the two gravely bowed again.

Then the Frenchman resumed, in conversational tones: "I have but one unmarried sister,—already nineteen, beautiful as an angel (in the eyes, at least, of fraternal affection), and undoubtedly as headstrong as any devil at present stoking the eternal fires below. You can conceive that the disposal of such a person is a delicate matter. In Poictesme there is no suitable match, and upon the other hand I grievously apprehend her presentation at our Court, where, as Arouet de Voltaire once observed to me, the men are lured into matrimony by the memories of their past sins, and the women by the immunity it promises for future ones. In England, where custom will permit a woman to be both handsome and chaste, I estimate she would be admirably ranged. Accordingly, my dear Jean, behold a fact accomplished. And now let us embrace, my brother!"

This was done. The next day they settled the matter of dowry, jointure, the widow's portion, and so on, and de Puysange returned to render his report at Marly. The wedding had been fixed by the Frenchman for St. Anne's day, and by Ormskirk, as an uncompromising churchman, for the twenty-sixth of the following July.

II

THAT EVENING THE DUKE OF Ormskirk sat alone in his lodgings. His Grace was very splendid in black-and-gold, wearing his two stars of the Garter and the Thistle, for there was that night a ball at Lady Sandwich's, and Royalty was to embellish it. In consequence, Ormskirk meant to show his plump face there for a quarter of an hour; and the rooms would be too hot (he peevishly reflected), and the light would tire his eyes, and Laventhrope would button-hole him again about that appointment for Laventhrope's son, and the King would give vent to some especially fat-witted jest, and Ormskirk would apishly grin and applaud. And afterward he would come home with a headache, and ghostly fiddles would vex him all night long with their thin incessancy.

"Accordingly," the Duke decided, "I shall not stir a step until eleven o'clock. The King, in the ultimate, is only a tipsy, ignorant old German debauchee, and I have half a mind to tell him so. Meantime, he can wait."

The Duke sat down to consider this curious lassitude, this indefinite vexation, which had possessed him.

"For I appear to have taken a sudden dislike to the universe. It is probably my liver.

"In any event, I have come now to the end of my resources. For some twenty-five years it has amused me to make a great man of John Bulmer. Now that is done, and, like the Moorish fellow in the play, 'my occupation's gone.' I am at the very top of the ladder, and I find it the dreariest place in the world. There is nothing left to scheme for, and, besides, I am tired.

"The tiniest nerve in my body, the innermost cell of my brain, is tired tonight.

"I wonder if getting married will divert me? I doubt it. Of course I ought to marry, but then it must be rather terrible to have a woman loitering around you for the rest of your life. She will probably expect me to talk to her; she will probably come into my rooms and sit there whenever the inclination prompts her,—in a sentence, she will probably worry me to death. Eh well!—that die is cast!

"'Beautiful as an angel, and headstrong as a devil.' And what's her name?—Oh, yes, Claire. That is a very silly name, and I suppose she is a vixenish little idiot. However, the alliance is a sensible one. De Puysange has had it in mind for some six months, I think, but certainly I did not think he knew of my affair with Marian. Well, but he affects omniscience, he delights in every small chicane. He is rather droll. Yesterday he knew from the start that I was leading up to a proposal for his sister,—and yet there we sat, two solemn fools, and played our tedious comedy to a finish. *Eh bien!* as he says, it is necessary to keep one's hand in.

"'Beautiful as an angel, and headstrong as a devil'—Alison was not headstrong."

Ormskirk rose suddenly and approached an open window. It was a starless sight, temperately cool, with no air stirring. Below was a garden of some sort, and a flat roof which would be that of the stables, and beyond, abrupt as a painted scene, a black wall of houses stood against a steel-colored, vacant sky, reaching precisely to the middle of the vista. Only a solitary poplar, to the rear of the garden, qualified this sombre monotony of right angles. Ormskirk saw the world as an ugly mechanical drawing, fashioned for utility, meticulously outlined with a ruler. Yet there was a scent of growing things to nudge the senses.

"No, Alison was different. And Alison has been dead near twenty years. And God help me! I no longer regret even Alison. I should have been more truthful in talking with poor Harry Heleigh. But, as always, the temptation to be picturesque was irresistible. Besides, the truth is humiliating.

"The real tragedy of life is to learn that it is not really tragic. To learn that the world is gross, that it lacks nobility, that to considerate persons it must be in effect quite unimportant,—here are commonplaces, sweepings from the tub of the immaturest cynic. But to learn that you yourself were thoughtfully constructed in harmony with the world you were to live in, that you yourself are incapable of any great passion—eh, this is an athletic blow to human vanity. Well! I acknowledge it. My love for Alison Pleydell was the one sincere thing in my life. And it is dead. I do not think of her once a month. I do not regret her except when I am tipsy or bored or listening to music, and wish to fancy myself the picturesque victim of a flint-hearted world. Which is a romantic lie; I move like a man of card-board in a card-board world. Certain faculties and tastes and mannerisms I undoubtedly possess, but if I have any personality at all, I am not aware of it; I am a mechanism that eats and sleeps and clumsily perambulates a ball that spins around a larger ball that revolves about another, and so on, *ad infinitum*. Some day the mechanism will be broken. Or it will slowly wear out, perhaps. And then it will go to the dust-heap. And that will be the end of the great Duke of Ormskirk.

"John Bulmer did not think so. It is true that John Bulmer was a magnanimous fool,—Upon the other hand, John Bulmer would never have stared out of an ugly window at an uglier landscape and have talked yet uglier nonsense to it. He would have been off post-haste after the young person who is 'beautiful as an angel and headstrong as a devil.' And afterward he would have been very happy or else very miserable. I begin to think that John Bulmer was more sensible than the great Duke of Ormskirk. I would—I would that he were still alive."

His Grace slapped one palm against his thigh with unwonted vigor. "Behold, what I am longing for! I am longing for John Bulmer."

Presently he sounded the gong upon his desk. And presently he said: "My adorable Pawsey, the great Duke of Ormskirk is now going to pay his respects to George Guelph, King of Britain, France, and Ireland, defender of the faith. Duke of Brunswick and Lunenburg, and supreme head of the Anglican and Hibernian Church. And tomorrow Mr. John Bulmer will set forth upon a little journey into Poictesme. You will obligingly pack a valise. No, I shall not require you,—for John Bulmer was entirely capable of dressing and shaving himself. So kindly go to the devil, Pawsey, and stop staring at me."

Later in the evening Pawsey, a thought mellowed by the ale of Dover, deplored with tears the instability of a nation whose pilots were addicted to tippling.

"Drunk as David's sow!" said Pawsey, "and 'im in the hactual presence of 'is Sacred Majesty!"

III

THUS IT CAME ABOUT THAT, five days later, arrived at Bellegarde Mr. John Bulmer, kinsman and accredited emissary of the great Duke of Ormskirk. He brought with him and in due course delivered a casket of jewels and a letter from the Duke to his betrothed. The diamonds were magnificent, and the letter was a paragon of polite ardors.

Mr. Bulmer found the château in charge of a distant cousin to de Puysange, the Marquis de Soyecourt; with whom were the Duchess, a gentle and beautiful lady, her two children, and the Demoiselle Claire. The Duke himself was still at Marly, with most of his people, but at Bellegarde momentarily they looked for his return. Meanwhile de Soyecourt, an exquisite and sociable and immoral young gentleman of forty-one, was lonely, and protested that any civilized company was, in the oafish provinces, a charity of celestial pre-arrangement. He would not hear of Mr. Bulmer's leaving Bellegarde; and after a little protestation the latter proved persuadable.

"Mr. Bulmer," the Duke's letter of introduction informed the Marquis, "is my kinsman and may be regarded as discreet. The evanishment of his tiny patrimony, spirited away some years ago by divers over-friendly ladies, hath taught the man humility, and procured for me the privilege of paying for his support: but I find him more valuable than his cost. He is tolerably honest, not too often tipsy, makes an excellent salad, and will convey a letter or hold a door with fidelity and despatch. Employ his services, monsieur, if you have need of them; I place him at your command."

In fine, they at Bellegarde judged Mr. Bulmer to rank somewhere between lackeyship and gentility, and treated him in accordance. It was an age of parasitism, and John Bulmer, if a parasite, was the Phormio of a very great man: when his patron expressed a desire Mr. Bulmer fulfilled it without boggling over inconvenient scruples, perhaps; and there was the worst that could with equity be said of him. An impoverished gentleman must live somehow, and, deuce take it! there must be rather pretty pickings among the broken meats of an Ormskirk. To this effect de Soyecourt moralized one evening as the two sat over their wine.

John Bulmer candidly assented. "I live as best I may," he said. "In a word 'I am his Highness' dog at Kew—' But mark you, I do not complete the quotation, monsieur."

"Which ends, as I remember it, 'I pray you, sir, whose dog are you?' Well, Mr. Bulmer, each of us wards his own kennel somewhere, whether it be in a king's court or in a woman's heart, and it is necessary that he pay the rent of it in such coin as the owner may demand. Beggars cannot be choosers, Mr. Bulmer." The Marquis went away moodily, and John Bulmer poured out another glass.

"Were I Gaston, you would not kennel here, my friend. The Duchess has too many claims to be admired,—for undoubtedly people do go about unchained who can admire a blonde,—and always your eyes follow her. I noticed it a week ago."

And during this week Mr. Bulmer had seen a deal of Claire de Puysange, with results that you will presently ascertain. It was natural she should desire to learn something of the man she was so soon to marry, and of whose personality she was so ignorant; she had not even seen a picture of him, by example. Was he handsome?

John Bulmer believed him rather remarkably handsome, when you considered how frequently his love-affairs had left disastrous souvenirs: yes, for a man in middle life so often patched up by quack doctors, Ormskirk looked wholesome enough, said Mr. Bulmer. He may have had his occult purposes, this poor cousin, but of Ormskirk he undoubtedly spoke with engaging candor. Here was no parasite cringingly praising his patron to the skies. The Duke's career was touched on, with its grimy passages no whit extenuated: before Dettingen Cousin Ormskirk had, it must be confessed, taken a bribe from de Noailles, and in return had seen to it that the English did not follow up their empty victory; and 'twas well known Ormskirk got his dukedom through the Countess of Yarmouth, to whom the King could deny nothing. What were the Duke's relations with this liberal lady?—a shrug rendered Mr. Bulmer's avowal of ignorance tolerably explicit. Then, too, Mr. Bulmer readily conceded, the Duke's atrocities after Culloden were somewhat over-notorious for denial: all the prisoners were shot out-of-hand; seventy-two of them were driven into an inn-yard and massacred *en masse*. Yes, there were women among them, but not over a half-dozen children, at most. Mademoiselle was not to class his noble patron with Herod, understand,—only a few brats of no importance.

In fine, he told her all the highly colored tales that envy and malice and ignorance had been able to concoct concerning the great Duke. Many of them John Bulmer knew to be false; nevertheless, he had a large mythology to choose from, he picked his instances with care, he narrated them with gusto and discretion,—and in the end he got his reward.

For the girl rose, flame-faced, and burlesqued a courtesy in his direction. "Monsieur Bulmer, I make you my compliments. You have very fully explained what manner of man is this to whom my brother has sold me."

"And wherefore do you accord me this sudden adulation?" said John Bulmer.

"Because in France we have learned that lackeys are always powerful. Le Bel is here omnipotent, Monsieur Bulmer; but he is lackey to a satyr only; and therefore, I felicitate you, monsieur, who are lackey to a fiend."

John Bulmer looked rather grave. "Civility is an inexpensive wear, mademoiselle, but it becomes everybody."

"Lackey!" she flung over her shoulder, as she left him.

John Bulmer began to whistle an air then popular across the Channel. Later his melody was stilled.

"'Beautiful as an angel, and headstrong as a devil!'" said John Bulmer. "You have an eye, Gaston!"

IV

THAT EVENING CAME A LETTER from Gaston to de Soyecourt, which the latter read aloud at supper. Gossip of the court it was for the most part, garrulous, and peppered with deductions of a caustic and diverting sort, but containing no word of a return to Bellegarde, in this vocal rendering. For in the reading one paragraph was elided.

"I arrive," the Duke had written, "within three or at most four days after this will be received. You are to breathe not a syllable of my coming, dear Louis, for I do not come alone. Achille Cazaio has intimidated Poictesme long enough; I consider it is not desirable that a peer of France should be at the mercy of a chicken-thief, particularly when Fortune whispers, as the lady now does:

> *"Viens punir le coupable;*
> *Les oracles, les dieux, tout nous est favorable.*

"Understand, in fine, that Madame de Pompadour has graciously obtained for me the loan of the dragoons of Entréchat for an entire fortnight, so that I return not in submission, but, like Cæsar and Coriolanus and other exiled captains of antiquity, at the head of a glorious army. We will harry the Taunenfels, we will hang the vile bandit more high than Haman of old, we will, in a word, enjoy the supreme pleasure of the chase, enhanced by the knowledge we pursue a note-worthy quarry. Homicide is, after all, the most satisfying recreation life affords us, since man alone knows how thoroughly man deserves to be slaughtered. A tiger, now, has his deficiencies, perhaps, viewed as a roommate; yet a tiger is at least acceptable to the eye, a vision very pleasantly suggestive, we will say, of buttered toast; whereas, our fellow-creatures, my dear Louis,—" And in this strain de Puysange continued, with intolerably scandalous examples as parapets for his argument.

That night de Soyecourt re-read this paragraph. "So the Pompadour has kindly tendered him the loan of certain dragoons? She is very fond of Gaston, is la petite Étoiles, beyond doubt. And accordingly her dragoons are to garrison Bellegarde for a whole fortnight. Good, good!" said the Marquis; "I think that all goes well."

He sat for a long while, smiling, preoccupied with his imaginings, which were far adrift in the future. Louis de Soyecourt was a subtle little man, freakish and amiable, and, on a minute scale, handsome. He reminded people of a dissipated elf; his excesses were notorious, yet always he preserved the face of an ecclesiastic and the eyes of an aging seraph; and bodily there was as yet no trace of the corpulence which marred his later years.

Tonight he slept soundly. His conscience was always, they say, to the very end of his long life, the conscience of a child, vulnerable by physical punishment, but by nothing else.

V

Next day John Bulmer rode through the Forest of Acaire, and sang as he went. Yet he disapproved of the country.

"For I am of the opinion," John Bulmer meditated, "that France just now is too much like a flower-garden situate upon the slope of a volcano. The eye is pleasantly titillated, but the ear catches eloquent rumblings. This is not a very healthy country, I think. These shaggy-haired, dumb peasants trouble me. I had thought France a nation of de Puysanges; I find it rather a nation of beasts who are growing hungry. Presently they will begin to feed, and I am not at all certain as to the urbanity of their table manners."

However, it was no affair of his; so he put the matter out of mind, and as he rode through the forest, carolled blithely. Trees were marshalled on each side with an effect of colonnades; everywhere there was a sniff of the cathedral, of a cheery cathedral all green and gold and full-bodied browns, where the industrious motes swam, like the fishes fairies angle for, in every long and rigid shaft of sunlight,—or rather (John Bulmer decided), as though Time had just passed by with a broom, intent to garnish the least nook of Acaire against Spring's occupancy of it. Then there were tiny white butterflies, frail as dream-stuff. There were anemones; and John Bulmer sighed at their insolent perfection. Theirs was a frank allure; in the solemn forest they alone of growing things were wanton, for they coquetted with the wind, and their pink was the pink of flesh.

He recollected that he was corpulent—and forty-five. "And yet, praise Heaven," said John Bulmer, "something stirs in this sleepy skull of mine."

Sang John Bulmer:

> *"April wakes, and the gifts are good*
> *Which April grants in this lonely wood*
> *Mid the wistful sounds of a solitude,*
> *Whose immemorial murmuring*
> *Is the voice of Spring*
> *And murmurs the burden of burgeoning.*
>
> *"April wakes, and her heart is high,*
> *For the Bassarids and the Fauns are nigh,*
> *And prosperous leaves lisp busily*
> *Over flattered brakes, whence the breezes bring*
> *Vext twittering*
> *To swell the burden of burgeoning.*
>
> *"April wakes, and afield, astray,*
> *She calls to whom at the end I say.*
> Heart o' my Heart, I am thine alway,—
> *And I follow, follow her carolling,*
> *For I hear her sing*
> *Above the burden of burgeoning.*
>
> *"April wakes;—it were good to live*
> (*Yet April passes*), *though April give*
> *No other gift for our pleasuring*
> *Than the old, old burden of burgeoning—"*

He paused here. Not far ahead a woman's voice had given a sudden scream, followed by continuous calls for aid.

"Now, if I choose, will begin the first fytte of John Bulmer's adventures," he meditated, leisurely. "The woman is in some sort of trouble. If I go to her assistance I shall probably involve myself in a most unattractive mess, and eventually be arrested by the constable,—if they have any constables in this operatic domain, the which I doubt. I shall accordingly emulate the example of the long-headed Levite, and sensibly pass by on the other side. Halt! I there recognize the voice of the Duke of Ormskirk. I came into this country to find John Bulmer; and John Bulmer would most certainly have spurred his gallant charger upon the craven who is just now molesting yonder female. In consequence, my gallant charger, we will at once proceed to confound the dastardly villain."

He came presently into an open glade, which the keen sunlight lit without obstruction. Obviously arranged, was his first appraisal of the tableau there presented. A woman in blue half-knelt, half-lay, upon the young grass, while a man, bending over, fettered her hands behind her back. A swarthy and exuberantly bearded fellow, attired in green-and-russet, stood beside them, displaying magnificent teeth in exactly the grin which hieratic art imputes to devils. Yet farther off a Dominican Friar sat upon a stone and displayed rather more unctuous amusement. Three horses and a mule diversified the background. All in all, a thought larger than life, a shade too obviously posed, a sign-painter's notion of a heroic picture, was John Bulmer's verdict. From his holster he drew a pistol.

The lesser rascal rose from the prostrate woman. "Finished, my captain,—" he began. Against the forest verdure he made an excellent mark. John Bulmer shot him neatly through the head.

Startled by the detonation, the Friar and the man in green-and-russet wheeled about to find Mr. Bulmer, with his most heroical bearing, negligently replacing the discharged pistol. The woman lay absolutely still, face downward, in a clump of fern.

"Gentlemen," said John Bulmer, "I lament that your sylvan diversions should be thus interrupted by the fact that an elderly person like myself, quite old enough to know better, has seen fit to adopt the pursuit of knight-errantry. You need not trouble yourselves about your companion, for I have blown out most of the substance nature intended him to think with. One of you, I regret to observe, is rendered immune by the garb of an order which I consider misguided, indeed, but with which I have no quarrel. With the other I beg leave to request the honor of exchanging a few passes as the recumbent lady's champion."

"Sacred blue!" remarked the bearded man; "you presume to oppose, then, of all persons, me! You fool, I am Achille Cazaio!"

"I deplore the circumstance that I am not overwhelmed by the revelation," John Bulmer said, as he dismounted, "and I entreat you to bear in mind, friend Achille, that in Poictesme I am a stranger. And, unhappily, the names of many estimable persons have not an international celebrity." Thus speaking, he drew and placed himself on guard.

With a shrug the Friar turned and reseated himself upon the stone. He appeared a sensible man. But Cazaio flashed out a long sword and hurled himself upon John Bulmer.

Cazaio thus obtained a butcherly thrust in the shoulder, "Friend Achille," said John Bulmer, "that was tolerably severe for a first hit. Does it content you?"

The hairy man raged. "Eh, my God!" Cazaio shrieked, "do you mock me, you misbegotten one! Before you can give me such another I shall have settled you outright. Already hell gapes for you. Fool, I am Achille Cazaio!"

"Yes, yes, you had mentioned that," said his opponent. "And, in return, allow me to present Mr. John Bulmer, thoroughly enjoying himself for the first time in a quarter of a century, Angelo taught me this thrust. Can you parry it, friend Achille?" Mr. Bulmer cut open the other's forehead.

"Well done!" Cazaio grunted. He attacked with renewed fury, but now the blood was streaming down his face and into his eyes in such a manner that he was momentarily compelled to carry his hand toward his countenance in order to wipe away the heavy trickle. John Bulmer lowered his point.

"Friend Achille, it is not reasonable I should continue our engagement to its dénouement, since by that boastful parade of skill I have inadvertently turned you into a blind man. Can you not stanch your wound sufficiently to make possible a renewal of our exercise on somewhat more equal terms?"

"Not now," the other replied, breathing heavily,—"not now, Monsieur Bulmaire. You have conquered, and the woman is yours. Yet lend me my life for a little till I may meet you more equitably. I will not fail you,—I swear it—I, Achille Cazaio."

"Why, God bless my soul!" said John Bulmer, "do you imagine that I am forming a collection of vagrant females? Permit me, pray, to assist you to your horse. And if you would so far honor me as to accept the temporary loan of my handkerchief—"

Solicitously Mr. Bulmer bound up his opponent's head, and more lately aided him to mount one of the grazing horses. Cazaio was moved to say:

"You are a gallant enemy, Monsieur Bulmaire. I shall have the pleasure of cutting your throat on Thursday next, if that date be convenient to you."

"Believe me," said John Bulmer, "I am always at your disposal. Let this spot, then, be our rendezvous, since I am wofully ignorant concerning your local geography. And meantime, my friend, if I may be so bold, I would suggest a little practice in parrying. You are of Boisrobert's school, I note, and in attack undeniably brilliant, whereas your defence—unvarying defect of Boisrobert's followers!—is lamentably weak."

"I perceive that monsieur is a connoisseur in these matters," said Cazaio; "I am the more highly honored. Till Thursday, then." And with an inclination of his bandaged head—and a furtive glance toward the insensate woman,—he rode away singing.

Sang Achille Cazaio:

> *"But, oh, the world is wide, dear lass,*
> *That I must wander through,*
> *And many a wind and tide, dear lass,*
> *Must flow 'twixt me and you,*
> *Ere love that may not be denied*
> *Shall bring me back to you,*
> *—Dear lass!*
> *Shall bring me back to you."*

Thus singing, he disappeared; meantime John Bulmer had turned toward the woman. The Dominican sat upon the stone, placidly grinning.

"And now," said John Bulmer, "we revert to the origin of all this tomfoolery,—who, true to every instinct of her sex, has caused as much trouble as lay within her power and then fainted. A little water from the brook, if you will be so good. Master Friar,—Hey!—why, you damned rascal!"

JAMES BRANCH CABELL

As John Bulmer bent above the woman, the Friar had stabbed John Bulmer between the shoulders. The dagger broke like glass.

"Oh, the devil!" said the churchman; "what sort of a duellist is this who fights in a shirt of Milanese armor!" He stood for a moment, silent, in sincere horror. "I lack words," he said,—"Oh, vile coward! I lack words to arraign this hideous revelation! There is a code of honor that obtains all over the world, and any duellist who descends to secret armor is, as you are perfectly aware, guilty of supersticery. He is no fit associate for gentlemen, he is rather the appropriate companion of Korah, Dathan, and Abiram in their fiery pit. Faugh, you sneak-thief!"

John Bulmer was a thought abashed, and for an instant showed it. Then, "Permit me," he equably replied, "to point out that I did not come hither with any belligerent intent. My undershirt, therefore, I was entitled to regard as a purely natural advantage,—as much so as would have been a greater length of arm, which, you conceive, does not obligate a gentleman to cut off his fingers before he fights."

"I scent the casuist," said the Friar, shaking his head. "Frankly, you had hoodwinked me: I was admiring you as a second Palmerin; and all the while you were letting off those gasconades, adopting those heroic postures, and exhibiting such romantic magnanimity, you were actually as safe from poor Cazaio as though you had been in Crim Tartary rather than Acaire!"

"But the pose was magnificent," John Bulmer pleaded, "and I have a leaning that way when one loses nothing by it. Besides, I consider secret armor to be no more than a rational precaution in any country where the clergy are addicted to casual assassination."

"It is human to err," the Friar replied, "and Cazaio would have given me a thousand crowns for your head. Believe me, the man is meditating some horrible mischief against you, for otherwise he would not have been so damnably polite."

"The information is distressing," said John Bulmer; and added, "This Cazaio appears to be a personage?"

"I retort," said the Friar, "that your ignorance is even more remarkable than my news. Achille Cazaio is the bugbear of all Poictesme, he is as powerful in these parts as ever old Manuel was."

"But I have never heard of this old Manuel either—"

"In fact, your ignorance seems limitless. For any child could tell you that Cazaio roosts in the Taunenfels yonder, with some hundreds of brigands in his company. Poictesme is, in effect, his pocket-book, from which he takes whatever he has need of, and the Duc de Puysange, our nominal lord, pays him an annual tribute to respect Bellegarde."

"This appears to be an unusual country," quoth John Bulmer; "where a brigand rules, and the forests are infested by homicidal clergymen and harassed females. Which reminds me that I have been guilty of an act of ungallantry,—and faith! while you and I have been chatting, the lady, with a rare discretion, has peacefully come back to her senses."

"She has regained nothing very valuable," said the Friar, with a shrug, "Alone in Acaire!" But John Bulmer had assisted the woman to her feet, and had given a little cry at sight of her face, and now he stood quite motionless, holding both her unfettered hands.

"You!" he said. And when speech returned to him, after a lengthy interval, he spoke with odd irrelevance. "Now I appear to understand why God created me."

He was puzzled. For there had come to him, unheralded and simply, a sense of something infinitely greater than his mind could conceive; and analysis might only pluck at it, impotently, as a wearied swimmer might pluck at the sides of a well. Ormskirk and Ormskirk's powers now somehow dwindled from the zone of serious consideration, as did the radiant world, and even the woman who stood before him; trifles, these: and his contentment spurned the stars to know that, somehow, this woman and he were but a part, an infinitesimal part, of a scheme which was ineffably vast and perfect. . . That was the knowledge he sensed, unwordably, as he regarded this woman now.

She was tall, just as tall as he. It was a blunt-witted devil who whispered John Bulmer that, inch paralleling inch, the woman is taller than the man and subtly renders him absurd; and that in a decade this woman would be stout. There was no meaning now in any whispering save hers. John Bulmer perceived, with a blurred thrill,—as if of memory, as if he were recollecting something once familiar to him, a great while ago,—that the girl was tall and deep-bosomed, and that her hair was dark, all crinkles, but (he somehow knew) very soft to the touch. The full oval of her face had throughout the rich tint of cream, so that he now understood the blowziness of pink cheeks; but her mouth was vivid. It was a mouth not wholly deficient in attractions, he estimated. Her nose managed to be Roman without overdoing it. And her eyes, candid and appraising, he found to be the color that blue is in Paradise; it was odd their lower lids should be straight lines, so that when she laughed her eyes were converted into right-angled triangles;

and it was still more odd that when you gazed into them your reach of vision should be extended until you saw without effort for miles and miles.

And now for a longish while these eyes returned his scrutiny, without any trace of embarrassment; and whatever may have been the thoughts of Mademoiselle de Puysange, she gave them no expression. But presently the girl glanced down toward the dead man.

"It was you who killed him?" she said. "You!"

"I had that privilege," John Bulmer admitted. "And on Thursday afternoon, God willing, I shall kill the other."

"You are kind, Monsieur Bulmer. And I am not ungrateful. And for that which happened yesterday I entreat your pardon."

"I can pardon you for calling me a lackey, mademoiselle, only upon condition that you permit me to be your lackey for the remainder of your jaunt. Poictesme appears a somewhat too romantic country for unaccompanied women to traverse in any comfort."

"My thought to a comma," the Dominican put in,—"unaccompanied ladies do not ordinarily drop from the forest oaks like acorns. I said as much to Cazaio a half-hour ago. Look you, we two and Michault,— who formerly incited this carcass and, from what I know of him, is by this time occupying hell's hottest gridiron,—were riding peacefully toward Beauséant. Then this lady pops out of nowhere, and Cazaio promptly expresses an extreme admiration for her person."

"The rest," John Bulmer said, "I can imagine. Oh, believe me, I look forward to next Thursday!"

"But for you," the girl said, "I would now be the prisoner of that devil upon the Taunenfels! Three to one you fought,—and you conquered! I have misjudged you, Monsieur Bulmer. I had thought you only an indolent old gentleman, not very brave,—because—"

"Because otherwise I would not have been the devil's lackey?" said John Bulmer. "Eh, mademoiselle, I have been inspecting the world for more years than I care to confess; I have observed the king upon his throne, and the caught thief upon his coffin in passage for the gallows: and I suspect they both came thither through taking such employment as chance offered. Meanwhile, we waste daylight. You were journeying—?"

"To Perdigon," Claire answered. She drew nearer to him and laid one hand upon his arm. "You are a gallant man, Monsieur Bulmer. Surely you understand. Two weeks ago my brother affianced me to the Duke of

Ormskirk. Ormskirk!—ah, I know he is your kinsman,—your patron,—but you yourself could not deny that the world reeks with his infamy. And my own brother, monsieur, had betrothed me to this perjurer, to that lewd rake, to that inhuman devil who slaughters defenceless prisoners, men, women, and children alike. Why, I had sooner marry the first beggar or the ugliest fiend in hell!" the girl wailed, and she wrung her plump little hands in desperation.

"Good, good!" he cried, in his soul. "It appears my eloquence of yesterday was greater than I knew of!"

Claire resumed: "But you cannot argue with Gaston—he merely shrugs. So I decided to go over to Perdigon and marry Gérard des Roches. He has wanted to marry me for a long while, but Gaston said he was too poor. And, O Monsieur Bulmer, Gérard is so very, very stupid!—but he was the only person available, and in any event," she concluded, with a sigh of resignation, "he is preferable to that terrible Ormskirk."

John Bulmer gazed on her considerately. "'Beautiful as an angel, and headstrong as a devil,'" was his thought, "You have an eye, Gaston!" Aloud John Bulmer said: "Your remedy against your brother's tyranny, mademoiselle, is quite masterly, though perhaps a trifle Draconic. Yet if on his return he find you already married, he undoubtedly cannot hand you over to this wicked Ormskirk. Marry, therefore, by all means,—but not with this stupid Gérard."

"With whom, then?" she wondered.

"Fate has planned it," he laughed; "here are you and I, and yonder is the clergyman whom Madam Destiny has thoughtfully thrown in our way."

"Not you," she answered, gravely. "I am too deeply in your debt, Monsieur Bulmer, to think of marrying you."

"You refuse," he said, "because you have known for some days past that I loved you. Yet it is really this fact which gives me my claim to become your husband. You have need of a man to do you this little service. I know of at least one person whose happiness it would be to die if thereby he might save you a toothache. This man you cannot deny—you have not the right to deny this man his single opportunity of serving you."

"I like you very much," she faltered; and then, with disheartening hastiness, "Of course, I like you very much; but I am not in love with you."

JAMES BRANCH CABELL

He shook his head at her, "I would think the worse of your intellect if you were. I adore you. Granted: but that constitutes no cut-throat mortgage. It is merely a state of mind which I have somehow blundered into, and with which you have no concern. So I ask nothing of you save to marry me. You may, if you like, look upon me as insane; it is the view toward which I myself incline. However, mine is a domesticated mania and vexes no one save myself; and even I derive no little amusement from its manifestations. Eh, Monsieur Jourdain may laugh at me for a puling lover!" cried John Bulmer; "but, heavens! if only he could see the unplumbed depths of ludicrousness I discover in my own soul! The mirth of Atlas could not do it justice."

Claire meditated for a while, her eyes inscrutable and yet not unkindly. "It shall be as you will," she said at last. "Yes, certainly, I will marry you."

"O Mother of God!" said the Dominican, in profound disgust; "I cannot marry two maniacs." But, in view of John Bulmer's sword and pistol, he went through the ceremony without further protest.

And something embryonic in John Bulmer seemed to come, with the knave's benediction, into flowerage. He saw, as if upon a sudden, how fine she was; all the gracious and friendly youth of her: and he deliberated, dizzily, the awe of her spirited and alert eyes; why, the woman was afraid of him! That sunny and vivid glade had become, to him, an island about which past happenings lapped like a fretted sea. "Dear me!" he reflected, "but I am really in a very bad way indeed."

Now Mistress Bulmer gazed shyly at her husband. "We will go back to Bellegarde," Claire began, "and inform Louis de Soyecourt that I cannot marry the Duke of Ormskirk, because I have already married you, Jean Bulmer,—"

"I would follow you," said John Bulmer, "though hell yawned between us. I employ the particular expression as customary in all these cases of romantic infatuation."

"Yet I," the Friar observed, "would, to the contrary, advise removal from Poictesme as soon as may be possible. For I warn you that if you return to Bellegarde, Monsieur de Soyecourt will have you hanged."

"Reverend sir," John Bulmer replied, "do you actually believe this consideration would be to me of any moment?"

The Friar inspected his countenance. By and by the Friar said: "I emphatically do not. And to think that at the beginning of our acquaintanceship I took you for a sensible person!" Afterward the Friar mounted his mule and left them.

Then silently John Bulmer assisted his wife to the back of one of the horses, and they turned eastward into the Forest of Acaire. Mr. Bulmer's countenance was politely interested, and he chatted pleasantly of the forenoon's adventure. Claire told him something of her earlier memories of Cazaio. So the two returned to Bellegarde. Then Claire led the way toward the western façade, where her apartments were, and they came to a postern-door, very narrow and with a grating.

"Help me down," the girl said. Immediately this was done; Claire remained quite still. Her cheeks were smouldering and her left hand was lying inert in John Bulmer's broader palm.

"Wait here," she said, "and let me go in first. Someone may be on watch. There is perhaps danger—"

"My dear," said John Bulmer, "I perfectly comprehend you are about to enter that postern, and close it in my face, and afterward hold discourse with me through that little wicket. I assent, because I love you so profoundly that I am capable not merely of tearing the world asunder like paper at your command, but even of leaving you if you bid me do so."

"Your suspicions," she replied, "are prematurely marital. I am trying to protect you, and you are the first to accuse me of underhand dealing! I will prove to you how unjust are your notions." She entered the postern, closed and bolted it, and appeared at the wicket.

"The Friar was intelligent," said Claire de Puysange, "and beyond doubt the most sensible thing you can do is to get out of Poictesme as soon as possible. You have been serviceable to me, and for that I thank you: but the master of Bellegarde has the right of the low, the middle, and the high justice, and if my husband show his face at Bellegarde he will infallibly be hanged. If you claim me in England, Ormskirk will have you knifed in some dark alleyway, just as, you tell me, he disposed of Monsieur Traquair and Captain Dungelt. I am sorry, because I like you, even though you are fat."

"You bid me leave you?" said John Bulmer. He was comfortably seated upon the turf.

"For your own good," said she, "I advise you to." And she closed the wicket.

"The acceptance of advice," said John Bulmer, "is luckily optional. I shall therefore go down into the village, purchase a lute, have supper, and I shall be here at sunrise to greet you with an aubade, according to the ancient custom of Poictesme."

The wicket remained closed.

VI

"I WILL GO TO MARLY, inform Gaston of the entire matter, and then my wife is mine. I have tricked her neatly.

"I will do nothing of the sort. Gaston, can give me the woman's body only. I shall accordingly buy me a lute."

VII

ACHILLE CAZAIO ON THE TAUNENFELS did not sleep that night. . .

The two essays* dealing with the man have scarcely touched his capabilities. His exploits in and about Paris and his Gascon doings, while important enough in the outcome, are but the gesticulations of a puppet: the historian's real concern is with the hands that manoeuvered above Cazaio; and whether or no Achille Cazaio organized the riots in Toulouse and Guienne and Béarn is a question with which, at this late day, there can be little profitable commerce.

One recommends this Cazaio rather to the spinners of romance: with his morality—a trifle buccaneerish on occasion—once discreetly palliated, history affords few heroes more instantly taking to the fancy. . . One casts a hankering eye toward this Cazaio's rumored parentage, his hopeless and life-long adoration of Claire de Puysange, his dealings with d'Argenson and King Louis le Bien-Aimé, the obscure and mischievous imbroglios in Spain, and finally his aggrandizement and his flame-lit death, as du Maillot, say, records these happenings: and one finds therein the outline of an impelling hero, and laments that our traffic must be with a stolid and less livelily tinted Bulmer. And with a sigh one passes on toward the labor prearranged. . .

Tonight Cazaio's desires were astir, and consciousness of his own power was tempting him. He had never troubled Poictesme much: the Taunenfels were accessible on that side, and so long as he confined his depredations to the frontier, the Duc de Puysange merely shrugged

---

* The twenty-first chapter of Du Maillot's *Hommes Illustres*; and the fifth of d'Avranches's *Ancêtres de la Révolution*. Löwe has an excellent digest of this data.

and rendered his annual tribute; it was not a great sum, and the Duke preferred to pay it rather than forsake his international squabbles to quash a purely parochial nuisance like a bandit, who was, too, a kinsman. . .

Meanwhile Cazaio had grown stronger than de Puysange knew. It was a time of disaffection: the more violent here and there were beginning to assert that before hanging a superfluous peasant or two de Puysange ought to bore himself with inquiries concerning the abstract justice of the action. For everywhere the irrational lower classes were grumbling about the very miseries and maltreatments that had efficiently disposed of their fathers for centuries: they seemed not to respect tradition: already they were posting placards in the Paris boulevards,—"Shave the King for a monk, hang the Pompadour, and break Machault on the wheel,"—and already a boy of twelve, one Joseph Guillotin, was running about the streets of Saintes yonder. So the commoners flocked to Cazaio in the Taunenfels until, little by little, he had gathered an army about him.

And at Bellegarde, de Soyecourt had only a handful of men, Cazaio meditated tonight. And the woman was there,—the woman whose eyes were blue and incurious, whose face was always scornful.

In history they liken Achille Cazaio to Simon de Montfort, and the Gracchi, and other graspers at fruit as yet unripe; or, if the perfervid word of d'Avranches be accepted, you may regard him as "*le Saint-Jean de la Révolution glorieuse.*" But I think you may with more wisdom regard him as a man of strong passions, any one of which, for the time being, possessed him utterly.

Now he struck his palm upon the table.

"I have never seen a woman one-half so beautiful, Dom Michel. I am more than ever in love with her."

"In that event," the Friar considered, "it is, of course, unfortunate she should have a brand-new husband. Husbands are often thought much of when they are a novelty."

"You bungled matters, you fat, mouse-hearted rascal. You could quite easily have killed him."

The Dominican spread out his hands, and afterward reached for the bottle. "Milanese armor!" said Dom Michel Frégose.[*]

---

[*] The same ecclesiastic who more lately dubbed himself, with Maréchal de Richelieu's encouragement, l'Abbé de Trans, and was discreditably involved in the forgeries of Madame de St. Vincent.

JAMES BRANCH CABELL

"Yet I am master of Poictesme," Cazaio thundered, "I have ten men to de Soyecourt's one. Am I, then, lightly to be thwarted?"

"Undoubtedly you could take Bellegarde—and the woman along with the castle,—if you decided they were worth the price of a little killing. I think they are not worth it, I strongly advise you to have up a wench from the village, to put out the light, and exercise your imagination."

Cazaio shook his head. "No, Dom Michel, you churchmen live too lewdly to understand the tyranny of love."

"—Besides, there is that trifling matter of your understanding with de Puysange,—and, besides, de Puysange will be here in two days."

Cazaio snapped his fingers. "He will arrive after the fair." Cazaio uncorked the ink-bottle with an august gesture.

"Write!" said Achille Cazaio.

VIII

As John Bulmer leisurely ascended from the village the birds were waking. Whether day were at hand or no was a matter of twittering debate overhead, but in the west the stars were paling one by one, like candles puffed out by the pretentious little wind that was bustling about the turquoise cupola of heaven; and eastward Bellegarde showed stark, as though scissored from a painting, against a sky of gray-and-rose. Here was a world of faint ambiguity. Here was the exquisite tension of dawn, curiously a-chime with John Bulmer's mood, for just now he found the universe too beautiful to put any actual faith in its existence. He had strayed into Faëry somehow—into Atlantis, or Avalon, or "a wood near Athens,"—into a land of opalescence and vapor and delicate color, that would vanish, bubble-like, at the discreet tap of Pawsey fetching in his shaving-water; meantime John Bulmer's memory snatched at each loveliness, jealously, as a pug snatches bits of sugar.

Beneath her window he paused and shifted his lute before him. Then he began to sing, exultant in the unreality of everything and of himself in particular.

Sang John Bulmer,

> *"Speed forth, my song, the sun's ambassador,*
> *Lest in the east night prove the conqueror,*

The day be slain, and darkness triumph,—for
The sun is single, but her eyes are twain.

"And now the sunlight and the night contest
A doubtful battle, and day bides at best
Doubtful, until she waken. 'Tis attest
The sun is single.

"But her eyes are twain,—
And should the light of all the world delay,
And darkness prove victorious? Is it day
Now that the sun alone is risen?

"Nay,
The sun is single, but her eyes are twain,—
Twain firmaments that mock with heavenlier hue
The heavens' less lordly and less gracious blue,
And lit with sunlier sunlight through and through,

"The sun is single, but her eyes are twain,
And of fair things this side of Paradise
Fairest, of goodly things most goodly,"

He paused here and smote a resonant and louder chord. His voice ascended in dulcet supplication.

"Rise,
And succor the benighted world that cries,
The sun is single, but her eyes are twain!"

"Eh—? So it is you, is it?" Claire was peeping disdainfully from the window. Her throat was bare, and her dusky hair was a shade dishevelled, and in her meditative eyes he caught the flicker of her tardiest dream just as it vanished.

"It is I," John Bulmer confessed—"come to awaken you according to the ancient custom of Poictesme."

"I would much rather have had my sleep out," said she, resentfully. "In perfect frankness, I find you and your ancient customs a nuisance."

"You lack romance, my wife."

"Oh—?" She was a person of many cryptic exclamations, this bride of his. Presently she said: "Indeed, Monsieur Bulmer, I entreat you to leave Poictesme. I have informed Louis of everything, and he is rather furious."

John Bulmer said, "Do you comprehend why I have not already played the emigrant?"

After a little pause, she answered, "Yes."

"And for the same reason I can never leave you so long as this gross body is at my disposal. You are about to tell me that if I remain here I shall probably be hanged on account of what happened yesterday. There are grounds for my considering this outcome unlikely, but if I knew it to be inevitable—if I had but one hour's start of Jack Ketch,—I swear to you I would not budge."

"I am heartily sorry," she replied, "since if I had known you really cared for me—so much—I would never have married you. Oh, it is impossible!" the girl laughed, with a trace of worriment. "You had not laid eyes on me until a week ago yesterday!"

"My dear," John Bulmer answered, "I am perhaps inadequately acquainted with the etiquette of such matters, but I make bold to question if love is exclusively regulated by clock-ticks. Observe!" he said, with a sort of fury: "there is a mocking demon in me who twists my tongue into a jest even when I am most serious. I love you: and I dare not tell you so without a grin. Then when you laugh at me I, too, can laugh, and the whole transaction can be regarded as a parody. Oh, I am indeed a coward!"

"You are nothing of the sort! You proved that yesterday."

"Yesterday I shot an unsuspecting man, and afterward fenced with another—in a shirt of Milanese armor! Yes, I was astoundingly heroic yesterday, for the simple reason that all the while I knew myself to be as safe as though I were snug at home snoring under an eider-down quilt. Yet, to do me justice, I am a shade less afraid of physical danger than of ridicule."

She gave him a womanly answer. "You are not ridiculous, and to wear armor was very sensible of you."

"To the contrary, I am extremely ridiculous. For observe: I am an elderly man, quite old enough to be your father; I am fat—No, that is kind of you, but I am not of pleasing portliness, I am just unpardonably fat; and, I believe, I am not possessed of any fatal beauty of feature such as would by ordinary impel young women to pursue me with unsolicited affection: and being all this, I presume to love you. To me, at least, that appears ridiculous."

"Ah, do not laugh!" she said. "Do not laugh, Monsieur Bulmer!"

But John Bulmer persisted in that curious laughter. "Because," he presently stated, "the whole affair is so very diverting."

"Believe me," Claire began, "I am sorry that you care—so much. I—do not understand. I am sorry,—I am not sorry," the girl said, in a new tone, and you saw her transfigured; "I am glad! Do you comprehend?—I am glad!" And then she swiftly closed the window.

John Bulmer observed. "I am perhaps subject to hallucinations, for otherwise the fact had been previously noted by geographers that heaven is immediately adjacent to Poictesme."

IX

PRESENTLY THE OLD FLIPPANCY CAME back to him, since an ancient custom is not lightly broken; and John Bulmer smiled sleepily and shook his head. "Here am I on my honeymoon, with my wife locked up in the château, and with me locked out of it. My position savors too much of George Dandin's to be quite acceptable. Let us set about rectifying matters."

He came to the great gate of the castle and found two sentries there. He thought this odd, but they recognized him as de Soyecourt's guest, and after a whispered consultation admitted him. In the courtyard a lackey took charge of Monsieur Bulmer, and he was conducted into the presence of the Marquis de Soyecourt. "What the devil!" thought John Bulmer, "is Bellegarde in a state of siege?"

The little Marquis sat beside the Duchesse de Puysange, to the rear of a long table with a crimson cover. Their attitudes smacked vaguely of the judicial, and before them stood, guarded by four attendants, a ragged and dissolute looking fellow whom the Marquis was languidly considering.

"My dear man," de Soyecourt was saying as John Bulmer came into the room "when you brought this extraordinary epistle to Bellegarde, you must have been perfectly aware that thereby you were forfeiting your life. Accordingly, I am compelled to deny your absurd claims to the immunity of a herald, just as I would decline to receive a herald from the cockroaches."

"That is cowardly," the man said. "I come as the representative of an honorable enemy who desires to warn you before he strikes."

"You come as the representative of vermin," de Soyecourt retorted, "and as such I receive you. You will therefore, permit me to wish you a pleasant journey into eternity. Why, holà, madame! here is that vagabond guest of ours returned to observation!" The Marquis rose and stepped forward, all abeam. "Mr. Bulmer, I can assure you that I was never more delighted to see anyone in my entire life."

"Pardon, monseigneur," one of the attendants here put in,—"but what shall we do with this Achon?"

The Marquis slightly turned his head, his hand still grasping John Bulmer's. "Why, hang him, of course," he said. "Did I forget to tell you? But yes, take him out, and have him confessed by Frère Joseph, and hang him at once." The four men removed their prisoner.

"You find us in the act of dispensing justice," the Marquis continued, "yet at Bellegarde we temper it with mercy, so that I shall ask no indiscreet questions concerning your absence of last night."

"But I, monsieur," said John Bulmer, "I, too, have come to demand justice."

"Tête-bleu, Mr. Bulmer! and what can I have the joy of doing for you in that respect?"

"You can restore to me my wife."

And now de Soyecourt cast a smile toward the Duchess, who appeared troubled. "Would you not have known this was an Englishman," he queried, "by the avowed desire for the society of his own wife? They are a mad race. And indeed, Mr. Bulmer, I would very gladly restore to you this hitherto unheard-of spouse if but I were blest with her acquaintance. As it is—" He waved his hand.

"I married her only yesterday," said John Bulmer, "and I have reason to believe that she is now within Bellegarde."

He saw the eyes of de Soyecourt slowly narrow. "Jacques," said the Marquis, "fetch me the pistol within that cabinet." The Marquis resumed his seat to the rear of the table, the weapon lying before him. "You may go now, Jacques; this gentleman and I are about to hold a little private conversation." Then, when the door had closed upon the lackey, de Soyecourt said, "Pray draw up a chair within just ten feet of this table, monsieur, and oblige me with your wife's maiden name."

"She was formerly known," John Bulmer answered, "as Mademoiselle Claire de Puysange."

The Duchess spoke for the first time. "Oh, the poor man! Monsieur de Soyecourt, he is evidently insane."

"I do not know about that," the Marquis said, fretfully, "but in any event I hope that no more people will come to Bellegarde upon missions which, compel me to have them hanged. First there was this Achon, and now you, Mr. Bulmer, come to annoy me.—Listen, monsieur," he went on, presently: "last evening Mademoiselle de Puysange announced to the Duchess and me that her impending match with the Duke of Ormskirk must necessarily be broken off, as she was already married. She had, she stated, encountered you and a clergyman yonder the forest, where, on the spur of the moment, you two had espoused each other; and was quite unable to inform us what had become of you after the ceremony. You can conceive that, as a sensible man, I did not credit a word of her story. But now, as I understand it, you corroborate this moonstruck narrative?"

John Bulmer bowed his head. "I have that honor, monsieur."

De Soyecourt sounded the gong beside him. "In that event, it is uncommonly convenient to have you in hand. Your return, to Bellegarde I regard as opportune, even though I am compelled to attribute it to insanity; personally, I disapprove of this match with Milor Ormskirk, but as Gaston is bent upon it, you will understand that in reason my only course is to make Claire a widow as soon as may be possible."

"It is intended, then," John Bulmer queried, "that I am to follow Achon?"

"I can but trust," said the Marquis, politely, "that your course of life has qualified you for a superior flight, since Achon's departing, I apprehend, is not unakin to a descent."

"No!" the Duchess cried, suddenly; "Monsieur de Soyecourt, can you not see the man is out of his senses? Let Claire be sent for. There is some mistake."

De Soyecourt shrugged. "Yen know that I can refuse you nothing. Jacques," he called, to the appearing lackey, "request Mademoiselle de Puysange to honor us, if it be convenient, with her presence. Nay, I pray you, do not rise, Mr. Bulmer; I am of a nervous disposition, startled by the least movement, and my finger, as you may note, is immediately upon the trigger."

So they sat thus, John Bulmer beginning to feel rather foolish as time wore on, though actually it was not a long while before Claire had appeared in the doorway and had paused there. You saw a great wave of color flood her countenance, then swiftly ebb. John Bulmer observed, with a thrill, that she made no sound, but simply waited, composed and alert, to find out how much de Soyecourt knew before she spoke.

The little Marquis said, "Claire, this gentleman informs us that you married him yesterday."

Tranquilly she inspected her claimant. "I did not see Monsieur Bulmer at all yesterday, so far as I remember. Why, surely, Louis, you did not take my nonsense of last night in earnest?" she demanded, and gave a mellow ripple of laughter. "Yes, you actually believed it; you actually believed that I walked into the forest and married the first man I met there, and that this is he. As it happens I did not; so please let Monsieur Bulmer go at once, and put away that absurd pistol—at once, Louis, do you hear?"

The Duchess shook her head. "She is lying, Monsieur de Soyecourt, and undoubtedly this is the man."

John Bulmer went to the girl and took her hand. "You are trying to save me, I know. But need I warn you that the reward of Ananias was never a synonym for felicity?"

"Jean Bulmer! Jean Bulmer!" the girl asked, and her voice was tender; "why did you return to Bellegarde, Jean Bulmer?"

"I came," he answered, "for the absurd reason that I cannot live without you."

They stood thus for a while, both her hands clasped in his, "I believe you," she said at last, "even though I do not understand at all, Jean Bulmer." And then she wheeled upon the Marquis, "Yes, yes!" Claire said; "the man is my husband. And I will not have him harmed. Do you comprehend?—you shall not touch him, because you are not fit to touch him, Louis, and also because I do not wish it."

De Soyecourt looked toward the Duchess as if for advice. "It is a nuisance, but evidently she cannot marry Milor Ormskirk so long as Mr. Bulmer is alive. I suppose it would be better to hang him out-of-hand?"

"Monsieur de Puysange would prefer it, I imagine," said the Duchess; "nevertheless, it appears a great pity."

"In nature," the Marquis assented, "we deplore the loss of Mr. Bulmer's company. Yet as matters stand—"

"But they are in love with each other," the Duchess pointed out, with a sorry little laugh. "Can you not see that, my friend?"

"Hein?" said the Marquis; "why, then, it is doubly important that Mr. Bulmer be hanged as soon as possible." He reached for the gong, but Claire had begun to speak.

"I am not at all in love with him! You are of a profound imbecility, Hélène. I think he is a detestable person, because he always looks at you as if he saw something extremely ridiculous, but was too polite to notice it. He is invariably making me suspect I have a smut on my nose. But in spite of that, I consider him a very pleasant old gentleman, and I will not have him hanged!" With which ultimatum she stamped her foot.

"Yes, madame," said the Marquis, critically; "after all, she is in love with him. That is unfortunate, is it not, for Milor Ormskirk,—and even for Achille Cazaio," he added, with a shrug.

"I fail to see," a dignified young lady stated, "what Cazaio, at least, has to do with your galimatias."

"Simply that I received this morning a letter demanding you be surrendered to Cazaio," de Soyecourt answered as he sounded the gong. "Otherwise, our amiable friend of the Taunenfels announces he will attack Bellegarde. I, of course, hanged his herald and despatched messengers to Gaston, whom I look for tomorrow. If Gaston indeed arrive tomorrow morning, Mr. Bulmer, I shall relinquish you to him; in other circumstances will be laid upon me the deplorable necessity of summoning a Protestant minister from Manneville, and, after your spiritual affairs are put in order, of hanging you—suppose we say at noon?"

"The hour suits me," said John Bulmer, "as well as another. But no better. And I warn you it will not suit the Duke of Ormskirk, either, whose relative—whose very near relative—" He posed for the astounding revelation.

But little de Soyecourt had drawn closer to him. "Mr. Bulmer, I have somehow omitted to mention that two years ago I was at Aix-la-Chapelle, when the treaty was in progress, and there saw your great kinsman. I cut no particular figure at the convocation, and it is unlikely he recalls my features; but I remember his quite clearly."

"Indeed?" said John Bulmer, courteously; "it appears, then, that monsieur is a physiognomist?"

"You flatter me," the Marquis returned. "My skill in that science enabled me to deduce only the veriest truisms—such as that the man who for fifteen years had beaten France, had hoodwinked France, would in France be not oversafe could we conceive him fool enough to hazard a trip into this country."

"Especially alone?" said John Bulmer.

"Especially," the Marquis assented, "if he came alone. But, ma foi! I am discourteous. You were about to say—?"

"That a comic subject declines to be set forth in tragic verse," John Bulmer answered, "and afterward to inquire the way to my dungeon."

X

BUT JOHN BULMER ESCAPED A dungeon after all; for at parting de Soyecourt graciously offered to accept Mr. Bulmer's parole, which he gave willingly enough, and thereby obtained the liberty of a tiny enclosed garden, whence a stairway led to his new apartment on the second floor of what had been known as the Constable's Tower, since du Guesclin held it for six weeks against Sir Robert Knollys. This was a part of the ancient fortress in which, they say, Poictesme's most famous hero, Dom Manuel, dwelt and performed such wonders, a long while before Bellegarde was remodeled by Duke Florian.

The garden, gravel-pathed, was a trim place, all green and white. It contained four poplars, and in the center was a fountain, where three Nereids contended with a brawny Triton for the possession of a turtle whose nostrils spurted water. A circle of attendant turtles, half-submerged, shot inferior jets from their gaping mouths. It was an odd, and not unhandsome piece,* and John Bulmer inspected it with appreciation, and then the garden, and having found all things satisfactory, sat down and chuckled sleepily and waited.

"De Soyecourt has been aware of my identity throughout the entire week! Faith, then, I am a greater fool than even I suspected, since this fop of the boulevards has been able to trick me so long. He has some card up his sleeve, too, has our good Marquis—Eh, well! Gaston comes tomorrow, and thenceforward all is plain sailing. Meantime I conjecture that the poor captive will presently have visitors."

He had dinner first, though, and at this meal gave an excellent account of himself. Shortly afterward, as he sat over his coffee, little de Soyecourt unlocked the high and narrow gate which constituted the one entrance to the garden, and sauntered forward, dapper and smiling.

"I entreat your pardon, Monsieur le Duc," de Soyecourt began, "that I have not visited you sooner. But in unsettled times, you comprehend, the master of a beleaguered fortress is kept busy. Cazaio, I now learn,

---

* Designed by Simon Guillain. This fountain is still to be seen at Bellegarde, though the exuberancy of Revolutionary patriotism has bereft the Triton of his head and of the lifted arm.

means to attack tomorrow, and I have been fortifying against him. However, I attach no particular importance to the man's threats, as I have despatched three couriers to Gaston, one of whom must in reason get to him; and in that event Gaston should arrive early in the afternoon, accompanied by the dragoons of Entréchat. And subsequently—eh bien! if Cazaio has stirred up a hornets'-nest he has only himself to thank for it." The Marquis snapped his fingers and hummed a merry air, being to all appearance in excellent spirits.

"That is well," said John Bulmer,—"for, believe me, I shall be unfeignedly glad to see Gaston once more."

"Decidedly," said the Marquis, sniffing, "they give my prisoners much better coffee than they deign to afford me, I shall make bold to ask you for a cup of it, while we converse sensibly." He sat down opposite John Bulmer. "Oh, about Gaston," said the Marquis, as he added the sugar—"it is deplorable that you will not see Gaston again, at least, not in this naughty world of ours."

"I am the more grieved," said John Bulmer, gravely, "for I love the man."

"It is necessary, you conceive, that I hang you, at latest, before twelve o'clock tomorrow, since Gaston is a little too fond of you to fall in with my plans. His premature arrival would in effect admit the bull of equity into the china-shop of my intentions. And day-dreams are fragile stuff, Monsieur d'Ormskirk! Indeed, I am giving you this so brief reprieve only because I am, unwilling to have upon my conscience the reproach of hanging without due preparation a man whom of all politicians in the universe I most unfeignedly like and respect. The Protestant minister has been sent for, and will, I sincerely trust, be here at dawn. Otherwise—really, I am desolated, Monsieur le Duc, but you surely comprehend that I cannot wait upon his leisure."

John Bulmer cracked a filbert. "So I am to die tomorrow? I do not presume to dictate, monsieur, but I would appreciate some explanation of your motive."

"Which I freely render," the Marquis replied. "When I recognized you a week ago—as I did at first glance,—I was astounded. That you, the man in all the world most cordially hated by Frenchmen, should venture into France quite unattended was a conception to confound belief. Still, here you were, and I comprehended that such an opportunity would not rap twice upon the door. So I despatched a letter post-haste to Madame de Pompadour at Marly—"

"I begin to comprehend," John Bulmer said. "Old Tournehem's daughter* hates me as she hates no other man alive. Frankly, monsieur, the little strumpet has some cause to,—may I trouble you for the nut-crackers? a thousand thanks,—since I have outwitted her more than once, both in diplomacy and on the battle-field. With me out of the way, I comprehend that France might attempt to renew the war, and our late treaty would be so much wasted paper. Yes, I comprehend that the woman would give a deal for me—But what the devil! France has no allies. She dare not provoke England just at present; she has no allies, monsieur, for I can assure you that Prussia is out of the game. Then what is the woman driving at?"

"Far be it from me," said the Marquis, with becoming modesty, "to meddle with affairs of state. Nevertheless, madame is willing to purchase you—at any price."

John Bulmer slapped his thigh, "Kaunitz! behold the key. Eh, eh, I have it now; not long ago the Empress despatched a special ambassador to Versailles,—one Anton Wenzel Kaunitz, a man I never heard of. Why, this Moravian count is a genius of the first water. He will combine France and Austria, implacable enemies since the Great Cardinal's time. Ah, I have it now, monsieur,—Frederick of Prussia has published verses against the Pompadour which she can never pardon—eh, against the Czaritza, too! Why, what a thing it is to be a poet! now Russia will join the league. And Sweden, of course, because she wants Pomerania, which King Frederick claims. Monsieur de Soyecourt, I protest it will be one of the prettiest messes ever stirred up in history! And to think that I am to miss it all!"

"I regret," de Soyecourt said, "to deny you the pleasure of participation. In sober verity I regret it. But unluckily, Monsieur d'Ormskirk, your dissolution is the sole security of my happiness; and in effect"—he shrugged,—"you comprehend my unfortunate position."

"One of the prettiest messes ever stirred up in all history!" John Bulmer lamented; "and I to miss it! The policy of centuries shrugged aside, and the map of the world made over as lightly as if it were one of last year's gowns! Decidedly I shall never again cast reflections upon the woman in politics, for this is superb. Why, this coup is worthy of

---

* Mr. Bulmer here refers to a venerable scandal. The Pompadour was, in the eyes of the law, at least, the daughter of François Poisson.

me! And what is Petticoat the Second to give you, pray, for making all this possible?"

"She will give me," the Marquis retorted, "according to advices received from her yesterday, a lettre-de-cachet for Gaston de Puysange. Gaston is a man of ability, but he is also a man of unbridled tongue. He has expressed his opinion concerning the Pompadour, to cite an instance, as freely as ever did the Comte de Maurepas. You know what happened to de Maurepas. Ah, yes, Gaston is undoubtedly a peer of France, but the Pompadour is queen of that kingdom. And in consequence—on the day that Madame de Pompadour learns of your death,—Gaston goes to the Bastile."

"Naturally," John Bulmer assented, "since imprisonment in the Bastile is by ordinary the reward of common-sense when manifested by a Frenchman. What the devil, monsieur! The Duchess' uncle, Maréchal de Richelieu, has been there four times, and Gaston himself, if I am not mistaken, has sojourned there twice. And neither is one whit the worse for it."

The Marquis sipped his coffee. "The Bastile is not a very healthy place. Besides, I have a friend there,—a gaoler. He was formerly a chemist."

John Bulmer elevated the right eyebrow. "Poison?"

"Dieu m'en garde!" The Marquis was appalled. "Nay, monsieur, merely an unforeseeable attack of heart-disease."

"Ah! ah!" said John Bulmer, very slowly. He presently resumed: "Afterward the Duchesse de Puysange will be a widow. And already she is fond of you; but unfortunately the Duchess—with every possible deference,—is a trifle prudish. I see it all now, quite plainly; and out of pure friendliness, I warn you that in my opinion the Duchess is hopelessly in love with her husband."

"We should suspect no well bred lady of provincialism," returned the Marquis, "and so I shall take my chance. Believe me, Monsieur le Duc, I profoundly regret that you and Gaston must be sacrificed in order to afford me this same chance."

But John Bulmer was chuckling. "My faith!" he said, and softly chafed his hands together, "how sincerely you will be horrified when your impetuous error is discovered—just too late! You were merely endeavoring to serve your beloved Gaston and the Duke of Ormskirk when you hanged the rascal who had impudently stolen the woman intended to cement their friendship! The Duke fell a victim to his own folly, and you acted precipitately, perhaps, but out of pure zeal. You will probably weep. Meanwhile your lettre-de-cachet is on the road, and presently Gaston, too, is trapped and murdered. You weep yet more tears—oh, vociferous tears!—and the Duchess succumbs to you because you were so devotedly attached to her former husband. And England will sit snug while France reconquers Europe. Monsieur, I make you my compliments on one of the tidiest plots ever brooded over."

"It rejoices me," the Marquis returned, "that a conspirator of many years' standing should commend my maiden effort." He rose. "And now, Monsieur d'Ormskirk," he continued, with extended hand, "matters being thus amicably adjusted, shall we say adieu?"

John Bulmer considered. "Well,—no!" said he, at last; "I commend your cleverness, Monsieur de Soyecourt, but as concerns your hand I must confess to a distaste."

The Marquis smiled. "Because at the bottom of your heart you despise me," he said. "Ah, believe me, monsieur, your contempt for de Soyecourt is less great than mine. And yet I have a weakness for him,—a weakness which induces me to indulge all his desires."

He bowed with ceremony and left the garden.

XI

John Bulmer sat down to consider more at leisure these revelations. He foreread like a placard Jeanne d'Étoiles' magnificent scheme: it would convulse all Europe. England would remain supine, because Henry Pelham could hardly hold the ministry together, even now; Newcastle was a fool; and Ormskirk would be dead. He would barter his soul for one hour of liberty, he thought. A riot, now,—ay, a riot in Paris, a blow from within, would temporarily stupefy French enterprise and gain England time for preparation. And a riot could be arranged so easily! Meanwhile he was a prisoner, Pelham's hands were tied, and Newcastle was a fool, and the Pompadour was disastrously remote from being a fool.

"It is possible to announce that I am the Duke of Ormskirk—and to what end? Faith, I had as well proclaim myself the Pope of Rome or the Cazique of Mexico: the jackanapes will effect to regard my confession as the device of a desperate man and will hang me just the same; and his infernal comedy will go on without a hitch. Nay, I am fairly trapped, and Monsieur de Soyecourt holds the winning hand—Now that I think of it he even has, in Mr. Bulmer's letter of introduction, my formally signed statement that I am not Ormskirk. It was tactful of the small rascal not to allude to that crowning piece of stupidity: I appreciate his forbearance. But even so, to be outwitted—and hanged——by a smirking Hop-o'-my-thumb!

"Oh, this is very annoying!" said John Bulmer, in his impotence.

He sat down once more, sulkily, like an overfed cat, and began to read with desperate attention: "'Here may men understand that be of worship, that he was never formed that at every time might stand, but sometimes he was put to the worse by evil fortune. And at sometimes the worse knight putteth the better knight into rebuke.' Behold a niggardly salve rather than a panacea." He turned several pages. "'And then said Sir Tristram to Sir Lamorake, "I require you if ye happen to meet with Sir Palomides—"'" Startled, John Bulmer glanced about the garden.

It turned on a sudden into the primal garden of Paradise. "I came," she loftily explained, "because I considered it my duty to apologize in person for leading you into great danger. Our scouts tell us that already Cazaio is marshalling his men upon the Taunenfels."

"And yet," John Bulmer said, as he arose, and put away his book, "Bellegarde is a strong place. And our good Marquis, whatever else he may be, is neither a fool nor a coward."

Claire shrugged. "Cazaio has ten men to our one. Yet perhaps we can hold out till Gaston comes with his dragoons. And then—well, I have some influence with Gaston. He will not deny me,—ah, surely he will not deny me if I go down on my knees to him and wear my very prettiest gown. Nay, at bottom Gaston is kind, my friend, and he will spare you."

"To be your husband?" said John Bulmer.

Twice she faltered "No." And then she cried, with a sudden flare of irritation: "I do not love you! I cannot help that. Oh, you—you unutterable bully!"

Gravely he shook his head at her.

"But indeed you are a bully. You are trying to bully me into caring for you, and you know it. What else moved you to return to Bellegarde, and to sit here, a doomed man, tranquilly reading? Yes, but you were,—I happened to see you, through the key-hole in the gate. And why else should you be doing that unless you were trying to bully me into admiring you?"

"Because I adore you," said John Bulmer, taking affairs in order; "and because in this noble and joyous history of the great conqueror and excellent monarch, King Arthur, I find much diverting matter; and because, to be quite frank, Claire, I consider an existence without you neither alluring nor possible."

She had noticeably pinkened. "Oh, monsieur," the girl cried, "you are laughing because you are afraid that I will laugh at what you are saying to me. Believe me, I have no desire to laugh. It frightens me, rather. I had thought that nowadays no man could behave with a foolishness so divine. I had thought all such extravagancy perished with the Launcelot and Palomides of your book. And I had thought—that in any event, you had no earthly right to call me Claire."

"Superficially, the reproach is just," he assented, "but what was the name your Palomides cried in battle, pray? Was it not *Ysoude!* when his searching sword had at last found the joints of his adversary's armor, or when the foe's helmet spouted blood? *Ysoude!* when the line of adverse spears wavered and broke, and the Saracen was victor? Was it not *Ysoude!* he murmured riding over alien hill and valley in pursuit of the Questing Beast?—'the glatisant beast'? Assuredly, he cried *Ysoude!* and meantime La Beale Ysoude sits snug in Cornwall with Tristram, who dons his armor once in a while to roll Palomides in the sand *coram populo*. Still the name was sweet, and I protest the Saracen had a perfect right to mention it whenever he felt so inclined."

"You jest at everything," she lamented—"which is one of the many traits that I dislike in you."

"Knowing your heart to be very tender," he submitted, "I am endeavoring to present as jovial and callous an appearance as may be possible—to you, whom I love as Palomides loved Ysoude. Otherwise, you might be cruelly upset by your compassion and sympathy. Yet stay; is there not another similitude? Assuredly, for you love me much as Ysoude loved Palomides. What the deuce is all this lamentation to you? You do not value it the beard of an onion,—while of course grieving that your friendship should have been so utterly misconstrued, and wrongly interpreted,—and—trusting that nothing you have said or done has misled me—Oh, but I know you women!"

"Indeed, I sometimes wonder," she reflected, "what sort of women you have been friends with hitherto? They must have been very patient of nonsense."

"Ah, do you think so?—At all events, you interrupt my peroration. For we have fought, you and I, a—battle which is over, so far as I am concerned. And the other side has won. Well! Pompey was reckoned a very pretty fellow in his day, but he took to his heels at Pharsalia, for all that; and Hannibal, I have heard, did not have matters entirely his own way at Zama. Good men have been beaten before this. So, without stopping to cry over spilt milk,—heyho!" he interpolated, with a grimace, "it was uncommonly sweet milk, though,—let's back to our tents and reckon up our wounds."

"I am decidedly of the opinion," she said, "that for all your talk you will find your heart unscratched." Irony bewildered Claire, though she invariably recognized it, and gave it a polite smile.

John Bulmer said: "Faith, I do not intend to flatter your vanity by going into a decline on the spot. For in perfect frankness, I find no mortal wounds anywhere. No, we have it on the best authority that, while many men have died from time to time, and worms have eaten them, it was never for love. I am inclined to agree with Rosalind: an aneurism may be fatal, but a broken heart kills nobody. Lovers have died in divers manners since the antique world was made, but not the most luckless of them was slain by love. Even Palomides, as my book informs me, went abroad with Launcelot and probably died an old man here in France,—peaceably, in his bed, with the family physician in attendance, and every other circumstance becoming to a genteel demise. And I dare assert that long before this he had learned to chuckle over his youthful follies, and had protested to his wife that La Beale Ysoude squinted, or was freckled, or the like; and had insisted, laughingly, that the best of us must sow our wild oats. And at the last it was his wife who mixed his gruel and smoothed his pillow and sat up with him at night; so that if he died thinking of Madame Palomides rather than of La Beale Ysoude, who shall blame him? Not I, for one," said John Bulmer, stoutly; "If it was not heroic, it was at least respectable, and, above all, natural; and I expect some day to gasp out a similar valedictory. No, not tomorrow at noon, I think: I shall probably get out of this, somehow. And when, in any event, I set about the process of dying, I may be thinking of you, O fair lost lady! and again I may not be thinking of you. Who can say? A fly, for instance, may have lighted upon my nose and his tickling may have distracted my ultimate thoughts. Meanwhile, I love you consumedly, and you do not care a snap of your fingers for me."

"I—I am sorry," she said, inadequately.

"You are the more gracious." And his face sank down into his hands, and Claire was forgotten, for he was remembering Alison Pleydell and that ancient bankruptcy of his heart in youth, and this preposterous old John Bulmer (he reflected) was simply revelling in pity for himself.

A hand, feather-soft, fell upon, his shoulder, "And who was your Ysoude, Jean Bulmer?"

"A woman who died twenty years ago,—a woman dead before you were born, my dear."

Claire gave a little stifled moan, "Oh—oh, I loathe her!" she cried.

But when he raised his head Claire was gone.

XII

HE SAT LONG IN THE twilight, now; rising insensibly about him. The garden had become a grave, yet not unfriendly, place; the white straining Nereids were taking on a tinge of violet, the verdure was of a deeper hue, that was all; and the fountain plashed unhurriedly, as though measuring a reasonable interval (he whimsically imagined) between the asking of a riddle and its solution given gratis by the asker.

He loved the woman; granted: but did not love rise the higher above a corner-stone of delusion? And this he could never afford. He considered Claire to be not extravagantly clever, he could have improved upon her ears (to cite one instance), which were rather clumsily modelled; her finger-tips were a thought too thick, a shade too practical, and in fine she was no more the most beautiful woman in the world than she was the tallest: and yet he loved her as certainly he had loved none of his recent mistresses. Even so, here was no infatuation, no roseate and kindly haze surrounding a goddess, such as that which had by ordinary accompanied Alison Pleydell. . .

"I am grown older, perhaps. Perhaps it is merely that I am fashioned of baser stuff than—say, Achille Cazaio or de Soyecourt. Or perhaps it is that this overmastering, all-engulfing love is a mere figment of the poet, an age-long superstition as zealously preserved as that of the inscrutability of women, by men who don't believe a syllable of the nonsense they are transmitting. Ysoude is dead; and I love my young French wife as thoroughly as Palomides did, with as great a passion as was possible to either of us oldsters. Well! all life is a compromise; I compromise with tradition by loving her unselfishly, by loving her with the very best that remains in John Bulmer.

"And yet, I wish—

"True, I may be hanged at noon tomorrow, which would somewhat disconcert my plan. I shall not bother about that. Always there remains the chance that, somehow, Gaston may arrive in time: otherwise—why, otherwise I shall be hanged, and as to what will happen afterward I decline to enter into any discussion even with myself. I have my belief, but it is bolstered by no iota of knowledge. Faith, let us live this life as a gentleman should, and keep our hands and our consciences as clean as may be possible, and for the outcome trust to God's common-sense. There are people who must divert Him vastly by their frantic efforts to keep out of hell. For my own part, I would not think of wearing a pelisse in the Desert of Sahara merely because I happened to be sailing for Greenland during the ensuing week. I shall trust to His common-sense.

"And yet, I wish—

"I wish Reinault would hurry with the supper-trays. I am growing very hungry."

XIII

THAT NIGHT HE WAS ROUSED by a tapping at his door. "Jean Bulmer, Jean Bulmer! I have bribed Reinault. I have the keys. Come, and I will set you free."

"Free to do what?" said John Bulmer.

"To escape—to flee to your foggy England," said the voice without,— "and to your hideous Englishwomen."

"Do you go with me?" said John Bulmer.

"I do not." This was spoken from the turrets of decision.

"In that event," said John Bulmer, "I shall return to my dreams, which I infinitely prefer to the realities of a hollow existence. And, besides, now one thinks of it, I have given my parole."

An infuriate voice came through the key-hole. "You are undoubtedly a bully," it stated. "I loathe you." Followed silence.

Presently the voice said, "Because if you really loved her you were no better than she was, and so I hate you both."

"'Beautiful as an angel, and headstrong as a devil,'" was John

Bulmer's meditation. Afterward John Bulmer turned over and went back to sleep.

For after all, as he reflected, he had given his parole.

XIV

HE WAS AWAKENED LATER BY a shriek that was followed by a hubbub of tumult. John Bulmer sat erect in bed. He heard a medley of yelling, of musketry, and of crashes, like the dilapidation of falling battlements. He knew well enough what had happened. Cazaio and his men were making a night attack upon Bellegarde.

John Bulmer arose and, having lighted two candles, dressed himself. He cast aside the first cravat as a failure, knotted the second with scrupulous nicety, and afterward sat down, facing the door to his apartment, and trimmed his finger nails. Outside was Pandemonium, and the little scrap of sky visible from his one window was now of a sullen red.

"It is very curious I do not suffer more acutely. As a matter of fact, I am not conscious of any particular feeling at all. I believe that most of us when we are confronted with a situation demanding high joy or agony find ourselves devoid of emotion. They have evidently taken de Soyecourt by surprise. She is yonder in that hell outside and will inevitably be captured by its most lustful devil—or else be murdered. I am here like a trapped rat, impotent, waiting to be killed, which Cazaio's men will presently attend to when they ransack the place and find me. And I feel nothing, absolutely nothing.

"By this she has probably fallen into Cazaio's power—"

And the man went mad. He dashed upon the locked door, and tore at it with soft-white hands, so that presently they were all blood. He beat his face upon the door, cutting open his forehead.

He shook his bleeding hands toward heaven. "In my time I have been cruel. I am less cruel than You! Let me go!"

The door opened and she stood upon the threshold. His arms were about her and repeatedly he kissed her, mercilessly, with hard kisses, crushing her in his embrace.

"Jean, Jean!" she sobbed, beneath his lips, and lay quite still in his arms. He saw how white and tender a thing she was, and the fierce embrace relaxed.

"You came to me!" he said.

"Louis had forgotten you. They had all retreated to the Inner Tower.* Cazaio cannot take that, for he has no cannon. Louis can hold out there until Gaston comes with help," Claire rapidly explained. "But the thieves are burning Bellegarde. I could bribe no man to set you free. They were afraid to venture."

"And you came," said John Bulmer—"you left the tall safe Inner Tower to come to me!"

"I could not let you die, Jean Bulmer."

"Why, then I must live not unworthily the life which, you have given me. O God!" John Bulmer cried, "what a pitiful creature was that great Duke of Ormskirk! Now make a man of me, O God!"

"Listen, dear madman," she breathed; "we cannot go out into Bellegarde. They are everywhere—Cazaio's men. They are building huge fires about the Inner Tower; but it is all stone, and I think Louis can hold out. But we, Jean Bulmer, can only retreat to the roofing of this place. There is a trap-door to admit you to the top, and there— there we can at least live until the dawn."

"I am unarmed," John Bulmer said; "and weaponless, I cannot hold even a trap-door against armed men."

"I have brought you weapons," Claire returned, and waved one hand toward the outer passageway. "Naturally I would not overlook that. There were many dead men on my way hither, and they had no need of weapons. I have a sword here and two pistols."

"You are," said John Bulmer, with supreme conviction, "the most wonderful woman in the universe. By all means let us get to the top of this infernal tower and live there as long as we may find living possible. But first, will you permit me to make myself a thought tidier? For in my recent agitation as to your whereabouts I have, I perceive, somewhat disordered both my person and my apparel."

Claire laughed a little sadly. "You have been sincere for once in your existence, and you are hideously ashamed, is it not? Ah, my friend, I would like you so much better if you were not always playing at life, not always posing as if for your portrait."

"For my part," he returned, obscurely, from the rear of a wet towel, "I fail to perceive any particular merit in dying with a dirty face. We are

---

* The inner ward, or ballium, which (according to Quinault) was defended by ten towers, connected by an embattled stone wall about thirty feet in height and eight feet thick, on the summit of which was a footway; now demolished to make way for the famous gardens.

about to deal with a most important and, it well may be, the final crisis of our lives. So let us do it with decency."

Afterward John Bulmer changed his cravat, since the one he wore was soiled and crumpled and stained a little with his blood; and they went up the winding stairway to the top of the Constable's Tower. These two passed through the trap-door into a moonlight which drenched the world; westward the higher walls of the Hugonet Wing shut off that part of Bellegarde where men were slaughtering one another, and turrets, black and untenanted, stood in strong relief against a sky of shifting crimson and gold. At their feet was the tiny enclosed garden half-hidden by the poplar boughs. To the east the Tower dropped sheer to the moat; and past that was the curve of the highway leading to the main entrance of the château, and beyond this road you saw Amneran and the moonlighted plains of the Duardenez, and one little tributary, a thread of pulsing silver, in passage to the great river which showed as a smear of white, like a chalk-mark on the world's rim.

John Bulmer closed the trap door. They stood with clasped hands, eyes straining toward the east, whence help must arrive if help came at all.

"No sign of Gaston," the girl said. "We most die presently, Jean Bulmer."

"I am sorry," he said,—"Oh, I am hideously sorry that we two must die."

"I am not afraid, Jean Bulmer. But life would be very sweet, with you."

"That was my thought, too. . . I have always bungled this affair of living, you conceive. I had considered the world a healthy and not intolerable prison, where each man must get through his day's work as best he might, soiling his fingers as much as necessity demanded— but no more,—so that at the end he might sleep soundly—or perhaps that he might go to heaven and pluck eternally at a harp, or else to hell and burn eternally, just as divines say we will. I never bothered about it, much, so long as there was my day's work at hand, demanding performance. And in consequence I missed the whole meaning of life."

"That is not so!" Claire replied. "No man has achieved more, as everybody knows."

This was an odd speech. But he answered, idly: "Eh, I have done well enough as respectable persons judge these matters. And I went to church on Sundays, and I paid my tithes. Trifles, these, sweetheart; for in every man, as I now see quite plainly, there is a god. And the god must judge, and the man himself must be the temple and the instrument of the god. It is very simple, I see now. And whether he go to church or no is a matter of trivial importance, so long as the man obeys the god who is within him." John Bulmer was silent, staring vaguely toward the blank horizon.

"And now that you have discovered this," she murmured, "therefore you wish to live?"

"Why, partly on account of that," he said, "yet perhaps mostly on account of you. . . But heyho!" said John Bulmer; "I am disfiguring my last hours by inflicting upon a lady my half-baked theology. Let us sit down, my dear, and talk of trifles till they find us. And then I will kill you, sweetheart, and afterward myself. Presently come dawn and death; and my heart, according to the ancient custom of Poictesme, is crying, '*Oy Dieus! Oy Dieus, de l'alba tantost ve!*' But for all that, my mouth will resolutely discourse of the last Parisian flounces, or of your unfathomable eyes, or of Monsieur de Voltaire's new tragedy of *Oreste*,—or, in fine, of any topic you may elect."

He smiled, with a twinging undercurrent of regret that not even in impendent death did he find any stimulus to the heroical. But the girl had given a muffled cry.

"Look, Jean! Already they come for us."

Through the little garden a man was running, running frenziedly from one wall to another when he found the place had no outlet save the gate through which he had scuttled. It was fat Guiton, the steward of the Duc de Puysange. Presently came Achille Cazaio with a wet sword, and harried the unarmed old man, wantonly driving him about the poplars, pricking him in the quivering shoulders, but never killing him. All the while the steward screamed with a monotonous shrill wailing.

After a little he fell at Cazaio's feet, shrieking for mercy.

"Fool!" said the latter, "I am Achille Cazaio. I have no mercy in me."

He kicked the steward in the face two or three times, and Guiton, his countenance all blood, black in the moonlight, embraced the brigand's and wept. Presently Cazaio slowly drove his sword into the back of the prostrate man, who shrieked, "O Jesu!" and began to cough and choke. Five times Cazaio spitted the writhing thing, and afterward was Guiton's soul released from the tortured body.

"Is it well, think you," said John Bulmer, "that I should die without first killing Achille Cazaio?"

"No!" the girl answered, fiercely.

Then John Bulmer leaned upon the parapet of the Constable's Tower and called aloud, "Friend Achille, your conduct disappoints me."

The man started, peered about, and presently stared upward. "Monsieur Bulmaire, to encounter you is indeed an unlooked-for pleasure. May I inquire wherein I have been so ill-fated as to offend?"

"You have an engagement to fight me on Thursday afternoon, friend Achille, so that to all intent I hold a mortgage on your life. I submit that, in consequence, you have no right to endanger that life by besieging castles and wasting the night in assassinations."

"There is something in what you say, Monsieur Bulmaire," the brigand replied, "and I very heartily apologize for not thinking of it earlier. But in the way of business, you understand,—However, may I trust it will please you to release me from this inconvenient obligation?" Cazaio added, with a smile. "My men are waiting for me yonder, you comprehend."

"In fact," said John Bulmer, hospitably, "up here the moonlight is as clear as day. We can settle our affair in five minutes."

"I come," said Cazaio, and plunged into the entrance to the Constable's Tower.

"The pistol! quick!" said Claire.

"And for what, pray?" said John Bulmer.

"So that from behind, as he lifts the trap-door, I may shoot him through the head. Do you stand in front as though to receive him. It will be quite simple."

XV

"My dear creature," said John Bulmer, "I am now doubly persuaded that God entirely omitted what we term a sense of honor when He created the woman. I mean to kill this rapscallion, but I mean to kill him fairly." He unbolted the trap-door and immediately Cazaio stood upon the roof, his sword drawn.

Achille Cazaio stared at the tranquil woman, and now his countenance was less that of a satyr than of a demon. "At four in the morning! I congratulate you, Monsieur Bulmaire," he said,—"Oh, decidedly, I congratulate you."

"Thank you," said John Bulmer, sword in hand; "yes, we were married yesterday."

Cazaio drew a pistol from his girdle and fired full in John Bulmer's face; but the latter had fallen upon one knee, and the ball sped harmlessly above him.

"You are very careless with fire-arms," John Bulmer lamented, "Really, friend Achille, if you are not more circumspect you will presently injure somebody, and will forever afterward be consumed with unavailing regret and compunctions. Now let us get down to our affair."

They crossed blades in the moonlight, Cazaio was in a disastrous condition; John Bulmer's tolerant acceptance of any meanness that a Cazaio might attempt, the vital shame of this new and baser failure before Claire's very eyes, had made of Cazaio a crazed beast. He slobbered little flecks of foam, clinging like hoar-frost to the tangled beard, and he breathed with shuddering inhalations, like a man in agony, the while that he charged with redoubling thrusts. The Englishman appeared to be enjoying himself, discreetly; he chuckled as the other, cursing, shifted from tierce to quart, and he met the assault with a nice inevitableness. In all, each movement had the comely precision of finely adjusted clockwork, though at times John Bulmer's face showed a spurt of amusement roused by the brigand's extravagancy of gesture and Cazaio's contortions as he strove to pass the line of steel that flickered cannily between his sword and John Bulmer's portly bosom.

Then John Bulmer, too, attacked. "For Guiton!" said he, as his point slipped into Cazaio's breast. John Bulmer recoiled and lodged another thrust in the brigand's throat. "For attempting to assassinate me!" His foot stamped as his sword ran deep into Cazaio's belly. "For insulting my wife by thinking of her obscenely! You are a dead man, friend Achille."

Cazaio had dropped his sword, reeling as if drunken against the western battlement. "My comfort," he said, hoarsely, while one hand tore at his jetting throat—"my comfort is that I could not perish slain by a braver enemy." He moaned and stumbled backward. Momentarily his knees gripped the low embrasure. Then his feet flipped upward, convulsively, so that John Bulmer saw the man's spurs glitter and twitch in the moonlight, and John Bulmer heard a snapping and crackling and swishing among the poplars, and heard the heavy, unvibrant thud of Cazaio's body upon the turf.

"May he find more mercy than he has merited," said John Bulmer, "for the man had excellent traits. Yes, in him the making of a very good swordsman was spoiled by that abominable Boisrobert."

But Claire had caught him by the shoulder. "Look, Jean!"

He turned toward the Duardenez. A troop of horsemen was nearing. Now they swept about the curve in the highway and at their head was de Puysange, laughing terribly. The dragoons went by like a tumult in a sick man's dream, and the Hugonet Wing had screened them.

"Then Bellegarde is relieved," said John Bulmer, "and your life, at least, is saved."

The girl stormed. "You—you abominable trickster! You would not be content with the keys of heaven if you had not got them by outwitting somebody! Do you fancy I had never seen the Duke of Ormskirk's portrait? Gaston sent me one six months ago."

"Ah!" said John Bulmer, very quietly. He took up the discarded scabbard, and he sheathed his sword without speaking.

Presently he said, "You have been cognizant all along that I was the Duke of Ormskirk?"

"Yes," she answered, promptly.

"And you married me, knowing that I was—God save the mark!— the great Duke of Ormskirk? knowing that you made what we must grossly term a brilliant match?"

"I married you because, in spite of Jean Bulmer, you had betrayed yourself to be a daring and a gallant gentleman,—and because, for a moment, I thought that I did not dislike the Duke of Ormskirk quite so much as I ought to."

He digested this.

"O Jean Bulmer," the girl said, "they tell me you were ever a fortunate man, but I consider you the unluckiest I know of. For always you are afraid to be yourself. Sometimes you forget, and are just you—and then, ohé! you remember, and are only a sulky, fat old gentleman who is not you at all, somehow; so that at times I detest you, and at times I cannot thoroughly detest you. So that I played out the comedy, Jean Bulmer. I meant in the end to tell Louis who you were, of course, and not let them hang you; but I never quite trusted you; and I never knew whether I detested you or no, at bottom, until last night."

"Last night you left the safe Inner Tower to come to me—to save me at all hazards, or else to die with me—And for what reason, did you do this?"

"You are bullying me!" she wailed.

"And for what reason, did you do this?" he repeated, without any change of intonation.

"Can you not guess?" she asked. "Oh, because I am a fool!" she stated, very happily, for his arms were about her.

"Eh, in that event—" said the Duke of Ormskirk. "Look!" said he, with a deeper thrill of speech, "it is the dawn."

They turned hand in hand; and out of the east the sun came statelily, and a new day was upon them.

HEART OF GOLD

As Played at Paris, in the May of 1750

Cette amoureuse ardeur qui dans les coeurs s'excite N'est point, comme l'on sçait, un effet du merite; Le caprice y prend part, et, quand quelqu'un nous plaist, Souvent nous avons peine à dire pourquoy c'est. Mais on vois que l'amour se gouverne autrement."

Dramatis Personæ

Duc de Puysange, somewhat given to women, and now and then to good-fellowship, but a man of excellent disposition.

Marquis de Soyecourt, his cousin, and loves de Puysange's wife.

Duke of Ormskirk.

Duchesse de Puysange, a precise, but amiable and patient, woman.

Antoine, Lackeys to de Puysange, Etc.

Scene

Paris, mostly within and about the Hôtel de Puysange.

HEART OF GOLD

PROEM:—Necessitated by a Change of Scene

You are not to imagine that John Bulmer debated an exposure of de Soyecourt. "Live and let live" was the Englishman's axiom; the exuberant Cazaio was dead, his men were either slain or dispersed, and the whole tangle of errors—with judicious reservations—had now been unravelled to Gaston's satisfaction. And Claire de Puysange was now Duchess of Ormskirk. Why, then, meddle with Destiny, who appeared, after all, to possess a certain sense of equity?

So Ormskirk smiled as he presently went about Paris, on his own business, and when he and Louis de Soyecourt encountered each other their friendliness was monstrous in its geniality.

They were now one and all in Paris, where Ormskirk's marriage had been again, and more publicly, solemnized. De Puysange swore that his sister was on this occasion the loveliest person affordable by the resources of the universe, but de Soyecourt backed another candidate; so that over their wine the two gentlemen presently fell into a dispute.

"Nay, but I protest to you she is the most beautiful woman in all Paris!" cried the Marquis de Soyecourt, and kissed his finger-tips gallantly.

"My dear Louis," the Duc de Puysange retorted, "her eyes are noticeable, perhaps; and I grant you," he added, slowly, "that her husband is not often troubled by—that which they notice."

"—And the cleverest!"

"I have admitted she knows when to be silent. What more would you demand of any woman?"

"And yet—" The little Marquis waved a reproachful forefinger.

"Why, but," said the Duke, with utter comprehension, "it is not for nothing that our house traces from the great Jurgen—"

He was in a genial midnight mood, and, on other subjects, inclined to be garrulous; for the world, viewed through a slight haze, of vinous origin, seemed a pleasant place, and inspired a kindly desire to say diverting things about the world's contents. He knew the Marquis to be patient, and even stolid, under a fusillade of epigram and paradox; in short, de Puysange knew the hour and the antagonist for midnight talk to be at hand. And a saturnalia of phrases whirled in his brain, demanding utterance.

He waved them aside. Certain inbred ideas are strangely tenacious of existence, and it happened to be his wife they were discussing. It would not be good form, de Puysange felt, for him to evince great interest in this topic. . .

I

"AND YET," DE PUYSANGE QUERIED, as he climbed democratically into a public hackney coach, "why not? For my part, I see no good and sufficient reason for discriminating against the only woman one has sworn to love and cherish and honor. It is true that several hundred people witnessed the promise, with a perfect understanding of the jest, and that the keeping of this oath involves a certain breach of faith with society. Eh bien! let us, then, deceive the world—and the flesh—and the devil! Let us snap our fingers at this unholy trinity, and assert the right, when the whim takes us, to make unstinted love to our own wives!"

He settled back in the *fiacre* to deliberate. "It is bourgeois? Bah! the word is the first refuge of the unskilful poseur! It is bourgeois to be born, to breathe, to sleep, or eat; in which of the functions that consume the greater part of my life do I differ from my grocer? Bourgeois! why, rightly considered, to be a human being at all is quite inordinately bourgeois! And it is very notably grocer-like to maintain a grave face and two establishments, to chuckle privily over the fragments of the seventh commandment, to repent, upon detection, and afterward—ces bêtes-là!—to drink poison. Ma foi, I infinitely prefer the domestic coffee!"

The Duc de Puysange laughed, and made as though to wave aside the crudities of life. "All vice is bourgeois, and fornication in particular tends to become sordid, outworn, vieux jeu! In youth, I grant you, it is the unexpurgated that always happens. But at my age—misericorde!—the men yawn, and les demoiselles—bah! les demoiselles have the souls of accountants! They buy and sell, as my grocer does. The satiation of carnal desires is no longer a matter of splendid crimes and sorrows and kingdoms lost; it is a matter of business."

The harsh and swarthy face relaxed. With, a little sigh the Duc de Puysange had closed his fevered eyes. About them were a multitude of tiny lines, and of this fact he was obscurely conscious, in a wearied fashion, when he again looked out on the wellnigh deserted streets, now troubled by a hint of dawn. His eyes were old; they had seen much. Two workmen shambled by, chatting on their way to the day's work; in the attic yonder a drunken fellow sang, "Ah, bouteille ma mie," he bellowed, "pourquoi vous vuidez-vous?"

De Puysange laughed. "I suppose I have no conscience, but at least, I can lay claim to a certain fastidiousness. I am very wicked,"—he smiled, without mirth or bitterness,—"I have sinned notably as the world accounts it; indeed, I think, my repute is as abominable as that of any man living. And I am tired,—alas, I am damnably tired! I have found the seven deadly sins deadly, beyond, doubt, but only deadly dull and deadly commonplace. I have perseveringly frisked in the high places of iniquity, I have junketed with all evil gods, and the utmost they could pretend to offer any of their servitors was a spasm. I renounce them, as feeble-minded deities, I snap my fingers, very much as did my progenitor, the great Jurgen, at all their over-rated mysteries."

His glance caught and clung for a moment to the paling splendor of the moon that hung low in the vacant, dove-colored heavens. A faint pang, half-envy, half-regret, vexed the Duke with a dull twinge. "I wish too that by living continently I could have done, once for all, with this faded pose and this idle making of phrases! Eheu! there is a certain proverb concerning pitch so cynical that I suspect it of being truthful. However,—we shall see."

De Puysange smiled. "The most beautiful woman in all Paris? Ah, yes, she is quite that, is this grave silent female whose eyes are more fathomless and cold than oceans! And how cordially she despises me! Ma foi, I think that if her blood—which is, beyond doubt, of a pale-pink color,—be ever stirred, at all, it is with loathing of her husband. Well, life holds many surprises for madame, now that I become quite as virtuous as she is. We will arrange a very pleasant comedy of belated courtship; for are we not bidden to love one another? So be it,—I am henceforth the model père de famille."

Now the *fiacre* clattered before the Hôtel de Puysange.

The door was opened by a dull-eyed lackey, whom de Puysange greeted with a smile, "Bon jour, Antoine!" cried the Duke; "I trust that your wife and doubtless very charming children have good health?"

"Beyond question, monseigneur," the man answered, stolidly.

"That is excellent hearing," de Puysange said, "and it rejoices me to be reassured of their welfare. For the happiness of others, Antoine, is very dear to the heart of a father—and of a husband." The Duke chuckled seraphically as he passed down the hall. The man stared after him, and shrugged.

"Rather worse than usual," Antoine considered.

II

Next morning the Duchesse de Puysange received an immoderate armful of roses, with a fair copy of some execrable verses. De Puysange spent the afternoon, selecting bonbons and wholesome books,—"for his fiancée," he gravely informed the shopman.

At the Opéra he never left her box; afterward, at the Comtesse de Hauteville's, he created a furor by sitting out three dances in the conservatory with his wife. Mademoiselle Tiercelin had already received his regrets that he was spending that night at home.

III

The month wore on.

"It is the true honeymoon," said the Duke.

In that event he might easily have found a quieter place than Paris wherein to spend it. Police agents had of late been promised a premium for any sturdy beggar, whether male or female, they could secure to populate the new plantation of Louisiana; and as the premium was large, genteel burgesses, and in particular the children of genteel burgesses, were presently disappearing in a fashion their families found annoying. Now, from nowhere, arose and spread the curious rumor that King Louis, somewhat the worse for his diversions in the Parc-aux-Cerfs, daily restored his vigor by bathing in the blood of young children; and parents of the absentees began to manifest a double dissatisfaction, for the deduction was obvious.

There were riots. In one of them Madame de Pompadour barely escaped with her life,* and the King himself on his way to Compiègne, was turned back at the Porte St. Antoine, and forced to make a détour rather than enter his own capital. After this affair de Puysange went straight to his brother-in-law.

---

* This was on the afternoon of the famous ball given by the Pompadour in honor of the new Duchess of Ormskirk.

"Jean," said he, "for a newly married man you receive too much company. And afterward your visitors talk blasphemously in cabarets and shoot the King's musketeers. I would appreciate an explanation."

Ormskirk shrugged. "Merely a makeshift, Gaston. Merely a device to gain time wherein England may prepare against the alliance of France and Austria. Your secret treaty will never be signed as long as Paris is given over to rioters. Nay, the Empress may well hesitate to ally herself with a king who thus clamantly cannot govern even his own realm. And meanwhile England will prepare herself. We will be ready to fight you in five years, but we do not intend to be hurried about it."

"Yes," de Puysange assented;—"yet you err in sending Cumberland to defend Hanover. You will need a better man there."

Ormskirk slapped his thigh. "So you intercepted that last despatch, after all! And I could have sworn Candale was trustworthy!"

"My adored Jean," replied de Puysange, "he has been in my pay for six months! Console yourself with the reflection that you overbid us in Noumaria."

"Yes, but old Ludwig held out for more than the whole duchy is worth. We paid of course. We had to pay."

"And one of course congratulates you upon securing the quite essential support of that duchy. Still, Jean, if there were any accident—" De Puysange was really unbelievably ugly when he smiled. "For accidents do occur. . . It is war, then?"

"My dear fellow," said Ormskirk, "of course it is war. We are about to fly at each other's throats, with half of Europe to back each of us. We begin the greatest game we have ever played. And we will manage it very badly, I dare say, since we are each of us just now besotted with adoration of our wives."

"At times," said de Puysange, with dignity, "your galimatias are insufferable. Now let us talk like reasonable beings. In regard to Pomerania, you will readily understand that the interests of humanity—"

IV

STILL THE SUGGESTION HAUNTED HIM. It would be a nuance too ridiculous, of course, to care seriously for one's wife, and yet Hélène de Puysange was undeniably a handsome woman. As they sat over the remains of their dinner,—*à deux*, by the Duke's request,—she seemed to her husband quite incredibly beautiful. She exhaled the effects of a water-color in discreet and delicate tinctures. Lithe and fine and proud she was to the merest glance; yet patience, a thought conscious of itself, beaconed in her eyes, and she appeared, with urbanity, to regard life as, upon the whole, a countrified performance. De Puysange liked that air; he liked the reticence of every glance and speech and gesture,—liked, above all, the thinnish oval of her face and the staid splendor of her hair. Here was no vulgar yellow, no crass and hackneyed gold. . . and yet there was a clarified and gauzier shade of gold. . . the color of the moon by daylight, say. . . Then, as the pleasures of digestion lapsed gently into the initial amenities of sleep, she spoke.

"Monsieur," said she, "will you be pleased to tell me the meaning of this comedy?"

"Madame," de Puysange answered, and raised his gloomy eyebrows, "I do not entirely comprehend."

"Ah," said she, "believe me, I do not undervalue your perception. I have always esteemed your cleverness, monsieur, however much"—she paused for a moment, a fluctuating smile upon her lips,—"however much I may have regretted its manifestations. I am not clever, and to me cleverness has always seemed to be an infinite incapacity for hard work; its results are usually a few sonnets, an undesirable wife, and a warning for one's acquaintances. In your case it is, of course, different; you have your statesmanship to play with—"

"And statesmen have no need of cleverness, you would imply, madame?"

"I do not say that. In any event, you are the Duc de Puysange, and the weight of a great name stifles stupidity and cleverness without any partiality. With you, cleverness has taken the form of a tendency to intoxication, amours, and—amiability. I have acquiesced in this. But, for the past month—"

"The happiest period of my life!" breathed the Duke.

"—you have been pleased to present me with flowers, bonbons, jewels, and what not. You have actually accorded your wife the courtesies you usually preserve for the ladies of the ballet. You have dogged my footsteps, you have attempted to intrude into my bedroom, you have talked to me as—well, very much as—"

"Much as the others do?" de Puysange queried, helpfully. "Pardon me, madame, but, in one's own husband, I had thought this very routine might savor of originality."

The Duchess flushed, "All the world knows, monsieur, that in your estimation what men have said to me, or I to them, has been for fifteen years a matter of no moment! It is not due to you that I am still—"

"A pearl," finished the Duke, gallantly,—then touched himself upon the chest,—"cast before swine," he sighed.

She rose to her feet. "Yes, cast before swine!" she cried, with a quick lift of speech. She seemed very tall as she stood tapping her fingers upon the table, irresolutely; but after an instant she laughed and spread out her fine hands in an impotent gesture. "Ah, monsieur," she said, "my father entrusted to your keeping a clean-minded girl! What have you made of her, Gaston?"

A strange and profoundly unreasonable happiness swept through the Duke's soul as she spoke his given name for the first time within his memory. Surely, the deep contralto voice had lingered over it?—half-tenderly, half-caressingly, one might think.

The Duke put aside his coffee-cup and, rising, took his wife's soft hands in his. "What have I made of her? I have made of her, Hélène, the one object of all my desires."

Her face flushed. "Mountebank!" she cried, and struggled to free herself; "do you mistake me, then, for a raddle-faced actress in a barn? Ah, les demoiselles have formed you, monsieur,—they have formed you well!"

"Pardon!" said the Duke. He released her hands, he swept back his hair with a gesture of impatience. He turned from his wife, and strolled toward a window, where, for a little, he tapped upon the pane, his murky countenance twitching oddly, as he stared into the quiet and sunlit street. "Madame," he began, in a level voice, "I will tell you the meaning of the comedy. To me,—always, as you know, a creature of whims,—there came, a month ago, a new whim which I thought attractive, unconventional, promising. It was to make love to my own wife rather than to another man's. Ah, I grant you, it is incredible," he cried, when the Duchess raised her hand as though to speak,—"incredible, fantastic, and ungentlemanly! So be it; nevertheless, I have played out my rôle. I have been the model husband; I have put away wine and—les demoiselles; for it pleased me, in my petty insolence, to patronize, rather than to defy, the laws of God and man. Your perfection irritated me, madame; it pleased me to demonstrate how easy is this trick of treating the world as the antechamber of a future existence. It pleased me to have in my life one space, however short, over which neither the Recording Angel nor even you might draw a long countenance. It pleased me, in effect, to play out the comedy, smug-faced and immaculate,—for the time. I concede that I have failed in my part. Hiss me from the stage, madame; add one more insult to the already considerable list of those affronts which I have put upon you; one more will scarcely matter."

She faced him with set lips. "So, monsieur, your boasted comedy amounts only to this?"

"I am not sure of its meaning, madame. I think that, perhaps, the swine, wallowing in the mire which they have neither strength nor will to leave, may yet, at times, long—and long whole-heartedly—" De Puysange snapped his fingers. "Peste!" said he, "let us now have done with this dreary comedy! Beyond doubt de Soyecourt has much to answer for, in those idle words which were its germ. Let us hiss both collaborators, madame."

"De Soyecourt!" she marveled, with, a little start. "Was it he who prompted you to make love to me?"

"Without intention," pleaded the Duke. "He twitted me for my inability, as your husband, to gain your affections; but I do not question his finest sensibilities would be outraged by our disastrous revival of Philemon and Baucis."

"Ah—!" said she. She was smiling at some reflection or other.

There was a pause. The Duc de Puysange drummed upon the window-pane; the Duchess, still faintly smiling, trifled with the thin gold chain that hung about her neck. Both knew their display of emotion to have been somewhat unmodern, not entirely *à la mode*.

"Decidedly," spoke de Puysange, and turned toward her with a slight grimace, "I am no longer fit to play the lover; yet a little while, madame, and you must stir my gruel-posset, and arrange the pillows more comfortably about the octogenarian."

"Ah, Gaston," she answered, and in protest raised her slender fingers, "let us have no more heroics. We are not well fitted for them, you and I."

"So it would appear," the Duc de Puysange conceded, not without sulkiness.

"Let us be friends," she pleaded. "Remember, it was fifteen years ago I made the grave mistake of marrying a very charming man—"

"Merci!" cried the Duke.

"—and I did not know that I was thereby denying myself the pleasure of his acquaintance. I have learned too late that marrying a man is only the most civil way of striking him from one's visiting-list." The Duchess hesitated. "Frankly, Gaston, I do not regret the past month."

"It has been adorable!" sighed the Duke.

"Yes," she admitted; "except those awkward moments when you would insist on making love to me."

"But no, madame," cried he, "it was precisely—"

"O my husband, my husband!" she interrupted, with a shrug of the shoulders; "why, you do it so badly!"

The Duc de Puysange took a short turn about the apartment. "Yet I married you," said he, "at sixteen—out of a convent!"

"Mon ami," she murmured, in apology, "am I not to be frank with you? Would you have only the connubial confidences?"

"But I had no idea—" he began.

"Why, Gaston, it bored me to the very verge of yawning in my lover's countenance. I, too, had no idea but that it would bore you equally—"

"Hein?" said the Duke.

"—to hear what d'Humières—"

"He squints!" cried the Duc de Puysange.

"—or de Créquy—"

"That red-haired ape!" he muttered.

"—or d'Arlanges, or—or any of them, was pleased to say. In fact, it was my duty to conceal from my husband anything which might involve him in duels. Now that we are friends, of course it is entirely different."

The Duchess smiled; the Duke walked up and down the room with the contained ferocity of a caged tiger.

"In duels! in a whole series of duels! So these seducers besiege you in platoons. Ma foi, friendship is a good oculist! Already my vision improves."

"Gaston!" she cried. The Duchess rose and laid both hands upon his shoulders. "Gaston—?" she repeated.

For a heart-beat the Duc de Puysange looked into his wife's eyes; then he sadly smiled and shook his head. "Madame," said the Duke, "I do not doubt you. Ah, believe me, I have comprehended, always, that in your keeping my honor was quite safe—far more safe than in mine, as Heaven and most of the fiends well know. You have been a true and faithful wife to a worthless brute who has not deserved it." He lifted her fingers to his lips. De Puysange stood very erect; his heels clicked together, and his voice was earnest. "I thank you, madame, and I pray you to believe that I have never doubted you. You are too perfect to err—Frankly, and between friends." added the Duke, "it was your cold perfection which frightened me. You are an icicle, Hélène."

She was silent for a moment. "Ah!" she said, and sighed; "you think so?"

"Once, then—?" The Duc de Puysange seated himself beside his wife, and took her hand.

"I—it was nothing." Her lashes fell, and dull color flushed through her countenance.

"Between friends," the Duke suggested, "there should be no reservations."

"But it is such a pitiably inartistic little history!" the Duchess protested. "Eh bien, if you must have it! For I was a girl once,—an innocent girl, as given as are most girls to long reveries and bright, callow day-dreams. And there was a man—"

"There always is," said the Duke, darkly.

"Why, he never even knew, mon ami!" cried his wife, and laughed, and clapped her hands. "He was much older than I; there were stories about him—oh, a great many stories,—and one hears even in a convent—" She paused with a reminiscent smile. "And I used to wonder shyly what this very fearful reprobate might be like. I thought of him with de Lauzun, and Dom Juan, and with the Duc de Grammont, and all those other scented, shimmering, magnificent libertines over whom les ingénues—wonder; only, I thought of him, more often than of the others, I made little prayers for him to the Virgin. And I procured a tiny miniature of him. And, when I came out of the convent, I met him at my father's house.* And that was all."

"All?" The Duc de Puysange had raised his swart eyebrows, and he slightly smiled.

"All," she re-echoed, firmly. "Oh, I assure you he was still too youthful to have any time to devote to young girls. He was courteous—no more. But I kept the picture,—ah, girls are so foolish, Gaston!" The Duchess, with a light laugh, drew upward the thin chain about her neck. At its end was a little heart-shaped locket of dull gold, with a diamond sunk deep in each side. She regarded the locket with a

---

* She was of the Aigullon family, and sister to d'Agenois, the first and very politic lover of Madame de la Tournelle, afterward mistress to Louis Quinze under the title of Duchesse de Châteauroux. The later relations between the d'Aigullons and Madame du Barry are well-known.

quaint sadness. "It is a long while since I have seen that miniature, for it has been sealed in here," said she, "ever since—since some one gave me the locket."

Now the Duc de Puysange took this trinket, still tepid and perfumed from contact with her flesh. He turned it awkwardly in his hand, his eyes flashing volumes of wonderment and inquiry. Yet he did not appear jealous, nor excessively unhappy. "And never," he demanded, some vital emotion catching at his voice—"never since then—?"

"I never, of course, approved of him," she answered; and at this point de Puysange noted—so near as he could remember for the first time in his existence,—the curve of her trailing lashes. Why but his wife had lovely eyelashes, lashes so unusual that he drew nearer to observe them more at his ease. "Still,—I hardly know how to tell you—still, without him the world was more quiet, less colorful; it held, appreciably, less to catch the eye and ear. Eh, he had an air, Gaston; he was never an admirable man, but, somehow, he was invariably the centre of the picture."

"And you have always—always you have cared for him?" said the Duke, drawing nearer and yet more near to her.

"Other men," she murmured, "seem futile and of minor importance, after him." The lashes lifted. They fell, promptly. "So, I have always kept the heart, mon ami. And, yes, I have always loved him, I suppose."

The chain had moved and quivered in his hand. Was it man or woman who trembled? wondered the Duc de Puysange. For a moment he stood immovable, every nerve in his body tense. Surely, it was she who trembled? It seemed to him that this woman, whose cold perfection had galled him so long, now stood with downcast eyes, and blushed and trembled, too, like any rustic maiden come shamefaced to her first tryst.

"Hélène—!" he cried.

"But no, my story is too dull," she protested, and shrugged her shoulders, and disengaged herself—half-fearfully, it seemed to her husband. "Even more insipid than your comedy," she added, with a not unkindly smile. "Do we drive this afternoon?"

"In effect, yes!" cried the Duke. He paused and laughed—a low and gentle laugh, pulsing with unutterable content. "Since this afternoon, madame—"

"Is cloudless?" she queried.

"Nay, far more than that," de Puysange amended; "it is refulgent."

V

WHAT TIME THE DUCHESS PREPARED her person for the drive the Duke walked in the garden of the Hôtel de Puysange. Up and down a shady avenue of lime-trees he paced, and chuckled to himself, and smiled benignantly upon the moss-incrusted statues,—a proceeding that was, beyond any reasonable doubt, prompted by his happiness rather than by the artistic merits of the postured images, since they constituted a formidable and broken-nosed collection of the most cumbrous, the most incredible, and the most hideous instances of sculpture the family of Puysange had been able to accumulate for, as the phrase is, love or money. Amid these mute, gray travesties of antiquity and the tastes of his ancestors, the Duc de Puysange exulted.

"Ma foi, will life never learn to improve upon the extravagancies of romance? Why, it is the old story,—the hackneyed story of the husband and wife who fall in love with each other! Life is a very gross plagiarist. And she—did she think I had forgotten how I gave her that little locket so long ago? Eh, ma femme, so 'some one'—'some one' who cannot be alluded to without a pause and an adorable flush—presented you with your locket! Nay, love is not always blind!"

The Duke paused before a puff-jawed Triton, who wallowed in an arid basin and uplifted toward heaven what an indulgent observer might construe as a broken conch-shell. "Love! Mon Dieu, how are the superior fallen! I have not the decency to conceal even from myself that I love my wife! I am shameless, I had as lief proclaim it from the house-tops. And a month ago—tarare, the ignorant beast I was! Moreover, at that time I had not passed a month in her company,—eh bien, I defy Diogenes and Timon to come through such a testing with unscratched hearts. I love her. And she loves me!"

He drew a deep breath, and he lifted his comely hands toward the pale spring sky, where the west wind was shepherding a sluggish flock of clouds. "O sun, moon, and stars!" de Puysange said, aloud: "I call you to witness that she loves me! Always she has loved me! O kindly little universe! O little kings, tricked out with garish crowns and sceptres, you are masters of your petty kingdoms, but I am master of her heart!

"I do not deserve it," he conceded, to a dilapidated faun, who, though his flute and the hands that held it had been missing for over a quarter of a century, piped, on with unimpaired and fatuous mirth. "Ah, heart of gold—demented trinket that you are, I have not merited that you

JAMES BRANCH CABELL

should retain my likeness all these years! If I had my deserts—parbleu! let us accept such benefits as the gods provide, and not question the wisdom of their dispensations. What man of forty-three may dare to ask for his deserts? No, we prefer instead the dealings of blind chance and all the gross injustices by which so many of us escape hanging" . . .

VI

"So madame has visitors? Eh bien, let us, then, behold these naughty visitors, who would sever a husband from his wife!"

From within the Red Salon came a murmur of speech,—quiet, cordial, colorless,—which showed very plainly that madame had visitors. As the Duc de Puysange reached out his hand to draw aside the portières, her voice was speaking, courteously, but without vital interest.

"—and afterward," said she, "weather permitting—"

"Ah, Hélène!" cried a voice that the Duke knew almost as well, "how long am I to be held at arm's-length by these petty conventionalities? Is candor never to be permitted?"

The half-drawn portière trembled in the Duke's grasp. He could see, from where he stood, the inmates of the salon, though their backs were turned. They were his wife and the Marquis de Soyecourt. The Marquis bent eagerly toward the Duchesse de Puysange, who had risen as he spoke.

For a moment she stayed as motionless as her perplexed husband; then, with a wearied sigh, the Duchess sank back into a *fauteuil*. "You are at liberty to speak," she said, slowly, and with averted glance—"what you choose."

The portière fell; but between its folds the Duke still peered into the room, where de Soyecourt had drawn nearer to the Duke's wife. "There is so little to say," the Marquis murmured, "beyond what my eyes have surely revealed a great while ago—that I love you."

"Ah!" the Duchess cried, with a swift intaking of the breath which was almost a sob. "Monsieur, I think you forget that you are speaking to the wife of your kinsman and your friend."

The Marquis threw out his hands in a gesture which was theatrical, though the trouble that wrung his countenance seemed very real. He was, as one has said, a slight, fair man, with the face of an ecclesiastic and the eyes of an aging seraph. A dull pang shot through the Duke as he thought of the two years' difference in their ages, and of his own tendency to embonpoint, and of the dismal features which calumniated him. Yonder porcelain fellow was in appearance so incredibly young!

"Do you consider," said the Marquis, "that I do not know I act an abominable part? Honor, friendship and even decency!—ah, I regret their sacrifice, but love is greater than these petty things!"

The Duchess sighed. "For my part," she returned, "I think differently. Love is, doubtless, very wonderful and beautiful, but I am sufficiently old-fashioned to hold honor yet dearer. Even—even if I loved you, monsieur, there are certain promises, sworn before the altar, that I could not forget." She looked up, candidly, into the flushed, handsome face of the Marquis.

"Words!" he cried, with vexed impatiency.

"An oath," she answered, sadly,—"an oath that I may not break."

There was hunger in the Marquis' eyes, and his hands lifted. Their glances met for a breathless moment, and his eyes were tender, and her eyes were resolute, but very, very compassionate.

"I love you!" he said. He said no more than this, but none could doubt he spoke the truth.

"Monsieur," the Duchess replied, and the depths of her contralto voice were shaken like the sobbing of a violin, and her hands stole upward to her bosom, and clasped the gold heart, as she spoke,—"monsieur, ever since I first knew you, many years ago, at my father's home, I have held you as my friend. You were more kind to the girl, Monsieur de Soyecourt, than you have been to the woman. Yet only since our stay in Poictesme yonder have I feared for the result of our friendship. I have tried to prevent this result. I have failed." The Duchess lifted the gold heart to her lips, and her golden head bent over it. "Monsieur, before God, if I had loved you with my whole being,—if I had loved you all these years,—if the sight of your face were to me today the one good thing life holds, and the mere sound of your voice had power to set my heart to beating—beating"—she paused for a little, and then rose, with a sharp breath that shook her slender body visibly,—"even then, my Louis, the answer would be the same; and that is,—go!"

"Hélène—!" he murmured; and his outstretched hands, which trembled, groped toward her.

"Let us have no misunderstanding," she protested, more composedly; "you have my answer."

De Soyecourt did not, at mildest, lead an immaculate life. But by the passion that now possessed him the tiny man seemed purified and transfigured beyond masculinity. His face was ascetic in its reverence as he waited there, with his head slightly bowed. "I go," he said, at last, as if picking his way carefully among tumbling words; then bent over her hand, which, she made no effort to withdraw. "Ah, my dear!" cried the Marquis, staring into her shy, uplifted eyes, "I think I might have made you happy!"

His arm brushed the elbow of the Duke as de Soyecourt left the salon. The Marquis seemed aware of nothing: the misery of both the men, as de Puysange reflected, was of a sort to be disturbed by nothing less noticeable than an earthquake.

VII

"If I had loved you all these years," murmured the Duc de Puysange. His dull gaze wandered toward the admirable "Herodias" of Giorgione which hung there in the corridor: the strained face of the woman, the accented muscles of her arms, the purple, bellying cloak which spread behind her, the livid countenance of the dead man staring up from the salver,—all these he noted, idly. It seemed strange that he should be appraising a painting at this particular moment.

"Well, now I will make recompense," said the Duke.

VIII

He came into the room, humming a tune of the boulevards; the crimson hangings swirled about him, the furniture swayed in aerial and thin-legged minuets. He sank into a chair before the great mirror, supported by frail love-gods, who contended for its possession. He viewed therein his pale and grotesque reflection, and he laughed lightly. "Pardon, madame," he said, "but my castles in the air are tumbling noisily about my ears. It is difficult to think clearly amid the crashing of the battlements."

"I do not understand." The Duchess had lifted a rather grave and quite incurious face as he entered the salon.

"My life," laughed the Duc de Puysange, "I assure you I am quite incorrigible. I have just committed another abominable action; and I cry *peccavi!*" He smote himself upon the breast, and sighed portentously. "I accuse myself of eavesdropping."

"What is your meaning?" She had now risen to her feet.

"Nay, but I am requited," the Duke reassured her, and laughed with discreetly tempered bitterness. "Figure to yourself, madame! I had planned for us a life during which our new-born friendship was always to endure untarnished. Eh bien, man proposes! De Soyecourt is of a jealous disposition; and here I sit, amid my fallen aircastles, like that tiresome Marius in his Carthaginian débris."

"De Soyecourt?" she echoed, dully.

"Ah, my poor child!" said the Duke and, rising, took her hand in a paternal fashion, "did you think that, at this late day, the disease of matrimony was still incurable? Nay, we progress, madame. You shall have grounds for a separation—sufficient, unimpeachable grounds. You shall have your choice of desertion, infidelity, cruelty in the presence of witnesses—oh, I shall prove a yeritabie Gilles de Retz!" He laughed, not unkindlily, at her bewilderment.

"You heard everything?" she queried.

"I have already confessed," the Duke reminded her. "And speaking as an unprejudiced observer, I would say the little man really loves you. So be it! You shall have your separation, you shall marry him in all honor and respectability; and if everything goes well, you shall be a grand duchess one of these days—Behold a fact accomplished!" De Puysange snapped his fingers and made a pirouette; he began to hum, "Songez de bonne à suivre—"

There was a little pause.

"You, in truth, desire to restore to me my freedom?" she asked, in wonder, and drew near to him.

The Duc de Puysange seated himself, with a smile. "Mon Dieu!" he protested, "who am I to keep lovers apart? As the first proof of our new-sworn friendship, I hereby offer you any form of abuse or of maltreatment you may select."

She drew yet nearer to him. Afterward, with a sigh as if of great happiness, her arms clasped about his neck. "Mountebank! do you, then, love me very much?"

"I?" The Duke raised his eyebrows. Yet, he reflected, there was really no especial harm in drawing his cheek a trifle closer to hers, and he found the contact to be that of cool velvet.

"You love me!" she repeated, softly.

"It pains me to the heart," the Duke apologized—"it pains me, pith and core, to be guilty of this rudeness to a lady; but, after all, honesty is a proverbially recommended virtue, and so I must unblushingly admit I do nothing of the sort."

"Gaston, why will you not confess to your new friend? Have I not pardoned other amorous follies?" Her cheeks were warmer now, and softer than those of any other woman in the world.

"Eh, ma mie," cried the Duke, warningly, "do not be unduly elated by little Louis' avowal! You are a very charming person, but—'*de gustibus*—'"

"Gaston—!" she murmured.

"Ah, what is one to do with such a woman!" De Puysange put her from him, and he paced the room with quick, unequal strides.

"Yes, I love you with every nerve and fibre of my body—with every not unworthy thought and aspiration of my misguided soul! There you have the ridiculous truth of it, the truth which makes me the laughing-stock of well bred persons for all time. I adore you. I love you, I cherish you sufficiently to resign you to the man your heart has chosen. I—But pardon me,"—and he swept a white hand over his brow, with a little, choking laugh,—"since I find this new emotion somewhat boisterous. It stifles one unused to it."

She faced him, inscrutably; but her eyes were deep wells of gladness. "Monsieur," she said, "yours is a noble affection. I will not palter with it, I accept your offer—"

"Madame, you act with your usual wisdom," said the Duke.

"—Upon condition," she continued,—"that you resume your position as eavesdropper."

The Duke obeyed her pointing finger. When he had reached the portières, the proud, black-visaged man looked back into the salon, wearily. She had seated herself in the *fauteuil*, where the Marquis de Soyecourt had bent over her and she had kissed the little gold locket. Her back was turned toward, her husband; but their eyes met in the great mirror, supported by frail love-gods, who contended for its possession.

"Comedy for comedy," she murmured. He wondered what purblind fool had called her eyes sea-cold?

"I do not understand," he said. "You saw me all the while—Yes, but the locket—?" cried de Puysange.

"Open it!" she answered, and her speech, too, was breathless.

Under his heel the Duc de Puysange ground the trinket. The long, thin chain clashed and caught about his foot; the face of his youth smiled from the fragment in his not quite steady hands. "O heart of gold! O heart of gold!" he said, with, a strange meditative smile, now that his eyes lifted toward the glad and glorious eyes of his wife; "I am not worthy! Indeed, my dear, I am not worthy!"

IX
THE SCAPEGOATS

As Played at Manneville, September 18, 1750

L'on a choisi justement le temps que je parlois à mon traiste de fils. Sortons! Je veux aller querir la justice, et faire donner la question à toute ma maison; à servantes, à valets, à fils, à fille, et à moi aussi."

Dramatis Personæ

Prince de Gatinais, an old nobleman, who affects yesterday's fashion.

Louis Quillan, formerly Louis de Soyecourt, son to the Prince, and newly become Grand Duke of Noumaria.

Vanringham, valet to the Prince.

Nelchen Thorn, daughter to Hans Thorn, landlord of the *Golden Pomegranate*, and loves Louis Quillan.

And In the Proem, Duke of Osmskirk.

Scene

The Dolphin Room of the *Golden Pomegranate*, an inn at Manneville-en-Poictesme.

THE SCAPEGOATS

PROEM:—To Present Mr. Vanringham as Nuntius

However profoundly the Duc de Puysange now approved of the universe and of its management, it is not to be supposed that in consequence he intended to overlook de Soyecourt's perfidy. De Puysange bore his kinsman no malice; indeed, he was sincerely fond of the Marquis, sympathized with him at bottom, and heartily regretted that the excellence of poor Louis' taste should be thus demonstrably counterbalanced by the frailty of his friendship. Still, one cannot entirely disregard the conventions: Louis had betrayed him, had before the eyes of de Puysange made love to de Puysange's wife. A duel was the inevitable consequence, though of course the Duke did not intend to kill poor Louis, who might before long be very useful to French statesmanship. So the Duke sent Ormskirk to arrange a meeting.

A floridly handsome man in black was descending the stairway of the Hôtel de Soyecourt at the moment the Duke of Ormskirk stepped cheerily from his coach. This person saluted the plump nobleman with due deference, and was accorded in return a little whistling sound of amazement.

"Mr. Vanringham, as I live—and in Paris! Man, will you hare-brained Jacobites never have done with these idiotic intrigues? Nay, in sincerity, Mr. Vanringham, this is annoying."

"My Lord Duke," said the other, "I venture to suggest that you forget I dare no longer meddle with politics, in light of my recent mishap at Tunbridge. Something of the truth leaked out, you comprehend— nothing provable, thank God!—but while I lay abed Captain Audaine was calling daily to inquire when would my wound be healed sufficiently for me to have my throat cut. I found England unsalubrious, and vanished."

Ormskirk nodded his approval. "I have always esteemed your common-sense. Now, let us consider—yes, I might use you here in Paris, I believe. And the work is light and safe,—a trifle of sedition, of stirring up a street riot or two."

Vanringham laughed. "I might have recognized your hand in the late disturbances, sir. As matters stand, I can only thank your Grace and regret that I have earlier secured employment. I've been, since April, valet to the old Prince de Gâtinais, Monsieur de Soyecourt's father."

"Yet lackeyship smacks, however vaguely, of an honest livelihood. You disappoint me, Mr. Vanringham."

"Nay, believe me, I yet pilfer a cuff-button or perhaps a jewel, when occasion offers, lest any of my talents rust. For we reside at Beaujolais yonder, my Lord Duke, where we live in retirement and give over our old age to curious chemistries. It suits me well enough. I find the air of Beaujolais excellent, my duties none too arduous, and the girls of the country-side neither hideous nor obdurate. Oho, I'm tolerably content at Beaujolais—the more for that 'tis expedient just now to go more softly than ever Ahab did of old."

"Lest your late associates get wind of your whereabouts? In that I don't question your discretion, Mr. Vanringham. And out of pure friendliness I warn you Paris is a very hotbed of hot-headed Jacobites who would derive unmerited pleasure from getting a knife into your ribs."

"Yet on an occasion of such importance—" Vanringham began; then marvelled in reply to the Duke's look of courteous curiosity: "You han't heard, sir, that my master's son is unexpectedly become the next Grand Duke of Noumaria!"

"Zounds!" said his Grace of Ormskirk, all alert, "is old Ludwig dead at last? Why, then, the damned must be holding a notable carnival by this, in honor of his arrival. Hey, but there was a merry rascal, a thorough-paced—" He broke off short. He laughed. "What the devil, man! Monsieur de Soyecourt is Ludwig's nephew, I grant you, on the maternal side, but Ludwig left a son. De Soyecourt remains de Soyecourt so long as Prince Rudolph lives,—and Prince Rudolph is to marry the Elector of Badenburg's daughter this autumn, so that we may presently look for any number of von Freistadts to perpetuate the older branch. Faith, you should study your *Genealogischer Hofkalender* more closely, Mr. Vanringham."

"Oh, but very plainly your Grace has heard no word of the appalling tragedy that hath made our little Louis a reigning monarch—"

With gusto Francis Vanringham narrated the details of Duke Ludwig's last mad freak* which, as the world knows, resulted in

* In his *Journal* Horace Calverley gives a long and curious account of the disastrous masque at Breschau of which he, then on the Grand Tour, had the luck to be an eye-witness. His hints as to the part played in the affair by Kaunitz are now, of course, largely discredited by the later confessions of de Puysange.

JAMES BRANCH CABELL

the death of both Ludwig and his son, as well as that of their five companions in the escapade,—with gusto, for in progress the soul of the former actor warmed to his subject. But Ormskirk was sensibly displeased.

"Behold what is termed a pretty kettle of fish!" said the Duke, in meditation, when Vanringham had made an end. "Plainly, Gaston cannot fight the rascal, since Hop-o'-my-thumb is now, most vexatiously, transformed into a quasi-Royal Personage, Assassination, I fear, is out of the question. So all our English plans will go to pot. A Frenchman will reign in Noumaria,—after we had not only bought old Ludwig, but had paid for him, too! Why, I suppose he gave that damnable masquerade on the strength of having our money,—good English money, mark you, Mr. Vanringham, that we have to squeeze out of honest tax-payers to bribe such, rascals with, only to have them, cheat us by cooking themselves to a crisp! This is annoying, Mr. Vanringham."

"I don't entirely follow your Grace—"

"It is not perhaps desirable you should. Yet I give you a key. It is profoundly to be deplored that little Louis de Soyecourt, who cannot draw a contented breath outside of his beloved Paris, should be forced to marry Victoria von Uhm, in his cousin's place,—yes, for Gaston will arrange that, of course,—and afterward be exiled to a semi-barbarous Noumaria, where he must devote the rest of his existence to heading processions and reviewing troops, and signing proclamations and guzzling beer and sauerkraut. Nay, beyond doubt, Mr. Vanringham, this is deplorable. 'Tis an appalling condition of affairs: it reminds me of Ovid among the Goths, Mr. Vanringham!"

"I'm to understand, then—?" the valet stammered.

"You are to understand that I am more deeply your debtor than I could desire you to believe; that I am going to tell the Marquis de Soyecourt all which I have told you, though I must reword it for him, as eloquently as may be possible; and that I even now feel myself to be Ciceronic." The Duke of Ormskirk passed on with a polite nod.

NEXT DAY THEY GOSSIPED BUSILY at Versailles over the sudden disappearance of Louis de Soyecourt. No more was heard of him for months. The mystery was discussed, and by the wits embroidered, and by the imaginative annotated, but it was never solved until the following September.

I

FOR IT WAS IN SEPTEMBER that, upon the threshold of the *Golden Pomegranate*, at Manneville in Poictesme, Monsieur Louis Quillan paused, and gave the contented little laugh which had of late become habitual with him. "We are en fête tonight, it appears. Has the King, then, by any chance dropped in to supper with us, Nelchen?"

Silently the girl bestowed a provisional pat upon one fold of the white table-cloth and regarded the result with critical approval. All being in blameless order, she moved one of the candlesticks the width of a needle. The table was now garnished to the last resource of the *Golden Pomegranate*: the napery was snow, the glassware and the cutlery shone with a frosty glitter, and the great bowl of crimson roses afforded the exact splurge of vainglorious color and glow she had designed. Accordingly, being now at leisure, Nelchen now came toward Monsieur Quillan, lifting her lips to his precisely as a child might have done.

"Not quite the King, my Louis. None the less I am sure that Monseigneur is an illustrious person. He arrived not two hours ago—" She told how Monseigneur had come in a coach, very splendid; even his lackeys were resplendent. Monseigneur would stay overnight and would tomorrow push on, to Beauséant. He had talked with her,—a kindly old gentleman, but so stately that all the while she had been the tiniest thought afraid of him. He must be some exalted nobleman, Nelchen considered,—a marquis at the very least.

Meantime diminutive Louis Quillan had led her to the window-seat beneath the corridor, and sat holding one plump trifle of a hand, the, while her speech fluttered bird-like from this topic to that; and be regarded Nelchen Thorn with an abysmal content. The fates, he considered, had been commendably generous to him.

So he leaned back from her a little, laughing gently, and marked what a quaint and eager child it was. He rejoiced that she was beautiful, and triumphed still more to know that even if she had not been beautiful it would have made slight difference to him. The soul of Nelchen was enough. Yet, too, it was desirable this soul should be appropriately clad, that she should have, for instance, these big and lustrous eyes,—plaintive eyes, such as a hamadryad would conceivably possess, since they were beyond doubt the candid and appraising eyes of some woodland creature, and always seemed to find the world not precisely intimidating, perhaps, yet in the ultimate a very curious place where one trod gingerly. Still, this Nelchen was a practical body, prone to laughter,—as in nature, any person would be whose mouth was all rotund and tiny scarlet curves. Why, it was, to a dimple, the mouth which François Boucher bestowed on his sleek goddesses! Louis Quillan was sorry for poor Boucher painting away yonder at a noisy garish Versailles, where he would never see that perfect mouth the artist had so often dreamed of. No, not in the sweet flesh at least; lips such as these were unknown at Versailles. . .

And but four months ago he had fancied himself to be in love with Hélène de Puysange, he remembered; and, by and large, he still considered Hélène a delightful person. Yes, Hélène had made him quite happy last spring: and when they found she was with child, and their first plan failed, she had very adroitly played out their comedy to win back Gaston in time to avoid scandal. Yes, you could not but admire Hélène, yet, even so. . .

"—and he asked me, oh, so many questions about you, Louis—"

"About me?" said Louis Quillan, blankly. He was all circumspection now.

"About my lover, you stupid person. Monseigneur assumed, somehow, that I would have a lover or two. You perceive that he at least is not a stupid person." And Nelchen tossed her head, with a touch of the provocative.

Louis Quillan did what seemed advisable. "—and, furthermore, your stupidity is no excuse for rumpling my hair," said Nelchen, by and by.

"Then you should not pout," replied Monsieur Quillan. "Sanity is entirely too much to require of any man when you pout. Besides, your eyes are so big and so bright they bewilder one. In common charity you ought to wear spectacles, Nelchen,—in sheer compassion toward mankind."

"Monseigneur, also, has wonderful eyes, Louis. They are like the stars,—very brilliant and cool and incurious, yet always looking at you as though you were so insignificant that the mere fact of your presuming to exist at all was a trifle interesting."

"Like the stars!" Louis Quillan had flung back the shutter. It was a tranquil evening in September, with no moon as yet, but with a great multitude of lesser lights overhead. "Incurious like the stars! They do dwarf one, rather. Yet just now I protest to you, infinitesimal man that I am, I half-believe le bon Dieu loves us so utterly that He has kindled all those pretty tapers solely for our diversion. He wishes us to be happy,

Nelchen; and so He has given us the big, fruitful, sweet-smelling world to live in, and our astonishing human bodies to live in, with contented hearts, and with no more vain desires, no loneliness—Why, in a word, He has given us each other. Oh, beyond doubt, He loves us, my Nelchen!"

For a long while the girl was silent. Presently she spoke, half-hushed, like one in the presence of sanctity. "I am happy. For these three months I have been more happy than I had thought was permissible on earth. And yet, Louis, you tell me that those stars are worlds perhaps like ours,—think of it, my dear, millions and millions of worlds like ours, and on each world perhaps a million of lovers like us! It is true that among them all no woman loves as I do, for that would be impossible. Yet think of it, mon ami, how inconsiderable a thing is the happiness of one man and of one woman in this immensity! Why, we are less than nothing, you and I! Ohé, I am afraid, hideously afraid, Louis,—for we are such little folk and the universe is so big. And always the storms go about it, and its lightnings thrust at us, and the waters of it are clutching at our feet, and its laws are not to be changed—Oh, it is big and cruel, my dear, and we are adrift in it, we who are so little!"

He again put forth his hand toward her. "What a morbid child it is!" said Louis Quillan. "I can assure you I have resided in this same universe just twice as long as you, and I find that upon the whole the establishment is very creditably conducted. There arrives, to be sure, an occasional tornado, or perhaps an earthquake, each with its incidental inconveniences. On the other hand, there is every evening a lavishly arranged sunset, like gratis fireworks, and each morning (I am credibly informed) a sunrise of which poets and energetic people are pleased to speak highly; while every year spring comes in, like a cosmical upholsterer, and refurnishes the entire place, and makes us glad to live. Nay, I protest to you, this is an excellent world, my Nelchen! and likewise I protest to you that in its history there was never a luckier nor a happier man than I."

Nelchen considered. "Well," she generously conceded; "perhaps, after all, the stars are more like diamonds."

Louis Quillan chuckled. "And since when were you a connoisseur of diamonds, my dear?"

"Of course I have never actually seen any. I would like to, though— yes, Louis, what I would really like would be to have a bushelful or so of diamonds, and to marry a duke—only the duke would have to be you, of course,—and to go to Court, and to have all the fine ladies very jealous of me, and for them to be very much in love with you, and for you not to care a sou for them, of course, and for us both to see the King." Nelchen paused, quite out of breath after this ambitious career in the imaginative.

"To see the King, indeed!" scoffed little Louis Quillan. "Why, we would see only a very disreputable pockmarked wornout lecher if we did."

"Still," she pointed out, "I would like to see a king. Simply because I never have done so before, you conceive."

"At times, my Nelchen, you are effeminate. Eve ate the apple for that identical reason. Yet what you say is odd, because—do you know?—I once had a friend who was by way of being a sort of king."

Nelchen gave a squeal of delight. "And you never told me about him! I loathe you."

Louis Quillan did what seemed advisable. "—and, furthermore, your loathsomeness is no excuse for rumpling my hair," said Nelchen, by and by.

"But there is so little to tell. His father had married the Grand Duke of Noumaria's daughter,—over yonder between Silesia and Badenburg, you may remember. And so last spring when the Grand Duke and the Prince were both killed in that horrible fire, my friend quite unexpectedly became a king—oh, king of a mere celery-patch, but still a sort of king. Figure to yourself, Nelchen! they were going to make my poor friend marry the Elector of Badenburg's daughter,—and Victoria von Uhm has perfection stamped upon her face in all its odious immaculacy,—and force him to devote the rest of his existence to heading processions and reviewing troops, and signing proclamations, and guzzling beer and sauerkraut. Why, he would have been like Ovid among the Goths, my Nelchen!"

"But he could have worn such splendid uniforms!" said Nelchen. "And diamonds!"

"You mercenary wretch!" said he. Louis Quillan then did what seemed advisable; and presently he added, "In any event, the horrified man ran away."

"That was silly of him," said Nelchen Thorn. "But where did he run to?"

Louis Quillan considered. "To Paradise," he at last decided. "And there he found a disengaged angel, who very imprudently lowered herself to the point of marrying him. And so he lived happily ever afterward. And so, till the day of his death, he preached the doctrine that silliness is the supreme wisdom."

"And he regretted nothing?" Nelchen said, after a meditative while.

Louis Quillan began to laugh. "Oh, yes! at times he profoundly regretted Victoria von Uhm."

Then Nelchen gave him a surprise, for the girl bent toward him and leaned one hand upon each shoulder. "Diamonds are not all, are they, Louis? I thank you, dear, for telling me of what means so much to you. I can understand, I think, because for a long while I have tried to know and care for everything that concerns you."

The little man had risen to his feet. "Nelchen—!"

"Hush!" said Nelchen Thorn; "Monseigneur is coming down to his supper."

II

It was a person of conspicuous appearance, both by reason of his great height and leanness as well as his extreme age, who now descended the straight stairway leading from the corridor above. At Court they would have told you that the Prince de Gâtinais was a trifle insane, but he troubled the Court very little, since he had spent the last twenty years, with brief intermissions, at his château near Beaujolais, where, as rumor buzzed it, he had fitted out a laboratory, and had devoted his old age to the study of chemistry. "Between my flute and my retorts, my bees and my chocolate-creams," the Prince was wont to say, "I manage to console myself for the humiliating fact that even Death has forgotten my existence." For he had a child's appetite for sweets, and was at this time past eighty, though still well-nigh as active as Antoine de Soyecourt had ever been, even when—a good half-century ago—he had served, with distinction under Louis Quatorze.

Tonight the Prince de Gâtinais was all in steel-gray, of a metallic lustre, with prodigiously fine ruffles at his throat and wrists. You would have found something spectral in the tall, gaunt old man, for his periwig was heavily powdered, and his deep-wrinkled countenance was of an absolute white, save for the thin, faintly bluish lips and the inklike glitter of his narrowing eyes, as he now regarded the couple waiting hand in hand before him, like children detected in mischief.

Little Louis Quillan had drawn an audible breath at first sight of the newcomer. Monsieur Quillan did not speak, however, but merely waited.

"You have fattened," the Prince de Gâtinais said, at last, "I wish I could fatten. It is incredible that a man who eats pounds of sugar daily should yet remain a skeleton." His voice was guttural, and a peculiar slur ran through his speech, caused by the loss of his upper front teeth at Ramillies.

Louis Quillan came of a stock not lightly abashed. "I have fattened on a new diet, monsieur,—on happiness. But, ma foi! I am discourteous. Permit me, my father, to present Mademoiselle Nelchen Thorn, who has so far honored me as to consent to become my wife. 'Nelchen, I present to you my father, the Prince de Gâtinais."

"Oh—?" observed Nelchen, midway in her courtesy.

But the Prince had taken her fingers and he kissed them quite as though they had been the finger-tips of the all-powerful Pompadour at Versailles yonder. "I salute the future Marquise de Soyecourt. You young people will sup with me, then?"

"No, monseigneur, for I am to wait upon the table," said Nelchen, "and Father is at Sigéan overnight, having the mare shod, and there is only Leon, and, oh, thank you very much indeed, monseigneur, but I had much rather wait on the table."

The Prince waved his hand. "My valet, mademoiselle, is at your disposal. Vanringham!" he called.

From the corridor above descended a tall red-headed fellow in black. "Monseigneur—?"

"Go!" quickly said Louis de Soyecourt, while the Prince spoke with his valet,—"go, Nelchen, and make yourself even more beautiful if such a thing be possible. He will never resist you, my dear—ah, no, that is out of nature."

"You will find more plates in the cupboard, Monsieur Vanringham," remarked Nelchen, as she obediently tripped up the stairway, toward her room in the right wing. "And the knives and forks are in the second drawer."

So Vanringham laid two covers in discreet silence; then bowed and withdrew by the side door that led to the kitchen. The Prince had seated himself beside the open fire, where he yawned and now looked up with a smile.

"Well, Louis," said the Prince de Gâtinais—"so Monsieur de Puysange and I have run you to earth at last. And I find you have determined to defy me, eh?"

III

"I TRUST THERE IS NO question of defiance," Louis de Soyecourt equably returned. "Yet I regret you should have been at pains to follow me, since I still claim the privilege of living out my life in my own fashion."

"You claim a right which never existed, my little son. It is not demanded of any man that he be happy, whereas it is manifestly necessary for a gentleman to obey his God, his King, and his own conscience without swerving. If he also find time for happiness, well and good; otherwise, he must be unhappy. But, above all, he must intrepidly play out his allotted part in the good God's scheme of things, and must with due humbleness recognize that the happiness or the unhappiness of any man alive is a trivial consideration as against the fulfilment of this scheme."

"You and Nelchen are much at one there," the Marquis lightly replied; "yet, for my part, I fancy that Providence is not particularly interested in who happens to be the next Grand Duke of Noumaria."

The Prince struck with his hand upon the arm of his chair. "You dare to jest! Louis, your levity is incorrigible. France is beaten, discredited among nations, naked to her enemies. She lies here, between England and Prussia, as in a vise. God summons you, a Frenchman, to reign in Noumaria, and in addition affords you a chance to marry that weathercock of Badenburg's daughter. Ah, He never spoke more clearly, Louis. And you would reply with a shallow jest! Why, Badenburg and Noumaria just bridge that awkward space between France and Austria. Your accession would confirm the Empress,—Gaston de Puysange has it in her own hand, yonder at Versailles! I tell you it is all planned that France and Austria will combine, Louis! Think of it,—our France on her feet again, mistress of Europe, and every whit of it your doing, Louis,—ah, my boy, my boy, you cannot refuse!"

Thus he ran on in a high, disordered voice, pleading, clutching at his son with a strange new eagerness which now possessed the Prince de Gâtinais. He was remembering the France which he had known; not the ignoble, tawdry France of the moment, misruled by women,

　　　　　JAMES BRANCH CABELL

rakes, confessors, and valets, but the France of his dead Sun King; and it seemed to Louis de Soyecourt that the memory had brought back with it the youth of his father for an instant. Just for a heart-beat, the lank man towered erect, his cheeks pink, and every muscle tense.

Then Louis de Soyecourt shook his head. In England's interest, as he now knew, Ormskirk had played upon de Soyecourt's ignorance and his love of pleasure, as an adept plays upon the strings of a violin; but de Soyecourt had his reason, a gigantic reason, for harboring no grudge against the Englishman.

"Frankly, my father, I would not give up Nelchen though all Europe depended upon it. I am a coward, perhaps; but I have my chance of happiness, and I mean to take it. So Cousin Otto is welcome to the duchy. I infinitely prefer Nelchen."

"Otto! a general in the Prussian army, Frederick's property, Frederick's idolater!" The old Prince now passed from an apex of horror to his former pleading tones. "But, then, it is not necessary you give up Nelchen. Ah, no, a certain latitude is permissible in these matters, you understand. She could be made a countess, a marquise,—anything you choose to demand, my Louis. And you could marry Princess Victoria just the same—"

"Were you any other man, monsieur," said Louis de Soyecourt, "I would, of course, challenge you. As it is, I can only ask you to respect my helplessness. It is very actual helplessness, sir, for Nelchen has been bred in such uncourtly circles as to entertain the most provincial notions about becoming anybody's whore."

Now the Prince de Gâtinais sank back into the chair. He seemed incredibly old now. "You are right," he mumbled,—"yes, you are right, Louis. I have talked with her. With her that would be impossible. These bourgeois do not understand the claims of noble birth."

The younger man had touched him upon the shoulder. "My father,—" he began.

"Yes, I am your father," said the other, dully, "and it is that which puzzles me. You are my own son, and yet you prefer your happiness to the welfare of France, to the very preservation of France. Never in six centuries has there been a de Soyecourt to do that. God and the King we served. . . six centuries. . . and today my own son prefers an innkeeper's daughter. . ." His voice trailed and slurred like that of one speaking in his sleep, for he was an old man, and by this the flare of his excitement had quite burned out, and weariness clung about his senses like a drug. "I will go back to Beaujolais. . . to my retorts and my bees. . . and forget there was never a de Soyecourt in six centuries, save my own son. . ."

"My father!" Louis de Soyecourt cried, and shook him gently. "Ah, I dare say you are right, in theory. But in practice I cannot give her up. Surely you understand—why, they tell me there was never a more ardent lover than you. They tell me—And you would actually have me relinquish Nelchen, even after you have seen her! Yet remember, monsieur, I love her much as you loved my mother,—that mettlesome little princess whom you stole from the very heart of her court.* Ah, I have heard tales of you, you conceive. And Nelchen means as much to me as once my mother meant to you, remember—She means youth, and happiness, and a tiny space of laughter before I, too, am worm's-meat, and means a proper appreciation of God's love for us all, and means everything a man's mind clutches at when he wakens from some forgotten dream that leaves him weeping with sheer adoration of its beauty. Ho, never was there a kinder father than you, monsieur. You have spoiled me most atrociously, I concede; and after so many years you cannot in decency whip about like this and deny me my very life. Why, my father it is your little Louis who is pleading with you,—and you have never denied me anything! See, now, how I presume upon your weakness. I am actually bullying you into submission—bullying you through your love for me. Eh, we love greatly, we de Soyecourts, and give all for love. Your own life attests that, monsieur. Now, then, let us recognize the fact we are de Soyecourts, you and I Ah, my father,—"

Thus he babbled on, for the sudden languor of the Prince had alarmed him, and Louis de Soyecourt, to afford him justice, loved his father with a heartier intensity than falls to the portion of most parents. To arouse the semi-conscious man was his one thought. And now he got his reward, for the Prince de Gâtinais opened his keen old eyes, a trifle dazedly, and drew a deep breath which shook his large frail body through and through.

"Let us recognize that we are de Soyecourts, you and I," he repeated, in a new voice. "After all, I cannot drag you to Noumaria by the scruff

---

* The curious may find further details of the then Marquis de Soyecourt's abduction of the Princess Clotilda in the voluminous pages of Hulot, under the year 1708.

of your neck like a truant school-boy. Yes, let us recognize the fact that we are de Soyecourts, you and I."

"Heh, in that event," said the Marquis, "we must both fall upon our knees forthwith. For look, my father!"

Nelchen Thorn was midway in her descent of the stairs. She wore her simple best. All white it was, and yet the plump shoulders it displayed were not put to shame. Rather must April clouds and the snows of December retire abashed, as lamentably inefficient analogues, the Marquis meditated; and as she paused starry-eyed and a thought afraid, it seemed to him improbable that even the Prince de Gâtinais could find it in his heart greatly to blame his son.

"I begin to suspect," said the Prince, "that I am Jacob of old, and that you are a very young cherub venturing out of Paradise through motives of curiosity. Eh, my dear, let us see what entertainment we can afford you during your visit to earth." He took her hand and led her to the table.

IV

Vanringham served. Never was any one more blithe than the lean Prince de Gâtinais. The latest gossip of Versailles was delivered, with discreet emendations; he laughed gayly; and he ate with an appetite. There was a blight among the cattle hereabouts? How deplorable! witchcraft, beyond doubt. And Louis passed as a piano-tuner?— because there were no pianos in Manneville. Excellent! he had always given Louis credit for a surpassing cleverness; now it was demonstrated. In fine, the Prince de Gâtinais became so jovial that Nelchen was quite at ease, and Louis de Soyecourt became vaguely alarmed. He knew his father, and for the Prince to yield thus facilely was incredible. Still, his father had seen Nelchen, had talked with Nelchen. . .

Now the Prince rose. "Fresh glasses, Vanringham," he ordered; and then: "I give you a toast. Through desire of love and happiness, you young people have stolen a march on me. Eh, I am not Sgarnarelle of the comedy! therefore, I drink cheerfully to love and happiness, I consider Louis is not in the right, but I know that he is wise, my daughter, as concerns his soul's health, in clinging to you rather than to a tinsel crown. Of Fate I have demanded—like Sgarnarelle of the comedy,—prosaic equity and common-sense; of Fate he has in turn demanded happiness; and Fate will at her convenience decide between us. Meantime I drink to love and happiness, since I, too, remember. I know better than to argue with Louis, you observe, my Nelchen; we de Soyecourts are not lightly severed from any notion we may have taken up. In consequence I drink to your love and happiness!"

They drank. "To your love, my son," said the Prince de Gâtinais,— "to the true love of a de Soyecourt." And afterward he laughingly drank: "To your happiness, my daughter,—to your eternal happiness."

Nelchen sipped. The two men stood with drained glasses. Now on a sudden the Prince de Gâtinais groaned and clutched his breast.

"I was always a glutton," he said, hoarsely. "I should have been more moderate—I am faint—"

"Salts are the best thing in the world," said Nelchen, with fine readiness. She was half-way up the stairs. "A moment, monseigneur,—a moment, and I fetch salts." Nelchen Thorn had disappeared into her room.

V

THE PRINCE SAT DRUMMING UPON the table with his long white fingers. He had waved the Marquis and Vanringham aside. "A passing weakness,—I am not adamant," he had said, half-peevishly.

"Then I prescribe another glass of this really excellent wine," laughed little Louis de Soyecourt. At heart he was not merry, and his own unreasoning nervousness irritated him, for it seemed to the Marquis, quite irrationally, that the atmosphere of the cheery room was, without forerunnership, become tense and expectant, and was now quiet with much the hush which precedes the bursting of a thunder-storm. And accordingly he laughed.

"I prescribe another glass, monsieur," said he. "Eh, that is the true panacea for faintness—for every ill. Come, we will drink to the most beautiful woman in Poictesme—nay, I am too modest,— to the most beautiful woman in France, in Europe, in the whole universe! *Feriam sidera*, my father! and confound all mealy-mouthed reticence, for you have both seen her. Confess, am I not a lucky man? Come, Vanringham, too, shall drink. No glasses? Take Nelchen's, then. Come, you fortunate rascal, you shall drink to the bride from the bride's half-emptied glass. To the most beautiful woman—Why, what the devil—?"

Vanringham had blurted out an odd, unhuman sound. His extended hand shook and jerked, as if in irresolution, and presently struck the proffered glass from de Soyecourt's grasp. You heard the tiny crash, very audible in the stillness, and afterward the irregular drumming of the old Prince's finger-tips. He had not raised his head, had not moved.

Louis de Soyecourt came to him, without speaking, and placed one hand under his father's chin, and lifted the Prince's countenance, like a dead weight, toward his own. Thus the two men regarded each other. Their silence was rather horrible.

"It was not in vain that I dabbled with chemistry all these years," said the guttural voice of the Prince de Gâtinais, "Yes, the child is dead by this. Let us recognize the fact we are de Soyecourts, you and I."

But Louis de Soyecourt had flung aside the passive, wrinkled face, and then, with a straining gesture, wiped the fingers that had touched it upon the sleeve of his left arm. He turned to the stairway. His hand grasped the newelpost and gripped it so firmly that he seemed less to walk than by one despairing effort to lift an inert body to the first step. He ascended slowly, with a queer shamble, and disappeared into Nelchen's room.

VI

"What next, monseigneur?" said Vanringham, half-whispering.

"Why, next," said the Prince de Gâtinais, "I imagine that he will kill us both. Meantime, as Louis says, the wine is really excellent. So you may refill my glass, my man, and restore to me my vial of little tablets" . . .

He was selecting a bonbon from the comfit-dish when his son returned into the apartment. Very tenderly Louis de Soyecourt laid his burden upon a settle, and then drew the older man toward it. You noted first how the thing lacked weight: a flower snapped from its stalk could hardly have seemed more fragile. The loosened hair strained toward the floor and seemed to have sucked all color from the thing to inform that thick hair's insolent glory; the tint of Nelchen's lips was less sprightly, and for the splendor of her eyes Death had substituted a conscientious copy in crayons: otherwise there was no change; otherwise she seemed to lie there and muse on something remote and curious, yet quite as she would have wished it to be.

"See, my father," Louis de Soyecourt said, "she was only a child, more little even than I Never in her brief life had she wronged any one,—never, I believe, had she known an unkind thought. Always she laughed, you understand—Oh, my father, is it not pitiable that Nelchen will never laugh any more?"

"I entreat of God to have mercy upon her soul," said the old Prince de Gâtinais. "I entreat of God that the soul of her murderer may dwell eternally in the nethermost pit of hell."

"I would cry amen," Louis de Soyecourt said, "if I could any longer believe in God."

The Prince turned toward him. "And will you kill me now, Louis?"

"I cannot," said the other. "Is it not an excellent jest that I should be your son and still be human? Yet as for your instrument, your cunning butler—Come, Vanringham!" he barked. "We are unarmed. Come, tall man, for I who am well-nigh a dwarf now mean to kill you with my naked hands."

"Vanringham!" The Prince leaped forward. "Behind me, Vanringham!" As the valet ran to him the old Prince de Gâtinais caught a knife from the table and buried it to the handle in Vanringham's breast. The lackey coughed, choked, clutched his assassin by each shoulder; thus he stood with a bewildered face, shuddering visibly, every muscle twitching. Suddenly he shrieked, with an odd, gurgling noise, and his grip relaxed, and Francis Vanringham seemed to crumple among his garments, so that he shrank rather than fell to the floor. His hands stretched forward, his fingers spreading and for a moment writhing in agony, and then he lay quite still.

"You progress, my father," said Louis de Soyecourt, quietly. "And what new infamy may I now look for?"

"A valet!" said the Prince. "You would have fought with him—a valet! He topped you by six inches. And the man was desperate. Your life was in danger. And your life is valuable."

"I have earlier perceived, my father, that you prize human life very highly."

The Prince de Gâtinais struck sharply upon the table. "I prize the welfare of France. To secure this it is necessary that you and no other reign in Noumaria. But for the girl you would have yielded just now. So to the welfare of France I sacrifice the knave at my feet, the child yonder, and my own soul. Let us remember that we are de Soyecourts, you and I."

"Rather I see in you," began the younger man, "a fiend. I see in you a far ignobler Judas—"

"And I see in you the savior of France. Nay, let us remember that we are de Soyecourts, you and I. And for six centuries it has always been our first duty to serve France. You behold only a man and a woman assassinated; I behold thousands of men preserved from death, many thousands of women rescued from hunger and degradation. I have sinned, and grievously; ages of torment may not purge my infamy; yet I swear it is well done!"

"And I—?" the little Marquis said.

"Why, your heart is slain, my son, for you loved this girl as I loved your mother, and now you can nevermore quite believe in the love God bears for us all; and my soul is damned irretrievably: but we are de Soyecourts, you and I, and accordingly we rejoice and drink to France, to the true love of a de Soyecourt! to France preserved! to France still mighty among her peers!"

Louis de Soyecourt stood quite motionless. Only his eyes roved toward his father, then to the body that had been Nelchen's. He began to laugh as he caught up his glass. "You have conquered. What else have I to live for now? To France, you devil!"

"To France, my son!" The glasses clinked. "To the true love of a de Soyecourt!"

And immediately the Prince de Gâtinais fell at his son's feet. "You will go into Noumaria?"

"What does that matter now?" the other wearily said. "Yes, I suppose so. Get up, you devil!"

But the Prince de Gâtinais detained him, with hands like ice. "Then we preserve France, you and I! We are both damned, I think, but it is worth while, Louis. In hell we may remember that it was well worth while. I have slain your very soul, my dear son, but that does not matter: France is saved." The old man still knelt, looking upward. "Yes, and you must forgive me, my son! For, see, I yield you what reparation I may. See, Louis,—I was chemist enough for two. Wine of my own vintage I have tasted, of the brave vintage which now revives all France. And I swear to you the child did not suffer, Louis, not—not much. See, Louis! she did not suffer." A convulsion tore at and shook the aged body, and twitched awry the mouth that had smiled so resolutely. Thus the Prince died.

Presently Louis de Soyecourt knelt and caught up the wrinkled face between both hands. "My father—!" said Louis de Soyecourt.

Afterward he kissed the dead lips tenderly. "Teach me how to live, my father," said Louis de Soyecourt, "for I begin to comprehend—in part I comprehend." Throughout the moment Nelchen Thorn was forgotten: and to himself he too seemed to be fashioned of heroic stuff.

X

THE DUCAL AUDIENCE

As Played at Breschau, May 3, 1755

"Venez, belle, venez,
Qu'on ne sçauroit tenir, et qui vous mutinez.
Void vostre galand! à moi pour recompence
Vous pouvez faire une humble et douce reverence!
Adieu, l'evenement trompe un peu mes souhaits;
Mais tous les amoureux ne sont pas satisfaits."

Dramatis Personæ

Grand Duke of Noumaria, formerly Louis de Soyecourt, tormented beyond measure with the impertinences of life.

Comte de Châteauroux, cousin to the Grand Duchess, and complies with circumstance.

A Coachman and two Footmen.

Grand Duchess of Noumaria, a capable woman.

Baroness Von Altenburg, a coquette.

Scene
The Palace Gardens at Breschau.

The Ducal Audience

Proem:—In Default of the Hornpipe Customary
to a Lengthy Interval between Acts

L ouis de Soyecourt fulfilled the promise made to the old Prince
de Gâtinais, so that presently went about Breschau, hailed by
more or less enthusiastic plaudits, a fair and blue-eyed, fat little man,
who smiled mechanically upon the multitude, and looked after the
interests of France wearily, and (without much more ardor) gave over
the remainder of his time to outrivalling his predecessor, unvenerable
Ludwig von Freistadt, who until now had borne, among the eighteen
grand dukes (largely of quite grand-ducal morals) that had earlier
governed in Noumaria, the palm for indolence and dissipation.

At moments, perhaps, the Grand Duke recollected the Louis
Quillan who had spent three months in Manneville, but only, I think, as
one recalls some pleasurable acquaintance; Quillan had little resembled
the Marquis de Soyecourt, rake, tippler and exquisite of Versailles,
and in the Grand Duke you would have found even less of Nelchen
Thorn's betrothed. He was quite dead, was Quillan, for the man that
Nelchen loved had died within the moment of Nelchen's death. Hé,
the poor children! his Highness meditated. Dead, both of them, both
murdered four years since, slain in Poictesme yonder. . . Eh bien, it was
not necessary to engender melancholy.

So his Highness amused himself,—not very heartily, but at least
to the last resource of a flippant and unprudish age. Meantime his
grumbling subjects bored him, his duties bored him, his wife bored
him, his mistresses bored him after the first night or two, and, above all,
he most hideously bored himself. But I spare you a *chronique scandaleuse*
of Duke Louis' reign and come hastily to its termination, as more
pertinent to the matter I have now in hand.

Suffice it, then, that he ruled in Noumaria five years; that he did
what was requisite by begetting children in lawful matrimony, and
what was expected of him by begetting some others otherwise; and
that he stoutened daily, and by and by decided that the young Baroness
von Altenburg—not excepting even her lovely and multifarious
precursors,—was beyond doubt possessed of the brightest eyes in all
history. Therefore did his Highness lay before the owner of these eyes

a certain project, upon which the Baroness was in season moved to comment.

I

"The idea," said the Baroness, "is preposterous!"

"Admirably put!" cried the Grand Duke. "We will execute it, then, the first thing in the morning."

"—and, besides, one could take only a portmanteau—"

"And the capacity of a portmanteau is limited," his Highness agreed. "Nay, I can assure you, after I had packed my coronet this evening there was hardly room for a change of linen. And I found it necessary to choose between the sceptre and a tooth-brush."

"Ah, Highness" sighed the Baroness von Altenburg, "will you never be serious? You plan to throw away a duchy, and in the act you jest like a school-boy."

"Ma foi!" retorted the Grand Duke, and looked out upon the moonlit gardens; "as a loyal Noumarian, should I not rejoice at the good-fortune which is about to befall my country? Nay, Amalia, morality demands my abdication," he added, virtuously, "and for this once morality and I are in complete accord."

The Baroness von Altenburg was not disposed to argue the singularity of any such agreement, the while that she considered Louis de Soyecourt's latest scheme.

He had, as prologue to its elucidation, conducted the Baroness into the summer-house that his grandfather, good Duke Augustus, erected in the Gardens of Breschau, close to the Fountain of the Naiads, and had en tête-à-tête explained his notion. There were post-horses in Noumaria; there was also an unobstructed road that led you to Vienna, and thence to the world outside; and he proposed, in short, to quiet the grumbling of the discontented Noumarians by a second, and this time a final, vanishment from office and the general eye. He submitted that the Baroness, as a patriot, could not fail to weigh the inestimable benefit which would thus accrue to her native land.

Yet he stipulated that his exit from public life should be made in company with the latest lady on whom he had bestowed his variable affections; and remembering this proviso, the Baroness, without exactly encouraging or disencouraging his scheme, was at least not prone to insist on coupling him with morality.

She contented herself with a truism. "Indeed, your Highness, the example you set your subjects is atrocious."

"And yet they complain!" said the Grand Duke,—"though I swear to you I have always done the things I ought not to have done, and have left unread the papers I have signed. What more, in reason, can one ask of a grand duke?"

"You are indolent—" remonstrated the lady.

"You—since we attempt the descriptive," said his Highness,—"are adorable."

"—and that injures your popularity—"

"Which, by the way, vanished with my waist."

"—and moreover you create scandals—"

"'The woman tempted me,'" quoted the Grand Duke; and added, reflectively, "Amalia, it is very singular—"

"Nay, I am afraid," the Baroness lamented, "it is rather notoriously plural."

But the Grand Duke waved a dignified dissent, and continued, "—that I could never resist green eyes of a peculiar shade."

The Baroness, becoming vastly interested in the structure of her fan, went on, with some severity, "Your reputation—"

"*De mortuis*—" pleaded the Grand Duke.

"—is bad; and you go from bad to worse."

"By no means," said his Highness, "since when I was nineteen—"

"I will not believe it even of you!" cried the Baroness von Altenburg.

"I assure you," his Highness protested, gravely, "I was then a devil of a fellow! She was only twenty, and she, too, had big green eyes—"

"And by this late period," said the lady, "has in addition an infinity of grandchildren."

"I happen to be barely forty!" the Grand Duke said, with dignity.

"In which event the *Almanachen* dating, say, from 1710—"

"Are not unmarred by an occasional misprint. Truly I lament the ways of all typographers, and I will explain the cause of their depravity, in Vienna."

"But I am not going to Vienna."

"'And Sapphira,'" murmured his Highness, "'fell down straightway at his feet, and yielded up the ghost.' So beware, Amalia!"

"I am not afraid, your Highness,—"

"Nor in effect am I Then we will let Europe frown and journalists moralize, while we two gallop forward on the road that leads to Vienna and heaven?"

"Or—" the Baroness helpfully suggested.

"There is in this case no possible 'or.' Once out of Noumaria, we leave all things behind save happiness."

"Among these trifles, your Highness, is a duchy."

"Hein?" said the Grand Duke; "what is it? A mere dot on the map, a pawn in the game of politics. I give up the pawn and take—the queen."

"That is unwise," said the Baroness, with composure, "and, besides, you are hurting my hand. Apropos of the queen—the Grand Duchess—"

"Will heartily thank God for her deliverance. She will renounce me before the world, and in secret almost worship me for my consideration."

"Yet a true woman," said the Baroness, oracularly, "will follow a husband—"

"Till his wife makes her stop," said the little Grand Duke, his tone implying that he knew whereof he spoke.

"—and if the Grand Duchess loved you—"

"Oh, I think she would never mention it," said the Grand Duke, revolving in his mind this novel idea. "She has a great regard for appearances."

"Nevertheless—"

"She will be Regent"—and the Grand Duke chuckled. "I can see her now,—St. Elizabeth, with a dash of Boadicea. Noumaria will be a pantheon of the virtues, and my children will be reared on moral aphorisms and rational food, with me as a handy example of everything they should avoid. Deuce take it, Amalia," he added, "a father must in common decency furnish an example to his children!"

"Pray," asked the Baroness, "do you owe it to your children, then, to take this trip to Vienna—"

"Ma foi!" retorted the Grand Duke, "I owe that to myself."

"—and thereby break the Grand Duchess' heart?"

"Indeed," observed his Highness, "you appear strangely deep in the confidence of my wife."

Again the Baroness descended to aphorism. "All women are alike, your Highness."

"Ah, ah! Well, I have heard," said the Grand Duke, "that seven devils were cast out of Magdalene—"

"Which means—?"

"I have never heard of this being done to any other woman. Accordingly I deduce that in all other women must remain—"

"Beware, your Highness, of the crudeness of cynicism!"

"I age," complained the Grand Duke, "and one reaches years of indiscretion so early in the forties."

"You admit, then, discretion is desirable?"

"I admit that," his Highness said, with firmness, "of you alone."

"Am I, in truth," queried the Baroness, "desirable?" And in this patch of moonlight she looked incredibly so.

"More than that," said the Grand Duke—"you are dangerous. You are a menace to the peace of my Court. The young men make sonnets to your eyes, and the ladies are ready to tear them out. You corrupt us, one and all. There is de Châteauroux now—"

"I assure you," protested the Baroness, "Monsieur de Châteauroux is not the sort of person—"

"But at twenty-five," the Grand Duke interrupted, "one is invariably that sort of person."

"Phrases, your Highness!"

"Phrases or not, it is decided. You shall make no more bad poets."

"You will," said the Baroness, "put me to a vast expense for curl-papers."

"You shall ensnare no more admirers."

"My milliner will be inconsolable."

"In short, you must leave Noumaria—"

"You condemn me to an exile's life of misery!"

"Well, then, since misery loves company, I will go with you. For we should never forget," his Highness added, with considerable kindliness, "always to temper justice with mercy. So I have ordered a carriage to be ready at dawn."

The Baroness reflected; the plump little Grand Duke smiled. And he had reason, for there was about this slim white woman—whose eyes were colossal emeralds, and in show equivalently heatless, if not in effect,—so much of the *baroque* that in meditation she appeared some prentice queen of Faëry dubious as to her incantations. Now, though, she had it—the mislaid abracadabra.

"I knew that I had some obstacle in mind—Thou shalt not commit adultery. No, your Highness, I will not go."

"Remember Sapphira," said the Grand Duke, "recall Herodias who fared happily in all things, and by no means forget the portmanteau."

"I have not the least intention of going—" the Baroness iterated, firmly.

"Nor would I ever suspect you of harboring such a thought. Still, a portmanteau, in case of an emergency—"

"—although—"

"Why, exactly."

"—although I am told the sunrise is very beautiful from the Gardens of Breschau."

"It is well worth seeing," agreed the Grand Duke, "on certain days—particularly on Thursdays. The gardeners make a specialty of them on Thursdays."

"By a curious chance," the Baroness murmured, "this is Wednesday."

"Indeed," said the Grand Duke, "now you mention it, I believe it is."

"And I shall be here, on your Highness' recommendation, to see the sunrise—"

"Of course," said the Grand Duke, "to see the sunrise,—but with a portmanteau!"

The Baroness was silent.

"With a portmanteau," entreated the Grand Duke. "I am a connoisseur of portmanteaux. Say that I may see yours, Amalia."

The Baroness was silent.

"Say yes, Amalia. For to the student of etymology the very word portmanteau—"

The Baroness bent toward him and said:

"I am sorry to inform your Highness that there is some one at the door of the summer-house."

II

Inasmuch as all Noumaria knew that its little Grand Duke, once closeted with the lady whom he delighted to honor, did not love intrusions, and inasmuch as a discreet Court had learned, long ago, to regard the summer-house as consecrate to his Highness and the Baroness von Altenburg,—for these reasons the Grand Duke was inclined to resent disturbance of his privacy when he first peered out into the gardens.

His countenance was less severe when he turned again toward the Baroness, and it smacked more of bewilderment.

"It is only my wife," he said.

"And the Comte de Châteauroux," said the Baroness.

There is no denying that their voices were somewhat lowered. The chill and frail beauty of the Grand Duchess was plainly visible from where they sat; to every sense a woman of snow, his Highness mentally decided, for her gown this evening was white and the black hair powdered; all white she was, a cloud-tatter in the moonlight: yet with the Comte de Châteauroux as a foil, his uniform of the Cuirassiers a big stir of glitter and color, she made an undeniably handsome picture; and it was, quite possibly, the Grand Duke's æsthetic taste which held him for the moment motionless.

"After all—" he began, and rose.

"I am afraid that her Highness—" the Baroness likewise commenced.

"She would be sure to," said the Grand Duke, and thereupon he sat down.

"I do not, however," said the Baroness, "approve of eavesdropping."

"Oh, if you put it that way—" agreed the Grand Duke, and he was rising once more, when the voice of de Châteauroux stopped him.

"No, not at any cost!" de Châteauroux; was saying; "I cannot and I will not give you up, Victoria!"

"—though I have heard," said his Highness, "that the moonlight is bad for the eyes." Saying this, he seated himself composedly in the darkest corner of the summer-house.

"This is madness!" the Grand Duchess said—"sheer madness."

"Madness, if you will," de Châteauroux persisted, "yet it is a madness too powerful and sweet to be withstood. Listen, Victoria,"—and he waved his hand toward the palace, whence music, softened by the distance, came from the lighted windows,—"do you not remember? They used to play that air at Staarberg."

The Grand Duchess had averted her gaze from him. She did not speak.

He continued: "Those were contented days, were they not, when we were boy and girl together? I have danced to that old-world tune so many times—with you! And tonight, madame, it recalls a host of unforgettable things, for it brings back to memory the scent of that girl's hair, the soft cheek that sometimes brushed mine, the white shoulders which I so often had hungered to kiss, before I dared—"

"Hein?" muttered the Grand Duke.

"We are no longer boy and girl," the Grand Duchess said. "All that lies behind us. It was a dream—a foolish dream which we must forget."

"Can you in truth forget?" de Châteauroux demanded,—"can you forget it all, Victoria?—forget that night a Gnestadt, when you confessed you loved me? forget that day at Staarberg, when we were lost in the palace gardens?"

"Mon Dieu, what a queer method!" murmured the Grand Duke. "The man makes love by the almanac."

"Nay, dearest woman in the world," de Châteauroux went on, "you loved me once, and that you cannot have quite forgotten. We were happy then—very incredibly happy,—and now—"

"Life," said the Grand Duchess, "cannot always be happy."

"Ah, no, my dear! nor is it to be elated by truisms. But what a life is this of mine,—a life of dreary days, filled with sick, vivid dreams of our youth that is hardly past as yet! And so many dreams, dear woman of my heart! in which the least remembered trifle brings back, as if in a flash, some corner of the old castle and you as I saw you there,— laughing, or insolent, or, it may be, tender. Ah, but you were not often tender! Just for a moment I see you, and my blood leaps up in homage to my dear lady. Then instantly that second of actual vision is over, I am going prosaically about the day's business, but I hunger more than ever—"

"This," said the Grand Duke, "is insanity."

"Yet I love better the dreams of the night," de Châteauroux went on; "for they are not made all of memories, sweetheart. Rather, they are romances which my love weaves out of multitudinous memories,— fantastic stories of just you and me that always end, if I be left to dream them out in comfort, very happily. For there is in these dreams a woman who loves me, whose heart and body and soul are mine, and mine alone. Ohé, it is a wonderful vision while it lasts, though it be only in dreams that I am master of my heart's desire, and though the waking be bitter. . . ! Need it be just a dream, Victoria?"

"Not but that he does it rather well, you know," whispered the Grand Duke to the Baroness von Altenburg, "although the style is florid. Yet that last speech was quite in my earlier and more rococo manner."

The Grand Duchess did not stir as de Châteauroux bent over her jewelled hand.

"Come! come now!" he said. "Let us not lose our only chance of happiness. 'Come forth, O Galatea, and forget as thou comest, even as I already have forgot, the homeward way! Nay, choose with me to go a-shepherding—!'"

"Oh, but to think of dragging in Theocritus!" observed his Highness. "Can this be what they call seduction nowadays!"

"I cannot," the Grand Duchess whispered, and her voice trembled. "You know that I cannot, dear."

"You will go!" said de Châteauroux.

"My husband—"

"A man who leaves you for each new caprice, who flaunts his mistresses in the face of Europe."

"My children—"

"Eh, mon Dieu! are they or aught else to stand in my way, now that I know you love me!"

"—it would be criminal—"

"Ah, yes, but then you love me!"

"—you act a dishonorable part, de Châteauroux,—"

"That does not matter. You love me!"

"I will never see you again," said the Grand Duchess, firmly. "Go! I loathe you, I loathe you, monsieur, even more than I loathe myself for having stooped to listen to you."

"You love me!" said de Châteauroux, and took her in his arms.

Then the Grand Duchess rested her head upon the shoulder of de Châteauroux, and breathed, "God help me!—yes!"

"Really," said the Grand Duke, "I would never have thought it of Victoria. It seems incredible for any woman of taste to be thus lured astray by citations of the almanac and secondary Greek poets."

"You will come, then?" the Count said.

And the Grand Duchess answered, quietly, "It shall be as you will."

More lately, while the Grand Duke and the Baroness craned their necks, and de Châteauroux bent, very slowly, over her upturned lips, the Grand Duchess struggled from him, saying, "Hark, Philippe! for I heard some one—something stirring—"

"It was the wind, dear heart."

"Hasten!—I am afraid!—Oh, it is madness to wait here!"

"At dawn, then,—in the gardens?"

"Yes,—ah, yes, yes! But come, mon ami." And they disappeared in the direction of the palace.

III

THE GRAND DUKE LOOKED DISPASSIONATELY on their retreating figures; inquiringly on the Baroness; reprovingly on the moon, as though he rather suspected it of having treated him with injustice.

"Ma foi," said his Highness, at length, "I have never known such a passion for sunrises. Shortly we shall have them announced as 'Patronized by the Nobility.'"

The Baroness said only, with an ellipsis, "Her own cousin, too!"*

"Victoria," observed the Grand Duke, "has always had the highest regard for her family; but in this she is going too far—"

"Yes," said the Baroness; "as far as Vienna."

"—and I shall tell her that there are limits, Pardieu," the Grand Duke emphatically repeated, "that there are limits."

"Whereupon, if I am not mistaken, she will reply that there are—baronesses."

"I shall then appeal to her better nature—"

"You will find it," said the Baroness, "strangely hard of hearing."

"—and afterward I shall have de Châteauroux arrested."

"On what grounds, your Highness?"

"In fact," admitted the Grand Duke, "we do not want a scandal."

"It is no longer," the Baroness considered, "altogether a question of what we want."

"And, morbleu! there will be a horrible scandal—"

"The public gazettes will thrive on it."

"—and trouble with her father, if not international complications—"

"The armies of Noumaria and Badenburg have for years had nothing to do."

"—and later a divorce."

"The lawyers will call you blessed. In any event," the Baroness conscientiously added, "your lawyers will. I am afraid that hers—"

"Will scarcely be so courteous?" the Grand Duke queried.

"It is not altogether impossible," the Baroness admitted, "that in preparation of their briefs, they may light upon some other adjective."

"And, in short," his Highness summed it up, "there will be the deuce to pay."

"Oh, no! the piper," said the Baroness,—"after long years of dancing. That is what moralists will be saying, I suspect."

And this seemed so highly probable that the plump little Grand Duke frowned, and lapsed into a most un-ducal sullenness.

---

* By courtesy rather than legally; Mademoiselle Berlin was, however, undoubtedly the Elector of Badenburg's sister, though on the wrong side of the blanket; and to her (second) son by Louis Quinze his French Majesty accorded the title of Comte de Châteauroux.

JAMES BRANCH CABELL

"Your Highness," murmured the Baroness, "I cannot express my feelings as to this shocking revelation—"

"Madame," said the Grand Duke, "no more can I At least, not in the presence of a lady."

"—But I have a plan—"

"I," said the Grand Duke, "have an infinity of plans; but de Châteauroux has a carriage, and a superfluity of Bourbon blood; and Victoria has the obstinacy of a mule."

"—And my plan," said the Baroness, "is a good one."

"It needs to be," said the Grand Duke.

But thereupon the Baroness von Altenburg unfolded to his Highness her scheme for preserving coherency in the reigning family of Noumaria, and the Grand Duke of that principality heard and marvelled.

"Amalia," he said, when she had ended, "you should be prime-minister—"

"Ah, your Highness," said the lady, "you flatter me, for none of my sex has ever been sufficiently unmanly to make a good politician."

"—though, indeed," the Grand Duke reflected, "what would a mere prime-minister do with lips like yours?"

"He would set you an excellent example by admiring them from a distance. Do you agree, then, to my plan?"

"Why, ma foi, yes!" said the Grand Duke, and he sighed. "In the gardens at dawn."

"At dawn," said the Baroness, "in the gardens."

IV

THAT NIGHT THE GRAND DUKE was somewhat impeded in falling asleep. He was seriously annoyed by the upsetment of his escape from the Noumarian exile, since he felt that he had prodigally fulfilled his obligations, and in consequence deserved a holiday; the duchy was committed past retreat to the French alliance, there were two legitimate children to reign after him, and be the puppets of de Puysange and de Bernis,* just as he had been. Truly, it was diverting, after a candid

---

* The Grand Duke, however, owed de Puysange some reparation for having begot a child upon the latter's wife; and with de Bernis had not dissimilar ties, for the Marquis de Soyecourt had in Venice, in 1749, relinquished to him the beautiful nun of Muran, Maria Montepulci,—which lady de Bernis subsequently turned over to Giacomo Casanova, as is duly recorded in the latter's *Mémoires*, under the year 1753.

appraisal of his own merits, to reflect that a dwarfish Louis de Soyecourt had succeeded where quite impeccable people like Bayard and du Guesclin had failed; by four years of scandalous living in Noumaria he had confirmed the duchy to the French interest, had thereby secured the wavering friendship of Austria, and had, in effect, set France upon her feet. Yes, the deed was notable, and he wanted his reward.

To be the forsaken husband, to play Sgarnarelle with all Europe as an audience, was, he considered, an entirely inadequate reward. That was out of the question, for, deuce take it! somebody had to be Regent while the brats were growing up. And Victoria, as he had said, would make an admirable Regent.

He was rather fond of his wife than otherwise. He appreciated the fact that she never meddled with him, and he sincerely regretted she should have taken a fancy to that good-for-nothing de Châteauroux. What qualms the poor woman must be feeling at this very moment over the imminent loss of her virtue! But love was a cruel and unreasonable lord. . . There was Nelchen Thorn, for instance. . . He wondered would he have been happy with Nelchen? her hands were rather coarse about the finger-tips, as he remembered them. . . The hands of Amalia, though, were perfection. . .

Then at last the body that had been Louis Quillan's fell asleep.

V

Discontentedly the Grand Duke appraised the scene, and in the murky twilight which heralded the day he found the world a cheerless place. The Gardens of Breschau were deserted, save for a travelling carriage and its fretful horses, who stamped and snuffled within forty yards of the summer-house.

"It appears," he said, "that I am the first on the ground, and that de Châteauroux is a dilatory lover. Young men degenerate."

Saying this, he seated himself on a convenient bench, where de Châteauroux found him a few minutes later, and promptly dropped a portmanteau at the ducal feet.

"Monsieur le Comte," the Grand Duke said, "this is an unforeseen pleasure."

"Your Highness!" cried de Châteauroux, in astonishment.

"*Ludovicus*," said the Grand Duke, "*Dei gratia Archi Dux Noumariæ, Princeps Gatinensis*, and so on." And de Châteauroux caressed his chin.

"I did not know," said the Grand Duke, "that you were such an early riser. Or perhaps," he continued, "you are late in retiring. Fy, fy, monsieur! you must be more careful! You must not create a scandal in our little Court." He shook his finger knowingly at Philippe de Châteauroux.

"Your Highness,—" said the latter, and stammered into silence.

"You said that before," the Grand Duke leisurely observed.

"An affair of business—"

"Ah! ah! ah!" said the Grand Duke, casting his eye first toward the portmanteau and then toward the carriage, "can it be that you are leaving Noumaria? We shall miss you, Comte."

"I was summoned very hastily, or I would have paid my respects to your Highness—"

"Indeed," said the Grand Duke, "your departure is of a deplorable suddenness—"

"It is urgent, your Highness—"

"—and yet," pursued the Grand Duke, "travel is beneficial to young men."

"I shall not go far, your Highness—"

"Nay, I would not for the world intrude upon your secrets, Comte—"

"—But my estates, your Highness—"

"—For young men will be young men, I know."

"—There is, your Highness, to be a sale of meadow land—"

"Which you will find, I trust, untilled."

"—And my counsellor at law, your Highness, is imperative—"

"At times," agreed the Grand Duke, "the most subtle of counsellors is unreasonable. I trust, though, that she is handsome?"

"Ah, your Highness—!" cried de Châteauroux.

"And you have my blessing upon your culture of those meadow lands. Go in peace."

The Grand Duke was smiling on his wife's kinsman with extreme benevolence when the Baroness von Altenburg appeared in travelling costume and carrying a portmanteau.

VI

"Heydey!" said the Grand Duke; "it seems, that the legal representative of our good Baroness, also, is imperative."

"Your Highness!" cried the Baroness, and she, too, dropped her burden.

"Everyone," said the Grand Duke, "appears to question my identity." And meantime de Châteauroux turned from the one to the other in bewilderment.

"This," said the Grand Duke, after a pause, "is painful. This is unworthy of you, de Châteauroux."

"Your Highness—!" cried the Count.

"Again?" said the Grand Duke, pettishly.

The Baroness applied her handkerchief to her eyes, and plaintively said, "You do not understand, your Highness—"

"I am afraid," said the Grand Duke, "that I understand only too clearly."

"—and I confess I was here to meet Monsieur de Châteauroux—"

"Oh, oh!" cried the latter.

"Precisely," observed the Grand Duke, "to compare portmanteaux; and you had selected the interior of yonder carriage, no doubt, as an appropriate locality."

"And I admit to your Highness—"

"His Highness already knowing," the Grand Duke interpolated.

"—that we were about to elope."

"I can assure you—" de Châteauroux began.

"Nay, I will take the lady's word for it," said the Grand Duke— "though it grieves me."

"We knew you—would never give your consent," murmured the Baroness, "and without your consent I can not marry—"

"Undoubtedly," said the Grand Duke, "I would never have given my consent to such fiddle-faddle."

"And we love each other."

"Fiddle-de-dee!" said his Highness.

But de Châteauroux passed one hand over his brow. "This," he said, "is some horrible mistake—"

"It is," assented the Grand Duke, "a mistake—and one of your making."

"—For I certainly did not expect the Baroness—"

"To make a clean breast of it so readily?" his Highness asked. "Ah, but she is a lady of unusual candor."

"Indeed, your Highness—" began de Châteauroux.

"Nay, Philippe," the Baroness entreated, "confess to his Highness, as I have done."

"Oh, but—!" said de Châteauroux.

JAMES BRANCH CABELL

"I must beseech you to be silent," said the Grand Duke; "you have already brought scandal to our Court. Do not, I pray you, add profanity to the catalogue of your offences. Why, I protest," he continued, "even the Grand Duchess has heard of this imbroglio."

Indeed, the Grand Duchess, hurrying from a pleached walkway, was already within a few feet of the trio, and appeared no little surprised to find in this place her husband.

"I would not be surprised," said the Grand Duke, raising his eyes toward heaven, "if by this time it were all over the palace."

VII

Then, as his wife waited, speechless, the Grand Duke gravely asked: "You, too, have heard of this sad affair, Victoria? Ah, I perceive you have, and that you come in haste to prevent it,—even to pursue these misguided beings, if necessary, as the fact that you come already dressed for the journey very eloquently shows. You are self-sacrificing, you possess a good heart, Victoria."

"I did not know—" began the Grand Duchess.

"Until the last moment," the Grand Duke finished. "Eh, I comprehend. But perhaps," he continued, hopefully, "it is not yet too late to bring them to their senses."

And turning toward the Baroness and de Châteauroux, he said:

"I may not hinder your departure if you two in truth are swayed by love, since to control that passion is immeasurably beyond the prerogative of kings. Yet I beg you to reflect that the step you contemplate is irrevocable. Yes, and to you, madame, whom I have long viewed with a paternal affection—an emotion wholly justified by the age and rank for which it has pleased Heaven to preserve me,—to you in particular I would address my plea. If with an entire heart you love Monsieur de Châteauroux, why, then—why, then, I concede that love is divine, and yonder carriage at your disposal. But I beg you to reflect—"

"Believe me," said the Baroness, "we are heartily grateful for your Highness' magnanimity. We may, I deduce, depart with your permission?"

"Oh, freely, if upon reflection—"

"I can reflect only when I am sitting down," declared the Baroness. She handed her portmanteau to de Châteauroux, and stepped into the carriage. And the Grand Duke noted that a coachman and two footmen had appeared, from nowhere in particular.

"To you, Monsieur le Comte," his Highness now began, with an Olympian frown, "I have naught to say. Under the cover of our hospitality you have endeavored to steal away the fairest ornament of our Court; I leave you to the pangs of conscience, if indeed you possess a conscience. But the Baroness is unsophisticated; she has been misled by your fallacious arguments and specious pretence of affection. She has evidently been misled," he said to the Grand Duchess, kindly, "as any woman might be."

"As any woman might be!" his wife very feebly echoed.

"And I shall therefore," continued the Grand Duke, "do all within my power to dissuade her from this ruinous step. I shall appeal to her better nature, and not, I trust, in vain."

He advanced with dignity to the carriage, wherein the Baroness was seated. "Amalia," he whispered, "you are an admirable actress. O wonderful, wonderful, and most wonderful wonderful! and yet again wonderful, and after that out of all whooping!"

The Baroness smiled.

"And it is now time," said his Highness, "for me to appeal to your better nature. I shall do so in a rather loud voice, for I have prepared a most virtuous homily that I am unwilling the Grand Duchess should miss. You will at its conclusion be overcome with an appropriate remorse, and will obligingly burst into tears, and throw yourself at my feet—pray remember that the left is the gouty one,—and be forgiven. You will then be restored to favor, while de Châteauroux drives off alone and in disgrace. Your plan works wonderfully."

"It is true," the Baroness doubtfully said, "such was the plan."

"And a magnificent one," said the Grand Duke.

"But I have altered it, your Highness."

"And this alteration, Amalia—?"

"Involves a trip to Vienna."

"Not yet, Amalia. We must wait."

"Oh, I could never endure delays," said the Baroness, "and, since you cannot accompany me, I am going with Monsieur de Châteauroux."

The Grand Duke grasped the carriage door.

"Preposterous!" he cried.

"But you have given your consent," the Baroness protested, "and in the presence of the Grand Duchess."

JAMES BRANCH CABELL

"Which," said the Grand Duke, "was part of our plan."

"Indeed, your Highness," said the Baroness, "it was a most important part. You must know," she continued, with some diffidence, "that I have the misfortune to love Monsieur de Châteauroux."

"Who is in love with Victoria."

"I have the effrontery to believe," said the Baroness, "that he is, in reality, in love with me."

"Especially after hearing him last night," the Grand Duke suggested.

"That scene, your Highness, we had carefully rehearsed—oh, seven or eight times! Personally, I agreed with your Highness that the quotation from Theocritus was pedantic, but Philippe insisted on it, you conceive—"

The Grand Duke gazed meditatively upon the Baroness, who had the grace to blush.

"Then it was," he asked, "a comedy for my benefit?"

"You would never have consented—" she began. But the Grand Duke's countenance, which was slowly altering to a greenish pallor, caused her to pause.

"You will get over it in a week, Louis," she murmured, "and you will find other—baronesses."

"Oh, very probably!" said his Highness, and he noted with pleasure that he spoke quite as if it did not matter. "Nevertheless, this was a despicable trick to play upon the Grand Duchess."

"Yet I do not think the Grand Duchess will complain," said the Baroness von Altenburg.

And it was as though a light broke on the Grand Duke. "You planned all this beforehand?" he inquired.

"Why, precisely, your Highness."

"And de Châteauroux helped you?"

"In effect, yes, your Highness."

"And the Grand Duchess knew?"

"The Grand Duchess suggested it, your Highness, the moment that she knew you thought of eloping."

"And I, who tricked Gaston—!"

"Louis," said the Baroness von Altenburg, in a semi-whisper, "your wife is one of those persons who cling to respectability like a tippler to his bottle. To her it is absolutely nothing how many women you may pursue—or conquer—so long as you remain here under her thumb, to be exhibited, in fair sobriety, upon the necessary public occasions. I pity you, my Louis." And she sighed with real compassion.

He took possession of one gloved hand. "At the bottom of your heart," his Highness said, irrelevantly, "you like me better than you do Monsieur de Châteauroux."

"I find you the more entertaining company, to be sure—But what a woman most wants is to be loved. If I touch Philippe's hand for, say, the millionth part of a second longer than necessity compels, he treads for the remainder of the day above meteors; if yours—why, you at most admire my fingers. No doubt you are a connoisseur of fingers and such-like trifles; but, then, a woman does not wish to be admired by a connoisseur so much as she hungers to be adored by a maniac. And accordingly, I prefer my stupid Philippe."

"You are wise," the Grand Duke estimated, "I remember long ago. . . in Poictesme yonder. . ."

"I loathe her," the Bareness said, with emphasis. "Nay, I am ignorant as to who she was—but O my Louis! had you accorded me a tithe of the love you squandered on that abominable dairymaid I would have followed you not only to Vienna—"

He raised his hand, "There are persons yonder in whom the proper emotions are innate; let us not shock them. No, I never loved you, I suppose; I merely liked your way of talking, liked your big green eyes, liked your lithe young body. . . Hé, and I like you still, Amalia. So I shall not play the twopenny despot. God be with you, my dear."

He had seen tears in those admirable eyes before he turned his back to her. "Monsieur de Châteauroux," he called, "I find the lady is adamant. I wish you a pleasant journey." He held open the door of the carriage for de Châteauroux to enter.

"You will forgive us, your Highness?" asked the latter.

"You will forget?" murmured the Baroness.

"I shall do both," said the Grand Duke. "Bon voyage, mes enfants!"

And with a cracking of whips the carriage drove off.

"Victoria," said the plump little Grand Duke, in admiration, "you are a remarkable woman. I think that I will walk for a while in the gardens, and meditate upon the perfections of my wife."

VIII

HE STROLLED IN THE DIRECTION of the woods. As he reached the summit of a slight incline he turned and looked toward the road that leads from Breschau to Vienna. A cloud of dust showed where the carriage had disappeared.

"Ma foi!" said his Highness; "my wife has very fully proven her executive ability. Beyond doubt, there is no person in Europe better qualified to rule Noumaria as Regent."

As Played at Ingilby, October 6, 1755

Though marriage be a lottery, in which there are a wondrous many blanks, yet there is one inestimable lot, in which the only heaven on earth is written. Would your kind fate but guide your hand to that, though I were wrapt in all that luxury itself could clothe me with, I still should envy you."

Dramatis Personæ

DUKE OF ORMSKIRK.

LOUIS DE SOYECOURT, formerly GRAND DUKE OF NOUMARIA, and now a tuner of pianofortes.

DUC DE PUYSANGE.

DAMIENS, servant to Ormskirk.

In Dumb Show are presented LORD HUMPHREY DEGGE, CAPTAIN FRANCIS AUDAINE, MR. GEORGE ERWYN, DUCHESS OF ORMSKIRK, DUCHESSE DE PUYSANGE, LADY HUMPHREY DEGGE, MRS. AUDAINE, and MRS. ERWYN.

SCENE

The library, and afterward the dining-room, of Ormskirk's home at Ingilby, in Westmoreland.

Love's Alumni

Proem:—Wherein a Prince Serves His People

The Grand Duke did not return to breakfast nor to dinner, nor, in point of fact, to Noumaria. For the second occasion Louis de Soyecourt had vanished at the spiriting of boredom; and it is gratifying to record that his evasion passed without any train of turmoil.

The Grand Duchess seemed to disapprove of her bereavement, mildly, but only said, "Well, after all—!"

She saw to it that the ponds about the palace were dragged conscientiously, and held an interview with the Chief of Police, and more lately had herself declared Regent of Noumaria.

She proved a capable and popular ruler, who when she began to take lovers allowed none of them to meddle with politics: so all went well enough in Noumaria, and nobody evinced the least desire to hasten either the maturity of young Duke Anthony or the reappearance of his father.

I

Meantime had come to Ingilby, the Duke of Ormskirk's place in Westmoreland, a smallish blue-eyed vagabond who requested audience with his Grace, and presently got it, for the Duke, since his retirement from public affairs,* had become approachable by almost any member of the public.

The man came Into the library, smiling, "I entreat your pardon, Monsieur le Duc," he began, "that I have not visited you sooner. But in unsettled times, you comprehend, the master of a beleaguered fortress is kept busy. This poor fortress of my body has been of late most resolutely besieged by poverty and hunger, the while that I have been tramping about Europe—in search of Gaston. Now, they tell me, he is here."

The travesty of their five-year-old interview at Bellegarde so tickled Ormskirk's fancy that he laughed heartily. "Damiens," said Ormskirk, to the attendant lackey, "go fetch me a Protestant minister from

---

* He returned to office during the following year, as is well known, immediately before the attempted assassination of the French King, in the January of 1757.

Manneville, and have a gallows erected in one of the drawing-rooms. I intend to pay off an old score." Meantime he was shaking the little vagabond's hand, chuckling and a-beam with hospitality.

"Your Grace—!" said Damiens, bewildered.

"Well, go, in any event," said Ormskirk. "Oh, go anywhere, man!—to the devil, for instance."

His eyes, followed the retreating lackey. "As I suspect in the end you will," Ormskirk said, inconsequently. "Still, you are a very serviceable fellow, my good Damiens. I have need of you."

And with a shrug he now began, "Your Highness,—"

"Praise God, no!" observed the other, fervently.

And Ormskirk nodded his comprehension. "Monsieur de Soyecourt, then. Of course, we heard of your disappearance, I have been expecting something of the sort for years. And,—frankly, politics are often a nuisance, as both Gaston and myself will willingly attest,—especially," he added, with a grimace, "since war between France and England became inevitable through the late happenings in India and Nova Scotia, and both our wives flatly declined to let either of us take part therein,—for fear we might catch our death of cold by sleeping in those draughty tents. Faith, you have descended, sir, like an agreeable meteor, upon two of the most scandalously henpecked husbands in all the universe. In fact, you will not find a gentleman at Ingilby—save Mr. Erwyn, perhaps—but is an abject slave to his wife, and in consequence most abjectly content."

"You have guests, then?" said de Soyecourt. "*Ma foi*, it is unfortunate. I but desired to confer with Gaston concerning the disposal of Beaujolais and my other properties in France since I find that the sensation of hunger, while undoubtedly novel, is, when too long continued, apt to grow tiresome. I would not willingly intrude, however—"

"Were it not for the fact that you are wealthy, and yet, so long as you preserve your incognito, and remain legally dead, you cannot touch a penny of your fortune! The situation is droll. We must arrange it. Meanwhile you are my guest, and I can assure you that at Ingilby you will be to all Monsieur de Soyecourt, no more and no less. Now let us see what can be done about clothing Monsieur de Soyecourt for dinner—"

"But I could not consider—" Monsieur de Soyecourt protested.

"I must venture to remind you," the Duke retorted, "that dinner is almost ready, and that Claire is the sort of housewife who would more readily condone fratricide or arson than cold soup."

"It is odd," little de Soyecourt said, with complete irrelevance, "that in the end I should get aid of you and of Gaston. And it is odd you should be forgiving my bungling attempts at crime, so lightly—"

Ormskirk considered, a new gravity in his plump face. "Faith, but we find it more salutary, in looking back, to consider some peccadilloes of our own. And we bear no malice, Gaston and I,—largely, I suppose, because contentment is a great encourager of all the virtues. Then, too, we remember that to each of us, at the eleventh hour, and through no merit of his own, was given the one thing worth while in life. We did not merit it; few of us merit anything, for few of us are at bottom either very good or very bad. Nay, my friend, for the most part we are blessed or damned as Fate elects, and hence her favorites may not in reason contemn her victims. For myself, I observe the king upon his throne and the thief upon his coffin, in passage for the gallows; and I pilfer my phrase and I apply it to either spectacle: *There, but for the will of God, sits John Bulmer.* I may not understand, I may not question; I can but accept. Now, then, let us prepare for dinner" he ended, in quite another tone.

De Soyecourt yielded. He was shown to his rooms, and Ormskirk rang for Damiens, whom the Duke was sending into France to attend to a rather important assassination.

II

At dinner Louis de Soyecourt made divers observations.

First Gaston had embraced him. "And the de Gâtinais estates?—but beyond question, my dear Louis! Next week we return to France, and the affair is easily arranged. You may abdicate in due form, you need no longer skulk about Europe disguised as a piano-tuner; it is all one to France, you conceive, whether you or your son reign in Noumaria. You should have come to me sooner. As for your having been in love with my wife, I could not well quarrel with that, since the action would seriously reflect upon my own taste, who am still most hideously in love with her."

Hélène had stoutened. Monsieur de Soyecourt noted also that Hélène's gold hair was silvering now, as though Time had tangled cobwebs through it, and that Gaston was profoundly unconscious of the fact. In Gaston's eyes she was at the most seventeen. Well, Hélène had always been admirable in her management of all, and it would be diverting to see that youngest child of hers. . . Meanwhile it was diverting also to observe how conscientiously she was exerting a good influence over Gaston: and de Soyecourt smiled to find that she shook her head at Gaston's third glass, and that de Puysange did not venture on a fourth. Victoria, to do her justice, had never meddled with any of her husband's vices. . .

As for the Duchess of Ormskirk, Louis de Soyecourt had known from the beginning—in comparative youthfulness,—that Claire would placidly order her portion of the world as she considered expedient, and that Ormskirk would travesty her, and somewhat bewilder her, and that in the ultimate Ormskirk would obey her to the letter.

Captain Audaine Monsieur de Soyecourt considered at the start diverting, and in the end a pompous bore. Yet they assured him that Audaine was getting on prodigiously in the House of Commons,*—as, *ma foi*! he would most naturally do, since his *métier* was simply to shout well-rounded common-places,—and the circumstance that he shouted would always attract attention, while the fact that he shouted platitudes would invariably prevent his giving offence. Lord Humphrey Degge was found a ruddy and comely person, of no especial importance, but de Soyecourt avidly took note of Mr. Erwyn's waistcoat. Why, this man was a genius! Monsieur de Soyecourt at first glance decided. Staid, demure even, yet with a quiet prodigality of color and ornament, an inevitableness of cut—Oh, beyond doubt, this man was a genius!

As for the ladies at Ingilby, they were adjudged to be handsome women, one and all, but quite unattractive, since they evinced not any excessive interest in Monsieur de Soyecourt. Here was no sniff of future conquest, not one side-long glance, but merely three wives unblushingly addicted to their own husbands. *Eh bien*! these were droll customs!

Yet in the little man woke a vague suspicion, as he sat among these contented folk, that, after all, they had perhaps attained to something very precious of which his own life had been void, to a something of which he could not even form a conception. Love, of course, he understood, with thoroughness; no man alive had loved more ardently and variously than Louis de Soyecourt. But what the devil! love was a temporary delusion, an ingenious device of Nature's to bring about perpetuation of the species. It was a pleasurable insanity which induced

---

* The Captain's personal quarrel with the Chevalier St. George and its remarkable upshot, at Antwerp, as well as the Captain's subsequent renunciation of Jacobitism, are best treated of in Garendon's own memoirs.

JAMES BRANCH CABELL

you to take part in a rather preposterously silly and undignified action: and once this action was performed, the insanity, of course, gave way to mutual tolerance, or to dislike, or, more preferably, as de Soyecourt considered, to a courteous oblivion of the past.

And yet when this Audaine, to cite one instance only, had vented some particularly egregious speech that exquisite wife of his would merely smile, in a fond, half-musing way. She had twice her husband's wit, and was cognizant of the fact, beyond doubt; to any list of his faults and weaknesses you could have compiled she indubitably might have added a dozen items, familiar to herself alone: and with all this, it was clamant that she preferred Audaine to any possible compendium of the manly virtues. Why, in comparison, she would have pished at a seraph!—after five years of his twaddle, mark you. And Hélène seemed to be really not much more sensible about Gaston. . .

It all was quite inexplicable. Yet Louis de Soyecourt could see that not one of these folk was blind to his or her yoke-fellow's frailty, but that, beside this something very precious to which they had attained, and he had never attained, a man's foible, or a woman's defect, dwindled into insignificance. Here, then, were people who, after five years' consortment,—consciously defiant of time's corrosion, of the guttering-out of desire, of the gross and daily disillusions of a life in common, and even of the daily fret of all trivialities shared and diversely viewed,—who could yet smile and say: "No, my companion is not quite the perfect being I had imagined. What does it matter? I am content. I would have nothing changed."

Well, but Victoria had not been like that. She let you go to the devil in your own way, without meddling, but she irritated you all the while by holding herself to a mark. She had too many lofty Ideas about her own duties and principles,—much such uncompromising fancies as had led his father to get rid of that little Nelchen. . . No, there was no putting up with these rigid virtues, day in and day out. These high-flown notions about right and wrong upset your living, they fretted your luckless associates. . . These people here at Ingilby, by example, made no pretensions to immaculacy; instead, they kept their gallant compromise with imperfection; and they seemed happy enough. . . There might be a moral somewhere: but he could not find it.

CURTAIN

THE EPILOGUE

Spoken by Ormskirk, Who Enters in a Fret

A thankless task! to come to you and mar
Your dwindling appetite for caviar,
And so I told him!

(*He calls within.*)
Sir, the critics sneer,
And swear the thing is "crude and insincere"!
"Too trivial"! or for an instant pause
And doubly damn with negligent applause!
Impute, in fine, the prowess of the Vicar
Less to repentance than to too much liquor!
Find Louis naught! de Gâtinais inane!
Gaston unvital, and George Erwyn vain,
And Degge the futile fellow of Audaine!
Nay, sir, no Epilogue avails to save—
You're damned, and Bulmer's hooted as a knave.

(*He retires behind the curtain and is thrust out
again. He resolves to make the best of it.*)

The author's obdurate, and bids me say
That—since the doings of our far-off day
Smacked less of Hippocrene than of Bohea—
His tiny pictures of that tiny time
Aim little at the lofty and sublime,
And paint no peccadillo as a crime—
Since when illegally light midges mate,
Or flies purloin, or gnats assassinate,
No sane man hales them to the magistrate.

Or so he says. He merely strove to find
And fix a faithful likeness of mankind
About its daily business,—to secure

No full-length portrait, but a miniature,—
And for it all no moral can procure.

Let Bulmer, then, defend his old-world crew,
And beg indulgence—nay, applause—of you.

Grant that we tippled and were indiscreet,
And that our idols all had earthen feet;
Grant that we made of life a masquerade;
And swore a deal more loudly than we prayed;
Grant none of us the man his Maker meant,—
Our deeds, the parodies of our intent,
In neither good nor ill pre-eminent;
Grant none of us a Nero,—none a martyr,—
All merely so-so.
                    And *de te narratur*.

A Note About the Author

James Branch Cabell (1879–1958) was an American writer of escapist and fantasy fiction. Born into a wealthy family in the state of Virginia, Cabell attended the College of William and Mary, where he graduated in 1898 following a brief personal scandal. His first stories began to be published, launching a productive decade in which Cabell's worked appeared in both *Harper's Monthly Magazine* and *The Saturday Evening Post*. Over the next forty years, Cabell would go on to publish fifty-two books, many of them novels and short-story collections. A friend, colleague, and inspiration to such writers as Ellen Glasgow, H.L. Mencken, Sinclair Lewis, and Theodore Dreiser, James Branch Cabell is remembered as an iconoclastic pioneer of fantasy literature.

A Note from the Publisher

Spanning many genres, from non-fiction essays to literature classics to children's books and lyric poetry, Mint Edition books showcase the master works of our time in a modern new package. The text is freshly typeset, is clean and easy to read, and features a new note about the author in each volume. Many books also include exclusive new introductory material. Every book boasts a striking new cover, which makes it as appropriate for collecting as it is for gift giving. Mint Edition books are only printed when a reader orders them, so natural resources are not wasted. We're proud that our books are never manufactured in excess and exist only in the exact quantity they need to be read and enjoyed.

bookfinity™

Discover more of your favorite classics with Bookfinity™.

- Track your reading with custom book lists.
- Get great book recommendations for your personalized Reader Type.
- Add reviews for your favorite books.
- AND MUCH MORE!

Visit **bookfinity.com** and take the fun Reader Type quiz to get started.

Enjoy our classic and modern companion pairings!

Classic & Modern

Printed in the USA
CPSIA information can be obtained
at www.ICGtesting.com
JSHW022221140824
68134JS00018B/1188